Crossroads

A Novel

Lori Hicks

Crossroads

Cover photo by Toni D'Avello
Copyright © 2012 Lori Hicks
All rights reserved.
My Voices Publishing — Phoenix, Arizona - USA
First Edition Published July 2012
Second Edition Published October 2012
Third Edition Published March 2015
LCCN: 2012905663
ISBN-13: 978-0615600819 (Crossroads)
ISBN-10: 0615600816

The book is dedicated to the people in my life who have been supportive and challenging, and those who have been there through the many crossroads I have personally faced. And to all the people along my path who made this book possible—you encouraged me, guided me, and you critiqued me along the way.

But mostly I am immensely grateful to Toni: she has been a constant source of love and support, and my greatest fan, always. I appreciate her devotion to my happiness and my life.

*"I find myself at the Crossroads of life,
paths before me going every which way.
I can't go back and I can't go forward
until I sort some things out."*

— Author unknown

Chapter One

Lisa

I wake because I can't breathe. A hand covers my mouth. I can't speak. He pulls me from my bed, dragging my small body out the window with only my jammies covering my skin. He does it so easily. I yell for my cousin Matty, but she can't hear me. His hand tightly covers my mouth. I thrash my legs, hoping Matty will look. But no, it's as if I'm invisible. I make the motion and try to scream but nothing comes out. I swing my arms but he grips them tighter against his sweaty body. Matty is sleeping on the floor right next to my bed. Why isn't she waking up? Matty lies silent and undisturbed as this monster drags me through the window of my daddy's house. He turns and grabs my Buggsy as he closes the window behind us. Buggsy is my favorite stuffed animal. My mommy gave him to me. He hands me my best friend. It calms me for the moment as I pull it into my face, covering my eyes. *He can't be all bad,* I think. He sets me down on the ground and promises he won't *hurt* me because I'm a *good* little girl. It's cool outside—dark, scary.

"Honey," he says, "I'm just going to take you to my house for some food, maybe a little TV."

Seems like a nice enough guy. He looks funny. I've never seen him up close. He seems bigger than normal. His eyes are bulging, and his face is sweaty and red. His thin hair is very messed up, and there is lots of white spit in the corners of his mouth. Looks kinda like the time I put too much soap in the dishwasher; the suds kept seeping out the sides. For some reason he is pushing me on the back, forcing me to hurry across the dark street. Now I'm really scared. I'm not wearing shoes, so I feel the cold scratchy pavement and the little rocks under my feet. The wet grass between my toes as we run across his front yard feels better on my bare feet.

When we come up to his front door, I ask him, "Why are we eating so late? I'm so sleepy," I tell him. I'm sure my eyes must be droopy and half glazed over.

"Your daddy told me you like chicken nuggets. I got them plus I have some ice cream, too. Doesn't that sound yummy?" Staring at me, he rubs his belly. His eyebrows wiggle up and down.

Holding Buggsy up to my face, his squishy softness muffles my words, "I love 'em."

I have seen him across the street from my house. He has always been really nice. When I play in the yard, he always waves at me. Each time we talk, he offers me candy. I have seen him talk to my dad. My dad said he sees him out at all hours of the night, working in the yard, working on the car, going through things in the garage. My dad thinks he keeps weird hours. He says, "The guy keeps the lights on all night." Now I know why. He eats late. I'm kinda hungry. I do love chicken nuggets. *So I guess it's ok to eat late.*

"Come in here," he says, while opening the door to his house.

I do as he says, and then I stand there, waiting, as he latches his front door. My dad taught me good manners, always to behave with adults. But this doesn't seem right. *What should I do?* I do as he says.

"You're a nice little girl." He rubs my head, the way I sometimes do Sylvester, my cat. "I like that you're not sassing me," he says, continuing to pet me. "I want you to go in there." He points to a dark room at the back of his house. "I'm gonna take you home, back to your house after we eat."

I walk down the long, dark hall. I can see what looks like the glare from a TV set. He is very close to me as we move toward the gray flickering light. His footsteps are loud, heavy. I'm scared. It smells like stinky trash. I want to go home. I feel myself shaking. My stomach is twisting and turning. Reminds me of the time we found our dog in the street in front of the house. When I came up to him, I thought he was sleeping. Once I knelt beside him, I could see he was dead, run over by a car or something. He had blood coming out of his mouth.

"It's okay, baby, don't be scared." His voice is soft, but his touch is not.

He pushes me through the doorway of the room. I'm too afraid to run or scream. I can barely feel my legs. I do exactly what he tells me. I stand for a moment and look around the room, noticing a black sheet tacked up on the window, and the dirty floors that surround me. Trash is piled in the corner.

"Where are we going to eat?" I don't see a table.

"Come and sit by me." He walks around me and sits down. I look at him, at his big smile while he pats the spot on the bed next to him, insisting I sit. I walk over to where he is, and I do as he tells me.

"Where are my nuggets?" I ask, clinging to Buggsy.

"Oh, let me get those for you. I'll be right back." He stands up from the bed, he bends over and he gently kisses my forehead, the way my father sometimes does. Then he turns, walks over to the bedroom door and shuts it. Never leaving, he turns and faces me, walking back towards the bed. He begins to remove his pants.

Crossroads

Chapter Two

"Death is not the greatest loss in life. The greatest loss is what dies inside us while we live."

— Norman Cousins

Madison Morgan

My name is Madison, but Lisa called me Matty. I am the cousin that was sleeping on the floor next to the bed, the bed Lisa was stolen from. I am the one who did not hear her screams. I am the one who was left to wonder why a twenty-eight-year-old man would want my sweet little ten-year-old cousin. I was eleven when it happened. That perverted pig is the scumbag I often see in my nightmares all these year later. I'm twenty-five now, haunted for fourteen years by *him.* The thoughts, the dreams, the conversations, the anger, the resentment, the regret, I want him dead, and I want him to be killed in the worst way. Sometimes I even imagine it being at my own hand.

I was visiting from Phoenix, Arizona, spending part of my school break with Lisa. I was just there, in New Mexico, on a mini vacation. That's when the predator took her. I slept right through it. After being out with friends, Uncle Joe returned home at around 3:00 a.m. He looked in on us, noticing Lisa was not in her bed, he frantically startled me awake. We were big girls. I was eleven, and Lisa was ten. We were both already in bed when he left to meet his friends. No big deal. Or so we thought. That is until the media got a hold of it. The coverage was torturous for my uncle. Not being there when his daughter was snatched sounded awful by the time they were done with the story. Leaving two young girls alone with a predator living across the street was never a good idea.

When my uncle opened the door to the bedroom and didn't see Lisa in her bed, he woke me out of a dead sleep.

"Where is Lisa?" he screamed, yanking me right up to his face.

I had a comfortable pallet bed, made out of blankets we had stacked on the floor beside her twin bed. Lisa's bed was right under the window, the window with the torn curtain.

"I don't know where she is. She was asleep right there." I looked around dazed and confused, still half-asleep. She was no longer in her bed. Sylvester the cat was pacing the twin bed, his loud meow was like an alarm. I will never forget the whole incident. After noticing the drape hanging down the wall, I saw my Uncle Joe's face turn a glowing red. His eyes blinked hard and bulged out of his head, as if that would help him to see better. He began to run through the house, room to room, frantically yelling for Lisa. I never saw him freak out like that. I never saw anyone freak out like that.

Uncle Joe came running back into the room looking like a madman. "Where is her Buggsy?" He began tossing stuff around the room. He pulled the covers back on her bed, looking under everything as if she were hiding. Where is she?" he shouted. Then he ran outside and began screaming her name, "Lisa! Lisa! Lisa!" at the top of his lungs, and still no Lisa.

In the search for Lisa, I blindly followed Uncle Joe. I was in my pajamas, no shoes and no sense; I followed him into his hell, watching as panic turned him into someone else. I just remember not being able to control my sobbing, my shaking, as I listened to the sounds of a wild animal come out of my dad's brother. It is that tone, the crash of his voice, the shrill high pitch, the expression on his face, the sound of him calling Lisa's name, that so often now wakes me from my sleep.

At that moment, I remember wanting my own mom and dad. I needed my mother and father. When I saw my uncle falling apart, I wanted my father to come to his rescue, but more than that, I wanted him to come to mine.

I was six when my aunt Nancy died of cancer. Lisa even younger had became everything in Uncle Joe's world. He continued calling for her as we wandered the neighborhood, up and down the street. The damp, early morning air was seeping into my nightgown and caused the emotional weight I was carrying to get heavier. Porch lights started popping on as people began pouring out of their homes. Uncle Joe's panic was getting louder and louder each time he yelled Lisa's name. Realizing we had circled the area, and in the darkness of fear, we had returned to where we had started. Uncle Joe paused, falling to the ground on his knees, his head in his hands. He was lost. Lost in his own front yard.

I put my small hand on his shoulder, and in the course of my sobs, I sputtered out, "Uncle Joe, should we call 911?" I remember he looked up at me from his crouched position, both of us had tears in our eyes had tears. Grabbing me around the waist, he gave me a big hug.

"Yes, Matty, we should call 911." Jumping into action, he swept me up and we flew through the air. We were in the house and on the phone in seconds. Suddenly it was the eleven-year-old calling all the shots.

The police were everywhere in minutes. It didn't matter that it was a Thursday, a workday, a missing child report brought people from all over. I never remember seeing the sunrise before that morning. I walked around in a daze and clung to Sylvester, Lisa's cat. He was wondering what was going on. We forged a bond, kept each other company—he purred and I cried. The police asked me tons of questions, to which I had no answers. I didn't have the answers then, and I don't have all the answers now.

They went through every scrap of paper, tossed every toy, looked in every closet, every cupboard. They went through my clothes, my suitcase, my backpack. They got up into the attic, looked around outside, in the bushes, the shed, the garage. They dusted everywhere for fingerprints. I watched the man who brushed what looked like cocoa powder all over near the window, both inside and out. It was creepy. All the tiny prints of Lisa, probably me, and anyone else who had jumped on her bed, at times using the wall for balance. Fingerprints seemed to be everywhere near the bed and by the window. Some fingers appeared to drag across the wall while others lightly spotted the glass. It was the large thumbprint on the window that police really seemed to pay the most attention to. The officer even took my fingerprints, along with my uncle's.

They didn't seem to treat Uncle Joe with the same kindness that they did me. It was, after all, his heart that was being yanked out. The same heart the detectives trampled and crushed as they questioned him. I could see the guilt strangle my uncle as he spoke of Lisa. His voice held the sound of his madness as he answered their questions. The officers acted as if somehow this was his fault. I can still hear them badgering him.

"Why did you go out in the middle of the night?"

"Where did you go when you left here?"

"Was Lisa with you?"

"Are you sure Lisa wasn't with you?"

"Why would you leave two young girls home alone?"

"Did you harm your daughter?"

They asked me a hundred times if Lisa left the house with her father, and I told them a hundred different times, she and I were in bed when Uncle Joe left the house. We were in our pajamas, she was in the bed and I was on the floor beside her. We were talking about how much fun we had had during that day. We were looking forward to tomorrow. As I answered their questions, my heart felt like it was throbbing in the back of my throat; my mouth got so dry talking to the detectives that I thought I would actually choke on my own tongue. Air came out of my body, but I could not get the air to flow back in. At the same time I could feel a dripping sensation, like a sense everything good in me was slowly draining out. I had never experienced anything so awful. I imagined this must be what it felt like right before you die. I just ached so badly for my cousin and my Uncle Joe.

My father came as soon as I called. He immediately flew in to help find Lisa, and to take me back home to Phoenix. He was there for Uncle Joe and me. But really, my dad was there to comfort his brother. So, I was still alone, even though my dad had come to the rescue. I was alone to overhear the adults talking, and I was all alone to try and make sense of what was being said.

It turned out the pervert was a whiskey drinking, crack-head, tweaker that had a thing for little girls. The kidnapper lived across the street in a small house with a detached garage, where according to my dad, he drank, drugged, organized his stolen things and tore apart electronics, just for the sake of putting them back together again. His house was surrounded by a sea of junk: old clunkers and lawnmowers, stacks of tires and wooden pallets, and old appliances. Miscellaneous car parts littered the yard. None of the neighbors had a clue that a depraved individual lived on the same street with them. I can remember talking with him. I can remember him talking with Lisa. He seemed to be kind enough. Two separate times, in his frenzy and in his calm, Uncle Joe went to the man's house while looking for Lisa. Now we know the sicko had her all along. When I look back, I can see Uncle Joe needed his brother, even more than I needed my father.

It was the second day of Lisa's disappearance and everyone had been watching all the activity that had stirred around the house across the street. Lisa's cat, Sylvester, followed me around anxiously.

I picked him up, hoping we could comfort each other. Police had big overhead lights all around the house the night before. It was obvious, even to me, the eleven-year-old, something was just not right. I didn't even know what to think about what was happening, that is, until I overheard all the conversations, all the different scenarios the others tossed around as if they were playing catch on a sunny afternoon:

"Why are they digging so many holes?"

"Maybe he cut her up and buried her in pieces."

"He could have hauled her out of here by now."

"Oh, poor little Lisa."

"I am sure he molested her."

"He probably beat her."

"It's possible she's alive."

"Maybe he kept her hidden somewhere?"

"He's killed her by now."

"There is no doubt… She's dead."

I had to cover my ears. I couldn't take it anymore. Not another word. But I couldn't get away from it. Most of what was being said was coming from the two men I loved most in the world. Now as we stood and watched the house across the street, there was a certain amount of intensity and commotion as the crowd gathered. Sylvester, still confused, meowed and looked up to me for answers. We all watched the strange man's house, swarming as it was with men in blue, not realizing exactly what we were witnessing.

The cops never told my uncle what they thought, what they knew, or what they found—if anything. They left him alone with his thoughts, which I believe must have been worse. I think he just began putting it all together. As a kid, even I was starting to see the writing on the wall. Everyone gathered in Lisa's front yard, and we all just watched, and we waited for confirmation of our worst nightmare. My mind was racing with all the possibilities. I stood with the others, leaning on my father, holding his big hand, his arm wrapped around me, hoping he would never let me go. Sylvester's furry body brushed my calves as he nervously circled me. We watched from across the street. We were told to stay behind the yellow tape. The sun was moving higher in the sky, yet nothing could brighten this very dark hour.

The tension among us rose when we saw more police cars arriving, being closely followed by a white van. Soon after they pulled in across the street, my uncle saw them bring the man out of his house in handcuffs. It was at that moment my uncle took off running across the street. Out of control, he broke through the barricade and charged at the police car that was holding his neighbor. Still seeing no sign of Lisa, he was sure this man had his little girl, my cousin. He was desperately trying to get to him, kicking the car that now protected him, and banging the windows as the others fought to pull him back. With only his suspicions, compounded by the images in front of him, I think Uncle Joe's mind must have just snapped.

The way his fists lashed out at the glass window, I was sure it would explode any minute. I was afraid my uncle would be the next one going into the back seat of the police car. My dad ran to pull him back. Even as dad was told by the cops to stop, he pushed through. He wanted to protect his brother, not only from himself, but to shield him from the aggressively swarming police officers. I am convinced Uncle Joe would have killed that wicked man had he been able to bust into the police car that day. While two men held my father back, he begged his brother to hold it together, at the same time begging the police officers that held Uncle Joe down, smashing his face into the muddy grass.

"Please let him up... please let him go," Dad screamed as he thrashed in the officer's arms.

They did. They released Uncle Joe at the same time they released my dad. I stood frozen in the arms of a stranger. The woman next door had taken me under her wing. I leaned over and picked up Sylvester, squeezing his furry body close to my chest, my gaze never leaving the scene across the street. My eyes blurred with tears.

My dad flew to his younger brother, grabbed him and held him tight, guiding him as they moved slowly through the crowd that had gathered. For some reason the wall of people did not open. My father continued to hold his brother close. They stood in front of a large group of onlookers. This was like the train wreck people could not look away from. Only this was no train wreck, this was the shattering of a man's life.

Everything began to move so fast. All I could do was stand there and cry. So many cameras, so many people, so much pain. Now I had seen the two strongest people I knew fall to the ground in front of a wall of people and sob in each other's arms. I watched as the cops drove the bad man away. My eyes followed the back of the car that carried him. I watched until it turned the corner and was out of my sight. Still not knowing what he had done to Lisa, I was sure it was bad.

My father had just picked my uncle up off the ground when two men dressed in white coveralls came out rolling a stretcher. They were headed for the white van that was now backed up close to the monster's house. On the stretcher was a small black canvas bag. I just knew it was Lisa in the zipped carrier. The crowd let out a gasp of horror. The sight of that black bag was all it took for the pack of people to lose it. The cries were a chorus of pain, all different tones, different pitches and different lengths of notes. Everyone that had tried so hard to find Lisa alive—suddenly the realization hit them. They felt let down, sickened. I was not even a teenager, yet suddenly, I felt so grown-up. I'd had a lifetime of lessons in just a few days.

Her small body was found in his backyard. It was in a freshly dug grave that revealed her naked, raped remains which were tossed in a bag with a stuffed bunny rabbit. The killer had had her for two days. The autopsy showed no food in her stomach. Even after all I imagine she went through, besides the terror, I hated knowing she was probably hungry when she died. I remember standing back, kind of like an out-of-body thing—however out-of-body an eleven-year-old could be. I stood and I listened as the reporters wanted to get their story, her story, how they saw it, what they went through, what we all went through. Some of them added their take on Uncle Joe leaving us home alone that night. That didn't make him look so good. Even while they witnessed his greatest loss, his breakdown, and his remorse and guilt, it was as if they still wanted to see more suffering. That's a weird thing about human nature.

The news was getting out quick. "Little Girl Found Dead." Even more media swarmed the site, their trucks, their vans, their cameras, their attitudes, and their concern. Many of them had also helped search for Lisa, congratulating me for not being the one. Like that was some sort of victory or something. Like I was supposed to feel better because she was gone and I wasn't. There was one reporter who stood out as genuine, truly touched by Lisa's tragic end. I stared at him as he spoke into the camera.

"What made him prey on a helpless child who was sleeping?" He seemed to be talking to all of society. "What can we do as citizens to guarantee our safety in the future from the drug addicts who are making Americans their victims? From these predators that are making children their victims? We must have the courage to face this horror if we are to make the world safer for our children," he said. "We need to find out what went wrong with this man." I could see he was really trying to hold it together. His eyes began to well up. "Why do we, society, turn our backs on each other?" He ended with, "Maybe we shouldn't so easily cast aside the troubled. Maybe we all need to try harder." When the camera went off, the reporter dropped down to his knees before crumbling and melting into the ground. No cameras were rolling, no microphones recording. He sobbed uncontrollably, clutching his face.

While watching him fall apart on the job, I gripped Sylvester even tighter and I cried. Something shifted in me at that moment, and I made a decision. I promised myself I would grow up to help society's throwaways. I would never cast away the troubled and lost.

My father and I flew home the next day, back to Phoenix. We had a service a week later in Arizona. Uncle Joe was so devastated that he killed himself less than six months after Lisa died. That was the second saddest day of my life. That time I did not see my father cry. I'm not sure he did. Sylvester the cat came to live with me.

Chapter Three

Samantha 'Sam' Green

I sat up in bed when I heard the clanging of old pipes. I knew it meant Madison had just turned off the shower. That was a sure sign it would be at least fifteen minutes before she came thundering out of the bathroom. Awaken now, I stirred in bed, vaguely aware of the movements Madison was making as she prepared for work. I heard the medicine cabinet squeak open, the blow dryer come on, and then I pictured Madison briskly running her fingers through her short, dark hair. I rolled to my side with a completely full bladder, noticing a slice of sky peeking through my pink curtains. I squeezed my legs together and tried to will away the urge to use the restroom. But I couldn't.

"Madison, please hurry!" I yelled from my bed. We were roommates in a rented house with only one bathroom. Sometimes it really sucked. One bathroom, that is. That will be a nice thing about cashing in on my trust fund: having two bathrooms, perhaps even a separate family room and dining room. Looking for a nicer place will be one of the first things on the agenda.

A few minutes later the door opened, and in her raspy morning voice, Madison spoke, "All right, Crybaby." I heard her travel down the short hall. Her sturdy steps carried her into her bedroom, where she shut the door.

I jumped up and darted for the bathroom. "Thanks, Madison. I'm sorry. I drank tea before I went to bed. Not a good idea."

"That's okay. I'm in a hurry today, anyway. I need to get to the courthouse early. Mondays, they're always super busy." Madison talked to me through the wall as I peed.

I could hear her rustling through her closet. I don't know what she would be looking for. She wore the same type of thing every day. A white button-up blouse, tucked into a pair of black dress slacks, with a shiny black belt, a black blazer, and her flat, polished, slip-on loafers. This was her go-to outfit for work—drab, yet professional. I could faintly hear her sweet talking Charlie, her cat. Only he didn't know he was a cat. It was rare to hear Madison use a sweet-talking tone. It was a clear sign she was speaking to her loving pet, with that playful, baby-talk voice. I loved that light-hearted side of her. That is why I knew there was hope. There was a very soft, mushy person underneath the calloused exterior she put up for others.

Almost crashing into each other, I tumbled out of the bathroom at the same time Madison rushed through the hallway.

"Sorry, I'm in a hurry." Madison was struggling to put her jacket on. She slung her backpack over one shoulder. "I'll get coffee at the office." She grabbed her briefcase off the kitchen table with her free hand and spun around back toward the door.

"Do you have class tonight?" I stretched my arms overhead and yawned.

"No, but the court docket is pretty full, so I'll be home a little late anyway. Being a servant to the judge makes for a long day. What about you, are you on days or nights?" Madison stared at me with her mismatched eyes.

I never knew anyone before her who had one green eye and one brown one. "I go in this morning, work till six, or so. Give or take. Then I'll probably run by Gram's house before I come home." I followed Madison to the front door. "She always cooks on Mondays. I'll bring you dinner from Gram's tonight. You know how she loves to feed you."

20

"That sounds great! I want to do my part to keep your grandmother happy. Besides, next to my mother's enchiladas, your Gram's cooking is the best." Madison turned back, her usual unyielding glare. "Be safe, and hey, Sam—don't forget to lock-up the house." Charlie playfully grabbed at her ankles. Bye boy." She stooped to give him one last pat on the head.

"You really think you need to say that? Of course I'll lock the doors, Madison. Don't I always?" I reached out for a farewell hug. "Don't worry." I stood holding the front door as Madison stepped through and turned back to face me.

"Well, there is a crazy killer on the loose, after all. Three women killed, in three weeks—I'd say that's something worth worrying about." Madison raised her brow, her tone more serious. "All the bodies have turned up in the downtown area, Sam. Being that we live downtown, I'd say that's cause for alarm. For all we know it could even be one of your social outcasts. The ones you keep thinking can be rehabilitated." She gave me one of her sideways smiles.

Madison's quiet bitterness and persistent worry infused every aspect of her life. I knew she worried about the people I worked around. But it still upset me she always insinuated I was a bad judge of character. "You'd probably be happy if I wore a whistle around my neck." I pretended to put a whistle in my lips. "That would protect me from what you think are the derelicts I supposedly surround myself with. Have you forgotten I have a sixth sense?" I yawned, unintentionally.

"A whistle won't save you if someone cuts your throat." Sometimes Madison just couldn't help herself. That was the part of her I'd rather not have to deal with, especially first thing in the morning. That negative everyone-is-out-to-get-you attitude made me tired.

"Fine then, I am sure when they catch him, whoever he is, you can advocate for the worst punishment, and get what you call real justice, death." I had to work at keeping my expression from going hard. This was a difference that came up often in our friendship. I guess if Madison had actually witnessed an execution, it might have shaped the way she believed. It had for me. Madison typically thought the worst of people. And me, I preferred to give the benefit of the doubt.

"Alright, alright—I'm sorry. I can see I hit a nerve." She raised her arms in the air.

"Isn't that what you were trying to do? Hit a nerve?" My eyebrow felt as though it arched into my hairline.

"I just want you to be safe. That's what I was trying to do, Samantha."

Madison only used my full name when she was trying to make a point. "Social services is a good job, Madison. Helping the less fortunate, I thought that was what it was all about. Sometimes I just get tired of you acting as if it's not. There are many good and decent people who need help. One pill shy of being normal. They are not all losers; they're especially not killers."

"Did someone wake up on the wrong side of the bed this morning?" Madison softened, a smile crossed her face. When Madison smiled, she was most engaging. Unfortunately, not many people saw her the way I did.

When I had heard the pitch in my voice, I eased up. I didn't like to let her provoke me into an argument, even if it was playful, to a degree.

"Besides, I heard lightening rarely strikes twice in the same place. I really think we've both had enough misery for one lifetime." I told her. "Now go, you worry-wart." I pushed her through the entrance. "Go, and don't forget to lead with your heart today, Madison." I smiled mockingly. I, too, knew how to aggravate. She knew I thought that she led with her mouth more often than necessary.

I shut the security screen, locked it, and then closed the thick wooden door and latched all three locks on it. In the instant I latched the last deadbolt an explosive flash went off in my head. I leaned against the door, closed my eyes and let the vision in. Crime scene ribbon sparked in my mind's eye. The problem with these interrupting mental images was that I sometimes struggled to determine whether they were predicting some future event, or just rehashing my old memories, bad as they were. After all these years, thirteen to be exact, the idea that I would now see the yellow strip of plastic flapping in my brain, had me baffled. I blinked my eyes several times hoping to clear the image. It worked. The vivid, creepy picture was gone, for now.

I pushed away from the door and hauled my sleepy body to the microwave to heat a cup of water. I always started my day with a cup of hot tea. I leaned into the counter and waited for the timer to ding. The large, perfectly clear crystal my grandmother gave me years ago dangled from a string in the center of the kitchen window. The sun that pressed through the curtain went right for the crystal, creating a flickering light, its glimmer of fantastic colors spun around the room with a splendid display. I hummed my morning classic, the Beatles tune, *Here Comes the Sun*. It was one of my mom's favorites. I dipped my tea bag several times in the steaming cup, dribbled a bit of milk, plunked in a cube of sugar, then cradled the warm cup between my hands and shuffled back to bed before starting my day.

Madison always quickly and easily leaped into her day. Me, I was more the type to crawl into mine. I preferred to start my day a bit slower, leisurely, meditatively. I sat on the side of my bed, blew into the steaming cup, and slurped, realizing what opposites Madison and I actually were, in almost every way. She was so black and white, and I was so not.. Her taste in music, television and décor are different, in that she's boring, and I have style. Compared to my room, her room is sparsely decorated; it seems more tailored

23

to suit a man rather than a young woman. Yet we are kindred spirits, the origin of our similarity is suffering. Our friendship is connected by tragedy and heartbreak.

I sat on my bed, sipped my warm tea, and watched flecks of dust float through the sunlight that was streaming through the thin window covering. My dream catcher gently twirled from the ceiling fan above. I reached out and grabbed the small, fluffy, stuffed brown bear that sat atop the night stand beside my bed. This little lifeless object evoked so many memories, none of them good. Its fur was matted in areas, one spot from a coke spill, another from fingernail polish. I fluffed the little bear and brushed off the incense ash on its paw. It had been a special friend who brought me comfort when I needed. Regrettably, my little friend also managed to provoke a horrible tenderness that will always be with me. I squeezed him into my chest and closed my eyes.

* * *

I was eleven when I finally told my mother about my stepfather. We sat at the kitchen table, just her and me, having an after school snack while I divulged my secret. It was almost as if she didn't believe me. Her crystal blue eyes stared into mine with skepticism. The wrinkles that crossed her face were of disbelief. I'll never forget the moment of truth, of the devastation I felt by her doubt. She had no idea how hard it was for me to tell her this. I wanted to take it back, but I didn't.

"Oh, Honey. How can you say that about him? Karl loves you. He would never do anything to hurt you. He has legally adopted you, Samantha. He has set up a trust fund for you and everything. If anything, God forbid, ever happened to us, Karl wants you to be taken care of, as if you were his own." There was a convincing quality to her voice. "I am sure there is some misunderstanding. Karl loves you. He brings home special gifts for you, all the time."

She twisted a paper napkin into shreds. "How could you think he wants to hurt you?" My mother had a distorted look on her face. She kicked back from the table and drew me to my feet, forcing our eyes to meet. "I love you, Samantha. I wouldn't let anyone hurt you." She pulled me into her chest and compressed our two bodies together.

Her neck, it was soft. My mother was small, too. Though, at eleven years old, I fit nicely against her. Her smell was always fresh, her hair often up in a beautiful twisting pony. Her makeup brightened her face, gave her creamy skin color, but it didn't change her true features. I felt her arms push me away slightly, and then her hand cupped my chin, raising it so our eyes met, once again.

"I promise I will have a talk with your stepfather. I am convinced whatever has happened between the two of you is a misunderstanding. I know he loves you, Baby." She kissed me on the forehead and that was that. She turned away and went about her day. I was hurt, and confused. She didn't become the protective mother I was so sure she was. She said she'd talk to him. I don't know what else I expected her to do.

A few weeks went by and he hadn't come back into my bedroom. I began to think maybe my mother had actually said something to Karl. I washed dishes with my mom, helped her make the beds, and we went grocery shopping, and also went to the mall several times. Not another word was mentioned. We talked about everything. Everything but that. I was so happy. I loved that I could finally sleep without the disturbance of my mother's husband wanting to touch me in the middle of the night. He never appeared to be mad about her talking to him, nor was he curt in his behavior with me. Karl still treated me well, like one of his own, as my mother would say. We watched TV together, played cards, ate dinners. I had persuaded myself she had taken care of things with Karl. I was convinced his touching was all in the past. Until one night, not even a month after my mother's promise to attend to things, I woke to his touch, his scent—a tang that exuded filth.

When my eyes opened, his hand was stroking my head. He was sitting beside me on my small, twin-sized bed. He began to vigorously rub my hair, then my shoulders, his free hand moved to his midsection. I stiffened, like I always had.

"Move over." He drew back the covers and began to stretch his long body beside mine.

I turned my gaze away from him, and I looked over to the wall where my laminated "Minerals Poster" was tacked up. My gram had given it to me. She liked rocks. A whopping 162 specimens were displayed. They were presented by class: native elements, carbonate, sulfates, sulfides, halides, oxides, phosphate, organic and silicates. I learned a lot about the rocks just by staring at the poster. I lifted my gaze slightly, that was when I saw them. My mother's eyes were wild as they peered through the small opening of my bedroom door. Then she pushed through the threshold and flipped on the light. Her long hair was even more untamed than her eyes. It was rare I ever saw it down, brushing her shoulders, stringing toward her face.

"What are you doing?" She had a pitch in her voice I hadn't heard before. "Get your hands off of her." Her jaw twitched, her teeth were clenched.

I was scared. I lay rigid in my bed, pulled the covers back up to my chin, and stared at my mother.

Karl abruptly stood. "It's not what you think." Becoming a statue, he froze in place.

"It isn't what I am thinking, Karl—it is what I see. I see you being a monster to my child." Her voice hitched mid sentence and sounded like ripping metal.

"You're crazy." He was trying to convince her she was delusional. "Tell her, Samantha." He turned back to me. "I just came in here to kiss you goodnight. Tell her!" All of a sudden his desperate stare was on me.

I sat up and twisted my body, swung my legs out from under the covers. I sat perched on the very edge of my mattress, speechless.

"Tell her, goddammit!" His words seemed to cut his tongue while slicing through my psyche.

I felt like a trapped animal, almost ready to chew my foot off for survival. My chest began to throb, like maybe his eyes were drilling a hole into me. I said nothing. I could no longer look at him. I diverted my eyes back to my mother. With a sinking heart, I saw my mom's arm swing around from behind her back, a handgun in her grip.

"Back-off, Karl! How could you do this to Samantha? For Christ's sake, Karl, she's eleven years old!" The gun shook in her clasp, even as both hands firmly gripped the handle.

"Whatever she told you is a lie, Carolyn." His tone was becoming more troubled as he reached out for her. "She's a liar," his cries pinged off the wall of my bedroom.

"You're the liar, Karl. We've been married seven years and I don't even know who you are." The tears rolled down her face.

"Samantha—tell her." His face twisted with angst, his hands went to prayer position. "Please, tell her."

"I already did," I said. A low moan escaped through my strangled voice.

"Do not even look at her, Karl." My mom screamed even louder and waived the weapon in his face. "I defended you, Karl. I doubted my own child. You said you loved her—loved me. You don't do those things to someone you love."

"I do love her, Carolyn. Honey, please—I love you." He extended his long arm toward her, his hand open, palm up. "Please, Carolyn."

"That's not love, Karl—that's abuse. It's sick is what it is." Her eyes were angry slits in her head.

27

My body began to tremble uncontrollably. I listened to my mother's resentment rise. Her cries came out in shrill heartbroken jags. She made him look her in the face as she pointed the gun toward his head. He was bigger than her, yet the fear was immense in his eyes. His posture was ramrod straight and unflinching. Swiftly, he made a lightning-fast motion for the gun.

The shot was loud.

I screamed at the top of my lungs, "NO!"

In one powerful moment the bullet exploded his head. A shower of blood sprayed me. My heartbeat was so loud it pounded in my head. An out-of-control sensation started in my extremities and coursed through my veins as I watched him limply fall to the floor beside my bed. His body bounced back on me before hitting the floor with an immense thud. I forced the bile that had crept into my throat back down, that and the small pieces of blackberries from my evening dessert tart. For one stunning moment, I felt relief and grief all at once. I'd spent so much time thinking of him as a cruel, vile man, someone who had stolen my childhood. It was hard to believe I still had a vein of compassion for him as his head lay in a spreading pool of blood. I looked through the red splatters that now coated my eyes. I could barely see my mother's horrified, apologetic gaze.

"My God, what have I done? My God—My God! What did I do? I'm sorry, baby. I'm so sorry. I should have protected you. I should have protected you sooner." Her eyes overflowed. She shuddered violently.

For a brief moment, time stood still. I looked at my lost mother and I swear she was encased in a blue-gray cloud. My gram called it an aura. I'd started seeing people's colors when I was real young. Though, I'd never seen anything like this. My mom's glow was flickering. Kinda like a broken wire that sparks just before bursting into flames.

"I failed you, Samantha. He should have never been able to do those things to you. I neglected my baby girl." Her cries were loud, blubbering, not really even directed toward me.

I was climbing off the side of my bed to reach for my mother, just as she raised the gun to her heart and looked me straight in the eyes.

"Please, forgive me." Her voice fell, confusion pleated her forehead, and then she pulled the trigger.

My screams rang out louder than the bang of the gun.

"NO!"

My stomach flipped with dread as I jumped toward her. But it was too late. Blood quickly soaked through her nightgown. She twitched and lay motionless, her legs bent in unnatural angles. For a brief moment, I was immobile, frozen in disbelief. It felt as if I was hovering from above, looking down on the scene. My stepfather and my mother lay on the floor beside my bed. Their blood began to mix together as it seeped into the white carpet that covered the floor. I turned back to collapse onto my bed but stopped abruptly when I noticed the red spots and clumping flecks on my covers, evidence of the spray of blood, of brain matter, and possibly pieces of my mother's heart, her husband's head. Instead, I dropped to the floor next to her and curled in a ball. I hugged up to her, close. I was in a place so dark, I couldn't even imagine light. It seemed I had dissolved into my tears, into her. Then I smelled her. She smelled pleasantly of face soap and night cream, which for me became the odor of profound, horrific grief. My cries became louder. There was a chill that had overtaken my bedroom. It was suddenly so cold. I swear I could see my breath while I wailed my pain.

Once I finally caught a gulp of air, my brain began to work again, and I realized there was no one to come to the rescue. The silence was as heavy as the burden of being alone. I felt panic take root. I jumped to my feet, ran down the hall to the kitchen, and jerked the phone off the wall and dialed 911 just as fast as I could.

Every kid was taught that was a sure way to get aid. I pressed the phone to my ear, trembling, my legs feeling as though they would buckle under me at any moment. I waited for a voice.

I screamed frantically into the mouthpiece, "There has been a shooting. My mother needs help. Please hurry." Once the woman on the other end repeated my address, I banged the receiver for a quick click and dialed my grandmother. "Gram, wakeup, I need you. We need you—now! Something terrible has happened. Grandma, please hurry. 911 is on the way." My tearful screams turned to grief-stricken hiccups, my hands slick and slimy with blood. Without waiting for Gram's response, I slammed down the phone and ran back to my bedroom and dropped to the floor next to my mother.

She was already beginning to look like a dead person. At least the dead people I've seen on TV. Her face was ashy, her small hands were colorless, except for the crusty crimson that drenched her right hand. The bloodied weapon lay on the floor between her and my stepfather's body. Mom didn't move as I cradled her twisted, limp body in my arms. On impulse, I began to hum one of my mother's favorite Beatle's songs. At the same time, the words slapped at my consciousness. *Yesterday—all my troubles were so far away, now it seems as though they're here to stay.* My mom was of the opinion the Beatles had a song for every occasion.

As I robotically hummed and chanted the words in my head, I could no longer look at her stillness. Instead, I glanced around my room and waited. I waited for someone—anyone. I glimpsed at the pink and white dresser my mother and I had painted together. The lace curtains we had put up in my room, with the pink ruffled valance to match my bedspread—my now blood-splattered bed cover. In the corner was a tall shelf with a mosaic of colors, representing the assortment of outfits on each of my dolls, the collection of dolls my mother had bought for me over the years.

Above my desk, tacked to a piece of memory-board, there were pictures of my mother, my grandmother and me, along with some of my friends from school. On top of my desk was the homework that she'd helped me with earlier, just before saying goodnight for the evening. Next to the spiral notebook was my beading tray. My mother and I were learning how to make earrings, bracelets and necklaces together. We had just brought home a gang of new beads, clasps and a roll of leather, and stretchy string. We were going to create something beautiful for Gram as a birthday present.

The doorbell chimed loudly through the house. I gently laid my mother's heavy body on the carpet and moved quickly in the direction of the thunderous wrapping noise that hammered at the front door.

"Police—Open up." A booming voice shot past the thick wood.

I rose on my tiptoes to look through the peep hole. There stood the officer, his weapon drawn, with a pack of others in uniform behind him.

"Yes, one minute. I'll let you in." I tried to yell back with the same force as the officer, but my voice quivered wildly.

I drew back to unlatch the locked door. My heartbeat felt like a nervous hamster's might. I was shocked by what I saw. Blood smears where everywhere on the backside of the white raised wood panels. My handprints framed the peep-hole, my fingertips, my cheek marks, my palms, even where my knees bumped the door, left reddish-brown smudges. My nightgown, my hair, my feet—I was covered in blood. I swung back the door.

"I'm Officer…" His words seemed to stick in his throat, his jaw hung open. The large man in uniform was momentarily rendered speechless. "Are you hurt? Do you need medical attention?" He knelt in front of me and lightly clutched my shoulders. "Is there anyone in the house with a weapon?" His breath smelled like bubblegum. He turned his head back toward the others. "We need social services—ASAP!" He shouted a few words out to the officers in the street, along with a few hand gestures, and they began moving. I was in a fog, at the same time, very alert. It's hard to explain. It was almost as if I were watching a movie.

I grabbed his arm, hoping to pull him toward my mother. "There is no one else here. Please help her. Please save my mother."

He firmly, but gently held me at the entrance, officers stormed passed us, an ambulance waited across the street, and a team of people gathered near our driveway.

"There is a gun on the floor in that front bedroom." I turned toward the hall and watched three policemen overtake my home. Guns waving, they maneuvered our living room and hallway, then broke off in different directions throughout the rest of the house. Everything was moving at lightning speed—yet it was the longest, drawn-out moment of my life.

"All clear sir," a strong voice shouted from the back of the house. "We've got one weapon and two dead."

"Officer!" Like the cracking of a whip, the large man's voice snapped in a reprimanding tone. He put his hand on my shoulder, turned his head out the front door. "Get in here, now!"

I saw him swing his glare to the young cop who walked toward us. It wasn't as if the big-mouthed policeman was saying something I didn't already know. Nevertheless, to hear it from someone else was unsettling. Karl was definitely dead. Even I knew that for sure. Half of his head was missing. I was afraid my mother was gone. I was pretty sure she was dead, too. But I held out hope. She never really moved once the bullet penetrated her. The insensitive, loud mouth cop had a plastic bag in his grasp, revealing what looked like the bloody gun my mom had had in her grip just before falling to the floor.

"Honey, do you have someone we can call to come and be with you?" The big policeman had a consoling stare as he looked into my face.

"I already called my grandma." I could barely hear myself speak. My vision seemed to close in around me.

"That's good, Honey, that's real good. I need you to sit right here for a few minutes." He pulled me toward our kitchen and gently settled me in the chair at the table. Then he turned and started shouting orders. "It's safe. Get the paramedics in here, now. First take care of her." He pointed to me. "Then, have 'em check on them." He head-nodded down the hallway toward the bodies. Then he looked at the cop holding the weapon. "They are trained professionals, not you." He towered over the guy. "They are the ones who make the call, not you." Again his fierce look went to the young man whose head was hanging low.

Even though his tone was muffled, I could hear him discipline the young officer. As I sat, I looked around at the blood I had transferred to the doorway, the counter top, the walls, and the telephone. Queasiness overtook me. It was like one of those horror films I'd always been restricted from watching, yet managed to see anyway. The officer in charge wheeled around and stepped back over to me.

"Can you tell me your name?" His bones popped and snapped as he stooped in front of me.

"Samantha, Sir." My knees were bouncing as my feet nervously sprung off the ground, even as I tried forcing them to stay down. My tears were unusually large as they flowed off my face. Through the hefty droplets, I looked down at my hands, crusty with my mother's blood. My cuticles were strangely outlined in burnt red. I wanted to wash myself.

"I need to get just a few pictures of you before I have them wipe you down, Samantha. Is that all right?" The officer lightly guided me out of the chair.

"Yeah." I stood. For some reason I touched my hair. I don't know why, as if I were going to fix myself for the photo, maybe. To my disgust, I felt the moist, clumped, bloody chunks that were caked to my head. I heard the top-cop snap his fingers, and in less than a second the flash of the camera was lighting up my horror. A crime-scene photographer was documenting the scene. Unfortunately that included pictures of me—covered in my parents' blood.

"What the hell is going on?" A large, heavy-set woman with darkish hair pulled into a modified up-do, something she obviously did in a hurry, stood before me. "There will be no more pictures." Her sharp eyes looked around the room filled with police officers and emergency personnel. "Get me a blanket—now!" She snatched the soft piece of material from the paramedic's hand, and wrapped me in it. I immediately felt safe. She dropped to one knee, and then pulled me into her arms. "Hi, Honey. My name is Elizabeth Hanson, you may call me Beth. I'm a social worker with the Child Protective Services. I'm here to look out for you. Are you hurt? Are you thirsty? Are you alone?"

She fired off her questions, fast, never letting up on the hold she had on me. I found such comfort in her strong embrace, even as I quaked inside. She looked to be my mother's age. My mom was thirty-eight. Ms. Beth was plump on top, soft and cuddly. Her clothes smelled clean. Her grip on me felt genuine. She handed me a soft, squishy stuffed bear to hold as she stood and stared down the large officer who remained at my side. I was only eleven years old, suffering through the worst tragedy of my life, and I had just figured out what I wanted to be when I grew up. I had never even heard of Child Protective Services.

"Hanson, don't look at me that way." He looked away from Ms. Beth's face. "I was just about to get Samantha a blanket." Now it was the big cop who was looking sheepish.

Ms. Beth pushed past the officer and turned back toward me. "Samantha, I want to have these nice people check you over for injuries." Ms. Beth pointed to the medic. "I want someone to take a look at this little girl, NOW!" Ms. Beth's eyes were kind and gentle, even as she became the bull in the room.

Check me over for injuries, I thought. I didn't know it was that easy to see I was wounded.

"Do you have any pain?"

"No," I lied. In fact, I had never felt such heart wrenching pain.

"There is an awful lot of blood—have you been cut?" One of the emergency worker's hands was exploring my head, picking through strands of hair.

"It's not my blood." I could see their eyes searching my nightgown for tears, cuts, holes, but there were none. I had a person on each limb as they washed me down while I sat at my own kitchen table. The table where only hours I ago I had had dinner with my mother.

The police officers were the first to arrive, and then the paramedic units were allowed to enter the crime scene. That was what everyone was calling it, "A Crime Scene." The officer in charge left me, only when Ms. Beth appeared. He took charge of securing the scene. A yellow plastic ribbon roped off the area. It appeared they wanted to bar the observers that were beginning to gather. A group of people carrying suitcases and bags began to descend on my home.

"Hi, my name is Detective Stevens." He didn't extend his hand, but he knelt to the floor in front of me and looked into my eyes. "I am a Crime Scene Investigator." His voice was deep, strong.

"Isn't that CSI?" I blurted. "That's my mom's favorite show!"

"I am the investigator who will oversee the crime scene. You know, I will find out exactly what happened here." He stood. His gaze went from me to Ms. Beth. "Hanson, we will need to ask her a few questions." He remained in the doorway of the kitchen, retrieved a pen from his shirt pocket and a small notebook from his coat pocket. He was wearing rubber gloves.

"What crime scene? What the hell happened here? My God, Samantha! Oh my God, are you all right? Where is Carolyn? Where is your mother? Where is my daughter?"

My grandmother made a thunderous entrance as she plowed through the barricade of people to get to me. Her flowered housedress was wrinkly, her hair flat, pressed to her head on one side, and her neck bared a slight crease, undoubtedly left behind by her bedcovers. Without hesitation, she took me in her arms and steadied me.

"Are you okay?" When she whispered into my ear, my chest loosened, my shaking turned to relief. "My God, Baby, where is your mother? What happened here? What have you been through? Where is Carolyn?" Her voice was quivering wildly.

"She's dead, Gram." I spat it out. I didn't even know the words were coming before I said them. "She's dead. Momma is dead, Grandma." I began to sob loudly.

Gram's skin turned a sickly shade of gray. She dropped her hold on me and started tearing through the house. Two police officers grabbed her before she reached my bedroom.

"Please, let me see her. Let me see my daughter." Gram pleaded with the two men that held her back. "Oh, God—please!" Her voice was as hollow as a cave while it echoed through the hallway of our home. "Why? Why? Why?" A great big howling scream filled the house. Gram's crying turned to brokenhearted sobs.

I had hated to be the one to tell her that her that mom was dead, her only child, my mother, dead. I watched my grandmother fall to her knees in our hallway. Ms. Beth immediately walked over to her. I followed. We both rested our hands on Gram's shoulder. Ms. Beth fished in her jacket pocket and came out with a tissue she offered. She pressed it into the palm of her hand. Gram wiped at her dripping nose.

"She was protecting me, Grandma. Momma was looking out for me." She lifted her upper body and turned to face me. The skin beneath her lower lids was almost lavender in color and loose with wrinkles as the tears unreservedly streamed.

Our eyes met. "Protect you—protect you from what?—From who?"

"From her husband, Grandma. She was protecting me from Karl." I stared at her. A puzzled sadness overtook my grandmother.

She reached out. "Oh, Sam. What did that son-of-a-bitch do to you?" She swept me up in her arms. "Why hasn't anyone washed this child?"

"They did," I muttered.

"Well… Grandma can do a better job than this. Let's get you cleaned up."

My body collapsed into her arms. Finally someone took control of me.

"Get out of the way." Gram's determined look was convincing as the sea of people parted.

I saw the officer in control give his nod of approval, and Ms. Beth was clearing our way. Gram sidestepped past all of them into the hall bathroom, me in her arms. She carried me in and we cuddled on the cool tile floor and sobbed. I thought my tears were big, until I saw hers. She smelled of fresh flowers, her skin was as soft as tissue paper. She was a young widow—my grandfather died when I was a baby. She never remarried, still lived alone. I knew she wouldn't be alone anymore.

My gram managed to bathe me, and with Ms Beth's assistance, get me a pair of underwear, jeans, a tee-shirt, socks, and a pair of tennis shoes, all without disturbing any evidence. After endless minutes in a small blue room that resembled a beautiful lagoon, in some tropical paradise, we emerged—red, swollen eyes and brokenhearted—but blood free, or so it appeared. We walked into the living room, and into a flurry of activity. It had become apparent by the site of brown paper sacks and Zip-lock bags that were scattered about the carpet, the CSI Unit had been busy. The photographer who snapped my picture was still clicking away. I never glimpsed at the photographs from the scene. Yet they are pictures that are vivid in my mind, today.

*   *   *

Recognizing it was time to get ready for work, I finished my cup of hot tea and returned my little stuffed bear to its place beside my alarm clock. I closed my eyes, placed my hands in prayer position near my heart, and I quietly said thanks to spirit, again, for bringing me through that terrible time of my life.

My goal had always been to grow up and become a protector of children, and thirteen years later I was on a veering path. Out of college for only three years, my first stop in social work was at a county facility. A place called Last Chance, located in the heart of the Capital Mall District of downtown Phoenix. It's nice because it is well located. I liked living and working near Gram's house. And with my odd hours, it made it very convenient to be at all three places regularly. I did placements for hundreds of people in a week, people coming from a broad range of settings. They included physical and mental health, child welfare, corrections, alcohol and drug abuse, and even sex offenders, or as Madison would call them, a bunch of low-life pedophiles. As it has turned out, rather than being the child protector, I mainly worked with adults. It is very sad, but it seems that in many of the cases, at one point or another, there was a very good chance these adults were once unprotected children.

Chapter Four

Madison Morgan

I slipped through the doorway of the Phoenix Metro light-rail, just before it slid shut. Holding my briefcase close to me, I took a seat in the far corner next to no one. My body made a jerking motion as the train jolted forward. I couldn't help but think about Sam's snappy attitude this morning. It was unusual that she ever even came back at me. Sam always seemed to wake up on the right side of the bed, humming some Beatles song and bouncing through the house with a joyful attitude. It would make me sound like a bitch if I said I thought she was often too happy, so I won't say it.

The train stopped and people poured on. A large man in a suit squeezed in beside me. I scooted over and gripped my personal items close. I didn't like it when people touched me. Especially strange people I didn't know. Sam was different when it came to strangers. Hugging them was no big deal. Sam was a good friend. In fact, she was my only *real* friend. But it scared me that she spent most her days and many of her nights working with penniless drunks, destitute drug addicts, and persuasive prostitutes. Generally speaking, Sam labored for a portion of society that most people were ready to discard. All that, and she made time to care for her aging grandmother.

*　　*　　*

When Lisa died, I was committed to doing great things for other people, yet I was so into me and my own suffering, I rarely had time to think of anyone else. But I was only eleven. No one expected any different. I could hardly comprehend the fact that my cousin was gone, much less departed, forever. Our dog had died a few months prior to Lisa, and that made sense, but my cousin— dead, murdered—that was almost inconceivable. Death was so final. The idea that I would never see Lisa again was almost too much for me to bear. The question I had continued to ask myself, over and over again, was, why. Why didn't he take me? Why did the killer take Lisa through the window and not me? For months after that night, demons would arrive in my bedroom, they'd wake me from my sleep, but they'd never take me either.

It was strange, I know. I regularly wondered what was wrong with me. Then I questioned why I'd even pose such a question. Worse, I began to ask myself things like: Was it because Lisa had blond hair and mine was dark? Was it her fair skin—compared to my muddy complexion? What was wrong with me? Or was it as simple as, Lisa was next to the window and I wasn't? My cousin was small compared to me. Maybe that was it. I was too big to kidnap. A million emotions have travelled the course of my mind since that night, a night that had turned into years. Unfortunately, fourteen years later, at twenty-five, I still had the demons. They woke me this morning.

Lisa wasn't just my cousin, she had been my best friend from birth. Had I not gone to visit her that haunting summer, it would have been our very first summer vacation apart. She and Uncle Joe moved from Phoenix to Albuquerque only months prior to her death. Before that, we were practically sisters. When Aunt Nancy got cancer, Lisa spent lots of time with my family, especially towards the end of her mother's life.

There were many nights Uncle Joe preferred staying at the hospital with his dying wife, while my mother gladly cared for his daughter. Lisa and I would sit up nights, a flashlight under the covers, and beneath our private tent, I would read to her for hours. I loved to read books and Lisa loved to hear the stories, as long as they weren't ghost stories. Our last happy summer together, we read: *Where the Red Fern Grows, The Little Mermaid,* and *Aladdin.*

When Lisa and I were together everything was an adventure. Every tree was a swing and every vacant corner of the yard was a magical land. A pile of stacked wood was our fort, and each leisurely walk was a treasure hunt. We played dress-up with the cat, fetch with the dog, and rescued a wounded pigeon. We'd run barefoot in my backyard and slide under the hedge and spy on the older boy next door. I can still see the shining eyes of the little girl lying on the grass next to me. We rarely argued, and we always shared everything, including our secrets.

One sticks out in my mind. It was a typical hot summer afternoon in downtown Phoenix. Lisa was nine. I was ten. We were at my house in the backyard running through the sprinklers, cooling our sweltering bodies. My father had forbidden us to ever go beyond our fenced yard. He especially gave a serious warning about going into the alley, but on this day, he wasn't home at the time. Lisa and I swore to secrecy just before we squeezed through the gap under the locked chain that held the gate together. Our tiny bodies pressed through the small opening without a problem and we ventured off, out of the confines of my backyard. Life was more carefree back then, before I knew how bad people could actually be.

The alley was cluttered with debris, old furniture, soiled mattresses and overflowing trash cans. The stench rose from the bulky black containers, and barking dogs bit at the chain-link fences that lined our route. Three doors down there was an old boat pulled into an unfenced yard on the back side of a neighbor's home. From the moment we had decided to climb into the hull, we knew we

41

could get in to trouble. We were trespassing. This was something else that required a pinky promise. That was always part of the fun.

Lisa and I sat in the small sail boat that was up on blocks, and through our imagination, we sailed around the world. We screamed and laughed at all the beautiful sites we encountered, including the friendly whales and dolphins that led us through the choppy waters of the sea. I commented on the fishy smell of the ocean. Lisa pointed out the snapping noise of the sails as gusts of wind drove us toward our destination. Just as we spotted our treasure island, the loud shouts of an elderly man startled us. I glanced up to see a short, stubby man with a full face of acne scars come running toward us. His arms were waving erratically.

"Go on! You kids get out of here. Get out of that boat." His gruff voice carried with it a shooing threat.

With that warning, we jumped from the bow and high-tailed it home. At first we were frightened as we darted down the path, barefoot, our clothes still damp. Once we safely made it back to the confines of my backyard, the uncontrollable giggles of accomplishment took over. Lisa and I returned to playing in the misty spray of the sprinkler. We clasped each other's upper arms and twirled in laughter through the soaking spurt. In the eighteen years I'd lived under my father's roof that was the only time I remember disobeying him.

* * *

The train continued to pick up passengers, so now I was uncomfortably smashed in between two large men. The downtown streets were filled with cars, the sidewalks with pedestrians. I was thrilled to know I would be reaching my destination soon. I wasn't sure how much more men's cologne and stale cigarette smoke I could take. Leaning forward, I realized my mind was still trapped in the past. That one night was stuck in my head, I was afraid, forever.

I just wanted him dead. Sam was right, "real justice," that was what I wanted. Maybe then the dread of that night would go away. But instead, he continued to sit on death row, haunting me, and haunting my family.

*   *   *

Just after the nightmare with my cousin, my dad and I were back home from Albuquerque less than a week, when without the approval of my mother, my father enrolled me in a boxing class. But not before cutting off all of my long hair. I'm still not sure if it was the haircut or the fact that my father was turning me into a hard-hitting little girl that upset my mother most. When I wore my favorite baggy shorts, tee-shirt and tennis shoes, next to my brothers, one might have thought I was one of the boys. I'm pretty sure that was what my dad was going for. That night when we came home and my mother saw my new hairstyle she was livid. It was the first time I could remember my parents quarrelling with one another. Unexpectedly, they were in a tug-of-war, arguing over which path my life should take.

"You think boxing is going to protect Matty? You think making her look like a boy instead of a little girl will keep her safe? Boxing is a violent activity. Is that what you think she needs—more violence?" My mother stared at my father. I remember her eyes. They were not just annoyed, but confused.

My dad quipped with something about how girls can get all the same benefits from boxing boys do. Boxing can give confidence and strength. And he made sure she knew how boxing could help me to face *any* situation.

"Will it help her to cope with loss—sadness and fear?" My mom's voice hitched mid-sentence. "My little girl is missing something since she's returned from New Mexico. I want her to find it, get it back." Her eyes scanned the room, as if she could find what I'd lost.

I hated hearing my parents argue over me. I remember how my throat lumped and my eyes swelled with water. Then my dad shot back at my mother.

"She's missing her cousin, Carmen. And we did find her—and she's not coming back," he told her.

"That is not what I'm talking about, Larry, and you know it." I could see my mother's temper rising.

The muscle along my father's jaw began to jump. "I want my little girl to be able to protect herself," he said. "I never ever want someone to be able to grab her like that creep got Lisa. Don't you remember what that man did to Lisa?"

"How can I not—you won't let us forget. Madison needs a professional counselor, Larry." My mom's voice ricocheted around the room.

They talked as if I wasn't standing in the middle of them. I slinked across the floor to gather my younger brothers. We were unfamiliar with the screaming between our parents.

"Oh, I'm sorry Carmen, but the YMCA doesn't offer psychotherapy. I make a plumber's wage for Christ's sake, and you, you clean houses. We can't afford that type of thing." He threw his arms up in the air. "I was just doing what I thought was best, that's all." His voice dropped an octave. He went into the kitchen, opened the refrigerator door, took out a beer, cracked it, and drank it, in a few gulps, until it was gone.

Even as a maid, my mother always retained a quality of self-assurance and grace. But that did not diminish her spunk. I believe being Mexican gave her a fiery attitude when necessary. At least that was what my father always said. When she was mad at him he often called her a "Hot Tamale."

She went on to fight for me, following him into the kitchen. "What about the reference the CPS officer in New Mexico gave you? I want the number to that social worker." I was wondering what the social worker could do for me that my dad hadn't already tried.

"I want Matty to have the qualified help she needs. I want my little girl to stop having nightmares. I want her to have a normal childhood." Using an authoritative voice, one hand rested on her hip, she held out the other hand and waited in the doorway, between the living room and the kitchen. In stature, my mother only went up to my dad's shoulder, but she exerted a subtle force that easily allowed him to forget her size. She may have been much smaller than he was, but he still looked up to her.

"She is going to stay in the boxing class," he said firmly, while digging in his pocket for his wallet, coming out with a business card, he handed it to my mother.

"Fine—she can stay in the class, as long as the professionals say it is the right thing for her to do." She snatched the card from his fingertips and mumbled something in Spanish. The look on her face would have scared anyone. My dad turned back toward the refrigerator.

I was glad she said I could continue to box. I actually liked it. It gave me a reason not to wear dresses. I never liked dresses. I liked my new short haircut, too. My mom was convinced I needed specialized help. My father was sure I needed to defend myself. I wasn't so sure I was the only one who needed the expert's help.

To keep Mom happy, besides boxing, I continued to read. I was already twelve by the time my mother went through all the red tape to get me into the system. While I waited to see the so-called experts I read four John Grisham novels, and also *Pleading Guilty* and *The Burden of Proof* by Scott Turow. And when I wasn't in my room reading, I was at the gym with my dad. He made sure I had my own pair of boxing gloves, protective headgear, and a mouthpiece. And before my thirteenth birthday, I could skip rope better than any of the boys my age. My dad would hold the heavy body-sized bag that hung from the ceiling and I would slug it, knee it, and kick at it. He made me practice striking it real hard until I built up lots of strength and control. And if I showed improvement, I would get to use what they called the speed bag. That was my favorite thing at the gym. It was smaller, kinda like a basketball that hung eye-level. I liked to punch at the smaller bag. My dad had me picture the killer's face on it as I swung my fists. Like rapid fire, I lashed out. I hated him.

"Hit it," he'd say. "Hit it hard, hit it fast, baby." The quicker I punched the bag the bigger the smile was that spread across my dad's face. "That's it, Honey. That's it. You've got it." He was puffed with pride at his tough little girl. I liked putting the gloves on, punching the bag as hard as I could, but I really liked pleasing him. But during it all, I discovered I took pleasure from hitting the killer in the face.

Finally, at the recommendation of the social worker, my mom got me into a child psychiatrist. I hated it. Someone you don't even know asks you questions like:

Do you feel sad or unhappy most of the time?

Do you get irritated with other people?

Do you feel guilty about surviving?

Do you blame yourself for everything bad that happens?

Do you wake often in the middle of the night?

I guess when I answered yes to all the questions, and after twelve months of therapy, the shrink determined I had Attachment Disorder, Survivor's Guilt, and PTSD caused by extreme emotional distress from being exposed to a traumatic event resulting in the death of Lisa. It was determined that my nightmares and disturbing recollections were what added to my jittery feelings and my untrusting attitude. The doctor told my mother and father that could very well be the reason I had a hard time showing affection. I was almost thirteen and had been prescribed Zoloft.

"She is not going to take those crazy pills," my dad argued.

"The doctor says it will help her with the anxiety, her anger. Madison is taking those pills until she improves, until she feels better—until the doctor says to stop." My mother stomped her small foot on the floor and turned away from my father and walked off.

"What ever happened to good, old fashion feelings—coping?" he muttered. My dad had his head down looking at his work boots. "My little girl is a lot stronger than you think." His voice was almost silent but not hushed enough to keep my mother from hearing.

"She's my daughter too, Larry."

I took the pill from my mother every day. And every day I flushed it down the toilet until the doctor said I was better and I didn't have to take the pills any more. I felt bad for wasting the money. I knew my parents were spending hard-earned dollars they didn't have. But I figured that was the cost of hope. Something my mom really needed.

My first day as a freshman in high school, a kid tried to steal my backpack right off my shoulder. Or so I thought. It turned out he was flirting. Either way, I clocked him—hard. Broke his nose, destroyed his ego, and made a name for myself—*Mad Madison*. That was when my social worker, Ms. Hanson, made the recommendation to my mother and father that I do something more constructive and less violent than boxing. My father argued, but not too vehemently, and in the end, everyone agreed that perhaps debate would advance me farther than boxing, and I could still remain a fighter. A deal was cut between the adults; I would work on my boxing skills less and my studies more. I became quite good at the speed bag while reading flash cards. Although I continued my training I backed off of my ring-time. No more matches. No more hand-to-face contact. My mom continued to remind me I was a girl. And girls don't fight she'd say. Apparently she was never confronted by the girls at my school.

Ms. Hanson knew I was an avid reader. She was aware of my fascination with the law. Regularly my social worker would try to get me to see two sides to a story where I frequently only saw one. That is how I became involved in the debate class.

I figured my mother and Ms. Hanson worked together, made a few calls, finagled a small number of things, and presto, I was enrolled in the closed class. I was finally on the path my mother had always wanted for me. She was determined to have a lawyer in our family. Paying for it, however, was something they'd worry about as we went. As it turned out, breaking that kid's nose was one of the best things I ever did, maybe not for him, but for me.

That one right hook changed the course of my life in a positive way. And *Mad Madison* was a name that followed me through high school and into college, but it was no longer for my right jab, but rather the madness I sometimes attached to my arguments while debating either side.

I was lucky—extremely fortunate to be assigned my social worker. She was a rare individual. She actually took an interest in my life. The very first time we met she insisted I called her Beth. I was never comfortable with that. I've always called her Ms. Hanson. She was a kind woman, with a commanding physique, yet a very warm presence. She really seemed to care about how I was feeling, always asked about my day, my week, my month.

Over the years, Ms. Hanson helped me prepare for court, build my courage to testify against a monster, and recover from the trauma that followed. A monster who stared at me through his evil eyes the entire time I was on the stand, every time, at each hearing—all of them, and there were many—his eyes were on me.

My debate class helped me to be a good witness, an expressive witness. I wanted to be clear about what I knew—and I knew I wanted him to die for what he did to Lisa. Like my dad said, "It's up to you, Honey. Tell the truth, the whole truth about that scumbag and he'll get the electric chair." His comments often carried bitterness, his eyes conveyed animosity, his thoughts I could only pretend to read, but I agreed with him.

We waited over four years for a Superior Court jury to convict that bastard of kidnapping, rape, and murder. Waiting was so upsetting, so frustrating, and frankly sometimes insulting with the unnecessary travel from Phoenix to Albuquerque, the missed school days and the time I'd taken to prepare—all for more delays. Ms. Hanson or my father had to accompany me, so it wasn't only my schedule, but theirs. Many times we were unable to get direct answers to our questions regarding the case.

There were actually times I envied Uncle Joe. By killing himself he was spared this grueling process over the course of many years. When I was on the stand they asked the questions as if I were the criminal. I later found out the four years between the killer's arrest for murder, and a conviction through the courts, was about the average time it took to prosecute a death penalty case.

Lisa's killer received the death penalty, yet he remained alive. Fourteen years later he was still here. Lisa was dead, long gone, and he was supposed to be dead, too. Never an admission of guilt, never an apology, he sat on death row, one appeal after another. And through it all, Ms. Hanson was there for me. She regularly asked about my relationships with my brothers, my mother, my father, and my friends. She took me to group meetings where I could meet other children who, just like me had experienced traumatic events at a young age. She was observant enough to know that wasn't my thing. In fact I hated group whining. All that *poor me, poor me* stuff was annoying. I wasn't about to share my experience with just anybody, certainly not my feelings.

One day I received a call from Ms. Hanson. She was working on a special project and she wanted my participation. I learned all her projects were *special*. She wanted me to meet someone who she would only preface by saying, "I think Samantha is someone you will really like. She's a sweet girl, someone your age, who like you, had a rough start at adolescence." She would always hug me when a mere mention of the past came up. "Samantha worked with me last summer at Miracle House, and is working there again this year. We could use some more help over there. They need someone to tutor the children in reading. I thought that would be a good place for you to start. There are many other things you can do, once you blend into the atmosphere of the facility." Ms. Hanson was one of those who believed that happiness comes from thinking about others, and all suffering comes from preoccupation with one's self.

She'd often say an idle mind was the devil's playground. Miracle House was meant to be a place I could go and lend a hand to others, but it turned out to be a place that gave me the hand up I needed.

*   *   *

Finally at my destination, I stepped off the railcar, walked less than a block, and entered the courthouse where I worked. I pitched my bag and briefcase on the conveyor belt and waited my turn to go through the metal detector. The April weather in Phoenix was perfect, so at least I wasn't waiting for everyone to strip down. The security guard, who I had so often seen, offered a friendly hello and a smile while I waited my turn. As I made my way through, I barely looked at him, briefly nodded, grabbed my things and headed to the elevators.

The courthouse building was a maze of linked, angled hallways and a blur of florescence. I approached the elevator, and as I waited for the doors to slide open, I glanced down and spied my faded reflection in the marble sheen. I suddenly felt the reminder of all that had changed in my life over the past fourteen years. The elevator doors opened, inviting me to enter, I moved forward into my day, hoping to somehow find redemption for being the one who lived.

Chapter Five

Samantha 'Sam' Green

My hot tea was gone. The worst part of my morning was an empty mug. I looked at the clock and realized I needed to get a move on. I stood from my bed to set my cup on the dresser, when I acknowledged the stack of papers that acted as a coaster was the Trust Documents I was supposed to have signed and dropped off at the attorney's office last week. These were the documents that for me aggravated a tremendous amount of emotion. Emotions I would rather avoid. Emotions I have tucked far away. Emotions I wasn't sure I was ready to uncover.

*   *   *

I was young and very innocent when Karl started touching me inappropriately. I didn't know how to do anything except trust the ones I loved. I loved him. He was a good stepfather, until he wasn't. I loved that my mother loved him; he made her smile and laugh, plenty. We were comfortable, a nice home, pretty things. Security was how my mom referred to it. I was five when my mom married him. We moved from our small run-down apartment in the center of the city, near Gram's house, to his big home on a country club golf course in the north section of Phoenix. It was a large ranch-style home, hillside, with views, a pool and beautiful gardens, and a

3-car garage. Very different from what we were used to. He had a good job—stock options—lots of them. I guess it paid to work for a computer start-up.

My mom, it seemed, for the sake of her husband, had worked her way into the cliquish world of the upper middle class. She was able to quit her job and become a homemaker, something she'd always wanted to do. And she was good at it. She made our home nice. Mom shopped, cooked, cleaned, and drove me here and there. She also ran Karl's errands and entertained his work people regularly. I noticed she was more cheerful with Karl than she was before him.

She appeared to love her new life. And all the while, my stepfather was shattering my life, one unpleasant occurrence at a time. It started with subtle touches. He'd drop the pop corn in my lap and burrow between my legs to retrieve it. Maybe he'd wipe a spill from the front of my shirt, his hand lingering in a place it shouldn't. There were times he'd put a strawberry in between his lips and make me take it with my mouth. He knew I loved strawberries. Other times he would just hold me, close. He especially liked it when I'd sit on his lap.

After about a year or so of living with Karl, my mom let him begin to help with my baths. I must have been about six or so, going on seven. I was a big girl. I didn't want the help. He would bring home a special floating toy that only he could show me how to play with. "It's our bonding time," he'd tell her. "Samantha loves baths. This will make her more comfortable with me, Carolyn," he used a warm and affectionate voice. That's when he started to touch me naked. He'd tell me to spread my legs wide so the soap could get me real clean down there. "Clean Samantha's pee-pee," he would say in a playful voice. Then he'd rub my entire body, his slippery hands went everywhere. No place was off limits. My mother would come in to help towel dry me, they'd smash my wrapped body between theirs and we'd all hug. So happy, my mother was.

I was nine when he started to come into my bedroom at night. My mom would be doing dishes. He would pretend he was playing a game with me and pull my nightgown up over my head so I couldn't find him. I now know, it was he who was looking for something. But it wasn't until just past my tenth birthday, when I saw Karl peering through the small opening in my bedroom door that I began to feel weird. My mother had bought me my first bra, and I was flitting around in front of my mirror, amazed how I was developing at such a young age. I was proud of the round bumps that where rising on my chest. None of my friends had them. When I saw his eyes, I turned to reach for a cover-up before turning back to find him gone. This was the first time I'd remembered being totally uncomfortable with his gawking stare. And then it started.

Lights out, Karl was always the last to go to bed. He was a successful business man after all. He had to stay up late and work, work, work. My mother always reminded me of how good our lives were because of him. My mother was an insomniac most of her life. I hated those sleeping pills. Every since I could remember, she needed pills to sleep.

Initially, his late-night visits started as loving caresses. The soft kisses on my neck tickled, felt good. He'd softly say, "Goodnight, Samantha." Most of the time, I had already been sound asleep when I'd wake to his words and gentle stroking. Sometimes I'd feel all tingly from his touch. Much of what he did felt good. That was what confused me. "You sure are maturing into a beautiful young woman, Samantha." Karl would always reward me the next day with some fantastic gift, my favorite candy, perhaps a package of fancy beads, maybe a dinner out at McDonalds. My mother assumed he was being such a thoughtful stepfather.

As his acts got more insistent, more invasive, the gifts became more extravagant. If he touched my breasts, I'd get to take my friends to the movies, treat and buy all the popcorn. If he touched my other privates, I could have a sleepover at someone else's home and he'd take me shopping for a new outfit. When his fingers started regularly going inside of me, I got a new bike, then a laptop. Our arrangement seemed to work out for all of us. I did what he wanted, I kept quiet, and my mother remained happily married.

At first, Karl made me believe what we were doing was okay. Then it changed. He would warn me that my mom might be hurt if she knew. He would tell me she would be mad at me because he treated me so special. When I turned eleven, he began to slink his entire body into my bed. The first time he took my panties off and got on top off me he almost squished me to death. When he forced himself in me, I yelped with pain. The blood that followed scared me. But what scared me even more was the way Karl stripped my bed and remade it, all as my mother slumbered.

He had never made any bed in our house. Those bloody sheets left the house. I never saw them again. I knew then what we were doing was wrong. What he was doing to me was wrong. Yet for some reason, I never told anyone about that night. Karl's visits to me in the middle of my sleep increased, sometimes weekly, depending on his work schedule. He intruded on my dreams—he became my nightmares. I began to feel nasty, hurt, angry, and betrayed. I hated feeling like a liar. The gifts he had been giving me could no longer keep me silent. I knew the gifts weren't out of love.

* * *

I slipped into my clothes, and then stood in front of the mirror and twisted my hair up into a ponytail on my head. Now, at twenty-four years old, I really resembled my mother. Sometimes it was startling to see my own refection looking back at me. When I thought of my mother, I had misty-edged memories of her, always coming back around to the night she killed herself. But I fought those off-putting memories, and I replaced them with fond recollections. Like the way she laughed, or how out of the blue she would grab me and begin to dance with me. Her special snuggles when she burrowed her face into my neck, her lips searching for "sugars," she'd say, while pressing into the ticklish part of my skin.

My mother loved to shop, she especially enjoyed being able to buy me nice things. I loved it when she'd bake me chocolate chip cookies; we'd sit together and watch her favorite soap opera, *All My Children*, and eat until we were sick. The warm cookies dipped in milk melted in my mouth. My mother would hum with joy when she ate them. Those are the things I tried to think of whenever I thought of my mother. My favorite times with my mother were when we did our arts and crafts projects together. We would create for hours on end, the times Karl wasn't around—the times I had her all to myself. We'd make all kinds of things: beautiful trinkets, rings, bracelets, necklaces. My mom had style with her bead designs, but her earrings were the best.

I opened the small jewelry box and selected one of my favorite pairs. On the mirror that hung on the wall over my dresser, tucked up in between the glass and the wood frame, was an old picture of my mom and grandmother and me, right before my mom died. It was one of my favorite pictures. We were all so happy that day. We'd been at some mother-daughter gathering for my grandma's church and each of us was dressed in pink, wearing matching flower necklaces my grandmother made from flowers she'd taken from her own yard. I smiled, realizing I had the best grandma in the world. I only wish I would have called on her to rescue me before talking to my mother. Then my mother might have still been alive. But when Gram did step in, she jumped in with both feet.

* * *

When Gram took me out of my home that night, I never returned. There was really no reason to. Unfortunately, I had many fitful nights on a bed that didn't seem to soften, before I called

Grandma's house home. It was less than a month after my mother's death and my grandmother had turned her favorite meditation, hobby, and everything else room into my bedroom. It was almost identical to my old room, right down to the memory board over my desk. The only thing that was tacked on it that wasn't there before was a dried rose—the one I saved from my mother's funeral. My gram paid special attention to make me feel at home. I knew she had to be tired of having me share a bed with her, especially those first few weeks—lots of restlessness and lots of crying. "Let it out, Sam. Let 'em roll. That's the only way, Honey." She'd fold her arms around me.

Gram had taken another assortment of my keepsakes and nicely displayed them along the window ledge of my new room. A blooming bougainvillea trailed along the outside of the glass; the smell of fresh paint filled the room. That April not only brought with it a new bedroom, the freshness of spring in the desert, and my twelfth birthday, but it was also the first time I actually thought of myself as an orphan. When Gram left me alone in my new room, I remember staring at the items on the wood-stained sill; I'd collected the treasures, usually when out with my mom and grandmother on one of our adventures.

I sat on my bed and put my shoes on, and looked to the windowsill in my room, still loaded with my treasures. I leaned over and picked up an arrowhead, the smallest knick-knack on the ledge, tossed it over in my hand, rubbed its sharp edges, and just like that I was taken back to the place I had found it.

It was in an area near the red rocks of Sedona, where it seemed we had hiked for miles along the winding Oak Creek. The crimson cliffs surrounded us. Large trees lined the creek, shadowing the crystal pools of deeper water. As a small child, I loved stepping from one large stone to the next, never letting my shoes touch the dirt beneath.

"Look, Honey, what's that?" My mother pointed to the ground beside the running creek.

My eyes searched with excitement. "Where? Where's it at, Mommy?" I called out.

"Keep looking, you'll see it. Look for the point," she hinted, slightly positioning her index finger toward the spot.

The small artifact blended with the other tossed, polished stones beside the flowing stream. Then finally I saw it. I reached out. "I found it—look, it's a perfect shape." I held the small stone in the direction of the sun, watching its sharp edges flicker.

My gram stepped forward and leaned on her walking stick. "It was probably an arrowhead. It looks too small to be the tip of a spear." She took the small stone from my hand as she evaluated my find—our rare unearthing. "Before you put that in your pocket, you need to visualize the journey this little stone has made to get here." She handed me back my precious new treasure.

"Mother, Samantha is only seven years old."

"It's never too soon to teach her respect for those spirits who walked the land before her." As my gram moved toward the creek's edge, I saw a figure moving in tandem, directly beside her. It stayed with her as she sat on a large boulder near the creek. Then the obscure shape vanished as quickly as it had appeared. Gram's hand fell to the spot beside her. "Sam, come here. Let's you and me sit for one minute, take a minuteof solitude and reflect. Your grandfather loved this part of the country, the lush beauty of this canyon, and all the wonderful colors. Oh, how I wish your granddad was here to see you, child." Her eyes glowed in the flickering sunlight as she spoke about him.

"He was here." I scooted up on the rock and found a flat spot to perch.

She went right over what I said, almost as if I hadn't said it. Like it was no big deal I just saw my grandpa. Then I saw her face scrunch, and her eyes lit up at the possibility of him being there.

"That is sweet, Sam. You are right. Your grandfather probably is here." She closed her eyes for a moment and took in a deep breath. When she opened her eyes, she told me how much she loved me. And then she reached her arm around my shoulders and pulled me close, and we gazed over the rushing rapids.

My mom kicked off her shoes and waded along the edge of the water. "Maybe an ancient Tuzigoot boy was looking to bring home dinner for his family and he dropped his satchel of arrows? Who knows?" My mom gave a teasing look toward Gram.

"You go ahead and make fun of me. That's all right." Gram waved her off with a sweeping motion of her hand. "But you know something, smart-aleck, you may be right. Did you know Tuzigoot is an Apache word for crooked water? They were probably called that cause there isn't one spot in this river that doesn't have a bend in it." Gram looked ahead at the creek that meandered like a snake through the canyon.

"I'm not making fun of you, Mom, it's just—Samantha is a little young for you to start introducing her to your spirit world, that's all." My mom lifted her foot and lightly sprayed us with the cool creek water from her toes. Her eyes sparkled like diamonds as she looked at my grandmother and me.

"Don't listen to your mother, Sam. She's what we call a skeptic. Heck, spirits are always around us." She made a sweeping, grandiose gesture with her hands. "You are never too young to know that." My gram reached out and took my hand in hers, the sacred stone pressed between our palms, and then she closed her eyes and invited me to do the same. "Just feel, Honey—feel with your heart, and just listen."

Our daytrips and hikes, and the many overnight trips, whether in town or out of town: it didn't matter, it always involved closing my eyes and listening to the hums of nature, all the different sounds in the silence of life. It was the rushing water of a river, the stillness of a lake, or the trickle of the fountain in Gram's own backyard, it didn't matter. Together we listened for the crackle of leaves, the chirping and singing of the birds, and the fluttering wings of the hummingbirds that surrounded her feeders. At night it was the crickets, the slight movement in the brush, the howl of a coyote, or the hoot of an owl; my gram was always honing my senses. Sometimes she'd tell me to listen for voices. "Don't stop 'em, just listen, let 'em in," she'd say. "You don't need to be afraid of 'em." I did hear voices. I saw things, too. Things other people didn't see. Except I didn't really understand the value of seeing dead people, until my mom died.

My mom always called Gram a tree-hugger and a thinker beyond her time. As I got older, I realized a tree-hugger was a compliment. When I moved in with Gram I am pretty sure I figured out the thinker part. Pretty quick, Gram taught me to meditate, said it was a good way to get in touch with myself. But I never saw anyone ponder life as much as her. I guess that's what my mom meant by, a thinker. At first, there were even times I mistook her meditation for her afternoon nap.

For the first few years after my mom's death, psychics, card readers and spiritualists became a familiar necessity for Gram, or had it always been an essential part of her life? I just never knew about it before we became roommates. But I often reminded myself, I hadn't just lost my mom, but she had lost her daughter.

Summer vacation started shortly after that ill-fated night, so Gram kept me connected to her hip. We regularly worked on our crafts together. A memory book was one of our first projects, pictures of us, of my mom when life was good. Gram knitted a lot, and me, I never made so many bracelets, earrings, and necklaces. My gram and her lady friends wore 'em, too. I don't know if they really liked them, or if they were showing pity for the little girl who lost her mom—the little girl who'd lost her childhood to a monster. That's what I'd heard 'em say.

Gram was retired when she took me in. She was a young sixty-five-year-old, caring for an aged eleven-year-old. On Mondays, Wednesdays, and Fridays she did yoga, and so of course, I did, too. I learned the downward-dog, a happy-baby, and a child's pose. But it was with the prayer position that I found the most comfort.

On Tuesdays and Thursdays we had lunch with "the girls," my gram called them that. The girls were her gang of friends ranging from Lois, who was fifty-five, to Gretchen, who was seventy-two and bragged she looked fifty-five. Betty, Dixie, and Phyllis were somewhere in between.

Helpful and doting, my gram's friends demonstrated a tremendous amount of compassion and strength when I needed it most. Lord knows they knew all too much about loss. My gram had lost her husband before his fiftieth birthday to a drunk driver. Her daughter, my mother, was killed by a skeleton that was hiding in my closet. Lois, the youngest of the group, the only one who never married, had just lost her mother. Mrs. Gretchen, still married, knew the pain of losing a child. And all the others were widows.

Besides their obvious commonalities, the shared aim of the friends was their desire to converse with the dearly departed. So, on Tuesdays before their regularly scheduled lunch, we would spend time sharpening our sixth sense, which included exercises using the subconscious mind to connect with the five senses. I was only eleven. But no one ever treated me like that. We would sit around my gram's large dining room table, passing different objects in a clockwise circle, our eyes closed, we'd touch, listen, sniff—mostly we'd feel.

"Don't just feel with your hands, Samantha. You must feel things from your heart center." Gram would say. "You must see not with your eyes, like everyone else, but rather with your mind's eye, Samantha, use your brow chakra." She tapped the spot on my forehead, right between my eyebrows.

We would each take a turn telling about our week, what we saw, in terms of visions. Dreams we may have had, or perhaps aura sightings and such. Mostly I listened; it took a while before I was comfortable discussing my clairvoyance with others. It wasn't until I was thirteen that I realized that's what they even called it.

Ms. Beth, my social worker, became a good friend to my gram and me. She'd stop in regularly to see how I was doing because I was living with a senior citizen and all. She and Gram got on well. They'd spend an hour at the small table in the kitchen, working on a cinnamon roll and a cup of coffee, chatting about everything and nothing. Ms. Beth seemed to understand I had undergone a drastic change in my life, but she also understood Gram did too. Ms. Beth stayed on top of my psychologist, even took me to some of my appointments when Gram was tied up. Sometimes I think she did it just to give Gram a break. She never went in with me or anything. But every time I hauled myself out of my shrink's office, my eyes swollen, tracks of tears running down my cheeks, Ms. Beth was right there, always offering an endearing smile and a warm embrace, an ear if I needed.

I never liked talking about what happened. But since that was all anyone wanted me to do, I was most comfortable with Ms. Beth. She never expected anything from me. I didn't have to lie to her and tell her I didn't feel sad and didn't have nightmares. She had a way of hearing what I was saying without me ever talking. There were times I thought she had special powers—clairvoyance.

Early on in our relationship, Ms. Beth introduced me to a place that helped victims of violence, mostly domestic. It was a safe haven for homeless folks, and people with addictions. Children were among the largest group of individuals at the home. It was actually more of a compound, really. Perhaps even a facility, but it was often referred to as a *house* or a *home*. I suppose it was because so many people wanted it to be one. I started out at Miracle House as a victim. At age eleven, I knew no better.

While in counseling, the group rants, everyone else's chatter about their pain and suffering, and I quickly became plagued by nightmares and frightening thoughts of brutal rape. Rape was a word I'd rarely even heard up to then. Certainly it was not a word that would speak about me. Yet, I became obsessed with its mere utterance. I repeatedly told myself I wasn't raped. Karl never even hit me. I hadn't ever put up a fight. I never screamed at him or scratched, clawed or punched him. Nevertheless, every time the word rape came up in the circle, I choked on my emotion, squirmed in my seat, and was reminded of what really happened to me.

Not soon enough, but soon after regularly going to Miracle House, I dropped the wounded sufferer's role, and graduated to volunteer. By the time I was fourteen, I could have run the place—me and my friend Ethan. Well, that is, I was a volunteer between school, yoga, counseling, and the additional psychic training my gram pursued, convinced I was gifted. By fifteen, I already knew the road map to life through palm reading, and was on my way to being a tarot card expert. Not always clear—on either account. And regrettably, the voices I heard weren't always the ones I listened for.

One day I was working with a group of kids—all younger than me. We were scrubbing down the toys in the infant department of Miracle House, giving the nursery a real good scouring. Germs were a problem in a facility like that; cleaning was an unending process. Not all volunteer work was fun and games. I was pressed against the sink, my hands deep into the soapy water, young ones all around helping, some not helping, when Ms. Beth walked into the room and called out my name. I turned toward the pleasant chorus of her voice. She approached me and leaned in for an embrace. We pressed out cheeks together, my hands dripped of soap and water.

Beside her stood a young girl, a lanky sort, her dark, thick eyelashes were long enough to brush my face from across the room. She had short hair, boyish features, dressed in big, baggy shorts, a scuffed pair of high-top tennis, and a purple Phoenix Sun's basketball tee-shirt that hung to the top of her thighs and looked like it had been washed a hundred times. Her arms dangled long at her sides, her face stern, unsympathetic, and unsmiling look I'd seen many times while working here, especially with teenagers who had been wronged by society.

"Samantha, I have someone I'd like you to meet." Ms. Beth turned back with her hand gesturing toward to the young woman beside her. "This is Madison. Madison Morgan. She lives pretty close to here, and not too far from you and your grandmother. Madison, this is Samantha Green."

"Hi Madison." I dried my hands on a towel as I stepped forward to greet her.

The youngsters that surrounded me scampered to Ms. Beth, mauling her, squeezing her calves, thighs, and waist, begging for her attention. Ms. Beth's deep laughter filled the room as she handed out hugs and kisses to the tiny, little people who were in desperate need of affection.

"You girls finish things in here, then show Madison around for me, Samantha—please. I'll take all these guys with me. Come on." Ms. Beth made a grand scooping motion, as if to pick up a bunch of flowers and out the door they all went, leaving Madison and me alone.

Madison extended her hand and I gently slapped it away with the damp towel.

"Oh, no—I'm a hugger." I wrapped my arms around her and felt her stiffen.

Madison's whole body went rigid. Most people loosen their embrace when they get that type of energy, but instead I held her, even tighter. And while we were connected, it was almost like a child's voice whispered in my ear. *"Hold on and don't let go. Hold her, hold her,"* it repeated. So I did as I was instructed. I held on to Madison. I held her until I felt her soften. I stepped back, realizing it was her turn to size me up. Would Madison notice my faded tie-dye shirt, my wrinkled cotton pants, or the Birkenstocks I'd worn for a full year, exposing my chipped toenail polish?

I moved across the room and began to towel-dry the Barbies, the Star Wars figures, Batman, and the Power Rangers and place them back in the box. Madison stood, staring, quiet.

"How long have you known Ms. Beth?" I asked.

"I don't know, a while I guess." Madison kicked at her feet.

"Here." I threw her a damp wash cloth. "Wipe all those tables and counters with this. You can use the water in that sink to rinse the rag. It's got Clorox in it. That keeps everything clean."

"What on earth did you do to get this crappy job?" Madison's tone was snotty.

A negative energy began to bubble inside me as I started tossing the toys in the box.

"So, is this what Ms. Hanson needs, a volunteer cleaning person? It would have been nice to know before she dragged me over here." Madison sauntered over to the sink to dip the cloth.

"Ms. Beth doesn't need anything. She brought you here because it is obvious you are the one in need. You are in need of some compassion." The words pushed through my clinched teeth. "If you must know what it is I did to get this crappy job," my tone indignant. "I was repeatedly molested and raped by my stepfather, before watching my mother shoot him in the head, just before shooting herself in the heart. So… this place is not my punishment. This place is my escape, my salvation." My eyes were unblinking. I stared Madison down, witnessing her mouth fall open and her eyes glaze over. She was so stunned by my assertion there wasn't even a nod of sympathy. I felt bad for my actions, but it quickly became obvious, with that statement I was able to knock the chip off her shoulder. "Come on, I'll show you around Miracle House." I grabbed her by the hand. "You can call me, Sam, if you like. My grandma calls me Sam."

*   *   *

I bent forward and put the arrowhead back on the window sill in my room. I was dressed and ready for work when I looked down and discovered I was still wearing Birkenstocks, and my pink toenail polish was still chipped. I scurried into the kitchen and placed my empty tea cup in the sink. I snatched the two brown paper sacks I'd packed the night before from the refrigerator. And then I went about grabbing my bag and purse, before heading off for work. First I had to find my car keys.

No matter what time I rose, I always seemed to run late for work. Not something I particularly liked about myself. Luckily I wasn't far from my place of employment. Finally, I dug them out of the bottom of my bag. I rushed through the front door. I always knew how lucky I was to have a grandmother like mine. She was someone who not only understood my sixth sense, but encouraged it. Too bad my insight didn't keep me from misplacing my keys.

Exactly six minutes in my car and I was approaching my job at Last Chance. It was a large, square, nondescript building of tan slump-block fronted by a raised flowerbed. It was surrounded by blacktop, with a few covered parking structures. That was when I caught sight of no less than five police vehicles, two TV vans, and hordes of people in several groupings. My back went stiff, my knees began to bounce with nervousness. I clutched the steering wheel in my car and awaited my chance to turn into the parking lot. A line of that ever haunting yellow plastic crime tape strung from the front end of the parking lot clear to the backside of the Q-Mart across the street from my job. Just as I began to make a left turn into work, I saw my friend and co-worker Ethan running across the street. He came toward me as I parked and stepped out of the car.

His black jeans fit tightly all the way down his thin legs to his unlaced red high-tops trimmed in speckled gold. His burgundy pullover clung to his upper body, and read: I'm a Fang-Banger, Bite me, and a bandana style scarf wrapped his long neck.

"Hi, Samantha." Ethan opened my car door.

"Hi, Honey." I stood and pressed my lips into his cheek. He smelled of his usual Calvin Klein cologne. "What happened over there?" My eyes traveled across the street to all the activity. We stood next to my car and gawked. "Why are all the police around?" My voice hitched with unease, my stomach swirled around the memories of that bright yellow reminder. "They found a woman's body behind the building." Ethan's sandy blond hair was combed forward and outlined his feminine features.

"I hope it's not someone we know." My gaze was fixed across the street.

"Girl—don't hold your breath. In this neighborhood if you're found dead in the back of a Q-Mart, you are most likely a street person, a drug addict, or a prostitute, and there aren't many of them we don't know. I spoke to the store manager, and he said her body was propped up next to the big trash bin in the back. He found her when he came on shift at eleven last night. He seemed pretty messed up by what he saw. I guess her throat was cut so deep it looked like her head was about to fall off." Ethan ripped into his pack of cigarettes and tapped them on the ball of his hand a few times until one came free.

"Oh jeez, Ethan, I could have gone without that little piece of information." I grabbed my purse and the remaining items from my car and used my foot to kick the door shut. We moved toward the employee entrance on the back side of the building. I felt Ethan tug at my blouse.

"Samantha, do you ever think to use an iron?" he said while assessing my outfit.

I turned and raised my brow. "I ran out of time."

"What's new?"

"I feel so bad for whoever it was. It gives me the creeps." We paused before reaching the corner of the building and stared across the street. The parking lot of Q-Mart bustled with activity. Ethan took another long draw of his cigarette. I watched wisps of smoke push through his lips.

"The dude at the counter told me she was a regular in the store, thinks she lived in the apartments beyond the block wall." Ethan's tone was shockingly blasé, almost unconcerned.

I instantly slapped his shoulder and stared in his face. "Hello—that's your apartment complex he's talking about." I was startled by this revelation.

"No shit, Sherlock. You don't think I know that? If someone is killing whores, it's only a matter of time before they start going for fags." With a blank stare, he breathed in a long drag of his cigarette. On the surface of his striking good looks Ethan embodied strength and confidence, but underneath, he was still a scared little boy—a little boy who was abandoned by his family.

"Ethan! Don't talk like that. It's not nice to call them whores." I halfheartedly smiled.

"Bitch," he countered.

"I kid the fags—I love the fags." I giggled nervously. My eyes were still narrowed in on the scene across the street. "I'm sorry, Ethan. I can hardly even say the F-word as a joke."

"Oh please, Sugar. I consider it a term of endearment." He batted his eyes and dipped his head toward my shoulder. "Kiss, Kiss," he said, while mock smacking his mouth on my face.

"Stop it—besides," I changed my tone to dismal, "someone died—we shouldn't even be talking like this. Have respect for the dead."

"Honey, that girl is dead and gone. It doesn't matter what we say now."

"I thought you were going to quit smoking?" I looked at him with a disapproving glance. My stern look wasn't so stern.

"Yeah, I thought so, too. It hasn't worked out that way." He swished away from me, taking another deep inhale. "It tastes too damn good to quit. I guess I'm not ready, yet." He smiled as he blew rings into the heavy morning air. "Come on, we better hurry, it's almost eight o'clock." He flipped his cigarette to the ground and smashed it out with his shoe.

"I wish it was only 8:00. But, I'm sure it's closer to 8:15 by now." I glanced back across the street. "Spirit, bless the survivors who loved her and will miss her." I whispered. Then I turned back around toward the private entrance of the building when I saw Willie sitting on the curb near the door.

"Hey Willie," I hollered from a distance. "I brought you something." Mondays were one of my regular day shifts. I could usually count on seeing Willie before entering the confines of my workplace. Today was no different. I always tried to bring him a little something: food, soda, a bag of clothes, a pair of shoes, some sort of gift. Yet I was the one who always felt gratitude after seeing him, with his toothless smile, and lost, but kind eyes. But today, as I neared him, I saw a trail of dried blood that had dripped off his ear and down his neck. The muscles in his jaw jumped in a peculiar way.

Chapter Six

Ethan Price

The air was cool, yet the morning sun was warming things nicely, as long as you were in the sun. April mornings in the desert could go either way. I walked up behind Samantha to find Willie sitting on the curb in front of us. When he tilted his head back, he cracked his eyes open and was looking right in the kind face of Samantha. I'm certain people rarely looked Willie in the face, especially in the eyes, but Samantha always did. And today was no different as she leaned over and greeted him. Samantha's pale arm extended out, the silver bangles on her arm collected at her wrist with a clinking noise when she reached down to Willie.

"Thanks Ms. Samantha." Lucid, he turned and reached up when she handed him a brown paper sack.

Samantha quickly wheeled back and pulled my gaze into hers. It was a troubled stare. It seemed she had to concentrate on each breath to remain upright. Willie was sitting on the curb in the shadow of the building. It appeared he was waiting for her, waiting for a meal, a friendly face, and kind eyes. I didn't really look at him closely, but when I did, I observed what looked like a whirlwind of half thoughts spinning in Willie's head, and the blood.

I stepped around Samantha. "Willie, what happened to you?" My voice pitched high.

Samantha stepped back, rendered speechless.

"I think I'd rather be hot than hungry. I'd rather be cold than hungry." He yelled out, and then looked up at the two of us. But I'm not sure he actually saw anything. I saw what seemed like a fog settle over him. He ignored us and riffled through the sack Samantha had handed him, repeating the word hungry so many times it was making me crazy. "Hungry, hungry, hungry, hungry, hungry, hungry…"

There was a sandwich of some sort, a small bag of chips, a green apple and a small container of juice.

"Willie! I want to know what happened to you. Where did all that blood come from?" I leaned down in front of him and tried to get him to look in my face. I wanted to get his attention. Really get his attention. "Who hit you? Where did all the blood come from?"

He said nothing. He stared into the bag of food.

I turned back toward Samantha, who was leaning over my shoulder, digging her hands into my skin. "It looks like he had a bloody nose or something."

"It looks worse than a bloody nose. He has scratches, Ethan. His ear looks like it was almost ripped off." Samantha's voice was queasy, but one of deep concern.

"Blood, blood, blood, blood, blood, blood." Willie put his hands in front of his face, as if to see them for the very first time.

"Why does he keep saying that?" Samantha pulled me toward the doorway. "He could be really hurt," her voice spiked. "I want to call the paramedics, or get someone from staff to come out here and check Willie out. Look at his jacket. That is a lot of blood, Ethan." She rushed into the building.

I pulled away and stepped back up beside him. "Willie, are you hurt?" Standing over him, I shook his shoulders. "Willie!" My gaze fell to his hands. His bloody hands.

Then I saw the gears in his mind slipping, everything appeared to be spinning out of control. Willie looked up at me and stood from his stooped position. His body protested with loud pops and snaps, causing him to grimace as he turned and limped away, shouting the words, "Silence!" over and over again. "Silence! Silence! Silence!"

"Willie, it's me!" I extended my hand.

Willie wasn't a young man. His grayish-brown, dreary hair matted to his head in big clumps. His overall looks told of a man who'd spent many hours on the breadline, so to speak. His soiled, ragged clothes were a dead giveaway of his destitution. He was lanky, his trousers too long, the loose threads dragged across the black pavement with each step, the dull black patch in his sagging seat looked like built up street oil. He had sweat patches under the arms of his filthy jacket, and plastic grocery bags tied around his feet to hold on his shoes. Or, perhaps they were his shoes, I couldn't really tell anymore.

"Willie, wait! Willie, I'm your friend—Ethan." I yelled one more time before he disappeared around the building. My experience with schizophrenia was little, but I knew enough not to follow Willie. His condition seemed to worsen over the years. Once he started talking to himself, things could get really ugly, very quick. Poor Willie, he's probably one pill away from being fairly normal, but he can't seem to stay on that one pill. And he had no one in his life to make sure he did.

Many younger people my age, twenty-six, usually looked at homeless people as thieves, drug users, or just smelly, lazy, dangerous, scary, losers. Me—I find them to be brave, desperate, resourceful people, trapped, depressed, struggling, and unlucky individuals. I know, because I, too, was down-and-out once, penniless and on the street.

* * *

I was fourteen when my father kicked me out of the house and told me never to come back. I thought it was something he'd get over at first, until I went home one afternoon to find the locks had been changed. The rock under the bush to the right of the door, the stone that always hid the family key was gone. No stone, no key, never an answer to any of my knocks, my pounding cries.

"I'd rather you got some girl pregnant. I would wish you were a criminal, a drug addict, a thief, anything but a fag." My father's expression was hard. "Get out! You are not my son. You will never amount to anything. Get out! I never want to see you again." Deep grooves ran the length of his mouth as he stared down on me with intimidating eyes.

He wanted me out without so much as a sleeping bag or a pillow. My mother reacted by not reacting. Her silence pierced my heart. Her eyes never even so much as looked up at me as my father pointed to the door. She never even voiced a protest, not even a huff, a mumble, a burble. Not a peep. I was her oldest son. I'm the one who spent time with her, kissed her, hugged her, complemented her. I'm the son who defended her from his vulgar slurs, his nasty comments. I helped her around the house, did the dishes, the laundry. I babysat my two younger brothers all the time. Yet, she remained motionless, speechless as I hauled my skinny, young, scared self to the exit. I turned back praying to see her eyes. I wanted to let her know I forgave her. She didn't look up. I paused. Those few seconds seemed like forever. Our eyes never met.

Given that kind of reaction it was not surprising that I left. I went out the door with nothing but the clothes on my back, and the four bucks I had in my jean pocket. The first week was the scariest. At fourteen, it wasn't like I had a car I could drive off in, and use as my hotel room. Finding shelter quickly became my first thought. The first night of homelessness all I did was walk around all night. I lived in the inner-city, so I spent the night walking the streets.

It was scary, so foreign being out after dark in these areas. I considered sleeping in several different abandoned buildings, but the screams of others, some of it laughter and other screeches of angry arguing, frightened me. At times, I felt as though I were in a labyrinth while moving aimlessly through the dark streets of downtown Phoenix, finding nothing but endless alleyways and windowless mortared walls.

Besides shelter and water—water of all things, who knew it would become such a precious resource in the middle of the city? Drinking, bathing, the bathroom, it all became so complicated. I had to be tricky, sly in a way, just to use something most people paid so little to have.

Each night of homelessness, I feared the sunset. My second week of being on my own I ran into a kid I knew from school. It was really weird, of all the times to see someone you know, of all places.

It was around ten o'clock at night. I was drifting through an alley on the backside of my new favorite Italian restaurant, ready to lift the lid on the large trash bin to see what was for dinner when I caught sight of them. There were two shapes in the shadows close to the rear of an unused warehouse adjacent to the trash can I was about to dive into. Startled, I paused at first. I didn't want to make a sound. I tried to avoid people in these types of places, especially in the dark, principally because I was alone, and I looked even younger than my fourteen years. There was a large, paunchy figure standing, leaning into the brick building, and the outline of a body kneeling on the ground in front of him.

I squeezed in between the garbage can and the restaurant, peering around the stinky, metal container, where I waited for the encounter to break up. Suddenly I saw them scuffling, the larger man shoved the other person back as they shouted. Then, by surprise, I saw someone I recognized. I was sure it was Jason's face. A slice of light from the distant street lamp pressed between the two buildings into the alley and lit up his youthful features. From where I was quietly hiding, I couldn't see his brilliant blue eyes, but I could picture them. What I could see for sure was the dimple that finished off his strong chin.

"You told me twenty bucks," Jason screamed at the man.

"Fuck off, kid." He pushed hard on Jason knocking him to the ground. He wadded something in his hand and threw it. "Take it or leave it, punk! Your blow job sucked."

"Wasn't that the fucking point." Jason jumped up and went for the man, but he went right back down, this time, he couldn't have seen it coming.

The large fist of the fat man connected with Jason's face. His limp body fell back; he was motionless. The belligerent man tugged at his trousers, straightened his collar, yanked at his sleeves and walked out of the alley. Jason left in the dark, alone and hurt—or possibly dead for all I knew. My heart pounded in my throat. I waited. I watched. No movement from me, no movement from him. I bolstered my courage with a deep breath and I stepped out of hiding. My eyes ran the length of the alley and back again several times. I crossed outside of the patch of light and knelt at Jason's side. Just as I approached, he was coming back to life. He was moving and moaning.

"Are you all right?" I grabbed his arm and pulled him to a sitting position on the pavement.

"Ethan—is that you? What the fuck are you doing here?" He pulled the tail of his shirt up to his face and wiped the blood that dripped from his nose and his lip.

"I was just stepping out for dinner." I concealed my embarrassment with sarcasm. "What the fuck are you doing?" I turned the questioning back onto him as I extended my arm to pull him off the ground. He was a sophomore, I was a freshman, he was a jock and I wasn't. I grunted as I heaved him from the grungy pavement.

"Did you see anything? How long have you been here?" His eyes were worried. He seemed less anxious about his bloody nose and swelling eye than what I possibly saw him doing in the alley.

I watched Jason brush himself off. His eyes weren't looking at mine.

"I walked around the corner just in time to see some guy clock you and send you flying," I lied. "I didn't get a good look at him. What happened between you?" I used a curious tone.

"Oh, nothing. He was some dirty old man trying to buy sex. When I told him no fucking way, he decked me." Jason ran his fingers through his wavy hair, and then slightly puffed his chest.

"It's going on eleven o'clock on a school night, what are you doing here?" He cast an assuming glare. "You smell like you could use a shower. What have you been doing—dumpster diving?" His split lip slightly smirked.

"Yes." I decided to be honest. "I have. I could also use some food, fresh clothes and a tall glass of fresh, cold water." I put my hands in my pockets and looked into the darkness behind him. It seemed neither of us wanted to look at each other. "I haven't been in school for almost two weeks." I look up at him.

"I hadn't noticed." Jason put his index finger to one side of his nose and aggressively blew out the other side of his nostril. Then he spit. When he saw me cringe, he apologized. "Sorry. I can't stand that blood dripping down the back of my throat."

Spitting and snorting really grossed me out. It reminded me of someone else.

"My dad hates me." I blurted out. I looked down. My hands were so filthy I wanted to just keep them in my pockets. The darkness was unable to hide the filth. I hated being dirty. That was almost worse than not being acknowledged by most people who simply just walked right by me, as if I were invisible, a ghost of the streets.

"Your dad hates you? Welcome to my fucking world. Come on, Pretty Boy. I'll take you to my house tonight. You can get a good meal, a hot shower, and a night's rest off the streets. I guess you can also have some of my clothes. I don't think we can wash the odor out of what you're wearing." He put his arm over me and led me out of the alley onto the lit roadway. "Don't get any funny ideas, Ethan. I'm not one of your kind." When we hit the brightness of the main street, he dropped his arm off my shoulder.

"One of my kind?" I acted naïve.

"You know, one of those..." He walked fast along the Central.

Was it that obvious? My father had called me a fag. Jason accused me of being something different, all within a few weeks. Yet I didn't even know for sure who I was. I had to run to stay up with him. Jason was nice enough, but this was not the same guy I knew from school. This person was agitated, sweaty and aged. Yet he was only fifteen.

"What are your parents going to say when you bring me home at midnight to eat and shower?" I was breathless racing to stay by Jason's side. The night air was chilling my moist skin. Yet I was feeling lucky it was April in Phoenix.

"Don't worry. My Dad doesn't give a shit, probably won't even hear us. And my mom is dead," his tone was flat. His expression fell to the concrete we trampled with each step. "So long as I live on the other end of the house, keep to myself, it's like I don't even exist, which is what he wants anyway."

"Oh, I'm sorry. I didn't know your mother died." I was damn near jogging to keep up with him. "What happened to your mom?" I solicited more information.

"Headache," he said. "You ever hear of anyone dying from a fucking headache?"

"What? No, I can't say I have." His pace finally slowed. "Aneurysm. That was the official name." Jason sadden with his statement.

We veered off the main street and walked the rest of the way to his house in the silence of the night. A light glow cast off the random porch lights, making it so I could see the sadness of his thoughts as we made our way to his place. The sprinklers watered the lawns on some of the residential homes causing the air to cool even more. The smell was fresh, clean, and hopeful. Jason took me to his home that night. An upper middle class home in the Encanto area of downtown Phoenix. We snuck in the back door. But, according to Jason, his father was passed out by then, anyway. We stopped off at the kitchen first before retiring to Jason's side of the house.

He and his father lived alone. Jason had a gigantic, nice bedroom, and his own private bathroom. That night, Jason did as he said he would. He fed me, let me shower, sleep, and he sent me off with a new outfit. Complete with underwear and socks. It didn't matter that the jeans and shirt were enormous on me, what mattered was they were clean, fresh, and they were now mine. I left Jason's house in the morning, the same time he did, with something he didn't even realize he had given me—a way to earn money.

That was when it started. I began to sell sex on the street. I launched myself into the underworld of deviant behavior for a buck, for a warm bed, and for a meal. I couldn't go home. Even if I had wanted to go home, my parents didn't want me. I was forced to quit school even though I liked it. I liked it because I was good at it. My teachers all liked me, too. I was smart, quick with numbers. Getting a roof over my head became my sole focus and I did whatever it took to get that. I had a baby face, soft features, a thin frame—business men couldn't refuse me. I was fourteen years old, very vulnerable, and suddenly exposed in a frightening new world.

No more sleeping in parks, alleys, and vacant buildings. I'd found a few tricks to pay me for blow jobs, amongst other sexual favors, and finally I had the money I needed to get my own room in a trashy hotel. They rented by the hour, the day, and by the week, and ID wasn't required. I quickly had the business to rent on a week to week tenancy. I never used my room for a trick. *No Johns allowed.* It was his room, his car, or a dark hideaway off the main street. Unfortunately, that rule didn't keep me safe.

My last night as a boy-toy came when I met two men in the foyer of the Wyndham Hotel in downtown Phoenix. I was sitting on the sofa in the upscale lobby, my legs tightly crossed, black skin-tight pants and a taut red pullover with short sleeves. I spied the two men. I caught the eye of the one guy out front. He was cute, taller than the other man, had a pretty smile, bright eyes and coal black hair. His clothes subtly hinted designer. He nudged his friend who was shorter; he had a large neck and crew-cut short hair, he was wearing Levis with a button-up shirt. They both eyed me. We communicated in glances. I was sure I had read the signals correctly. I rose and walked across the lobby, maneuvered my way around a large sculpture moving toward the men's room. In less than a minute we were standing at the urinal, me directly in the middle of them.

"So, is this something you're into?" he asked. His eyes seemed to flirt with me.

"And what is it I'm into?" I returned his glance, looking at his perfectly combed black hair.

The other man intervened, "Three-ways?" he blurted as he zipped his pants up.

I turned to look in his direction. "It depends."

"We have plenty of money." A smile played around the edges of his lips, his hand gestured toward his pocket.

"Fine," I said with confidence in my voice and uncertainty in my mind. "I'll follow you to your room." At sixteen, two at a time was something I hadn't yet experienced.

"Oh, no!" he snapped. "We have to go to your place. We'll pay extra."

"I don't have a place," I lied. Then I turned back to the guy with black hair, the one I thought was in control. Now I wasn't so sure.

"We have a car. Come on. We'll figure it out. He looked at his buddy and smiled." He was nicer than his gruff friend. He turned to walk to the sink.

We all washed our hands and formed a line as we each walked out of the men's room.

I liked this hotel because I typically met men who paid me well. In a jovial manner, I traveled through the extravagant lobby and through the revolving front doors and into the darkness of night. The two strangers were on my heels. Going outside to someone's vehicle wasn't uncommon. Some of the businessmen were leery of going back to their room. Others were afraid of being seen by associates who were traveling the same trade-show circuit.

We crossed the dimly lit parking lot to an Expedition that had been backed into a spot opposite the hotel entrance. A quarter-moon was high in the sky offering a bleak glow. The night air was warm and still, rather weighty. The handsome one slid in the driver's seat, told me to jump in the back, which I did. His bossy buddy went around to the other side of the vehicle and swung his body into the backseat with me. *Okay, so he wants to go first*, I thought. The heavy aroma of pot smoke hung in the air. In the close quarters of the vehicle the smell of stale alcohol became very pungent.

"So, you're a hustler, huh?" The burly man's eyes narrowed, sweat dripped from his closely-cut hair. His tone was deep, nasty. His hands moved to his crouch splaying open his pants.

"I prefer to think of myself as a determined business person." I looked at the spitefulness etched into the malice planes of his face and my stomach began to turn over with nerves.

The man beside me had colorless eyes. So colorless they didn't reflect light. Realizing I had made a grave error in judgment, I reached for the door, just as the vehicle jerked into motion. Before I could freak out about what I had gotten myself into, we were out of the parking lot and onto the main street headed through the city, going somewhere only God knew. I felt a numbing sensation as his large hand clamped the back of my neck. Pulling me toward him he forced my mouth over his penis. It seemed as if my neck were being slowly crushed in a vise.

"We don't like faggots." The driver finally spoke. His voice was low, but it carried clearly to the backseat.

I couldn't respond—my mouth was full.

Many hours later, when my eyes cracked open, I was in a hospital room with a strange woman slumped in the chair at my bedside. I think I actually heard her snoring.

"Hello." My swollen lips felt sliced to pieces, barely allowing the greeting to slip out. My eyelid drooped over one eye making it difficult for me to see.

Apparently startled by the sound of my raspy voice, the woman moved in her seat, and then she leaned in closer to me. "Hi there, young man, I've been waiting for you to wake. I'm Elizabeth Hanson, I'm with CPS." Her voice was soft, her touch velvety as she lightly stoked my hand.

"What day is it? How'd I get here?" I tried to open my bad eye wider, but couldn't.

She adjusted my bed, causing me to sit up slightly. "It's Sunday. A homeless man found you and saw to it you were brought in here on Saturday morning." Her soft voice radiated compassion. "You were naked, badly beaten and assaulted. Willie waited with you until the ambulance showed up." Her cheeks were round, her eyes somber as she stared into my face. She sounded like she knew Willie. Willie was a street person I had befriended.

"Naked? Damn, those were my favorite black jeans." Losing two days and perhaps much more, I don't know why I tried to make light of my dark circumstance. My head was throbbing and by the feeling in my backside, she didn't need to define the word assaulted.

I felt like I had shit a watermelon. For a moment I imagined how it must have been for Willie to find me this way. Tears began to flow down my face, stinging along the way. *What happened to me?* I asked myself the question without really being prepared for the answer.

As if reading my thoughts, this woman with all the bad news spoke. "You have numerous bruises to your body and a laceration on your scalp that required thirty-six stitches. There was no ID on you, and no reports of a missing person, that is why I am here." A simple smile curled at the edges of her mouth. "I couldn't just leave you alone." Elizabeth Hanson looked into my face and said nothing while her gemstone eyes began to mist. This plump, friendly stranger genuinely cared about me. "I'm sorry" was all she said for the next several minutes as she sat next to my bed and held my hand—something I'd wished my mother would have done.

"CPS—what's that?" I thought I knew, but I wasn't sure. It had been so long since anyone considered me a child I had second guessed myself.

"I'm with social services, the child protection agency." She stood and leaned into the rail of the bed. Her grip on my hand was unyielding. "When someone comes in unconscious, and without the proper identification, the doctors make their best judgment in age. Assuming you are less than eighteen years old, I am one of the authorities they call. Can you tell me your name?" Her brunette hair was pulled back into a messy ponytail. Her gaze concentrated on my good eye.

"No good can come out of you knowing my name." I was afraid to tell her who I really was. I barely even knew myself anymore.

She leaned into my face. "Let me just tell you, regardless of your identity, if you are under eighteen years old, I am here to protect you. I won't let anything else happen to you, so long as you'll allow me to help you. "

"My name is Ethan, I'm sixteen. I don't have any family." What I should have said was I don't have any family who cares.

"I'm sorry, Ethan." Tenderly and gently her hand combed the hair away from my face. She reached for a spoonful of ice chips and brought them to my lips. "Try this—if it hurts to chew just let 'em melt in your mouth."

I separated my lips and took great pleasure in not just the coolness of the ice, but I was elated with the attention this stranger expressed. She smelled of lilac, my mother's favorite flower. Like my mother, Ms. Beth Hanson was a large woman, age for me was impossible to guess, maybe thirty-five or forty. Her face was pretty, cheerful features, naturally redden skin tone. She probably spent the bulk of her life hearing how it was such a shame for a woman to have such a pretty face and be so fat. I didn't see a ring on any of her fingers, leaving me to assume she was unmarried.

I hummed with gratitude as this kind woman continued to spoon-feed crushed ice through my ballooned lips. A part of me wanted to ask her for a mirror, but the part of me that was afraid of what I'd see prevailed. I looked past her, to the window, the slices of light that peered through the blinds and cast bright lines through the room, and I became mindful of the fact that in the few minutes I had known this person she treated me with more dignity and respect than anyone ever had in all my sixteen years.

I was never able to identify the two men who did such terrible things to me. In fact I didn't try. I told the police I hadn't seen their faces. I let them know I was homeless, living on the streets, no family. Those were the same lies I told Ms. Hanson. I never wanted her to know about the hotel room I lived in, or what I did to survive. From that hospital bed, Ms. Elizabeth Hanson, social worker extraordinaire, got me totally hooked up. By the way she dressed, I could see she didn't have much sense of style, but the woman had clout when it came to caring for others. She was completely in charge of getting me on the right path, and nothing or nobody stood in her way, not even me, not then.

I never returned to that sleaze-bag hotel room, and I never returned to my life, the way it had been. Instead, I went into a home known as Miracle House. Living up to its name, it was truly a *house of miracles* for me. Mostly they helped the homeless and poor populations of the Phoenix area. As it turned out, violence, abuse, and neglect were not only things that pertained to me. Luckily I fell into the hands of not just one angel, but two. If not for Willie, a homeless man few people cared about, who knows what would have come of me? I found out Ms. Elizabeth Hanson had positioned herself beside my bed from the time she was called in, until the moment I actually awoke. Oddly, it was a bed I found myself grateful to have been in.

*   *   *

Because Willie had been the one who rescued me all those years ago I had a special place in my heart for him. But even I knew there was no saving a street man.

"Willie, wait! Willie, it's Ethan." He disappeared around the building. I turned around and was heading back through the doors to work at the same time Samantha came running through with the staff nurse to check Willie for injuries.

"Where is Willie?" Samantha was glancing past me into the parking lot.

"He's gone." I shrugged my shoulders and walked past her. "I need to clock in."

"How could you have just let him walk off, Ethan? My God, he was covered in blood." Samantha screeched. She turned and gave a nod to the nurse, sending her back to her duties inside the building.

"You know better than that. I have no control over that man. Shit, he doesn't even have control of himself, now come on. Let's get to work. There are other people who need us right now. Mainly the two employees who are waiting to be relieved of their duties." I tugged at her arm, her eyes continued to pan the parking area and beyond. "I'm telling you, I watched him walk away, Samantha. Willie is long gone, trust me, Sugar. If he were injured, he wouldn't have been able to disappear so quickly. I'm sure he's fine. I don't know where all that blood came from, but I'm sure he's okay."

"It's weird, Ethan. When I see Willie, his aura is always gray. Not dull or muted, but brilliant gray. I think that just means he's a lost soul or something because I don't see a gray aura very often. But today, today was different, Ethan. Today his aura was fading. It was much weaker than usual, more like a pale blue, but there were sparks. Gleaming silver sparks were popping off Willie. That's not good, Ethan."

"Oh Samantha, Honey, I'm sure there is an explanation for that." There was never a good way to respond to Samantha when she started talking like that.

"Yeah, I *guess* there is an explanation—death, Ethan." Her expression showed gloom.

Samantha shrugged her shoulders and retreated inside the building. I followed her. It was past time to get busy. I worked in admitting the poor souls into Last Chance, and Samantha was in placement, helping to get them out. We worked every day with people who had run out of money, food, drugs, alcohol, and luck. They were often brought to us by their own family members who could no longer cope with their loved one's disability, whatever it was.

Initially we checked them out for arrest warrants, and then we ran them through our admissions form. The first question on the list: have you had any alcohol or done drugs within the past twenty-four hours? The answer to that question must unequivocally be no, or they do not get to move on to question number two. Do you have anyone else you can call to come and pick you up? Anyone?

Chapter Seven

Madison Morgan

I worked in courtroom number four. There were six courtrooms in the building. I sat at my desk in the courtroom and prepared for our morning session. The air was cool around me. I adjusted the collar on my shirt, pulling it up slightly to cover my neck, since my short hair didn't. Because of my official status, my movements caused the others in the courtroom to begin to whisper, and stare in my direction. As usual for a Monday the docket was very full, so the judge would have little patience for all the crap that spewed from the defendants and their attorneys. The public defenders were so bogged down with the number of *lowlifes* they encountered.

A large percentage of the people who came into this courtroom were total liars and bullshit artists. Nearly every public defender would prefer to be sunk to the bottom of Saguaro Lake with cinder blocks strapped to their bodies, rather than to defend another crack addict or meth whore, who inevitably would be right back in their office in sometimes hours rather than days—most often arrested for another petty crime, all over again, causing the attorney to work too many hours for what would seem to be no valid reason. Yes, there are other types of cases that come across my desk, but, I would venture to say almost all are drug related in some kind of way.

I jumped from my seat. "All rise," I said, as the large door behind my desk opened into the chamber.

I'm a Court Clerk for Maricopa County, in Phoenix, Arizona. Some people referred to me as a Judicial Assistant or a Trial Clerk. I prefer Judge's Right Arm. It wasn't like my qualifications were exceptional or anything. My mother worked for the judge. She had cleaned her house for ten years. Yes, I had graduated high school, and yes, I had four years of college, and I was currently in law school working towards my law degree, but none of that mattered like the connection my mother had to the judge. Ten years cleaning her home, I have no doubt my mother always discussed me and my future. That was what she did. Anyway, it paid off. It also helped that I was able to speak Spanish. Once again, thanks to my mom, I was bilingual. Timing was everything. Justice Pittsman began her term as a Superior Court Judge three years ago, and I was hired then too, and began my job as a JA.

The judge and I were not allowed to speak to the litigants or to their attorneys about a case unless the conversation took place at a hearing when all concerned had an opportunity to be present. You would be surprised how often I ran into people outside of the courtroom, especially in my neighborhood, but mostly around the hallways of the courthouse. I often walked around with my head down. Sometimes I even pretended not to see certain people just to save us both from that uncomfortable moment. I even faked a call on my cell phone to get out of talking to some of the attorneys I came across.

As a judicial assistant, I was the staff member closest to the judge. I had a variety of responsibilities including scheduling hearings, preparing orders and correspondence, communicating with other judge's offices, and dealing with the public. When I am in the courtroom sitting beside the judge, I keep track of the minutes of the court proceedings, I act as evidence custodian, and I also administer the oath to witnesses and jurors if there are any.

Our court can handle various charges, including narcotic law violations, violent crimes, and property crimes. I am usually in the courtroom for three daily sessions, with about ten felony incidents of all types in each session for a total of approximately thirty cases per day. It sounds like a lot of work—that's because it is. Our courtroom presides over felony and misdemeanor trials for non-violent offenders. These defendants enter guilty pleas for sentences, which are mostly suspended because of the lack of space to house them. Some are turned over to the probation division of the courts, which is another branch of the system that is overtaxed, turning out criminals on a regular basis.

Mrs. Dedee Pittsman, the presiding justice, walked in and sat down behind her bench. The cases began. "Okay Madison, what do we start with today?" She held her hand out to me for the first file of the morning. "I just heard they found another woman's body down off of 24th Street and Roosevelt," she added.

I was jolted. That was close to Sam's job. "Where, exactly? How long had the body been there?" My mind was racing. I wanted to call Sam. I wanted to warn her.

"I think they said she hadn't been dead for long," the judge continued, "maybe killed last night sometime. They found her body behind the Q-Mart. Apparently her throat was slit just like the others." The judge talked while she was looking through the file I'd just handed her.

I stood and bellowed loudly, "The court calls Charles Tipton." My thoughts were on one thing.

A tall slender man dressed in a plaid shirt and torn blue jeans approached the bench. His public defender, dressed in a plain brown suit, stepped up from a bench seat that held a few other attorneys. He was a standard issue district attorney, lean as a shark, with a mouthful of capped teeth and a full head of hair. The defendant held up his hand and declared to tell the truth.

"Charles Tipton, could you take the stand? Please give your full name for the court reporter to record it properly.

"Charles Tipton. C-H-A-R-L-E-S T-I-P-T-O-N."

While he was reading in his name, I heard the door on the other side of the courtroom open, which meant the bailiff was leading the jail-held litigants into the courtroom. Their shackles clanged in unison as they walked into the box, a box made especially for them. One by one the sheriff handling the inmates unlatched the chains that restrained the criminals' legs to their hands, giving them an opportunity to approach the bench when called to do so.

Charles Tipton's attorney placed his hands on top of the judge's high desk and slightly leaned forward, giving reasons as to why his client's charges should be immediately dropped, or at the very least, lowered to a lesser charge with a minimal fine. In this court, that is usually what happened. Many of the criminals that came in here would steal just about anything from anybody. Most of the pilfering was committed against family members or companies who didn't want to take the time to prosecute these losers.

The drug addicted-criminals were continuously released back out onto the streets, most of the time to take right back up where they left off; only to elevate their drug use and their bad behavior. That was the part of the job that I hated. I hated that I saw the same people in court, over and over again, in such a short period of time. Most of them should have taken advantage of some of the drug rehab programs that were offered to them.

So, instead they became repeat offenders, some of them habitual repeat offenders, for years, their crimes escalating. Just like the miserable man who killed my cousin Lisa. Fourteen years later, my cousin and uncle are still dead, my dad is an alcoholic, and I was probably screwed up for the rest of my life—while that fucking killer lies around, collecting his three squares a day, and has the time to find God, or something. Maybe even become an attorney in jail—who the fuck knows?

When I started this job, I wanted to keep an open mind, somehow evaluate the system and provoke a change for the future. After being friends with Sam for more than ten years, she'd begun to wear off on me. It took some time; it didn't happen right away.

* * *

When I first met Samantha Green, I was taken by her eyes. A certain hard-won wisdom sparkled in her eyes, eyes that seemed to smile when she looked at you. Eyes that looked, depending on the light, brilliant green—almost like emeralds. She was tiny compared to me, yet when she reached out and hugged me upon introduction, she was like a giant in comparison. Her confidence, her coolness and assurance overtook me as she clung to my body. She seemed so mature for someone who was fourteen. Less than a year separated us, me being the elder.

My first impression of Sam was her obvious mature kindness. But in my mind, her kindness was to a fault. I thought it odd she was so nice to me. She didn't even know me. Then she reacted to my snide, infantile behavior, unleashing her inner anger by snapping off my head, and then I knew she was normal. That is, until she spilled the dirty details of her private horror. There was nothing normal about that. I immediately felt like an idiot. I always thought what I went through as a child was bad. I knew right away I had met a friend in Samantha. Sadly for her, she was someone who had suffered worse than I had—far worse.

I was speechless after learning of Sam's past and she picked up on it. She immediately switched back into this super charming individual. "Come on, I'll show you around Miracle House." Sam took me by the arm and led me through the halls of the enormous campus.

That's when I met Ethan, Sam's friend, another Miracle House protégé. I couldn't help but check him out, he was different. He was tall, very slender, and very loud. His arms flailed wildly as he walked in our direction. The neckline was cut out of his tee-shirt, and it was knotted up on one side, slightly revealing his midriff. A pair of faded jeans sucked to his body. They were rolled just below his knees, and his shoes were worn-out Converse, no socks.

"Hi, Samantha," he hollered in a high pitched scream. He bounced over to us and kissed Sam on the cheek. "Who is Miss Smiley, here?" He stared into my face and smiled glibly.

"Ethan, this is Madison." Sam gestured my direction, tilting her head slightly. "He is another Ms. Beth save."

"Yes indeed, we love us some Ms. Beth Hanson." Ethan swung out his hand in a flamboyant gesture. "Hi, I'm Ethan. I'm Queen of this here palace." He fluffed his hair and adjusted the thin cotton material he used as a headband. It actually looked like the missing neckline of his shirt.

I reached out and grabbed his hand, mumbling, "Hi."

"Christ, Honey—for a thin hand you have a firm grip. What, have you been clinching your fists as a strengthening pastime?" He jerked his hand back and began massaging it.

"Nice outfit," Samantha said, checking Ethan out.

He twirled at the compliment, giving us view of his backside as well. "It's not easy dressing out of the freebie bin. But hey, I'm not complaining. As long as I have a pair of scissors I can cut some style into anything. Taa-taa my Darlings. I don't have time to join your party. I have work to do, if I am to earn my keep." He swished away and disappeared down an intersecting hallway.

Over the ensuing months of that summer vacation, I managed to become quite dedicated to Miracle House. As volunteers, who regularly bumped into each other, Sam, Ethan, and I had developed a friendship founded on sadness and a shared reluctance for remembering our own pasts. I was pretty sure that is exactly what Ms. Beth had in mind.

*   *   *

While she was on the bench, I obeyed Judge Pittsman's every command as she followed my lead. We handled the courtroom like an exquisite dance pair; one couldn't make a move without the other. I looked up from the stack of files that sat before me. The judge had worked things out with Charles Tipton's attorney. Throwing me his file, she churned out instructions as to what kind of fines Charles would pay. I set him up in the system and called the next defendant.

No matter what was going on in the courtroom, my attention was always on the inmate box. They, well some of them, looked pretty scary. Sometimes when the courts would call an initial hearing, it required that an arrested person be taken promptly before a judicial officer, and often times that meant without showers and a change of clothing. The statute does not define promptly, but most courts have said that an initial hearing be held within 48 hours.

That is reasonable, although longer periods, such as over a weekend or a holiday, have been approved as well. So, consequently, not only are they dirty and smelly, some of these people are brought off the streets after being high, non-stop, for months. Some of them came straight into the courtroom from the drunk tank, which could easily be referred to as the *drug* tank.

It freaked me out to see the faces and the eyes of some of these drug heads. And it totally disturbed me to see the women who lived that way. I could only imagine where they had been, or what they had done to themselves just to get where they were. By the time the women got arrested and were brought into court, it almost seemed like they were more messed up then the men. So often a woman could use her own body to get her drugs. She was not forced to do the same petty crimes that brought the majority of the criminals in front of us.

The women, they were totally messed up by the time I'd see them. As an alternative to petty crimes, they were instead forced to give up their dignity. Most of the women were so bad that they could no longer earn their keep with their own body. Even the screwed up men that paid them in the past could no longer find worth or any value in these poor women—girls really.

I stood tall and once again bellowed over the crowded chamber. "The court calls Jason Magnus."

From the inmates' box, a medium height man rose. He raised his stare to one of the public defenders in the courtroom and waited for her instruction. The public defender walked toward the contained area, with the nod of her head, she gestured to Mr. Magnus. Still wearing the shackles that bound his hands together in front of him, he slowly and methodically moved around the partition, down the step, and toward the bench as directed by his attorney. He held up his right hand, clamped to the chain, his left hand dangled along the front of his chest. Without looking up, he declared to tell the truth. I asked the man to give his full name so the court reporter could record it properly. I handed the file over to Judge Pittsman and took my seat.

"Mr. Magnus, it seems this is not the first time you have been in my courtroom." With her prying stare, it was obvious the judge was trying to get him to look at her. "Do you understand why you are here today, Mr. Magnus?" Her tone was firm, again trying to get him to look her direction. This time judge Pittsman leaned forward, her face tipped over the tall desk that protected her from him. But her intent gaze didn't coerce him to look at her.

He did not lift his head. It was obvious to me he didn't want us to see his eyes. His chin tucked to his chest, finally, hesitantly, he fixed his eyes on me. Even through his sideways stare, I could see his eyes were deep pools of anger, sadness, and shame, all swirling in the redness of restlessness and fatigue. His slanted gaze revealed a brilliant shade of blue, but beneath was a dark, almost black tint that influenced his defiance. He looked like he was there, but not present.

"Jason Magnus, I asked you if you know why you are here." The judge prodded with even more authority.

"Yes your honor." He still did not look at her. "I'm accused of stealing." His voice was not gruff, but raspy.

"Good, Mr. Magnus. Thank you for responding." The judge used a condescending tone. "Can you tell me what you stole?"

"Yes." That was all he said. And then, for just a moment, an uncomfortable silence fell upon the courtroom.

"I am waiting, Mr. Magnus."

He looked to the ground. "Yes, your honor, I'm accused of stealing beer." He seemed to have an embarrassed agitation about him. "I haven't had a clear head, family issues. I wasn't thinking right, your honor."

I could tell by listening to him this was an excuse he had often used. I ran my fingers across the grain of my wood desk as I peered at him under the bright bank of florescent lighting. Beneath his street-worn hide, he was a pale, grayish-yellow tone. He had dark circles under his eyes and brown stained teeth. He looked like he could have been an attractive guy at one time. And maybe still, if he would stay off drugs, get some rest, take a shower, shave, and put on something besides jail attire.

According to his file, he was twenty-seven years old. I would have guessed he was closer to a thirty-seven-year-old man. His skin appeared tan, dry, tired and worn, the look of a laborer, or that of a tired drug addict. He had a blood-crusted scratch across his cheek and neck. I wondered what women he'd offended. It never ceased to amaze me the torn down individuals that came through this courtroom. But today, for some reason, this guy was sticking with me. I could not seem to take my eyes off him. When he would glance my way, I'd stared down at his reflection off the shine of marble floor beneath him.

"Now, we are finally getting to it, Mr. Magnus." The judge had a pleasing quality to her voice, once he admitted to doing wrong. "You have a very long record here, my friend. And you do not seem to be getting it together. Do you have anything else to add?" There was a period of silence. "Can you say anything for yourself, Jason Magnus?" She scrutinized him over the top of her eyeglasses.

With no response from him, her eyes moved to his public defender, who of course brought a motion to quash the whole case. When the victim of the crime didn't show up in court it was hard to convict for walking into a 24-hour store and stealing beer by the armload, just to sell on the streets to supply a drug habit. It was not financially beneficial for corporations to take the time to prosecute on such petty stuff. So of course it was most often pleaded out, getting the predatory thief off for the crimes he'd committed over and over again.

Instead, the criminal would go back out onto the streets with absolutely no help for his alcohol and drug addiction, and little to no punishment for his or her wrongdoings. A few days in county jail, a little rest for the weary, three square meals, a shower, and back out they would go, to do the same stupid shit, while living in squalor and the unpleasant unhappiness they called life. Recently, I found that I struggled with wanting to help them. But I also struggled with just locking them up and throwing away the key, too. These were the losers Sam tried to convince me were worth saving.

"I am remanding Mr. Magnus in the custody of the Maricopa County jail until Thursday." She closed the folder. "See if a few more days in jail will help you clear your head, Mr. Magnus." The judge tossed me his file.

The jittery young man, wearing an old man's mask turned to his public defender again for instructions. I watched as he twisted his shaking body and headed back over to the box on the other side of the courtroom. I don't know why I stared at him. I don't know why I pitied him—but I did.

"Madison. Madison!" The judge commanded my attention. She gave me the signal for recess and loudly banged her gavel.

I stood and yelled, "All rise."

Judge Dedee Pittsman walked back toward her private chamber. I glimpsed Jason Magnus looking back my way. Our eyes met. While he was being restrained at the ankles, his stare never left mine. I was now the one quickly looking away, refusing him eye contact. I was the one who didn't want him seeing inside of me. As they began to escort out the defendants who were dressed in jumpsuits, with their clanging chains, and as the large room cleared of spectators and the other defendants, I kept my head down, working the cases before me.

I remained at my desk in the echoing room with the expectation of getting my act together for the next session. The prior defendant's file lay in front of me. I couldn't help but open it. He didn't even look familiar, yet the justice said Jason Magnus had been before us on another occasion. I was surprised because usually I would recognize our past defendants. It was unlike me not to have been the one telling the judge he was a repeat offender in our courtroom. I wouldn't forget him again. For some reason he stood out for me now.

I once again raised my head, noticing he was the last of the inmates to walk through the door. I snuck another fleeting look at him, only to see his head unexpectedly snap back, trapping my gaze. Our eyes locked as he traveled through the threshold and disappeared. I flipped through his file and began to comb through his records. Jason Walker Magnus: in a ten year period he had a DUI, Driving with a Suspended License, Misdemeanor Probation Violation, Felony Drug Paraphernalia, Felony Dangerous Drug Possession, Failure to Pay Fines, Felony Count Possession of Narcotic Drug, Soliciting a Prostitute, Probation Violation, and now he was charged with Misdemeanor Theft.

While I perused through his folder, I noticed he had had issues since he was a very young man. I bet if I had access to his juvenile file it would have had just as many incidents prior to age eighteen. How does this guy keep coming back into the system? I don't know why we don't either help him or keep him. It seemed so simple to me. Regrettably, this was the kind of person who ended up back in our courtroom, each time the crimes were worse, until they eventually ended up being the guy who took someone's child through a bedroom window. I looked back down at his file, noticing a common thread in his arrests. Most of his incidents were in the month of April.

It was no wonder I didn't recognize him. Each time someone came through the court these young people looked a little older, gaunter, fewer teeth, visible sores on their bodies, and they had absolutely no hope left in their eyes. They were like the walking dead. It was haunting to see the dead stares from people who were still alive. I processed his file and set it in the completed pile. Then I was jolted back to my own reality. Someone was out killing women in our city. I immediately dialed Sam's cell phone.

Chapter Eight

Jason Magnus

My insides boiled with a drug fever, while my skin shivered uncontrollably with the cold of withdrawal. The lighting was bright and harsh, glinting off the shiny floors. The chains that bound me to the other men made it so we were closely connected as we walked. Too close. So close that my dick could go up the ass of the guy in front of me if he were to bend over. I knew the whole routine. I had to sit next to all the other losers who had done stupid-ass things and wait my turn to be unshackled, and then wait for my go-around with the judge.

This was not the first time I'd been in this courtroom over the years. Nothing had changed. The judge still sat behind a high, solid mahogany, hand-carved executive desk, where she yapped, each syllable coming out like a bullet. Beside the judge's perch was a matching hand carved table where the court assistant sat in a perfectly upright position, shuffling papers or whatever it was she did, besides stare. The floors were a polished limestone; the gloss so high I could see just how shitty I looked. That damn scratch across my face didn't help my appearance. It made me look far rougher than I was. And the fact that I was extremely dehydrated made my skin age by twenty years.

My eyes roamed the open room. Behind me was the Barney Fife who kept an eye on the courtroom. On the left side of the room, everyone else who was not an inmate sat in church-pew seating, awaiting their turns for the judge to hammer down her penalty. The women inmates brought over from the jail were in front of me. If anyone here was lucky enough to have someone who cared whether they'd go home or not, well, those people would be sitting over to the right. I can't say anyone had ever shown up for me.

My wandering eyes stopped on the older woman who was front and center. She was speed typing into a machine, sitting at a small desk in front of the judge. It resembled a school size desk. Just like the one I could remember myself sitting at as a kid, a desk that prodded my mind, pushing me back to another time.

I wasn't always this messed up. I had a great life once. It was lifetimes ago since things were actually good—it's almost hard to recall those times. But for some reason, every time I found myself in jail, feeling like shit, coming down off drugs, I went back in time. Since I could rarely see a future, it seemed all I had was the past. Besides the typical questions that bombarded me: What if I would have done this? What if I would have done that? It was the constant stream of thoughts that filtered through my wasted mind. Unfortunately, I couldn't seem to ever get away from them. They were always present to remind me what an idiot I was, what a fool I had been. But it always boiled down to the same thing. I was a fuck up, nothing more and nothing less.

I knew the customary, *Hi, I'm Jason, and I'm an alcoholic.* I had been there and so fucking done that. I knew the whole, *admit you are powerless* shit; *open your arms to God* stuff. It just didn't work for me. But where I really had problems was with the amends. The whole make-a-personal-inventory idea never took off with me. I have never been any good at claiming my own shit. In fact, that in and of itself is a pretty big claiming statement—especially for me. Really, I blamed my messed up life on my mother and my father, anyone but me—right? It all started fourteen years ago.

* * *

I was thirteen years old when I looked up from my desk and saw my aunt standing in the doorway of my homeroom. I called her Aunt Marie, even though she really wasn't related. She had a very strange look on her face as she signaled me to come to her. Her brown eyes were soft and her features seemed sad. Then I saw the school principle standing over her shoulder as if to gesture to my teacher that it was okay for me to leave the classroom. All very sudden and unexpected, I was getting pulled out of class by my mother's best friend. She came to take me to the hospital to meet my father. All she would tell me was my mother had been rushed in with an excruciating headache. A headache so bad she called an ambulance to pick her up.

"An ambulance?" I'm sure the shock in my pitch startled Aunt Marie.

All I could do was stare past her and into the metal lockers on the wall. The principle walked away; his footsteps echoed through the vacant hallway. Bewildered and stunned, she and I momentarily stood just outside the doorway of my classroom, alone, the two of us, accompanied only by our fear. An ambulance, that alone sounded serious. I never knew anyone who rode in an ambulance before. I could feel Aunt Marie's arms hug me tight, drawing me against her body.

"Everything will be okay, Jason. Pray for everything to be okay." I heard the pounding of her heart as she squeezed me into her.

That was when I felt the vibration. Like the quiver of an earthquake, the stress of what I was hearing caused a tremor that prompted an upheaval in my own body. I couldn't do anything else but pray. I knew by Marie's forceful embrace something was terribly wrong with my mother.

"She was home alone." Marie's whisper was one of extreme worry as she continued to grip me.

All of a sudden my world was no bigger than the dark tunnel I was suddenly staring into. Feeling nauseated, sick to my stomach, I pushed back from her. Like always, my dad was at work, I was at school, and my mom was home alone. She was home doing everything for my father and me. Marie and I rode to the hospital in silence. After what seemed like a cross-country drive that took an eternity, we finally arrived.

The disgusting odor of vomit greeted us in the emergency room. Moans from sick people created a painful melody. The waiting room overflowed with people. Less than a minute after walking into the emergency room, my dad came to meet me. I had never seen my father look that way. His red, swollen eyes seemed to search for words. His always perfectly combed hair was a mess. His flawless posture was slouched. My father, who was usually composed, wasn't. His hands trembled. I was terrified of the words he was trying to gather.

"It's your mother." He stared at me for a brief moment.

I watched him take a deep breath before lowering his head toward the polished tile of the hospital floor.

"What is it Dad?" My legs shook and the blood rose in my face. "Where is she? Where is Mom?"

"She's almost gone, Son." His sobs became wet hitches of breath.

His words hit me, first like a punch between the eyes, and then a gut punch dropped me to the ground. And before I knew it, we were both in a puddle on the hospital floor, trying desperately to hold each other together while facing our loss. My thirty-three-year-old, loving, kind, gentle, angel of a mother was brain-dead from a fatal cerebral aneurysm. Who knew you could die from a headache?

She had some sort of weak or thin spot on a vessel in her brain that ballooned out and filled with blood, some kind of rupture or something. I never heard of a cerebral anything before that day. From that point, things seemed to move rather quickly.

My father and I were asked to donate her organs, her tissues, and yes—her heart. We fulfilled my mother's wishes. She was very compassionate, even in her passing. It was heartbreaking listening to the sympathetic donor representative. It must not be easy to ask for someone's life. My mother, after all, was still breathing, her heart still beating. I gazed at my father and I could see his pain. I could see he would never be the same. I was thirteen years old, my dad was thirty-five, and I knew right then and there we were both doomed. I didn't know how either of us would ever be the same. My father turned and left the room, leaving me alone with my pain, alone with my mother.

In the dimly lit room, while standing beside her bed, I looked at my mother's still body as she lay on the hospital bed. The antiseptic aroma stung my nostrils. The flashing lights, steady beeping noises, and the low, persistent hum was sure proof technology was the only thing keeping my mother alive. I watched as her chest rose and fell at the rate of the machine. The person lying in the bed scarcely resembled my mother. Her smell, the way her brow was settled on her face, the shape of her lips, all unusually different.

Even after realizing this was no longer my mother, for just a moment, I pretended she was still alive. I acted as if she could feel me as I cupped her hand into mine. I wept and I inhaled the memories of her, the two of us together. The homemade chocolate chip cookies she'd sometimes let me have for breakfast, as long as I drank a glass of milk. Often she'd let me lick the cake frosting straight out of the bowl. I loved the way my mother packed my lunch daily, always attaching with it a hand written note of encouragement. *You will always have a chance—and there is always a choice,* was the one I remembered most. I think she told me someone famous said it first. The notes that I liked best were the ones that simply said *I love you, my baby boy*. I liked knowing I would always be her baby boy, even though I was already a teenager, bigger than her, and no longer a baby.

I squeezed my mother's hand and pressed my face into her palm. I couldn't get enough of her. I knew she would stroke me if she could. She always knew what to do, what to say to lessen my pain. I imagined she could hear me while she lay comatose in the hospital bed, the crisp white sheets pulled up over her chest. I cried and apologized to her for not being able to remember kissing her that morning. I sobbed because of all the memories we would no longer be able to share. I wanted to crawl up onto her bed and lay beside her, but I was too paranoid about what people would think. Here I was, this young strapping jock type, crying like a baby because I wanted my mom. I just wanted my mother back. I wanted that more than I ever wanted anything.

My sobbing became uncontrollable. The muscles in my body jumped and jerked ragingly. My pulse pounded in my ears, as if somebody else's loud footsteps were treading heavily through my head. Finally, I was able to set aside my thirteen-year-old self and climb onto the bed. I gently placed my arm over her and hugged our bodies close. She was not stiff, nor was she cold, like I expected she would be. But rather, she was soft and warm. I found comfort in her softness. I snuggled close. As close as all the tubes would allow.

Beneath the hospital odors that lingered on the surface of her skin, present was the slightest hint of my mother's perfume. My heart melted. Yet, for some reason, I began to think of every mean thing I'd ever said to her. All the times I hadn't obeyed her wishes. I felt guilty for all the Sundays I wanted to sleep in, when she wanted me to wake for church. I felt horrible for complaining about my chores, little as they were. My mother did everything for my father and me. Surprised by the emotion coming from my mother, I quickly jumped from her bed and darted across the room.

"Dad!" I screamed outside the door. "A tear just pressed through mom's eyelid. I saw it roll down mom's face. She's crying. I saw a tear." A rush of people swarmed the small space.

I tried to convince them she was alive. She wasn't ready to die. The doctors and nurses surrounded her, poked at her feet, shined a light in her eyes and reassured me my mother was gone. In my stupor of desperation, I was still very much aware of the sturdy hand of my father. His intense grip separated me from my mother as they rolled her out of the room.

*   *   *

I remember at that very moment, I could feel my life change, and not in a good way, in fact, in the worst way. When I lost my mother, it was unexpectedly as if I was missing all my favorite things: dessert, my squishy pillow, my blue Converse with the holes in the toes, and my favorite Steve Nash Suns jersey. But mostly, I missed her smell, her smile, her touch, and her head rubs. I could still feel the silkiness of my mother's fingertips as she lovingly massaged my scalp.

The month of April was never the same for me again. It no longer represented spring, perfect weather. or helping my mother in the flower garden care for her daisies, tomato plants and peppers. It represented a time for sadness, a time for escape. Some people were messed up and they never knew why. I'm one of the lucky ones. I knew exactly why. The day my mother died, I learned how to live without a heart. I soon found out one cannot live without a heart. I often wondered if the dead could see the future. If so, I'm pretty sure my mother was crying for me and my father. I'm almost certain she knew my dad would become an alcoholic and I would follow in his footsteps.

*   *   *

When I brought my attention back to the courtroom, people were still shuffling papers, wringing their hands, and silently praying for the right outcome. The air-conditioned air was cool as it whipped about my neck. I was still shivering. The smell coming off the guy next to me was pungent. Finally the sheriff dude in uniform, a real Dudley Do-right, began to unlock the leg-chains that kept me from running out of here. Or so I wished. That Do-right didn't always do right as he whispered "tweaker" every time he brushed by me. I should've shown him tweaker and tweaked my foot in his teeth while he was down on the floor in front of me releasing my shackles. But I didn't. I would never do something like that. It was just the irritation of withdrawal pestering my mind. My legs were free. Free to agitate like an old washing machine. This was the first day in a three-week run that I hadn't had any drugs injected into my system.

Crystal Meth was the monkey on my back, my reason for being in this predicament. I was long past the days of snorting or smoking my drugs, long ago having moved on to shooting up. I suppose I ran it up so that I could get to a mindless state much quicker. I don't know why I ever started using needles. Same reason I couldn't figure out why I kept coming back to court on brainless crimes. Probably the same reason I couldn't find a way out of Loserville.

Anticipation was throttling my mind. I was wondering what would be the outcome of my stupidity. Seems I'd lost a few hours again. Blackouts—I started getting them a few years back. Not all the time, just every time I went off on a binge—a binge that lasted days, sometimes weeks.

While I sat in the courtroom, irritability began to overwhelm me. The drug was a beast as it left my system, leaving behind a monster I had to contain. What I really needed was food. I was hungry. I'd probably lost about twenty-five pounds over the past three weeks, normally weighing in at about 195 lbs. I also lacked sleep, badly. Having to hang around in an overcrowded drunk tank all night had not helped my attitude. Sunday night was never a good time to be arrested.

While I watched the courtroom proceedings my legs jumped all over the place. I tried desperately to control my own body as it bounced around the seat. I was achy, just flat-out dragging ass, every muscle, every joint in my body hurt, weighed down with the anxiety of waiting for my name to be called. I felt the sweat building in my pits; a stream ran down my backbone, a gush spilled from my hairline, and I still shivered. I looked down at my arms. The sores that lined my forearm were red and bulging, slightly oozing. I guess the poison I had put into my bloodstream had to come out somewhere. The orange jumpsuit was short sleeved so the big boils on my skin were out there for everyone to see. I wanted to pick at the oozing lumps but I knew it only made them worse. Left alone for a few days and they'd ooze and go away on their own. My mind began to clang, *I'm coming down. I'm hungry. I'm tired. I'm coming down. I'm hungry. I'm tired.* Then the paranoia began to take over. I spied the room, glancing to see if anyone detected me getting fidgety. So to try and control my mind, I stared down, not allowing my drug induced suspicion to take over.

"The court calls Jason Magnus." The short-haired female just said my name. Younger than me by her appearance, her tone flat, she was unemotional and unsmiling as she stood and waited for me to make a move. The judgment from her eyes burned my skin. The tapping noise from her pen reverberated throughout the open room.

I drew my lengthy body out of the chair and briefly stared at the lady they assigned to be my attorney. She gave me a hand signal, so I followed her command. I kept my head down. I hated that everyone watched as the skinny, scruffy guy in the stupid orange jumpsuit, flip-flops and white socks walked to the front of the courtroom. Back, before the drugs, before the streets, you would never have thought of me as skinny or scruffy. Of course I never walked with a slight limp, either, or had sores all over my body. I hated being up in front of everyone. Especially in the state I was in. That's when it started, the stares, the disdain, the better than thou attitudes, and the whispers. I knew she wanted me to answer her silly questions, but I hated to give her the satisfaction. She was a persistent judge, looking down at me over the tops of her old lady glasses. The judge's assistant pecked away on her computer keyboard and stared at me sideways.

"Yes your honor," I said, still not giving her the fulfillment of eye contact. "I'm accused of stealing." *There, I said it, are you happy now? I want out of here. I'm embarrassed. I'm tired. I'm hungry. I'm humiliated.* My mind was loud and intrusive.

Then the judge had to act like she was so happy I could speak. Like I'm some sort of a dog or something. Okay, admitting I was a thief aloud in the courtroom, that wasn't easy for me. It was always embarrassing to acknowledge I was nothing more than a low life— someone who stole beer from a convenience store. I guess it could be worse. I could be admitting to stealing from an old lady. I never got caught stealing from an old lady. Not my thing. I never kicked dogs either, or hurt children. No, my brutality and disgust was saved for myself.

I could feel the eyes of the judge and her assistant intently looking at me. My back burned with the stares of the people in the courtroom.

"We'll see if another 72 hours in jail will help you clear your head, Mr. Magnus. I pray for you that it does."

Mr. Magnus, Mr. Magnus. Doesn't she know *Magnus* means *Great*. Every time she says Mr. Magnus, I heard my mother telling me how great I was. Yeah, Mom, I turned out to be real great, a real winner. I felt like a fraud. When I heard the judge tell me I would have to stay in jail for another 72 hours my body began shaking, way more than it was only a minute ago. I could feel the sweat on my brow. I almost felt as if I were going to dry heave. The adrenalin of the moment had taken hold of my psyche and my body. I had to totally talk myself off the ledge as I pivoted back to the box of losers. Breathing deeply through my nose, I looked at my attorney, who did nothing for me.

My legs spazzed-out. I struggled to step back into my place in the constrained area. And then before I knew it, with the bang of the gavel, the shackles were going back on my jumpy legs. I looked up and saw the judge's assistant staring at me. She wanted to take another look at the freak. I let her.

They walked us all back to the stinky putrid holding cell before taking us over to the other rank shit-hole—county jail, where I would serve out my seventy-two hours, where I would again fight off the anger, the resentment, and all the guilt. I hated to remain focused on the destruction I had left in my path, but there was little else that could hold my attention. I begged my own mind to give me peace, to give me will, and some sort of self control to change. It was funny—when I was straight, level-headed, it was like I really wanted to stay straight. Clean and sober. But, when I was high, I really wanted to be high, and regrettably, being high always won out. I guess that's why they called it addiction.

Crossroads

Chapter Nine

Samantha 'Sam' Green

I was at my desk, leaning over some files, trying to complete a few client placements when my cell phone began to vibrate across the top of my desk. I reached out just before it shimmied over the edge. My eyes went immediately to the screen. Madison's number flashed. When I said hello, right off, I could hear the unease in her voice. She was once again concerned about my being cautious, reminding me a killer was on the loose. She'd heard about the female's body being discovered across the street. I thought my grandmother and her friends were quick to tittle-tattle a story, but nothing compared to the buzz of the courthouse. Madison was already a paranoid individual, and now with a murderer at large, that just amplified her mistrust. I have never known her any other way. When I told her I would have Ethan hang around until I left tonight, and we'd leave together, she laughed, as if he had no chance in hell of protecting either one of us.

I remember as teenagers it took almost a year of us hanging out together for me to convince Madison that Ethan was an upright guy. He wasn't shady or crooked in any way. He talked fast, he was quick witted, and he said some damning things about others, but I loved him, and I didn't consider any of that to be criminal. Corrupt, maybe. Yet Madison thought of him as trouble with a capital T. I often found myself laughing at the things he'd say, many times at the expense of someone else. But really, I mostly cackled at his naughty stories of himself. He had a way of sharing too much information. Sometimes I think I giggled out of a lack of any other response. But I would always defend his intentions. And his loyalty. Ethan had a devotion unlike any other.

He was older than Madison and me by a few years. The other thing about Ethan was he had a life outside of his tragedy. He didn't remain as a resident at Miracle House long, too many rules. Not to mention a youth minister, a few minutes in a bathroom stall, and suddenly Ethan was faced with choices. He moved from Miracle House by the time he was seventeen, but he did remain on as a volunteer, but not the minister. Well, Bradley wasn't actually a minister. He was the preacher's son, with church responsibilities. He was older than Ethan by about five years. Old enough to know what he was doing with Ethan was wrong.

Ethan was street wise, smart, old beyond his years, yet he had a childish naïveté. Before Madison came into the picture, Ethan was my best friend. Now I had two best friends. When Ethan and I first met, I especially liked him because he wasn't interested in my breasts. Unlike most guys whose eyes would immediately go to my bulging bumps, Ethan could care less. He and I were able to talk about everything and anything. We talked about guys, how he had all the experience, and I had none. Well, that is if I didn't count Karl. It took me a while to stop counting him. Ethan and I were also able to not talk. We were both comfortable with the silence that sometime lay between us.

Before I ended the phone conversation with Madison, I promised to be extra alert, keep my eyes peeled and my senses peaked. As if I should even have to tell her that again. I reminded her of my natural instincts, my ability to pick up on energy vibrations. She laughed again, just as she did when I told her Ethan would act as my security. Few people enjoyed such insight. Madison never wanted to admit I had a keen sense of intuition. In fact, I'd seen her roll her eyes at the mere mention of karmic connections. Little did she know, I had already felt her energy.

Which reminded me, Willie seemed peculiar today. His energy was way off. Dark, very dark. While Madison and I were still on the phone, I stood from my desk and walked over to the window and looked between the blind slates to see if Willie had returned to the parking lot. He hadn't. I always felt sorry for the Willies of the world. I knew as the day moved towards darkness his main focus became looking for a safe place to hunker down for the night. I let Madison finish with her warning before returning to my desk.

I walked back over to my chair and sat. Skepticism for sixth sense intuition was widespread and Madison was among the majority. I loved the idea of being able to read my stones, or even tarot cards to predict the future. It was exhilarating when my energy would connect with someone who had crossed over. I was in touch with my spiritual and emotional body, something most people couldn't relate to. Clairvoyance: being able to see beyond the five senses, to see auras and feel energy, this has always been present in my mind. Receiving messages from other frequencies and realms was something that I had little control over. They just came.

I wanted to hone those skills. I tried to control them, even while people like Madison considered them far-out. She never said that exactly, but she often referred to me as creatively concocting reality. Call it what you want, I knew, without a doubt, I would sometimes see and hear things that other people didn't.

* * *

The setting sun pressed through the blinds of my office. Dusk was upon us, and my day was approaching its end. I sat at my desk and stared at the stack of files—clients who I hadn't been able to place today. I stretched my arms overhead, took in a deep breath, then brought my tired limbs back down, crossed them on my desk, then plopped my head down on them, realizing the day had defeated me. I quietly committed to trying again tomorrow.

"Hey you," Ethan leaned into my office door. He worked just outside my room in the admittance area.

I lifted my gaze but not my head. I continued to rest my head on my arms.

"I'm headed home," he said. "This girl had way too much fun this weekend and today kicked my ass." He often referred to himself as "girl." He walked over to me and leaned down. His lips grazed my cheek. "Besides, Bradley might call me tonight. It's been almost a week since his mother passed and I haven't seen him."

"Get out of here." I lifted my head. "You're nuts to still be seeing him." I cranked my finger at the side of my head. "Now that his mother is dead I can't wait to see what excuse he uses to keep his relationship with you a secret from his wife." I swished my hand, waiving him off. I got so tired of hearing him complain about Bradley, all while doing nothing to change the relationship. As far as I was concerned that was the definition of insanity.

"Bad day, huh?" Ethan tilted his head and stood with his hands on his hips. "Besides, who says he is keeping our relationship a secret from his wife? In fact, quite the contrary, Miss *I-know-everything*. Bradley says Amber knows about us." Ethan playfully pushed back on my desk chair, making me feel as though I was going to flip over.

I screamed. "Whatever. That is what he tells you. And we all know he isn't always honest." I waved him off with a sweeping hand gesture. "Fine! Go ahead, go home. There is only a killer roaming the streets of downtown Phoenix. But, I'm sure I'll be okay." I tried to make him feel guilty. It worked, sort of.

"I'll wait for you if you'd like." He turned back and cast a bogus, sympathetic gaze.

"No, really, go. I'm only kidding. It's okay to leave me by myself." My features became very pouty before slipping into snide.

"Go home and wait for your married man to come calling. I'll be all right." I poured it on. "Oh, and don't let the fact that it's my birthday week make you feel guilty, or anything."

"Like I would forget it was your birthday—get real, Sugar. And you're right. Someone did just get murdered across the street. Of course I'll wait for you." He stood defiant. "You can just drive me home," he said, "so I can wait for my Honey to call." His smile was wide, mischievous.

"I'm only kidding. I'm not afraid. Of course I'll give you a ride home if you want to wait, but I'll probably be close to another hour or so wrapping up a few files before I can get out of here."

"If you are sure you're all right?"

"I'm sure."

"All right then, last chance." He turned his soft eyes my direction.

I blew him a kiss, waived him on, and watched him turn and walk away. I teased Ethan so much, only because I loved him so much.

Just before reaching the door, he twisted back. "I can't believe you are finally turning twenty-five. You're catching up with me, at last. But, Bitch, you are still immature," he smiled. "See ya." He waived and then the door shut behind him.

"I'll never catch up," I said to no one, because Ethan was gone and my office was empty. But I did feel like I was catching up. I will be the same age as Madison, again. For about half the year we were the same age, and on my upcoming birthday, that made us both twenty-five.

I leaned back in my chair, hoping to take hold of a second wind I took a long breath. I glanced around at the few personal items I kept on my desk. On one corner there was a picture of my mother and grandmother, me in the middle, I was about ten. On the opposite corner sat a simple wood frame with a photo of me with Ms. Beth. That one was much more recent. It was my twenty-first birthday. Ms. Beth had been there for all of my birthdays since we met. And in the middle of my desk, next to a photograph of Ethan, Madison and me, back at Miracle House, was a small container that held a set of very special stones. They were the stones that I had used over the years to help guide me in my journey of self awareness. I reached out and picked up the small box. Reflecting, I mused over its predictions.

* * *

Madison and I had become roommates the summer before college. Before I went to college, that is. I started after Madison and finished before her. But at this time, Madison was well on her way in college, taking the longer route, part-time and night classes, all while holding down her job. She didn't have the benefit of a college fund to tap into for her education. Both of us opted for the local university, keeping us close to family and everything else that was important to us.

As teenagers and young women, Madison and I both continued to do our volunteer work together at Miracle House. And every year in May, Miracle House would have a fundraising event called *Spring Affair*. It was held on the campus, outdoors in the courtyard, a real park-like atmosphere, sometimes too hot, but mostly it was a perfect seventy-five to eighty-five degrees, sunny, with a slight breeze. We volunteers and all the organizers tried to help the cause by offering services, games, entertainment, and food, then donating the proceeds.

When it came to making money for a fair, I always did something around the area in which I happen to be most skilled, tarot card readings, predictions and forecasting people's lives. By seventeen I had already become rather proficient with the ancient form of mapping spiritual pathways. Tarot card reading seemed to be a more accepted practice. So *Tarot Card Readings* was what I scribbled on my makeshift sign. It was this particular event where I decided to try to develop my own technique in reading the hopes, dreams, and desires of others. It was something unique in the sea of *Fortune Tellers*. In fact I used this distinctive method to convince Madison she needed me as her roommate. That and a furry little creature I knew she couldn't refuse.

A few months back, prior to this particular Spring Affair, Madison's cat, Sylvester, had died. She'd had it almost nine years. It was the cat she was bequeathed. Her Cousin Lisa's beloved pet. I knew what a blow that had been to her. Not just the death of her cat, but for Madison, it also brought up the loss of Lisa all over again. She'd moped around, sulking her way through the days. She never cried in front of me, but when she talked about the loss, I could see she wanted to cry. I cried. Madison was always stoic—in control. She talked about wanting to get another cat, but she didn't. So as a surprise, I went to a shelter and picked out the cutest little, fluffy boy I could find. He became her adored Charlie.

I staged a *Fortune Teller's* booth at the affair, $5 donations. People especially liked that kind of stuff during a festival atmosphere. And for a measly five bucks people would actually spend the money. There was always a line at the entrance to my tent. Ethan was my helper. More like the carnival barker who attracted attention to the psychic. He had been my assistant before, and even though he didn't do so much for Miracle House after his little situation, he always did this for me. In an orderly fashion he took the money, kept me on my toes with our ten-minute rule, and for no extra donation, he had the clients laughing with his endless one-liners as they waited their turn to learn their futures.

Of course, Ethan was in charge of décor. He'd set up this really cool tent, a little larger than an outhouse, yet big enough for me to sit in there with a table and two chairs. It was lit by candlelight and a small table lamp, permeated with the fragrance of sandalwood incense. The entrance was draped with feather boas, and our sign was written in glittered bling. I wore a simple muumuu dress and wrapped my head with a scarf for effect. Ethan wore a genie outfit he thought made him look like *Aladdin*, whereas I believed he more embodied *I Dream of Jeannie*. Nonetheless, his enthusiastic, gay charm helped me to draw in clientele as they walked through the fair. So I did the readings, he collected the cash, and he also did plenty of flirting. That was something Ethan couldn't not do. Behaving playfully in an alluring way was as natural to Ethan as breathing.

Just as I wrapped up a reading, Ethan stuck his head into the dim tent and said, "Okay, Miss Fortuneteller, here she comes. Miss Smiley is next." He arched his brow and smiled mischievously. I knew he was referring to Madison. He couldn't understand how she seemed to be so serious all the time, naming her Miss Smiley years ago.

I reached down under the table and pulled back the dark table cloth that covered the cardboard box holding the small kitten. He was curled up in the corner resting peacefully on an old towel I had laid out. I gestured to Ethan, "Send her in."

"Madame Psychic Divine, I give to you a bundle of joy." He snickered and lifted the curtain high, revealing Madison. "Go on in tough girl," he said, pushing her through the entrance. He rarely let up on her with his teasing about her seriousness. He pressed her into the seat across from me and looked into my eyes. "You better give her a reading she won't soon forget." The curtain dropped behind him.

I shrugged my shoulders and cleared the space on the table between us. "Hello, welcome." For some reason my voice always dropped an octave when I did readings, my words were longer, my speech slower.

"Hi," she said. Madison looked around the small space, fanning the light smoke of the incense.

"Does it bother you?" I began to move to put it out.

"I can take anything for ten minutes." She adjusted herself in her seat.

I sat back in my chair and reached for her hands, then held them in the middle of the table, just for a few seconds, I slowed my breath, beckoning her to do the same. I always liked to try and harness the energy before beginning. It was a habit. There was a lamp on top of the table that was off to the side, the light was muted by a purple and red scarf that draped the shade. I could see Madison's inquisitive eyes, her skeptical look. I gripped her hands and drew her gaze into mine.

Her dark hair was short, just like it was when I first met her as a hardened young girl. Although, this time, as I looked at Madison, I saw softer features, kinder eyes, not the hard line, boyish young woman who originally came to volunteer at Miracle House years ago. She was eighteen now, tweezing her brows, her short hair was stylish, shaped with hair products, and she was wearing a tiny bit of make-up, softening her eyes. Plain, petite gold loop earrings hung on her lobes, and she wore tight shorts that covered her knees. Madison had on a snug tank top squeezing her upper body, as she often did—I think to show off her boxing physique. That hasn't changed. Outside of work, she still wears her clothes tight, fitted to her athletic figure.

I had a box of brilliantly colored stones along with a cotton cloth that lay on the table between us. I began to press out the wrinkles in the shiny fabric, striped in emerald, aqua, sapphire, and purple. I rubbed my hands across the colors until all of the creases in the cloth were gone.

"What is this, Sam—some kind of new magic?" Madison's voice dripped in sarcasm.

A slight squeak, not really an actual meow, but a noise non-the-less, slipped out from underneath the table.

"What was that?" Madison looked curiously around the small, tented space.

I made a funny noise with my mouth, hoping to distract Madison's attention. I dipped my toe in the box where the surprise awaited, hoping to preoccupy the restless little one. I could feel the tickle of claws playing with my toes. I struggled to ignore the distraction.

"Would you prefer the cards or the stones?" I pushed the stones forward.

"It looks like you've already decided for me. Come on now, Sam, I want something more than the festival special." Madison leaned back in the metal chair and crossed her arms. "Tell me what my future has in store for me. Make sure I get my five bucks worth with your little stones."

"These aren't just any stones." I smiled warmly. "They are special stones I've collected through unique moments of my life journey." I ran my hand over them, as if to cast a spell.

"Okay, whatever." She looked at her watch.

"Don't forget, it is a donation after all. Give me your hands, again." I drew her hands back to the middle of the table. Madison timidly placed her palms over mine. "I can feel you shaking. I promise I won't give you any bad news."

"I'm not too worried, Madame Divine." She raised her brow teasingly. "Give me the facts, as *you* see them."

I closed my eyes, and in a hushed tone, I whispered, "Madison, Madison, Madison," and then set her hands back on the table.

With my eyes shut, I shook the box that contained my colorful pebbles and blindly tossed them along the cloth between us. Opening my eyes, I looked at the variety of stones. Glancing to Madison, and then to the stones, I stared at their placement with trepidation. When I read tarot cards, death an instantly recognizable symbol. But when it came to stones, two stacked stones appeared to be two stacked stones. It was when they were both black, as these were, that the meaning became ominous. However, it doesn't always have to refer to the physical act of dying the way many people thought. It could represent transformation, and perhaps the death of one phase of a person's being that is necessary in order to give birth to the next phase of life.

"I see you have a positive future, Madison." With sleight of hand, the dark stones that were closest to me were quickly gone. "You see these, the farther a stone is from you means the farther I'm looking into the future. If the stone has spilled off the cloth, I'm looking into a future life. And if the stones are bunched up, one on top of the other, that represents family or close friends, a bonding of sorts." I stared into her questioning eyes and smiled. I looked back down and noticed three stones teetering on each other. Oddly enough, not like I planned it or made it happen, but they were closest to her, which indicated something present, or in the near future.

"So, tell me Madison." Using my *Fortune Teller* voice, I pulled her gaze into mine. "Are you excited to be going to college and moving into your own place? And moving away from your parents for the first time?" I already knew the answer.

"Yes, yes, and yes." She nodded matter-of-factly. "Why do you even ask? You know this is what I've been looking forward to for the past year." Madison's eyes left mine and narrowed on the stack of three stones. She studied the table, and for just a moment, I felt as though she had an actual interest in the magic of my visions.

"These three stones represent attachment, closeness." I waved my hand above the prediction.

"Attachment? I'm not really sure what you mean." She looked baffled.

"Well, I can never be sure. It is not a precise science, but my sense is that you might have met someone special."

"Okay, I get it. I could tell something was up. You feel sorry for me because I've never dated. You're setting me up." Madison pushed away from the table. "I knew this was bullshit." She started to rise.

I reached for her hands. "Whoa! Wait! Sit down. Give me a break, like I'm the relationship expert—please. Obviously, Madison, you haven't considered I'm the president of the *Lonely Hearts Club*—remember?" I wasn't expecting that.

Madison settled back into her chair. "What then? What are you trying to say?"

"I'm not seeing anything romantic. That's way off." I suddenly got all nervous inside. After all, I threw the stones, I didn't place them perfectly. The signs were the signs. From my perspective, it was clear. It was meant to be. I decided to just come out with it. "Are you opposed to having a roommate instead of living alone?"

Madison didn't speak for a few seconds. "Well, I don't know. I hadn't thought about it any other way. I don't know anyone who would want to live with me. I suppose it depended on the person." Bit by bit, she began to catch on. Her cheeks took on a red hue. Something I rarely witnessed.

"Madison, these stones are all about patterns. Every stone represents an event, and each event is linked to others in a chain. Each rock and its placement on my cloth have a basic meaning, but their specific meaning changes as time passes. For example, today I am telling you that you have a possibility of a connection with someone, possibly a child, or perhaps a pet. That is this small stone." My index finger grazed the surface of the shiny rock that rested atop the other two.

"What makes you think that?" She looked on with amusement.

I went on explaining myself. "These other two stones are roughly the same size, while the last one on the stack is smaller, possibly representing a dependent." I had to keep the reading honest, so I added, "It could also be that two adult people are depending on you for something, and you are the smaller stone. Are you sure your parents want you to move out?" Even though my reading had intentions from the beginning, by the end, I found I was trying to validate my vision.

"Are you kidding me? They want my bedroom for a TV room. Someplace to get a little peace from my brothers," she laughed.

The kitty under the table was beginning to get restless. His tiny teeth began gnawing on my big toe, and occasionally his nails would tug on my moo-moo.

"What if I told you I thought the rocks showed you and me as roommates?" I was silent waiting for her response.

Unexpectedly, her comeback was, "What about the smaller stone?" Her cynicism disappeared, momentarily.

I reached under the table and pulled the playful kitten from the box. "This is the smaller stone." I held his squirming body over the table and out to Madison. Her eyes lit up. She smiled so wide I saw her teeth. She immediately grabbed him from my hands and pressed her face into his belly.

"Oh... look how cute this little baby is." The pitch of her voice changed to something I'd never heard. "It's so fluffy. Where'd it come from? Whose kitten is it?"

"I got him from a shelter."

"You did this for me?" Madison was rubbing her face into his fur, patting his small body.

"He's yours if you want him. What I want is a housemate." I looked Madison in the eye, encouraging her to say yes.

"I can't believe you thought you had to go through this whole charade for a roommate. Why didn't you just ask?" Madison smirked. "I would have said yes, you know. You're my best friend." Her head tilted with compassion. She put the kitten high in the air and twirled his squirming body above her head, thoroughly checking the little guy out.

"I was afraid you'd say no. I know how you prefer being alone." I let the charade comment go. All along I was planning to ask Madison to be my roommate. But the placement of the stones convinced me it was the right thing to do. That was no charade.

She held up the dangling kitty as she spoke directly into his face. "You have a very bright future, my little friend. And I can tell you that without ever throwing any stones. Of course I want him. And I'd love to be roommates. You're the only one I know who puts up with me, besides my own family. We can start looking right away for a place together." Madison smiled and stood from the table holding her new four-legged baby.

Just then, Ethan poked his head in the makeshift room. "All right, all right—if you stay any longer I have to charge you another five bucks. People are waiting out here." Ethan waved flamboyantly and held the cloth back for Madison to exit the tent.

"We'll talk later." Madison twisted her body and headed out, then stopped abruptly, turned, and smiled. "By the way, I like the head scarf, roomy. I never thought I'd live with a gypsy."

"Thanks, I think. The scarf was Ethan's idea." I watched Madison shake her head as she walked through the hanging flap of the tent. The scarf that covered my head was to suggest fortune teller. Instead it implied Gypsy.

*   *   *

My cell phone burst out with the song *Wild Thing* startling me out of my thoughts of the past. Ten years ago, and it seemed like yesterday. I smiled and set my box of stones back on my desk, beside the picture of my friends, and reached for my phone. I knew by the special ringtone, it was Ethan.

"Hello."

"Samantha, the cops are everywhere in my complex." He sounded alarmed. "I had to get special permission to enter my own fucking apartment. The murdered woman behind the Q-Mart lived directly above me. It was Nasreen." I heard the distress in his voice.

122

"Are you all right? Do you want me to come and get you? I can be there in two minutes." I began to pack my purse and clear my desk as he continued to speak.

"No, I'm okay. I see the landlord talking to the police. Maybe I can find out what happened. She was no prostitute, Samantha. Nasreen was a nice girl, young and sweet, inexperienced. She'd come here from Iran a few years back to go to school, to work, to live a free life. She just wanted to experience having choices. Wearing short skirts, high heels and makeup doesn't make her a whore. I can't wait to give that asshole at Q-Mart a piece of my mind tomorrow."

"Oh... Ethan." I tried interjecting calmness.

"She never seemed to fit in this area. She was too, nice." A tremor made his voice skip.

"I'm sorry, Ethan. It sounds like you really liked her."

"Well, I didn't know her, know her. But I often sat at the bottom of the stairway that separated our apartments to smoke, chat on my cell, and she never once passed me without a kind expression, or even a few words. She never turned her nose up at my smoke, even though she was a non-smoker. I'll never forget her smile." Ethan's voice fell to a very low point.

"I'm getting a very bad vibe right now, Ethan. I don't like it. Are you sure you don't want to stay at my house tonight? I'm going to swing by and see my grandmother and get some food to take home for dinner with Madison. I'm sure Gram made enough, we can all have dinner together."

"It sounds good, but I think I'll pass, I wanna stick around here. I need to find out what happened to Nasreen. I'll keep you posted."

"I get it! Bradley..." I restrained an annoyed snip. I knew why he wouldn't leave. *Bradley. Bradley. Bradley.* Sometimes I just couldn't believe Ethan. He deserved better. It wasn't that I didn't like Bradley. In fact, given different circumstances there were things I admired about him. I just really hated to see Ethan hurt, over and over again.

"Thanks anyway, Sweetie. I'll call you later. Kiss, kiss. Bye-bye. Tell your gram hi."

I hit the end button on my phone. I was surprised it was already seven o'clock. I quickly cleared the work off my desk, grabbed my belongings, and headed for the door. I'm sure Gram was waiting for me, and worried, given the news. I called out goodbye to the people who had come in for the next shift and headed out the back door. The parking lot was dark. I heard the large metal door to the building slam behind me, shutting out the florescent light that had trailed me. When I turned the corner of the building, I was startled by his blank eyes.

Chapter Ten

Ethan Price

Sometimes it's hard to have a best friend who is perfect. Whether I like it or not, it holds me to a different standard. I just finished telling Samantha I found out it was the nice young woman living upstairs from me whose body had been discovered behind the store, and of course she consoled me, lovingly and thoughtfully. Samantha usually could sense my sadness. Still, after finishing our phone conversation it was her judgmental tone about Bradley that I clung to. Even though she didn't say it, I knew what she was thinking. She isn't the only one with a sixth sense. I know she hated that he was married. Hell, I hated that he was married.

I opened the front door and walked through my small, dark apartment, tossed my few pieces of mail on the counter and flipped on the lamp that sat atop the sofa end table. I hated the staleness of my downstairs unit. I suppose it came from a full day of being closed-up, locked in the mustiness of living beneath someone else.

I was feeling shook up about Nasreen. Seeing all the police and everything, all the commotion surrounding someone I sort of knew felt weird. The fact that she lived directly above me felt even more weird. I opened the kitchen drawer and pulled out a long lighter and lit the scented candle on the top of the kitchen bar. Nerves caused my hand to shake and the flame from the lighter to bounce.

My mouth was dry as Arizona dirt. I replaced the lighter before stepping over to my fridge and grabbing a bottle of water. Bradley's name rarely evoked positive conversations between Samantha and me. She would tell me things like, *Ethan, you are on your own path of discovery, but hey, who am I to comment?* It all sounded so mature, almost approving, until she added, *the road you are on can sometimes be a dark one.* Okay, when it came to Samantha, I almost had to wonder if she had actually seen my dark road. I didn't dare ask. It's no secret she sees things others don't. And she was often right. I leaned into the counter and drank down half a bottle of water.

I've told Samantha a lot about Bradley over the years, probably too much. I knew that couldn't possibly help the way she sometimes slid into protective best-friend-mode. For instance, Samantha knew Bradley was married to a straight girl he felt sorry for, claimed a kid that wasn't his, and worked for the church only because his father died unexpectedly. I hoped now that his mother had passed that was a job he would no longer keep. Bradley was an only child from a well-to-do Christian family. Not that the ministry didn't mean anything to him, it was just the pressure to continue the tradition had just died. The pressure was hopefully buried right alongside his mother. With a bit of luck it won't be replaced with guilt from the grave. His mother had had a lot of power over him.

I also informed Samantha that Bradley helped me with my rent, bought me gifts for no reason, and paid for my cell phone. That information alone made her gasp. All while shaking her head disapprovingly. There are some things I haven't told Samantha. Like how Bradley sometimes cried when we had sex, or the way his tongue has traced every inch of my body. I've never told her of the pleasure Bradley got from being inside of me. He also enjoys my touch, and he loves my mouth.

Samantha couldn't accept the fact that Bradley stayed with his wife out of honor to his family, and out of friendship. They were actually childhood friends. He did it as a favor to them both. It saved him from declaring his true identity to his family, becoming an outcast, rejected and unloved. And the same for her, part of a good Christian family who didn't favor having a daughter who was pregnant without a husband. And according to Bradley he rescued the child from being fatherless, a child I know he now treated as his own.

Samantha still believed that all those years ago, Bradley, a young, immature, under-sexed twenty-two-year-old church boy seduced me. Me, Ethan Price, man-whore, sexually advanced horny seventeen-year-old. To hear her tell it, Bradley took advantage of my vulnerability, him being a church youth counselor at Miracle House and all. Bradley only did that because his father was a Baptist minister. Bradley's whole life had constantly been about obligation. Nevertheless, Samantha always thought he crossed the line. And even though it had been almost ten years since then, not to mention I was an adult now, she still held it against him.

Samantha was the only one that ever knew what really happened at Miracle House. She never told the leadership. But the only person I really cared about finding out was Elizabeth. Elizabeth Hanson wasn't only an extraordinary social worker; at the time, she was the only authority figure in my life that cared about me. Really, truly cared about me—to the point I actually felt her love from the moment we met. If it weren't for her I'd have never escaped the streets. I couldn't stand the idea of disappointing her. Samantha promised she wouldn't tell anyone, so long as Bradley and I stopped what we were doing. I didn't want to stop. Instead, I left Miracle House, and Samantha never mentioned a word to anyone else about me and Bradley in the bathroom.

Fortunately I had just received my GED. I was able to get a job along with an apartment. My first legal, paying job was with a non-profit organization, helping homeless teens, mostly gays and lesbians. I loved it. I was never really around other gays until then. I'd probably still be working with the not-for-profit-group if the funding hadn't run out. I was pretty fortunate to land the job at Last Chance, full benefits, retirement, and all. The pay sucked, but with Bradley's help, I made ends meet. I suppose I was destined to work with the neglected, impoverished, desperate portion of society, only because I really like what I do. My past makes it so I can relate to what some of the people are going through. I've been with Last Chance longer than Samantha, but her degree shot her way past me right from the get go.

Samantha always said it would never last with Bradley and me. He's straight, she'd say. He's a preacher's son. All of those comments came before he was married. And here I was, standing in the kitchen of my apartment, looking down at my phone, still hoping to see his name light up across the screen. I hadn't heard a word from him in almost a week. I knew he would be busy with the funeral, the arrangements, casket, flowers, friends, family, services, and all the things you don't count on when someone dies. And it was his mother, so that made it that much more intense. I hate to admit it, but I felt slightly giddy at the idea she was gone. I wanted Bradley to have a chance to be himself for a change.

I took the last swig of water, crinkled the plastic bottle and tossed it into the trash under the sink. Tapping a cigarette out of my pack, I twisted back toward the front entrance. I swung the door open, flipped on my porch light, and stood still in the doorway, watching the hubbub outdoors. I could hear the rumbling and crashing of things in Nasreen's apartment above me. It made me feel sick inside knowing the police were up there looking through all of her things. Her face kept flashing in my mind. I let the cool night air run over me. The month of April had already been a month that, for me, had evoked bad memories. I now added Nasreen's murder to the collection.

I heard the voices atop the stairs, in front of Nasreen's apartment. It sounded as though the cops were questioning my landlord. I could picture Mr. Faranghi twisting the golden Allah that hung on a thick chain around his fat neck. I always thought Muslims were forbidden to display icons of Allah. Either I am wrong or he's a hypocrite. Possibly both. The thick, strong voice of my landlord rolled over the terrace, hitting me right upside the head. He often sounded as though he was clearing his throat when he spoke. I couldn't help but eavesdrop. It was obvious Mr. Faranghi wasn't even removing the chip from his shoulder for the police officer interviewing him. He always commented about how everyone blamed the Muslims for everything. It sounded as though he was doing the same thing now. I never trusted that man, and it most definitely wasn't because he was Muslim.

I hardly knew Nasreen. In fact I didn't really know her at all, yet hearing them talk about her made my stomach swirl nauseously at the thought of Nasreen's slit throat. A chill traced my spine. I was slapped with the mental image of Nasreen's body left beside the dumpster. A fucking garbage can behind the filthy convenient store. I hated the notion of never seeing her smiling face again, her big brown eyes, and her beautiful, full lips. Nasreen had a smile that would make any *normal* man sell his soul to have her. The way she wore her makeup was perfect. I couldn't have done it better myself.

As I stepped out through the threshold of my apartment, I dug my hand into the front pocket of my jeans for a lighter. I had to duck under the yellow tape to get out to the walkway. I lit my cigarette, turned and stared back at the chaotic scene, smoke swirling my head, sad thoughts, too. Nasreen, like me, was rejected by her family for being different. Scared of her own father, fearing for her life, Nasreen felt the need to leave her country. She told me he hated her Western desires. The fact that she wanted the power and knowledge to rule her own life was all too much for her father. My father hated things about me, too. Me, I only moved down the street, but I might as well have moved to another country.

I turned and tilted my gaze upstairs onto the balcony, right outside Nasreen's door. My landlord was flailing his hairy arms, his heavy accent bellowed through the air. He was probably telling the cops one of his ridiculous stories of how life was so different where he came from, or acting as if he actually knew something about Nasreen, since they were both Iranian. Funny, she'd been here, in America, only a short time, yet her English was perfect. Him—he'd been here quite some time, and it was still a struggle to understand many of his words. He was a large paunchy man with sweat patches under his arms, regularly.

I stamped my cigarette out and continued to gawk. He talked loud, and he talked a lot. Always had an opinion, whether you wanted to hear it or not. A mole sat on his right nostril like a dark droplet that had fallen from his eye. I always thought he looked like he needed a shave, or even a body wax for that matter, with the way his hair puffed out of his collar, front and back. His thick, black hair was fleck gray, his beard and mustache seemed to conceal most of his pockmarked features.

Every month when I paid my rent, I had the urge to tweeze the hair from his nose and ears. I could hardly stand talking to him long enough to say, "Give me my receipt." I hated the way he stared at me with disparaging eyes, often mumbling something about interrupting his prayers. Every time he went for his receipt book, Mr. Faranghi would leave his door cracked just enough for me to see a single tapestry that hung on the wall inside, with the sewn-in beads forming the word Allah-u-Akbar. Of course I had to Google it to find out it meant—*Allah is the Greatest*. Beneath the wall-hanging was a narrow, squatty table with candles, incense, and an aged book. It looked like the Bible, but was probably the Quran. And there was a large sword that rested on an elaborate stand atop the table next to the wall. The way it all seemed memorialized, maybe it was an ancient weapon or something. In front of the table, on the floor lay a rug, one I was sure Mr. Faranghi had knelt on numerous times.

I took from that that he was a religious man. I guess. But, to hear him talk, he was really more of a prejudiced man, a man who hated most people who weren't like him. And as he mouthed off on the balcony, I could hear there was someone else he didn't approve of. When he'd hand me the rent receipt, Mr. Faranghi would often drag his sweaty hand across mine in the exchange of the small slip of paper. But what really creeped me out were his long yellow fingernails as they lightly scraped over my skin. I really hated knowing he had a key to everyone's apartment, including mine.

I lit up another cigarette and pulled out my cell phone, looking to see if maybe I'd missed a call from Bradley. I hadn't. I glanced up to see a plainclothes detective walking my way, pen and pad in hand. The darkness of night couldn't hide the fact that this person was a cop. The towering lamp in the center of the cluster of apartments cast a light on the walking path.

"Excuse me." He approached. "I understand you live in apartment 103."

"Yes." I fanned the smoke that seeped from my lips.

"Did you know Ms. Karimi in unit 203, directly above you?" He looked me right in the eyes. He stood close to me.

"Not enough to know her as Ms. Karimi." I tossed my cigarette to the ground and smashed it out with the toe of my shoe. I found myself tossing my hair and looking at the detective through the prism of a horny gay man, which I was.

"Did you see or hear anything suspicious yesterday, or last night, today?"

"No."

"What about any strange people in the complex or unfamiliar faces in the parking lot?"

"I don't drive. I walk into the complex from the front, and I walk right down this sidewalk." I gestured widely, showing him my pattern.

He was cute, young, and tall. "Did you hear any noise above you last night?" His suit fit him nicely.

"Nothing that stands out."

"Did you hear anything at all from apartment 203?" His tone became stern, seemingly becoming desperate for answers. Finally he glanced back toward my face.

"No, I didn't hear anything. I'm sorry. I really liked Nasreen. I wish I could help you." I turned and took a step toward my apartment.

"Wait a minute. I thought you said you didn't know her." His hand clinched my upper arm, causing me to turn back toward him.

I caught a whiff of the detective's cologne. It was fresh, clean, like Bradley's. "No, what I said was, I didn't even know her last name. All I know is she kept to herself. I never saw any visitors coming or going. She was a trusting, inexperienced young woman." I pulled my arm from his grip.

"Okay, fine. That will be all for now. Can I get your name and number in case we have any more questions?" As we stood face to face, light from the overhead lamp popped on, and as it warmed up it slowly illuminated the area. He fumbled while balancing his pen and notebook.

I snatched the pen from his hand and wrote my name and number on his pad.

"Thank you, Mr. Price." The detective looked down at my writing as I pressed the pen back into his hand.

"Please—if you call me on the phone, call me Ethan." I twisted away from him and swished back to the confines of my apartment.

I looked down at my cell phone. The bright light beamed 8:25 p.m. Still—no missed call. I walked into my downstairs dwelling and shut the door behind me. I gave up on the idea Bradley was going to call, so I tossed my phone on the counter and made my way to the refrigerator. I rummaged through my freezer and came out with a frozen dinner that I popped into the microwave. *No big deal,* I said to myself. Not so convincingly. *Bradley must be very busy.* Today was only Monday. *There's always tomorrow.*

I felt a shiver run along my spine. The apartment felt cool and my thoughts became dark. While my dinner cooked, I moved around the breakfast bar, plopped on the couch, pulled my pot tray out from under the couch and loaded my pipe. I figured the cops were done with me for tonight. I took in a long inhale and held it while flipping open my laptop. The smoke pushed through my tightly closed lips. The computer screen in front of me brightened. The Internet site I wanted to search was just about to come up. I re-filled my one-hitter and indulged once again. A cloud of marijuana smoke filled the small space.

The bell on the microwave sounded, drawing me from the couch. I grabbed a fork and my meatloaf dinner, ripped off a paper towel, and went back to the sofa. With one hand, I slid the computer to the top of my thighs and began my search. With my free hand I shoveled food into my mouth. *Naughty-Hookups* appeared on the screen. It was one of my favorite cruising sites. I could always find someone out there who was horny and nearby. I hated to travel too far for a quick fuck. But really, since Phoenix decided to become a big city and install the light-rail, nothing seemed too far. I most always used the rail for my travels, especially since it stopped in front of my apartment. Besides, it was much cheaper than a taxi and the *Metro* was another good place to cruise for men.

First I saw his face on my computer screen. Then his well endowed body parts appeared in full color. A caption in the corner read, *Top Seeks Bottom.* I decided this was the man I would spend time with tonight. After seeing his picture, I scrolled through his profile. The words, *Available at the drop of a hat* rolled along the bottom of his bio. I hit the send button on my computer, took a mouthful of fake mashed potatoes and awaited his response. I knew he was dissecting my picture just as I had done his. He probably skipped over the lies I told about myself, the same way I disregarded his likely deception. Within seconds an address appeared on my screen, along with the words, *see you at eleven o'clock.*

I smiled, closed my computer, and went to finish my dinner when my phone rang. *Finally,* I thought, it had to be *him.* It wasn't. It was Madison tracking down Samantha, all the media publicity and all, not to mention the close proximity, had her nervous, thinking bad thoughts. That way of thinking wasn't totally uncommon for Madison, under any circumstance. We talked for a few minutes and I finished my dinner then took another few hits off my pipe.

I thought about the wonderful dinner I could have been eating had I gone with Samantha for the night. No one cooked better than her grandmother. But I suppose anything would have been better than a TV dinner. Madison passed her nervous energy onto me, so I decided to try and get a hold of Samantha, make sure she got over to her gram's house okay. My call went to voicemail.

"Hi Sugar, I am just checking in on you. Call me when you get this." A wave of guilt washed over me.

Here I was, worried about my best friend, waiting for my boyfriend to call me, anticipating, with excitement, my eleven o'clock date. I was sure meeting a stranger for a sexual rendezvous was something else Samantha wouldn't approve of, which is why I would not share this part of my life with her. But really, this was a piece of my life I wouldn't share with anyone.

Chapter Eleven

Madison Morgan

It was way past six o'clock and I was just wrapping up my day, finishing my paperwork, getting my zillion phone calls done, and assigning my case load for the next court session. While I stacked my files I could hear the buzzing from the florescent lights above. Other than that it was silent. It was a welcome stillness. Mondays were the toughest day of the week. And always, before I could leave my office, I needed to have the next day scheduled for Judge Pittsman. Every available slot filled, no free time. However, in the morning when I arrived, usually one hour before the justice, I'd probably have to reschedule most of the day anyway.

Oftentimes the cases would settle and the attorney would wait until the last minute to cancel. I scheduled hearings, changed and canceled them all day long. But when an attorney screwed up the judge's timetable by not calling in their cancelled hearings, they had to go through me for the availability of their new hearings, and they might find there was no time available on the judge's calendar for weeks. That was a part of the job that I really loved—punishing attorneys.

When I finally become an attorney myself, I would have respect for the judge's time, but I would have equal esteem for the judicial assistant as well. I opened the center drawer of my desk, set my pen

135

in the tray and slid it shut. I had scooped up tomorrow's files and walked over to the cabinet to lock them away when my phone rang.

"Matty, it's me. I'm glad I got you and not your voicemail."

"Hi Dad!" I hadn't talked to him much lately. Work, school and life just seemed to get in the way. I finished sliding all the files into the drawer.

"Have you heard?" He was loud, brief, to the point.

"Heard what? I'm just leaving the courthouse, been here all day." I gathered my things, turned off the lights and stood in the doorway with the phone pressed to my head.

"It was on the national news, Matty. I just saw it. They're finally gonna do it. The clemency plea didn't work. They are finally going to kill that son-of-a-bitch. The New Mexico attorney general said the questions raised on forensics had been asked and answered time and again and there was no longer any reason to delay the execution."

My body went rigid. I immediately knew who the *son-of-a-bitch* was. I stumbled back to my desk and sat in the dark. "Are you sure? How do you know? Did they set a date? How will he die?" Leaning back in the chair, I clutched my briefcase to my chest and reminded myself to breathe. It had been fourteen years since he had killed Lisa. Fourteen years of trials. Fourteen years of nightmares.

"They said he would die by lethal injection near the end of the month, Matty. It's finally here, the day we've been waiting for." My father's voice carried with it a certain enthusiasm, one he obviously expected me to share.

But for some reason I didn't. Along with my father, I'd waited all these years to hear this news, to actually get a date of execution, yet the pleasure I had expected to feel was not the sensation that was running over me just now. Sadness would better explain the way I instantly felt. The sickened and nauseating feeling took a few more seconds, but it came, just before my feet started tapping off of the floor, causing my knees to bounce erratically.

"Matty! Are you there? Can you hear me?" He raised his voice. I could picture him holding the phone away from his ear and speaking into the mouthpiece.

"Yes, dad—I'm here. I'm sorry, I guess I'm shocked. I don't really know what to say."

"You don't know what to say, I don't understand, Madison. This is what we've prayed for all these years."

I had prayed for Lisa's killer to die. Night after night I had pleaded for bad things to happen to him. I'd often punched the speed bag at the gym and imaged pulverizing his face with my own bare hands. But all I felt now was burden.

"I know, I know, Dad—you're right. He does deserve to die. I don't doubt that." I lied. "It's just unfortunate a fatal dose of drugs is his way out. That seems a little too humane." I used a spiteful tone as I rocked back and forth in my chair. I blankly stared into the darkness of my office.

"Lethal injection is like euthanasia for this guy. He deserves to die painfully—not in a humane way, but in the most inhumane way."

All these years I had felt torment, anguish, guilt, shame and fault. It wasn't until my father actually said the word that I realized I, too, had been tortured. The veins in my neck pulsated and my muscles tensed.

"Dad, it is capital punishment, not torture. That is the way things are done here in America. For his last supper, maybe they'll burn his steak, or serve his apple pie frozen, something dreadful like that. But dead is dead, we will just have to live with that." I heard the irony of my own statement. "I guess we should just be grateful it will finally be his day of reckoning." I could hardly believe I was able to say that. We had waited so many years for this day. I wasn't sure I could even begin to believe it would actually happen.

A custodian opened the door to my office and saw me sitting in the dark. She was slightly more alarmed than I was at the interruption.

"I've got to go, Dad." I jumped up, flipped the light on and held the door open for the lady to push her cleaning cart through. The pungent smell of industrial cleanser trailed her.

With the phone still smashed to my ear I heard my dad's voice take on a pressing tone. "Wait a minute. How about meeting me at the gym tonight? I know you don't have school." I heard him breathing, waiting for my response.

"I can't. I have class tomorrow night and I have a lot I still need to get done tonight. Tell Mom I love her." I certainly didn't feel like being around a lot of testosterone. The boxing gym was full of it. But mostly, I just didn't want to hate someone tonight.

"What about Wednesday night, then?" He waited for my answer.

"Wednesday—I'll have to wait and see, Dad. I've got a busy week, school, work, and Samantha's twenty-fifth birthday party. I told her grandmother I'd help her."

"You never make time for your old man anymore."

"Dad, that's not true."

"Okay, Honey, I guess we'll talk later then. If nothing else, we will see you on Friday for the big birthday party. Sometime this week I'm gonna take a few tables over to Samantha's grandmother's, along with some extra folding chairs. She called me last night and asked if she could borrow them. Your mother is making Samantha's favorite green chili enchiladas and some biscochitos cookies." He gushed pride. "Now we have two things we can celebrate."

I felt guilty. I wasn't sure if that was what he was going for, or if it was just me. "That sounds good, Dad. I gotta go. I love you." I hit the end button on my cell, grabbed my things and stepped out into the hallway that snaked through the courthouse building. It didn't make me feel good ditching my father. It was unfortunate that the worst thing that ever happened to me in my life was what bonded our relationship.

My office was back in the corner of the building, a full city block from the front where the exit was located. As I moved through the giant maze toward the elevators, I stared down at the patterns in the flooring. My mind raced with the news of the looming punishment for a man, who for over half my life had haunted my sleepless nights and intruded on my dreams. I had always felt he should shoulder culpability for his horrific actions. So I am not really sure why now I felt barbaric and cruel to root for his demise.

I quickly found myself in front of the elevator, robotically pushing the down arrow and waiting. He was a child killer—the worst of the worst, *certainly he should be executed*, I thought. The doors separated and I entered the confining box that held two other people. I looked at no one and I said nothing. Within seconds I was exiting on the bottom floor. For some reason I began to have thoughts of the killer's childhood, his loves, his losses, his reasons for becoming who he was. Who were his parents? I wondered if anyone ever loved him. In an instant, my pity turned to anger, and it built into a thick ball in the pit of my stomach. I told myself it shouldn't matter who loved him as a child, or even who didn't. He never thought of Lisa's loves. I'm sure it never occurred to him the life she would miss out on, or her family and friends who would have suffered because of his heinous actions.

I pushed through the doors to the exit. The coolness of the Arizona evening air was refreshing. I needed to force myself to breathe—such a natural instinct, yet it wasn't coming naturally. Startled by the sharp cracking sound of the American flag snapping in the wind high above me, I shot down the courthouse steps with a crooked stride. After my hard landing at the bottom of the stairs, I stood tall, regained my bearing, straightened the collar of my jacket, and took a firm grip on my belongings as I began to walk. I tried to keep my thoughts off the news my father had just unloaded on me. I couldn't understand the emotions that were running through my body. So I decided I would rather not deal with it for now.

The courthouse was downtown, which made it super convenient since I lived in the historic Coronado neighborhood of Phoenix. Some people called it the high crime district, but I thought referring to it as an historic area sounded much better. Basically, Sam and I shared a small rental house in the old part of town. I jumped off the curb, darted across the busy street and leapt up onto the raised platform where people had collected, waiting for the 7:10 inner-city Metro.

April evenings in Phoenix were comfortable. The breeze caused the smell of orange blossoms to fill the air, even in the business district. I leaned forward and glanced up Central and saw the train about three blocks away. I reached into my jacket pocket for my phone and dialed Sam's cell real quick. She should have been off work by now.

The train, sleek and shiny, and covered in advertisements, giving it the look of the Coors Light Silver Bullet, approached quicker than I'd expected. The doors slid back and people began to push through the small entry. With the phone to my ear, I took a seat opposite the doorway and sat while listening to Sam's voicemail. *Hi. You've reached Samantha Green. Leave a message. And please, commit a random act of kindness today.* I spoke into the mouthpiece of my cell. "Sam, it's Madison. I'm just touching base. Where are you? Call me. I wanted to see if you were still bringing dinner home. Or, maybe I should stop for something. Let me know." It wasn't like I actually had an appetite; I really just didn't feel like being home alone tonight. I returned the phone to my pocket and looked up to see people staring at me. I had a tendency to speak loudly on my cell, even though I hated it when other people did it.

I leaned back on the hard plastic seat and glanced around the crowded car. My body swayed and jerked with the movement of the car. The quick stops and starts made it impossible to actually relax. Consequently, I sat and thought about my day, as I often did. The buildings of downtown blurred as we sped past them. However, the soaring glass walls of the main library were hard to miss.

Working hard not to focus on the news, I began to make a mental list of all the things I needed to do for work and school in order to be prepared for tomorrow. Every day I parked myself beside the judge listening to all the pathetic stories of people who went before the bench, and every day I rode the light rail to and from work. But today, as I glimpsed the folks who now sat beside me, in front, and across from me, I noticed there was little difference between them and the people I processed all day long in Superior court. They were just everyday, ordinary people. People like me.

While I studied the group who sat directly in my view, it suddenly became obvious to me there was little that separated the hard-working from the desperate, and the desperate from the hopeless. I had seen my fair share of tweakers, drunks, prostitutes, and thieves in our courtroom, but as I sat stewing on my view of capital punishment, mostly what I saw surrounding me were hard working people trying to make it in this tough world. These were the same kind of people who might steal from K-mart to get school clothes for their kids, or drive with a suspended license because they needed to get to work to feed their family. Both stories I'd heard in my courtroom.

The weather-beaten skin and cavernous lines that etched the face of the man sitting across from me suggested a life of struggle. The dark circles around his eyes encased an untelling sadness, similar to that of the defendant, who in the courtroom earlier today had managed to lock eyes with me. I realized that that stranger in the orange jumpsuit had stolen a piece of me as he was taken from the court and back to jail. Jason Magnus, the shackled man whose body noticeably stirred with agitation, had managed to stay at the forefront of my mind. I was actually somewhat confused by this. Even his name still resonated with me. I rarely later thought of the litigants tried in our court, but this man, this man's glinting blue eyes I could not yet erase from my brain.

The train slowed as it approached my destination, and then with a loud, snapping jerk it stopped. The doors slid open and people shoved their way in, while at the same time, others pushed through to get out. Without thought, my arm flew out and clutched the rail near the exit.

"Hey man, watch it. Can't you see this woman wants to get out, too! Where's your manners, punk!" I pushed back. "Go ahead." I held my arm firmly across the aisle and blocked the young man, allowing a small, elderly Asian woman the opportunity to get out of her seat and through the door.

"Thank you." She gestured by tapping her heart.

I nodded. "You are most welcome." I couldn't help but think of Sam's voicemail as I faintly smiled back at the woman. I believed I had just committed my random act of kindness, without even trying. I turned back. "You see, it's called respect, boy." I glared at the young man with the brow piercing, the word BAD was tattooed along the side of his neck. "That wasn't so hard, now was it?" Our eyes met. There was a pause of intensity as we stood toe-to-toe. He smelled of cheap cologne, too much of it, and cigarettes. He reeked. I could tell he wanted to hit me, or say something rude, instead he darted past me and through the opening.

Relieved, I followed him out of the train onto the sidewalk and watched him trot off in the opposite direction. Quickly cutting across traffic, he pulled up his baggy pants after he stumbled up the curb. It was apparent to me his pants kept him from picking up his feet. Why wasn't it obvious to him? Showing off one's underwear, and putting one's ass on display in public wasn't a fashion statement—it was a ridiculous trend that made absolutely no sense.

I turned away from him and walked along the sidewalk toward my house. My blood pumped with adrenaline. A part of me wanted him to try and hit me earlier. I would have had a reason to lash out in my resentment. But he wasn't the person I resented. The actual individual I held such contempt for might soon be dead.

Exhaust fumes mixed with the smell of gasoline filled my nostrils. A loud bass thumping erupted from a passing car, causing my heart to feel as though it were beating in my throat. I wanted to yell out, *Turn it down you deaf fucker!* Instead, I kept a long stride, doing my best to ignore the obnoxious rap music. I had an attitude; I could feel it to my bones. This was a very busy intersection, with a grocery store on one corner and a popular fried chicken place on the other, along with a little strip plaza filled with Mexican specialty shops, including a bakery, a laundromat, and a tobacco shop. It wasn't that I didn't like the businesses of downtown, but this area in particular was not the kind of place I would want my mother to walk around at night. Once I became an attorney and started to make more money, I would be looking to move out of this section of the inner city.

With the green light, I crossed the street and turned off toward the residential neighborhood I lived in. That's when I noticed a small crowd gathered in front of the bus stop. Everyone stood staring at a man sprawled out using the bus bench as a cot. When I looked closer I noticed a bottle wrapped in a brown paper sack on the sidewalk beneath him. It was a booze bottle, and by the looks of the comatose man, it was an empty one. I had to walk right passed him to get to my house, and when I grew closer, I saw he had taken the bottom half of his leg, which was a fake limb, removed it, and put it under his head as a pillow. Disturbed by the image of this man's head resting on his calf, I stepped up my pace. But after a minute, and once I was out of ear-shot, I couldn't help but laugh aloud. For some reason I found it funny that a drunken man lay there on the bus bench with only a stump for a leg, and a leg for a pillow. The laughing eased my mind and relaxed my body, if only for a minute, and it allowed me to take a pause from my thoughts.

With just a few blocks to go until I arrived home, I reached into my pocket and tried Sam again. I got her voicemail again. I scrolled down my directory to her grandma's number and hit send. Within seconds there was a busy signal. This was not uncommon for Sam's grandma. Sam had always tried to talk her gram into getting call waiting, but I suppose there was a generational rationale for not doing so. Her reasoning was she could only talk to one person at a time.

I stepped through the front gate and up the walk, took both stairs at once, and was finally on the front porch of my little house. It was nice Sam remembered to leave the porch light on when she left. I could hear Charlie chattering on the other side of the door as I worked at the locks. I'm pretty sure that cat of mine could hear the jingle of my keys a block away. Once I entered, I tossed my things on the couch and leaned over to pick up my baby boy. The house was dark inside. Sam must not have made it home yet. I kind of figured Sam would have been here by now. But she always managed to find something to do for her grandmother whenever she stopped over. Running a vacuum or dusting took time.

"Hi, son." I kissed Charlie's furry lips, flipped him onto his back, and cradled his chunky body in my arms as I walked through the house, drew curtains, turned down blinds, and switched on a few lights before clicking on the TV. While I stroked Charlie's belly, the hum of happiness came through loud and clear with a rumbling purr. "Where is Sam, Charlie?" As if my cat was really going to answer me. I supported him in the crook of my arm while I reached down to pick the mail up off the floor. Our mail slot was in the wall near the entrance, with a basket on a table to catch the letters.

Inevitably, some items would fall from the table to the floor. At times, little teeth marks would give away the reason why.

I collected the items, tossed them on the kitchen table, and gently dropped Charlie to the floor. Then I went over toward the back door, reached in the little cubby where the cat box was, and scooped out the chunks, carried them down the hall to the toilet and flushed. Charlie was at my heels following me as I did my nightly routine. His bellowing meow was a cry for dinner. I returned to his space, leaned over and poured the dry bits into the food bowl on the floor beside the backdoor. I checked the locks, pulled the blinds, and went back into the kitchen.

I pulled out a chair, sat at the table, and began to sift through the day's mail. The only thing that had my name on it was a bill, one of my student loans. There were, however, many other colorful envelopes in a variety of sizes, all addressed to Samantha Green—a clear reminder it was her birthday week. While I stacked the items, I heard the faint sound of a newscaster's voice doing the evening news coming from the TV. I rose from the table and walked into the other room to turn it up a notch. I heard him say, *Another victim found in downtown Phoenix with her throat slashed.*

I backpeddled to the kitchen and dropped back into the chair at the table. Once again, I tried Sam's phone—still no answer. Now I was really worried. A wave of unease washed over me. Immediately I called Ethan. It was likely he saw Sam last. He answered on the first ring.

"Hello."

"Ethan, hi, it's Madison." I began to pace the kitchen floor.

"Madison, what's up? Is everything okay?" Ethan's tone was more somber than usual.

"Sam's not with you, is she? She isn't answering her phone."

"Hi, I'm good, too—thanks for asking. So now I'm supposed to be Samantha's keeper?" Now that was more like the sarcasm Ethan regularly dished out.

"I'm sorry, Ethan, how are you?" I did the obligatory greeting. "It's just I am a little worried, that's all." I cocked my head and pressed my phone to my shoulder with my ear. Then I poured soap on the sponge in the sink and washed out Sam's tea cup from this morning, along with few other dirty items in the sink.

"Let's just say I've had better days. Samantha told me she was going by her grandmother's house after work. That was a little over an hour ago. She probably has her phone tossed in the bottom of her purse or something. You know how she is. She doesn't always have it on her like I do." Ethan made a smacking noise. It sounded like he was chewing.

"I already tried her grandma's house and the number was busy." I tossed Sam's old tea bag in the trash and washed off all the countertops. "I will just feel better once she's home. There are too many crazies on the loose out there and one just happens to be running around in our neighborhood." It was easy falling into my normal routine of cleaning up after Sam.

"You don't need to tell me that. Just keep calling her." Ethan's voice sounded anxious. "Eventually she will hear her phone. But I'm sure she'll be home soon. Madison, why do you always have to think the worst? Never mind. I think I already know the answer to that." He paused for a moment. "I'm sure this won't help… but the girl who was murdered across the street from the office, well, she lived in my complex."

"Yeah, Sam told me about the woman they found near your work. And no, that doesn't make me feel better. I also just heard about the killing on the news. That's what's making me really worry. I didn't realize that was your complex she lived in." I opened the fridge door and stared inside. I never understood how Ethan lived down in that area. It was a well known drug-infested zone, which brought with it prostitution, homelessness, and everything thing else I wanted to stay away from.

"I knew her." Ethan's voice was suddenly gloomy. "She lived right upstairs from me. Her name was Nasreen."

This new revelation caused my head to spin with the what-ifs. "Oh Ethan, I'm sorry. That must be very sad for you." I shut the fridge, left empty handed, and sat back at the table. I found myself playing with some loose beads Sam had left in a bowl in the center of the table. It looked like she'd been working on a necklace or something and didn't finish.

"Thanks. It does make me sad." Ethan paused for a brief moment. "Nasreen and I weren't close or anything. I just liked her, that's all. She was a nice person. I only ran into her on occasion. But still, the thought of someone killing her sickens me. I can't seem to wrap my brain around it. It's just too weird. She was beautiful. She was nice, the innocent type, you know. The cops questioned me and all, but didn't tell me anything. I knew from what the store clerk said earlier that her throat had been slashed. That was enough information, I suppose. I can't seem to get rid of that image. Who could do such a terrible thing, Madison? Who could cut a beautiful young woman's throat like that?" I heard a long draw of breath. I could tell Ethan was smoking.

I wanted to ask him when he was going to give up the cancer sticks, but I thought better of it. Timing was everything.

"I know how you feel. Don't even try wrapping your head around it. Sometimes there is just no understanding a sick situation. But believe me, there is wickedness lurking amongst us." He knew all too well I had firsthand experience with the devil's offspring.

My mind immediately went back to the conversation with my father. "I got some upsetting news today, as well. My cousin's killer is finally going to be executed."

"That's awesome! That pig deserves to die. I hate people who harm children." His reaction was harsh and unexpected. "Isn't that what you wanted?"

"I thought so. I mean, I don't know, I guess. Every time I've thought of that bastard killing Lisa, raping her, and doing God only knows what, it made me feel sick." Ethan just listened as I poured out my reflections. "I thought I had already decided the judgment of Lisa's killer. So why can't I now come to terms with it? Why am I not excited?" I heard the confusion in my own voice. "I wanted him dead, Ethan. I wished for the death penalty for him. That was what I've wanted all along. He was never declared mentally ill or insane. He's a cold-hearted, calculated child killer bent on evil, who deserves to die for what he did." Every muscle in my body tensed. My voice raised several octaves while my seething anger poured through the phone.

"I agree with you, darling, but you need to just calm down. You've hated this man long enough. Listen, honey, once he is dead and gone you need to let him go. Oh God! Listen to me, I sound like that group counselor we had Miracle House."

I wasn't feeling comforted by this phone call, in so many ways. I glanced up at the clock on the wall. *Sam?* It was bad enough a dead girl was found across the street from Sam's office; to now hear it was someone Ethan actually knew quickly made my mind wander to the dark side.

"I've gotta go. I'm going to try Sam's grandma again." I remembered my comment earlier in the day about the whistle around Sam's neck. "She should have been home by now. Don't forget, it is Sam's birthday party on Friday at her grandmother's house. It's her twenty-fifth. We need to make it special for her. She always makes sure our birthdays are special. I know her grandmother has planned something nice and wants her good friends there." He was never the most dependable.

"I would never forget my best friend's birthday. But I think this year will be special for a few million other reasons. She's finally coming into her inheritance. I think that will be special enough? I mean really, who wouldn't want to be a trust fund baby." Ethan sounded somewhat envious.

It was funny how we both thought of Sam as our best friend. "I'm not so sure Sam is thrilled about getting that money, Ethan. For Sam, that money is nothing more than a reminder of what she has lost. If it weren't for that stepfather of hers, and if her mother was still alive, she wouldn't be getting any of that money. I just think it brings back too many bad memories for Sam, that's all." I also knew she wouldn't appreciate being called a *trust fund baby*.

"Yeah," Ethan agreed, "you're probably right. Bet you never thought I'd say that to you, huh? I'd hate for you to think you were any smarter than you already think you are." Ethan chuckled. That was more like the Ethan I knew. "I'm gonna let you go. Don't worry, I'm sure Samantha will walk in any minute. We'll talk later. Bye." Ethan hung up.

Anxious now, I tried Sam's phone once more. My stomach dropped when I got her voicemail, again. I knew I couldn't foresee the future, especially because I was so clouded by my past, but something wasn't setting right with me. I quickly redialed her grandma's house. It beeped busy.

Crossroads

Chapter Twelve

Jason Magnus

Stuffed in a jail cell with a bunch of strangers wasn't my idea of luxury. At twenty-seven-years-old, I had hoped this miserable part of my life was over. But yet here I sat, on a cold cement floor among the musty odors of wool bedding, sweat-saturated clothing, sour breath, and the stench of stale alcohol. Some people think jail is some extravagant place, where an inmate gets three squares a day, endless TV, and a phone to the outside world. I haven't even seen a television yet, I'd only had one shitty meal since coming in last night, and I had no one on the outside I could call, no one that would give a damn.

Most of my friends don't talk to me anymore. My family—what's left of it—my father is fed up with my addiction and won't even look at me, much less talk to me. Not until I'm clean and sober. You know—a track record. *Some time under my belt* were the words he would use. *Prove yourself*, he'd tell me. Maybe something longer than six months would be acceptable under his terms. He always chastised *me* on addiction as he pounded back a fifth of alcohol a day.

I sat back and reflected on the day I had had in court. It was never easy being ripped by a judge, humiliated. Today—well, today was no different. I hated it. I was still angry about the court hearing.

Being judged was never fun. Neither was being stared at. I remember the eye contact with the judge's assistant, her face, her disapproving gaze. Today I was embarrassed and extremely uncomfortable in my own skin. As the drugs left my system, paranoia was part of coming down—besides the guilt from my own stupidity. Paranoia made it so I felt not just her eyes, but the eyes of everyone in the courtroom. But it was hers that I remembered. Our eyes actually made contact. It was as if she were trying to figure out how I ended up this way. I couldn't help but look back with no explanation.

My body was still twitching on its own. The muscle spasms were random and uncontrollable from all the toxic drugs I had pumped into myself on this most recent relapse. After 48 hours behind bars, the meth that still remained in my blood crawled down the pathways of my body. And the self loathing I suffered became like a tourniquet around my neck. But no matter the pressure I applied, I couldn't stop the bleeding. I don't know why I couldn't just get a grip on my life. Every year I did the same stupid crap, no change. I wasn't sure how many more Aprils I could live through.

My mother loved this time of year—April showers, spring flowers, and all that. I don't know why I couldn't just remember her for that. But instead, I had to focus on this as the month I lost her. Every year about this same time, it was as if I held a gun and to my head, spun the cylinder, and pulled the trigger. Every year I was reminded of my grief, the pain I needed to escape. Instead, the anniversary of her death became my trigger and the drugs were the bullet in my weapon. If she were here right now she'd tell me to move on, to get over it. She would tell me again how the slightest negative thought harbors intense power. My mother often tried to teach me the power of my thoughts. Now I could see she was right. I could also see I had become powerless to myself.

I let my finger run across the throbbing, swollen scratch that stretched from my cheek down my neck to the top of my shoulder.

I couldn't tell you how I was sliced, scratched, or cut. That was the worst part of blackouts—the not knowing. But what I did know was it hurt like hell. By the pain and heat that radiated from the swollen wound, I'm guessing it was infected. The whimpers of withdrawal, the nonsensical conversations from the crazies, and the stifling smells of stinky feet and body odor filtered through the air of the confined jail area. *God help me.* I wanted to stop doing this to myself.

One of my cellmates was a tall, slender, teenage guy, who looked closer to thirteen rather than eighteen. But I knew he had to be at least eighteen to be in this cell. That or someone really fucked up. He sat on his mat in the corner and scratched himself compulsively. We said nothing to each other; meanwhile, the guys in the two cells next to us, one on either side, were practically having a party. They'd gotten some guards to buy them Cokes and were hollering and yelling back and forth. Two other dudes who were in the cell with us, they got the beds, while the kid and me had a spot on the floor. The older fellow on the top bunk was reading a book, kind of talked to himself some; the man beneath him, as far as I could tell, had been sleeping since I was brought in yesterday. I didn't even know what he looked like. I only knew he snored, loud. I'm surprised no one forcefully pressed a pillow over his head. Believe me, there were moments when I was tempted. Right now was one of them. I wanted to jump out of my skin.

Every time I'd been thrown in jail, every time I came off drugs, I told myself the same line of crap. *This time would be different. No more—I've really learned a valuable lesson. I don't want to be like all the other guys I was surrounded by.* The problem was: I was one of those guys. I tried to deny it, but it was getting harder to believe the lie I'd been telling myself all these years. The older I got, the more difficult it was to run from the shadow of meth. It followed me everywhere. I was an addict. I had gone through unpredictable mood swings, I had become very manipulative, I had lied, I had cheated, I was a thief, and I had neglected every responsibility and every relationship in my life for the past thirteen years. I am an addict. I would go to any length to get drugs. If I could only put that same ingenuity into living a clean life, maybe I would live up to the greatness my mother saw in me. My gut wrenched with remorse.

A burly female guard walked through the corridor and told us, with sadistic glee, that we were being locked down in ten minutes. *One more night.* I found comfort in that thought. After making it through tonight there would only be one more night to go. I scooted down onto my back, against the hard surface, and tried to find comfort where there wasn't any. The kid on the thin matt across from me broke down at the guard's announcement. I listened as he wept and continued to claw at himself.

"Hey guy, everything will be okay," I lied. "Just try to go to sleep." I told him. I knew it was easier said than done. I regretfully stared up at the cracks that spread across the plaster ceiling and I began to think of all my misfortune, and it always started with the loss of my mother.

After my mother's death my dad began to spiral out of control. The late night drinking turned to all-nighters. I was thirteen years old, my teen years, and I had no one watching me grow up, guiding me. No one cared about how my day was. Whether or not I had any homework, maybe a ballgame coming up, or if I had eaten dinner— none of that mattered to anyone anymore. My clothes never seemed to smell as good. Things around the house never looked as clean or colorful. Always out of place.

Most times I was with my dad there was an emptiness that it seemed only alcohol and anger could fill. This went on for several months after losing Mom. But then, one day he was different. The late-night crying stopped. He had someone come in and clean the house. He had all the holes in the walls repaired. No more unreasonable breakdowns. He packed my mom's things and took them away. That was when he gave me the cross my mother had worn around her neck—a cross I knew meant the world to her and now it meant the world to me. It was a simple piece of jewelry I had made for her in vacation bible school when I was eleven.

After all that, my father went back to sleeping in his bed. No more passing out in the Lazy Boy. It seemed he was dealing with his grief, so I decided to give it a try. I took his route of alcohol and anger—in that order. I began to sneak booze from his bottles, money from his pockets, and cigarettes from the carton in the refrigerator. Next thing I knew, I had become a teenager who lied and stole—often—and for no reason.

"Lock down."

"Lock down"

"Lock down."

It sounded like a choir of voices, from baritones to tenors, hollering throughout the area that caged us all in. The loud screams created an echo through the corridor as they mimicked the loud announcement over the intercom. It meant within minutes it would be lights out. First it would be the hushed whispers in the dark, then the squabbles over space, and finally the fart ripping would commence. Something that often bonded men, even the ones you didn't particularly like. I observed a detention officer flip open a rusted door along the wall and grab hold of a large iron hand crank. As the circular wheel labored through one revolution after another, the barred cell doors slowly slid shut with a grinding squeal.

It was 10:30 p.m. The hour of darkness had arrived. All of us inmates lay behind bars, many of us on the floor, the lucky few on beds. The concrete was hard and the mat wasn't worth a shit. Besides, it smelled of urine. Now that I was getting more clear-headed, all I wanted to do was go back to my apartment, my life, the way it was before this last setback, which was really setting my goals pretty low.

I closed my eyes, and silently began to pray for strength and forgiveness. That prayer was by habit. *Dear God, Forgive me for my sins, and Lord please give me strength to get through this.* The words were so routine I hardly heard them anymore. I begged God for help to stop my mind from running with maddening thoughts. I pleaded for sleep. I entrusted all this to a God I wasn't even sure I believed in.

Until the age of thirteen I was brought up to believe in God. I lived in a nice home, had lots of love, little alcohol, no drugs, good moral values. Neither one of my parents smoked, we ate meals together, and we actually had conversations with one another. I never even heard my mom say a bad word. My mom prided herself on getting us to church every Sunday morning, as a family. My dad, he could care less. He made that clear when my mom passed. I know it wasn't easy for him, after my mom died, to be thrown into parenthood, into responsibilities he was unfamiliar with. He never helped with homework, drove me to school, took care of a home, prepared a meal, or did laundry. My mom did all those things.

While laying in the dark I reached for the cross I wore around my neck. *It wasn't there.* My gut turned. Had I lost it? My mind scrambled. Then I remembered removing it and tucking my keepsake in a large paper envelope I received upon my check-in to jail, along with my wallet, my grandfather's pocket knife, three quarters, two one-dollar bills and my driver's license. The knife was a gift from my mother. Before my grandfather died my mom said her dad bragged about how that little pocket knife could gut, skin, and cut up a five-hundred pound buck. I had never used it for hunting. My finger ran along the base of my neck, around to my throat, across the spot where my mom's cross always lay. Regret pulsed through my skin.

It was the summer before high school when I started experimenting with drugs. And for the next fourteen years of my life I had tried everything to figure out a way of stopping—addicted to meth four years now. Before that it was mostly liquor, cocaine, crack, and some marijuana, mostly to help me sleep and eat. I never really cared for the buzz pot offered. I wish I would have, though. It would have been a much better choice. I never heard of a pothead ruining their life, losing their friends and family, and giving up all that they ever were, or ever wanted to become, for one toke of the fluffy, green stuff.

For a short while after my mom's passing, I had a connection to my grandmother, my mom's mom. That was before her memory totally left her. She couldn't remember her own daughter was dead, much less her only grandson. She had Alzheimer's. But I still liked being around her, short as it was. She would say things that reminded me of my mom, like; worsh instead of wash, supper, not dinner. And she called me sugar. I loved that name. Like my mother, my grandmother also used her bread to scoop food onto her fork, and Grandma had the same piercing blue eyes as my mother. But then she died, too. Lucky she didn't suffer the drawn-out death of Alzheimer's. Instead, she went quick and unexpected. An aortic aneurism took her to see my mother. Good for her, bad for me.

My dad's parents had already been dead for years. Like my father, I was an only child. I had no one. While cooped up in a stinky-ass jail cell, looking back on my life, as I always did in this situation, I finally came to the realization that he, too, had no one. Like me, my father was lost after my mother's death. He was lonely. I could now see he and I were more alike than I wanted to admit. I probably should have forgiven him for getting remarried so soon, but I never had. Not yet.

With no one to hold me accountable, no one to make proud, I forgot what it was like to have goals. I began to feel more and more like an outsider. I didn't know anyone else whose mother had died. None of my friends had an angry drunk for a father. I found no one could relate to me. I began to shut everyone out, everybody but Amber. She was all I had left. I cared what she thought of me. But because we went to different schools, had few of the same friends, plus the fact that she lived miles away, it was easy to hide my problems from her, especially my increased cravings and my excesses.

Amber and I had known each other from Sunday school. I could remember one summer in vacation bible school, we had built Noah's ark out of Popsicle sticks. Another year we created a picture of Jesus out of shell macaronis. And one holiday for the Christmas pageant, she was Mary and I was Joseph. My mother was very proud. For the first year after my mother's death I went along with Amber to church, just as I had gone with my mother all the other Sundays before. But then it began to seem senseless. I started to believe my soul wasn't worth saving.

Amber went through an extra effort to keep me in a place of worship. She and Bradley, both, my two best friends, continually pleaded with me to go with them to church. Bradley was the preacher's son, working on being a youth minister, so I'm guessing saving souls moved him up the ladder in God's eyes. He was a little older than us, but liked being around me and Amber anyway, and he had a car. I don't think he had many friends. The ones he did have were part of the flock. Being the preacher's son and all, he always said it was a lot to live up to. If only I had had something to live up to.

"Dude, you have to stop scratching! Christ, you're not going to have any fucking skin left by morning." I could no longer take the sound of his nails scraping across his skin. I felt bad for sayin' something, but I couldn't fucking take it anymore.

"Hey man, I'm trying to sleep here!" A gruff voice shot out from the bottom bunk.

"Give me a fucking break! I've been listening to you snore for twelve fucking hours." I rotated my body over, leaned up on my elbows, and he was already back to sleep, snoring. My heart was beating through my chest. My patience was running thin.

When I was younger, I had become extremely skilled at mistrust, becoming suspicious of just about everyone. I doubted my teachers, my dad's new wife, her perfect little daughter, the church, Bradley, God, and even Amber. I found it so ironic that every time I found myself sitting in a jail cell, I could always look back and see clearly where I went wrong. And clearly, I should have trusted these people more, and I should have never let Amber go.

I had hurt the one person in my life who had been a constant companion. She stood with me even when it was difficult to do so. Often telling me to hold my head high, urging me to not let the death of my mother dim the light in my heart. That was how Amber talked. She was mature and I was a punk. My gut wrenched at the memory. I closed my eyes and I could see that soft gaze of hers, her long brown hair sweeping the tops of her shoulders. I could picture Amber wearing her favorite baggy jeans and purple tunic top with long wide sleeves, gathered at her narrow waist, emphasizing the curve of her figure.

Again, I heard the kid across from me in the cell crying. But it was the wetness from my own tears I felt dripping down my face. I gritted my teeth and held in the emotion that was overtaking me. Chill bumps stretched all across my skin, sweat drenched my clothing, and my hair was damp against my head. I threw my leg out from underneath the scratchy wool blanket that covered me, hoping for a breeze to pass through the cellblock.

I closed my eyes; the tears continued to press through my lashes. My mother always loved my eyelashes. She said I'd be a lady killer someday; the girls would be swept up by my eyes. Boy was she wrong. When I brushed my tears away, my rough, calloused fingers felt as though they tore through the thin skin of my eyelids. I wanted to fall asleep, my body was exhausted, but my mind was not.

Blame now began to pummel my thoughts. I had always believed my life would have been different, if, and only if, my father would have just been different after my mom died. Maybe if he could have just told me he loved me or something. Possibly things could have been better if we would have talked about my mom after she was gone. My mother, his wife; the woman he loved and was married to for fifteen years.

By the time I was a senior in high school all I knew was resentment. But it was something I knew very well. It had become my trustworthy friend. Now, as I lay on the thin mat, on the floor of the jail cell, my body vacillating from fire hot to cold chills, I could now see how even my resentment had turned on me. Something else I could no longer count on.

My body bucked under the blanket. I tossed and turned until I finally gave up and pushed myself up against the wall. I tucked my knees to my chest and began to rock. Methodically, I tried to calm my shakes and shivers. It didn't work. I was getting myself worked up. I was angry—pissed at everything, and sad, I was really sad. Then I became light-headed. Gasping for air, I began hyperventilating. I desperately needed to fill my lungs with oxygen. Instead, the taste of stinky socks overwhelmed the back of my throat. The nausea and the hot and cold sweats I could deal with, even the body cramps were doable, but I would almost rather be dead than to live with the memories and guilt of my own life. I had committed so many egregious acts converting my sorrow to chaos and my chaos to anger. But nothing haunted me as much as the flagrant, offensive action I committed against Amber.

Chapter Thirteen

Samantha 'Sam' Green

Waking to silence, I couldn't help that my first thought of the day was on my homeless friend, Willie. He scared the crap out of me last night when I left the office. His vacant stare and his ranting shouts remained front and center in my mind.

I sat up, rubbed my eyes, and then looked at the clock on the nightstand. I popped up out of bed and peeked into Madison's room. Her bed was made and the lights were all off. When I walked past the bathroom, dampness lingered in the air. My feet dragged through the rest of the house as I looked for my roommate. There was no sign of her briefcase. A clear indication she was gone. I glanced over at Charlie, who was sitting on the backside of the couch peering through the split in the curtains, making a funny noise as he often did while stalking small birds on the porch. The morning light was soft as it washed across the aged, wood floors.

Madison must still be mad at me. It was unlike her to leave for work without so much as a whisper. No pleasant good morning, or even a rushed goodbye, no reminder of the things I've left lying around that need to find a place. I got nothing from her today. It wasn't like her to punish me. The brat must have forgotten it was my birthday week.

When I came home last night she was totally beside herself with worry. I couldn't believe she was so upset at me. I mean, I had told her I was going to stop at Gram's house after work. I even brought her a home-cooked meal, one of my grandmother's famous meatloaf dinners. I couldn't have known my phone was vibrating in the bottom of my bag and she had become Ms. Paranoid. And I'm sure not going to blame my grandmother for not knowing her phone was off the hook. I'm just glad we figured that out before I left her house last night. I hated the idea of not reaching her if I needed to.

With that thought in mind, I guess I could kind of understand Madison's overreaction, especially in light of her emotional history, her job with criminals, her incredulous attitude, and the fact that a murderer was on the loose in the city. I suppose those were all good reasons why I would forgive her ill-mannered behavior.

I walked into the kitchen, allowing my normal morning routine to play out. I warmed a cup of water in the microwave and hummed a Beatles tune as I reached in the cabinet for a tea bag and sweetener. I never really picked the melodies that randomly buzzed in my head. This morning the words that were crooning in my mind were 'I get by with a little help from my friends.' That was the song I was humming, while all along I was thinking *Madison could use a little help from her friends*. Her paranoid nature was a little much at times. But I knew all too well how fear could cause anger.

I remember when I was about four years old and my mom spanked my bottom for almost getting hit by a car. But then within minutes, maybe even seconds, she was so overwhelmed she swept me up into her arms and gripped me tightly. Grandma smacked my hand once when I almost touched the hot burner on her stove. I suppose the sting of her slap spared me the throbbing pain of a burn.

Getting upset when scared was a normal human reaction, but Madison's reaction last night wasn't normal. She was agitated and worried, extremely preoccupied. It was like she knew something I didn't. She kept saying she had a bad feeling. I'm the one who has premonitions, yet she's the one who was forewarning. More than once she said something about a looming threat that was giving her the creeps. God forbid I told her about Willie having a major flip-out in the parking lot at work, swinging his knife around shouting about killing himself. That would have sent her into an I-told-you-so tailspin.

I dipped my tea bag into the steaming cup of water until the liquid turned dark amber. My thoughts went to my friend, who I knew still struggled to cope with what happened to her cousin so many years ago. A wave of sadness washed over me, the remembrance of my own tragedy suddenly tugging at my gut.

I stepped back, turned and opened the fridge for some milk. I loved my tea creamy and sweet, the same way my mother drank it. I focused on our mornings at the kitchen table, her sipping warm tea, and me with my juice and cereal, about to head out to school for the day. I was immediately taken to a better time, so much so that I caught a whiff of my mother's familiar scent. When I reached for the milk container, I noticed a slip of paper rolled into the handle on the plastic jug. I gripped the bottle with two hands and moved it to the countertop, removed the rubber band, and rolled out the paper scroll. It was a note from Madison.

Hi Sam,

I'm really sorry I'm such an ass. I have a lot on my mind, and I was scared. I know I freaked out when I probably shouldn't have. Please know I love you; you're my best friend. I just want you to be safe. A little bit more cautious, that's all. I worry about you, that's all. There is a <u>killer on the loose.</u> I can't bear the idea of losing someone else who is so special to me. Thanks for bringing me home dinner last night. I took it to work today for lunch. I'll be sure to call your grandmother. I already know it will be delicious. I'm sorry I stormed off to my room last night. No dinner, what a fool. I've got school *tonight, so I'm the one who will be late and out of touch. Have a good day and a happy birthday week.*

Love M.

The friend in me was grateful to find such a lovely note. The trained psychoanalyst, however, saw a passive aggressive reminder to keep my phone on me and to be safe. The underscored killer on the loose was a dead giveaway. I poured a bit of milk into my tea, and turned to find Charlie looking up for his share. His meow was rather insistent. I reached into the cupboard for a small saucer.

"What can I say, boy, that mommy of yours needs help." I leaned over and set the bowl of milk on the floor. Then I realized I was talking to a cat. I shook my head, smiled, and returned the container to the fridge. I picked up my mug and leaned against the countertop, basking in my quiet time. The buzzing of the old refrigerator competed with the pulsating hum of the clock on the stove. I sipped my tea and watched Charlie enter into his own paradise. I loved the sound of Charlie's tongue as he lapped the milk.

The phone on the kitchen wall rang out, breaking the silence of the morning. My eyes went directly to the clock. It was strange to hear the phone ring before 8 a.m.

I answered. "Hello."

"Samantha, turn on the television!" It was my grandmother, and I knew it was serious when she called me Samantha.

"Gram, is everything okay? It's not even eight o'clock." I set my tea on the kitchen table.

"It's Madison, Sam. They're interviewing her on CNN." Her voice pitched with excitement, and it wasn't the good kind. "I just saw the whole back story on the murder of her cousin, Lisa. They even had Madison and her father on camera from all those years ago. The media was making a big deal about Madison being the one he left behind, the child who survived the kidnapping and murder.

You know, talking about how he snatched that little girl as she slept right beside Madison."

"What! Why now?" I quickly moved into the living room and hit the power button. I rarely watched TV, almost never before work. "What happened? Why is she on TV? What's going on?" I scrolled through the channels until I found the story.

My grandmother was talking a mile a minute. "It's that guy who killed her cousin, Sam. I guess they're finally going to put him to death. I'm thinkin' it's a pretty big deal. New Mexico has never executed anyone before now. The courts finally cleared the way for him to die by lethal injection."

"Gram, I've gotta call you back." I hung up without waiting for a response, and then I stared at Madison pushing through a crowd, making absolutely no headway. She was carrying the Tupperware container I had brought home from Gram's house. Questions were being fired at her from every direction. Madison was trying to push her way up the front steps of the courthouse while the mob of reporters pushed back, forcing themselves in her face, causing her to stop before reaching the entrance. She stood behind a bushel of microphones.

"Fourteen years and he is finally going to die for what he did. How does your family feel?" A voice shot out from a reporter.

"My family respects the decision of the courts." Madison adjusted the lapel of her black jacket and tucked the leftovers out of sight.

The man came back with, "Will his death give your family closure?"

"Capital punishment isn't closure. Instead it has been fourteen years of statements, endless courtroom testimonies, and mind boggling evidential proof, as we were forced to continually relive that horrendous time of our lives. It is my opinion that our system of capital punishment harms the survivors of murder victims, while it rewards the criminal. The judicial procedures may have been put in place to serve us, but in fact it is a colossal failure for the many families who are forced to deal with those actions. Mine has been no exception." Madison was stoic as they hammered her back into the past. These were opinions I'd never heard Madison share.

This must have been the *things on her mind*. I didn't know why she wouldn't have told me this was coming. I stared into the TV.

"Miss Morgan, do you think justice is finally going to be served?" The man was part of the barricade of people who stood in her pathway to the courthouse.

"I can't be the judge of that," she said. "If he had been suffering from terminal cancer and died today, would you be asking me the same question?" Madison turned her head and looked for a way out. I was feeling sorry for her. My anxiety was peaking.

"Will you be traveling to New Mexico to witness them carry out the sentence?" This was a local reporter I recognized.

"I haven't received my invitation." Madison's tone was sarcastic, her face flushed. Her mouth sounded like it was getting dry.

"Do you believe in the death penalty, Miss Morgan?" A woman's voice shouted the question.

"My cousin received a sentence of death at the age of ten. A brutal, vile end to what had been a beautiful, fun-loving life, cut short by a selfish executioner. My uncle, her father, was sentenced to death by way of grief. It was a heartbreaking way to go."

I could see Madison's features tensing, she paused and then she continued.

"As if it were yesterday, I remember when this all happened, and a reporter, someone just like all of you, made the most profound impact on me." Madison's eyes stared directly into the camera as she pointed her index finger out into the crowd before her. "To this day, I can still look back to myself as a child, watching that reporter, a kind man, he looked straight ahead at a camera and spoke into a microphone. As events continued to unfold, his true compassion for the situation was unbelievably convincing. He looked into the lens and talked to the other Americans who were horror-struck by the tragedy of my cousin's murder. I have never forgotten his words. He said, 'We must have the courage to face this horror if we are to make the world safer for our children.' Fourteen years later, and I don't think our children are any safer from pedophiles. That kind reporter also implored the viewers to demand to know what went wrong with this man. What made him want to harm children? I still don't have the answers to that question."

Madison paused and looked out over the mob. "The million dollar question was, why? This murderer preyed on a helpless child who was sleeping. Right now, as we speak, there is a murderer on the loose in our inner-city. Do you think the death penalty is going to keep him from killing again?" This was when her debate skills shined. She might as well have been at a podium. She was able to make a case for both life and death.

A man's voice yelled above the crowd. "It could have just as easily been you who was taken through the bedroom window, Miss Morgan. Do you want to see him die?" The question was direct. Madison's chin slightly dropped, the person I rarely saw falter seemed taken aback.

"Listen," she paused, her features appeared methodical. "Why don't you ask your viewers that question? Ask them if they want him to die. I know a jury who saw all the facts in the case sentenced him to death. Okay, so capital punishment as a crime deterrent is debatable. However, one thing is absolutely clear—the death penalty is 100 percent effective against recidivism in pedophile murder cases. It is a proven fact that pedophilia is a permanent condition. The high rate of repeat offenders plainly proves the abysmal success rate of rehabilitation. Are we to gamble with the lives of our children? How many times have these deviants killed children after being treated and released from prison? This is a question for you, for the American people. Ask the social workers and politically correct elitists if protecting our children takes priority over policies that endanger the most helpless members of our society. Ask them if pedophile child killers should be executed." I felt like she was talking to me.

"You are obviously affected by this decision, Miss Morgan. But you are still not telling us if you agree with it." The man was persistent.

I could see Madison's veins bulging in her neck. "Listen, there were hundreds of people, perhaps even thousands who were affected by the brutal killing of one little girl. Ask them if they want to see him die. For some time, my cousin Lisa had become a poster child for the most disturbing kind of pedophilia, the kind that ends in the senseless murder of a child. That man, who now sits awaiting his fate, was able to climb into the minds of many and remain as a horrendous nightmare. Why don't you ask them if they want to see him die?"

I watched Judge Pittsman push her way through the crowd to Madison. "That's enough." She had an authoritative voice. "No more questions." The judge waved her arms the way judges do, and then she put her elbows out and plowed through the crowd. The cameras cut away and I watched Madison and the judge enter the protective walls of the courthouse.

Madison had to have known this was coming. I can't believe she didn't tell me. She needed me and I wasn't there for her. That must have been why she was so upset last night. She had to have known. I wanted to talk to her right away. I wanted to be the best friend she desperately needed at a time like this. I ran through the house unsure of what to do next. The phone rang. It was my grandmother telling me I needed to go to Madison. With her confirming my thoughts, I hung up the phone and raced through the house. Within fifteen minutes I was out my front door and headed to the courthouse.

Chapter Fourteen

Madison Morgan

Judge Pittsman stepped into the fray and whisked me away from the vultures that were beginning to pick at my bones. It was dizzying how quickly everything was happening. I was thrilled to have been rescued from the surprise attack. Although she wasn't wearing her judicial robe, she drew the attention of the crowd as if she were. The bodies parted, and we made our escape to the open doors that awaited us. Courthouse security kept the reporters at bay while another guard took us to the head of the line and through the metal detectors. Both of us grabbed our personal items off the belt and headed to the elevator in a hurry. My usually quiet morning had turned into a flurry of loud activity, completely knocking me off balance.

"What the hell is going on? It sounds like New Mexico is finally going through with the execution. How did I not hear about this?" The judge looked me in the eyes. "Madison, are you okay? You look extremely pale." She placed the palm of her hand on my forehead.

"Yeah, I'm fine." I lied. "They just caught me off guard." I could feel my legs trembling. "I never expected to show up to a media circus this morning. I couldn't believe they trapped me. I wasn't prepared. I can't even remember half of what I said. It was like I blacked out or something." The elevator doors opened, and we both stepped into the hallway and began the trek through the marble pathway to our office.

"What time are we hearing the first case?" The judge looked at her watch.

"Not until ten o'clock." I was finally starting to get my stride while keeping up with my boss's brisk pace. She was smaller than me by a little bit, but she did everything with a certain urgency. She had the gait of a feline, and her high heels didn't diminish her swiftness as we rounded the corner and approached our destination.

"Ten, oh good, that should give you some time to get it together. Have some coffee and calm yourself down. "I'll see you at the bench in about an hour and a half." She entered her private office and shut the door behind her.

I quickly moved through the administrative area, got to my office, and closed the door. I tossed my briefcase on the floor beside my desk, peeled my jacket off, and plopped into my chair. Closing my eyes, I ran my fingers through my hair and took in a deep breath, recalling the bombardment of questions. I couldn't believe they wanted to remind me how easily it could have been me who that murdering bastard had taken. Like that was something I haven't thought about every fucking day for the past fourteen years.

My mind traveled back to that dreadful time, my uncle waking me from my sleep, the fear, and the devastating loss as the scene unfolded. Vivid images flashed in my head. It was like it all happened just yesterday. In my thoughts I could hear my uncle's screams and feel the dampness of his tears. The smell of his cologne as we ran through the house looking for Lisa suddenly flooded my senses.

"Madison!" The receptionist's voice shot out from the intercom. "It's Samantha on line one. She is downstairs and she can't get through security."

"Thanks, Darin, I'll take care of it." I clinked onto line one. "Sam, what are you doing here?" I could hear voices stirring loudly in the background. "Is that Ms. Beth I hear down there with you?" I heard her firm tone giving someone a hard time.

"Madison, they won't let us through to your office. Will you let security know who we are, please?" Sam was frustrated.

"I'll call right down. Once they let you in, go to the elevator, up to four, and I'll come meet you." I clicked the receiver and dialed the security desk. "Hi, this is Madison Morgan, Judge Dedee Pittsman's clerk. You have two women asking to get through to my office, Samantha Green and Elizabeth Hanson. Could you please see to it they find their way to the west tower elevators?"

He was very pleasant, informing me they were only trying to protect me from the mob of reporters, and then he assured me they would be granted entry. I didn't know why they were here, both of them, in my office, before nine o'clock. That was just something that never happened before. I walked quickly back down the long corridor to the elevators and arrived just as the doors slid back.

"Oh, Madison, why didn't you tell me?" Sam fell out of the elevator and draped her arms around me.

"I saw you on the news, and I could only imagine how upset you must be." Ms. Beth wrapped her arms around us both, and the three of us huddled in an embrace for a few brief moments, just outside the elevator doors. It felt good to relax in the supportive arms of people who I knew cared about me, yet at the same time I felt uneasy.

I stepped back slightly. "You really didn't need to come, either one of you. But since you are here, come on." I could feel Ms. Beth squeezing my hand, and she wasn't letting go. I turned and started walking, me in the middle of this threesome. "I only have a few minutes before I need to get ready for my day. What time do you have to be at work?" I looked directly at Sam.

"Not until ten. But don't worry about me. I want to know how you are doing. You were great with those reporters, the way you handled that barrage of questioning was truly remarkable. You are already starting to sound like a top-notch attorney. I can't believe they were asking you to say you wanted to see him die. Death brings out the vultures. I mean, you don't want to see him die, do you?" Sam's eyes were staring into mine.

Ignoring the question, I dropped Ms. Beth's hand and opened the door off the hallway and escorted them into a conference room on the right. I was only a judge's clerk. That meant I had two chairs and one desk, and one of those chairs was behind my desk.

"Come in and sit for a minute." I moved around the table to a chair opposite the door and sat.

"Isn't your birthday on Friday, Samantha? The big two-five." Ms. Beth sensed my need to sidestep.

"Yes, but you already know that." A smile played around the edges of Sam's lips.

Ms. Beth took a seat at the end of the long table. "When did you get the news?" She rested her arms on the polished wood surface and leaned forward onto her elbows. Concern was etched in the planes of her face.

"My father called me last night, just as I was leaving the office. He wanted to get together and celebrate the news." My eyebrow automatically shot up. "This is the day he's been waiting for."

"Why all the media? Why are they making such a big deal about another death penalty case?" Sam paced the floor of the conference room. She wore a sweater that dropped just below her knees. Wisps of cat hair clung to the dark wool material. Sam's hair was pulled up into a messy ponytail that was folded in half. Her linen pants were just short enough to reveal she had on a pair of paisley cotton socks with her Birkenstocks.

"I guess I hadn't really given it much thought, but New Mexico has never executed anyone. Lisa's murder sparked an outcry around the state. They established the death penalty just to punish that asshole for his crime. In a twenty-four hour media cycle, this should be good TV." I couldn't help the sarcasm that pushed out my words.

"It would be good TV, if only the fear of the death penalty would make people think twice before doing this kind of thing to some other child. I wish their reporting would somehow prevent this from happening to someone else, but it won't. They will only glorify the decision to kill." Sam was trying not to show her anger, unsuccessfully. It was a fine line for her to dance, promoting life for the killer of my cousin. "It's really sad because ninety percent of the time child molesters were abused and molested themselves as children. So if a child is molested, should he be killed by the state when he grows up to do the same if untreated?"

"Sam, I don't want to debate this with you right now." I looked away from her and stared at the floor.

"I don't mean… Sorry!" Sam caught herself.

"Have they set a date for execution?" Ms. Beth's soft voice came between us.

"No. But it is likely to happen within the next thirty days." I glanced over at Sam, her eyes were confused.

"As a child who was molested, no, I do not wish to advocate for child-raping killers. But I definitely think there are better ways than the death penalty to deter them." Sam stopped talking for a moment. "I'm sorry Madison, but you know what I believe."

Her words came from her heart, I knew that.

"All I am saying is you and I both know the death penalty does not discourage crime. I'm pretty certain that when a person is about to kill or rape or commit other heinous acts, he or she does not stop and think about the death penalty."

"Samantha, why don't you tell us how you really feel?" Ms. Beth snapped her head back in Sam's direction, before calmly turning back my way. "Madison, I just want you to know I'm here for you during this time, regardless of how I feel about capital punishment." Ms. Beth reached across the table and touched my hand. "Many people don't understand the impact this has had on you your entire life. His death won't put an end to that." She gripped my hand, as if to let me know she understood.

She had been a confidant, my sounding board over the years. I looked into her eyes and could see the signs aging were beginning to show. Her lids were heavier, kind of droopy, and the folding skin appeared loose and thin. Ms. Beth's hair now had wisps of gray that brushed up around the edges of her tightly pulled twist.

"Are you going to be able to work today with all these distractions?" Sam leaned against the wall while staring at me. Empathy had returned in her tone.

"I think working will be a diversion. It will give me something else to focus on." I noticed I was picking at the dry cuticle that lined my fingernails. I pushed back from the table and stood.

"I should get back to work. You two don't need to worry about me. I'll be fine." I smiled convincingly, and moved toward Ms. Beth, helping her rise; I embraced her plump figure and held her tight. "Thanks for always being there for me. I know it hasn't always been easy."

"Call me if you need anything." She put her hands on my cheeks and brought my face toward hers. "Promise me."

"I promise." I turned back toward Sam. "And you, I'll see you later. I have school tonight, so I will be late." I reached out to hug Sam as well.

"I'm sorry I wasn't there for you last night." Sam squeezed me tight. "I'm here for you now."

"You couldn't have known. Don't worry about it." I didn't want Sam to feel bad. Last night was about my issues, not hers. "I'll call you later. That is if you keep your cell phone on." I jerked away as Sam playfully reached out and slapped me on the arm.

"I will keep my phone with me at all times, just in case you need me." Sam patted the pocket of her sweater and smiled. "See, it's on right now."

"I just hope the reporters don't show up at the end of my day." I dreaded the idea of running into that crowd again.

"Well, if they do, you'll be ready for them. Just lead with your heart. Don't allow anger to get ahead of you." Sam leaned in for another hug. "See you later," she whispered.

"That is good advice. If all else fails, ignore them and run like hell." Ms. Beth let out a hearty laugh. "Just keep that right hook of yours out of the picture." She adjusted the large bag draped over her shoulder. "Remember who the enemy is, Madison." Ms. Beth wagged her finger my direction.

Unfortunately, I was often my own worst enemy. I walked over to the door and opened it. "You guys have a nice day." I walked them back out into the hall and watched them head down the busy corridor to the elevators. I turned on my heel, stopped in the break room for coffee, and then headed back to my office.

At first, after Lisa was murdered, I never really thought about issues like the death penalty. All I worried about was how I could get rid of the horrid thoughts of what that nasty man did to my little cousin. I was consumed with trying to understand how someone could have deliberately taken Lisa from the bed beside me as I slept. I was concerned about what to do with the emptiness in my heart.

But then something happened after the killer was put on trial. The conversations that were all around me had become all too consuming. "I hope they fry the bastard, so your family can get some peace." "He deserves to die." "They should hang him." I found this to be a common assumption people made. And this wasn't only coming from outsiders, but from my father. Then suddenly I was someone who wanted the death penalty for the person responsible for taking Lisa away.

I sat at my desk and stared into my creamy cup of coffee. The steam swirled into the air. I could feel a heavy weight on my chest. My mind wouldn't let go of the pounding questions from the reporters. But it was Sam's query that left me uncertain. I didn't have the answer. I just couldn't be sure I still wanted Lisa's killer to die for his crime.

A terrible dread filled me bit by bit. I sipped from the little white foam cup and took in the strong coffee aroma. I sat frozen, drained of energy, not sure where to start. I glared at the case files that needed my attention this morning, and I implored myself to pull it together. I gulped down the small cup, filled my lungs with air, stood and gathered my morning case load into my arms and headed for the courtroom.

Chapter Fifteen

Jason Magnus

The darkness of the concrete building began to dissipate as the fluorescent lights in the dayroom buzzed to life, flickering on just outside of the locked cell, signaling 6:30 a.m. My eyes adjusted to the brightness, and to the recollection of my predicament. I guess I finally dozed off last night or maybe even this morning. It was sleep, little as it was. It couldn't have been for more than a few hours, but it was a start to coming off the drugs, and a start to restoring my body and my brain cells. Sleep was one of the best ways to recover. It also helped my mind take a break from hashing over the failures of my life.

The clanging of the cell doors reverberated through the corridor as they slid open. The men began to emerge from their cells. Like clockwork, at 6:35 a.m., a chorus line of flushing toilets filled the silence as inmates awoke to the day.

I stood and shuffled to the back of the line at the bathroom. The body I inhabited didn't seem like my own. I was stiff and sore, achy all over, and my head throbbed. It was finally my turn to step up to the urinal. My pee was hot. It was like I was pissing razor blades. It hurt like hell. My insides felt like they were coming out of the end of my penis. I was thirsty. I had some dry flaky crap caked around the edges of my lips. I turned and walked over to the bank of sinks against the tiled wall, splashed water on my face and rinsed my dry mouth.

There was a distorted reflective material above the sink that was meant to serve as a mirror. The dim lights made my face a skeleton looking back at me. My gut twisted with the reality of where I was. I felt like punching my image, but I knew from experience the face would still be there mocking me, and my fist would then begin to throb. I leaned in to take a closer look at the glowing, raised, red streak on my face and neck. It was tender to the touch and was beginning to build a light scab in some areas of the scrape.

I walked back out to the community area just as an officer called for the inmates to prepare to receive food trays. In order to get my thoughts in order, food and sleep was what I so desperately needed. Two small fans mounted high in opposite corners of the corridor struggled to move stale air around. A small TV mounted to the wall was tuned into the morning news, capturing the attention of the room full of men.

A different crowd of men filtered into the group area. The large steel doors closed behind them. Now they were trapped, same as me. Many of them clung to their bundles of linen, the thin mat issued at check-in, and any other items they lay claim to in this shithole. They all stared about. I was pretty sure they were looking at the cinder block walls and bars that locked them away from the public, not to mention evaluating the other inmates who stared them down. Their personal articles were tightly tucked up under their arms while they stepped in line and waited for their morning meal tray.

A wiry young man walked over to the corner of the open space, away from the tables where we sat and ate, and he unrolled his thin, plastic looking body, and lay on the cement floor. No bedroll beneath him, no nothing, he just walked in and plopped to the floor of the common area. Everybody looked over to the corner of the room, watching his every move, but no one did or said anything. I shuffled a few steps closer to the food.

A big, huge black dude leaned out of the middle of the line and began to holler. "Did you hear about the cockroach someone found in his chow a few days ago?" He intently watched the scrawny guy at the front of the line. "You gonna be able to eat all that?" He rolled his pink tongue and licked his thick lips.

"Did you hear about the mother-fucking newbie who spread tuberculosis in the unit? I suggest you leave me the fuck alone." His spidery arms shot out to protect his plate as he walked by. His eyes looked just crazy enough that no one said anything.

Known as "Mr. B," Officer M. Brown, according to the badge on his pocket, paced down the center aisle, eyeballing the crowd. "Wrap it up ladies. Everyone wants to eat this morning."

An inmate, intending to amuse, told the story about two men who brawled the morning before. One got a tray smashed into his face and walked away spitting blood. "Never did get to eat his slop." He laughed loudly as he waited in line for breakfast. "Maybe that was good thing, who knows? We'll find out in about twelve hours when we get the shits." He laughed loudly.

The crowd of men cracked up. I even chuckled slightly. It was me who was up next to receive my share of the grub that I had no doubt would give me the shits. I grabbed my tray and returned to my cell. I had no choice but to get back down on the floor. I rolled my mat, along with the wool blanket I had managed to snatch. I created a cushiony seat and I sat where I could lean against the wall. Tangy smells of barf, combined with the stench of urine, and everyone's morning shit made this breakfast most undesirable, but I dug in and ate it anyway.

"So, was it Amber who left you that nice little mark across your face?" A voice came from the shadows of the bottom bunk. "She must have put up a nasty fight."

"Excuse me." I was startled at the mention of Amber's name.

The guy speaking was talking with a mouthful of food. "I figured since you were apologizing in your sleep all fucking night to someone named Amber, she must be the one who left you wounded." His voice was raspy, deep in the throat. His eyes were flat and bored. They were the eyes of a man who had spent all of his time hustling strangers.

I didn't feel like explaining my nightmare. "Oh, she left me wounded all right." I pressed my milk carton on the swollen, infected skin. The coolness gave me relief. "I didn't know you could hear me talking in my sleep through your loud, obnoxious snoring." I nervously adjusted my seat on the mat and folded my legs beneath me. I was feeling agitated, unprotected, very vulnerable to the thieves I was surrounded by, who knowingly intruded upon my private thoughts as I slept.

"My wife always said my snoring was loud. I never believed that lying bitch." He laughed and took a bite of the mush on his serving tray. "I guess she was right, huh?"

I sunk my plastic spoon into the blob on my plate and took another bite. You'd think I was eating shit as difficult as it was to swallow. The oatmeal had no flavor whatsoever, but I knew the nutrition was essential. I turned my head and glanced around as I picked at the dry piece of toast. I had to look at the other losers to keep from looking at myself. The shame, the disgrace, the regret I felt for the life I've lived was too much to stomach, especially while I was eating.

Not too many inmates returned to their cells to eat. Most would sit at a table out in the open, common area, just so they could bullshit with all the others. We received three meals a day in here: 7:00, 11:30 and 4:30. Most of these guys savored the time out of this box more than the food itself. As soon as mealtime was over, it was back to the confinement of the cells.

"I am not a drunk!" A Donald Trump look-alike said to no one in particular as he walked in circles around the common area. They were still bringing more offenders into the unit, even as crowded as it was.

"Of course you're not." A few men chuckled.

Donald twisted back toward them and cursed. The young kid sat slumped against the cinder block wall across from me, staring a hole into the filthy floor. His skin was spotted with red marks and open sores. I tried to stop him from doing that to himself.

I leaned in his direction. "You gotta go get something to eat before they stop serving." He never took his eyes off the spot on the floor. "It will help you come down off the drugs." He ignored me. I don't even think his eyes blinked.

Trump shuffled back and forth. His eyes were ruby red and swollen. His body swam in the orange jumpsuit he wore. He persistently twirled the identification bracelet on his wrist. Another man stood with his face pressed against the smudged glass and looked out on an adjoining room where other detainees huddled over a bank of phones.

"I never got my phone call." His voice went off like a fire alarm. "When do I get to make my fucking phone call?" He turned and dropped to the floor and leaned into the wall. "All I want is one fucking phone call!" He ran a trembling hand through his twisted dreadlocks.

Many of these guys would dial number after number, desperately trying to reach someone, anyone. They had fifteen minutes to make a connection or it was all over. When they came up empty, the look of distress would overtake them, sometimes anger would rage, and a fight would ensue.

I stood and walked over to return my empty tray. As I walked across the open room my eyes went directly to the picture on the TV screen. It was the woman from court. The judge's assistant.

"What's happening?" I leaned into one of the guys who seemed to be paying close attention to the story. The noise of the jail made it hard to hear the television.

"They're gonna fry some fucking child killer in New Mexico." He never took his eyes off the screen.

"What does she have to do with it?" The media was drilling her when I saw the same judge from yesterday whisk her away.

"It was her sister or some relative of hers that was killed, I'm not sure. But it happened years ago." The guy continued to tell me what he knew as he stared at the tube. "The little girl was swiped through the fucking window of a bedroom where they both slept." He finally turned and faced my direction. "I got a kid. I'd kill that motherfucker myself if he did that to my child. He'd never make it to a death penalty." His high, over-gaunt cheekbones appeared hollow next to his grey eyes.

I couldn't imagine him as a father. I guess I'm not the only one having troubles. I scraped the remains of my meal into the large trash can, tossed my empty milk container and returned to the bathroom. I couldn't help but think of that court clerk. Yesterday I thought she was a fucking bitch, and today I fucking felt sorry for her. It goes to show you, people all have their own shit.

I made my way in and out of the stinky-ass bathroom as quick as I could. But still, as I washed my hands, I was forced to see myself again. This time I quickly turned away.

I worked myself back to the cell I was calling home for a few days, rolled out the mat that had become my bed, and then I crawled down to the floor and flipped onto my back. My body began to revolt, jumping and twitching; again the goose pimples stretched the length of my legs, along my torso and up and down my arms. Another day without drugs added to both my success and my misery. Coming down and detoxing from meth caused a mental suffering that left hopelessness in its path.

I turned onto my side and stared through the cell bars out to the community area. "Mr. B" was shouting at the newcomers to find a spot in a cell. I knew the lock-up announcement would be coming soon and the new guys would press in, so I wanted to lay claim to my spot on the floor. I felt like I was finally tiring. I begged my body to stop twitching.

I noticed a tall, willowy, black-haired man, whose appearance was more like a woman, work his way into our cell. He-she slumped up against the wall beside the psychotic scratcher. He folded his knees over to one side and leaned into the bars. Dried mascara lined the tear tracks on his sharp cheekbones. He stared down at a spot on his thigh, where I noticed him methodically tracing his index finger, as if he were writing a note to himself, and then reading it.

It reminded me of the many times Amber would calm me by tracing a smiley face on my leg. Or she would draw a heart on my palm and tell me I would always hold her heart. I often yelled at no one while raging inside of myself, yet Amber was there, getting the brunt end of my emotions, always. But she saw through it. She knew it wasn't about her, but rather about me and my demons. Still, she was there for me. She stayed with me when many others abandoned the newly-fangled, angry, unpredictable Jason. With a full belly, I felt dozy, the jumping tremors of my body slowed.

* * *

Since Amber and I attended different high schools, I was able to have two separate lives. We mostly saw each other on the weekend. She had strict parents, who had a strict curfew, with strict rules about me. With Amber, I was able to be vulnerable without feeling exposed. We laughed and teased each other, and she was always hugging me, going on about how important the human touch was to the growth of the human spirit. She knew my mother and I often brought her up in conversation—something no one else did. I became someone totally different when Amber wasn't around.

I remained popular with my school peers—especially the partiers—you know the ones who liked to get glazed over and then go to class. I knew how to have a good time, and I had a knack for livening things up. I just didn't have the self-control to know when to stop. I could never figure out when enough was enough.

My alcohol and drug use continued to escalate in high school, leading to my first shoplifting episode. I was a freshman when I got caught stealing a bottle of Jack Daniel's from a supermarket in our neighborhood. They called my dad and the police. He came down and they issued a ticket and let him take me home. That night he barely scolded me, and then he sat in the darkness of our den and stared into the bottom of his glass of scotch.

It wasn't long after the shoplifting incident that I was caught tearing up one of the classrooms at my school. I don't really know what came over me that night. Possibly it was my dad's happiness that made me break. It was in the middle of the week on a school night, I was buying some blow with the fifty bucks I stole out of my dad's wallet, just regular old cocaine, and this guy claimed he had something better and cheaper. He called it crank, said it, too, would send me flying high, only much faster than cocaine. As it turned out, another name for crank was crystal meth, more toxic than crack and more addictive than heroin—probably why I liked it so much. *My bad luck.* My first time of snorting it the rush was the most intense feeling ever. It was fucking awesome, a sensation I've been chasing every since.

It took me two seconds to fork over the cash, snatch the shit from his hands and be gone. The white powdery substance burned my nose like a son-of-a-bitch. But I was immediately pepped up. My blood pulsed in my veins, and everything within my view was brilliant, extremely radiant, and clear. I didn't feel like going home, so I went walking around the school yard under the bright light of the full moon. The next thing I knew, I was testing the doors, and after about ten doors one suddenly opened. It was the biology room. I walked in and let my eyes adjust to the darkness before moving over to the desk at the front of the room. I kicked out the chair, plopped my ass down and threw my legs up on the table.

I glanced around the room lit only by the moonlight. It pushed through the small windows located high on the wall, just beneath the ceiling. I counted them; there were twenty-eight windows in all. I guess they wanted the kids to have natural light in the classroom, but the obvious intent was for them not to be able to look outside.

I don't know why, but for no apparent reason I slammed my head down on the desk. I immediately felt the rising pain on my left cheek. My throat swelled, my chest tightened, and I started crying. Then I abruptly stood and tossed the chair I was sitting in up against the wall. I pitched tables, threw books, classroom chairs, anything I could get my hands on. Then suddenly the lights came on. I dropped the chair I had over head and bolted toward the exit.

"Boy, there is no use tryin' to run. I done called the cops on your ass." A tall black man stood in the doorway with a baseball bat.

I could feel my heart beating a thousand beats too fast. There was nothing I could do but wait. That was my first real trip in a police car. I was escorted into the police station downtown and told to sit on a bench behind a waist-high wall, right next to a bullpen area of desks. I did as I was told. I figured this was when they called my father. My head was throbbing where I had pounded myself. I don't know why they'd bother call my father—he'd be busy with his new wife and her kid. I lowered my body into the metal chair, dropped my chin to my chest and stared down at my feet. The floors were bright white, twelve inch, square linoleum tiles. Under the florescent lighting they looked filthy, stained with dribble from who knows what.

Men and women, some in uniform, others were wearing regular street clothes, occupied a few of the desks behind the half wall. I rocked forward and back, the drugs, my nerves, and all my fear had grabbed ahold. My mouth was dry, and my tongue was as thick as my fist. It was a struggle to swallow. My palms were dripping with sweat and my head throbbed. I pressed my hand onto my cheekbone and felt a large lump. I glanced up to see the clock on the wall read 11:15 p.m., and then I noticed a woman walking toward me. She was a wide-shouldered woman, wearing jeans, tennis shoes, and a yellow collared blouse with a brown blazer that I am certain she thought dressed it all up. Her hair was messily pulled up on her head, and she had little makeup on her chubby face. She didn't look like your typical cop.

Unexpectedly she stopped in front of me and knelt to the floor. "Hi, I'm Elizabeth Hanson, I work for CPS. It's a division of…"

"I know what CPS is." I looked away from her kind eyes. I was embarrassed for the predicament I had now found myself in.

"Good! Not everyone knows what CPS means." She twisted her body onto the chair beside me. "Your father was called, and he isn't answering the number you gave us. Is there another way of reaching him?"

"Yeah, you can call his girlfriend's house. But then again, he might choose to leave me here anyway. I only get in the way of him moving on. I remind him of a family he once had." I momentarily tilted my head her way. My legs were trembling, causing them to bounce off the floor slightly. I pressed my palms to my knees to hold them down.

"I want to know if you are afraid to go home. Has your father ever hit you?" Concern wrapped her words. I gave no response. "What happened to your face?" Her fingers lightly touched my cheek.

"Oh, I get it. You think my father did this? That would require him paying attention to me." I was taken aback by her questioning. "He wouldn't hit me. He can't even see me. He doesn't even know I still exist."

"How did you get the bruise on your face?" She searched my eyes for answers while grazing the bump on my face with her index finger.

"I did a head plant into a wood table. I'm the one who did this to myself." I put my head in my hands and began to cry. I felt her hand rubbing my back. She did big circles, and then small ones with her palm pressing firm. It reminded me of my mother. She rubbed my back the same exact way. This Hanson woman had the same tender warmth as my mother. I melted to her touch.

"I want to sit here with you until they reach someone in your family." Her hand felt warm through my shirt as she continued to stroke me. "You know there are places that can help you, right?"

"Do they have a way of giving me back my mother? That is all I need." I bounced out of my seat and looked down at her, but only for a moment before she was up in my face.

"Sit back down!" Her hand firmly guided me back into the chair. She was now standing over me. "I know you're high on something. These people down here, they don't give a crap about you, but I do. They will turn you over to your father and call it a night. What, you gonna to tell me your mom died, your dad ignores you, or worse, he's already remarried, so you've got to go out and become a juvenile delinquent just to get a little attention?" She forced our eyes to meet. "Am I close?"

"You're more than close, you're dead on. Well, he's not married yet, but I am sure that's coming. My mom's body is barely cold and my dad has already found another family." I put my head in my hands again and began to sob loudly. This time she knelt in front of me and wrapped her arms around me. "He has not only forgotten about her, he's forgotten about me."

"I hate to hear that," she said. "But that is still no reason to ruin your life, Jason. What would your mother think?" She rocked me in her arms as I sobbed even harder. "I can help you, Jason, but only if you let me." She spun back around and sat beside me. "I can help you get back on the right path, stay off drugs, and stay in school."

Just then a uniformed officer walked up and announced the arrival of my father. I turned and saw him. She was there, too. The CPS lady walked with me through the hall, reminding me she was there for me, tucking her card into my pocket before delivering me to my father. He pretended to show an interest, insincerely thanked the kind woman and the others for their troubles, apologized for me, promised to take care of the damages, and out the door we went. I felt the eyes of the CPS officer follow me through the exit.

When my father wasn't looking, I picked the card from my pocket and read it. On one side it was a very official looking business card. It identified her by name and position, and it also included the state emblem. I flipped the card over between my fingers. It read: *Miracle House Volunteer—A Place Where Everyone Gets a Chance to Start Over.* There was an address and phone number beneath the slogan. I tucked the card in my wallet.

* * *

"Lock down."
"Lock down."
"Lock down."
Once again the choir of voices sounded off in harmony with the intercom announcement, marking the end of the morning break as the barred cell doors slid shut with a high-pitched screech. I couldn't help but think of that woman, all those years ago. If only I had called. Her kind offer to help me has always remained in my thoughts, yet always in the outside edge, never really within my reach. I lingered between sleep and wakefulness, with the disturbing realization that when time passes, blame turns to shame.

Chapter Sixteen

Ethan Price

When I left my apartment this morning, my landlord, Mr. Faranghi, stared my direction as I crossed the courtyard nearing his unit. He leaned out of his doorway, a wife beater tee-shirt and a pair of green workpants covered his fat body, barely. He was always twisting the golden Allah that draped his thick neck. His stare was so intense it forced me to keep my head down and my eyes elsewhere as I walked the meandering concrete trail through the complex. Then I could sense him following me.

The morning air was fresh, crisp, and the first scent of spring awakened my senses. Then I realized all the other smells of the city lingered in the atmosphere. The grounds were a combination of desert lawn, which basically were small pieces of rock. The tiny amounts of actual Bermuda grass lawn was mostly worn down by foot traffic, turning it to patches of compacted, brown earth. Fencing in the apartment complex was a tall wall of oleanders, all of which were in full bloom, with splashes of white, red and pink flowers.

I was always reminded of Bradley when I saw the overgrown plants. They were reminiscent of my time as a boarder at Miracle House. It was my short stint as a resident victim. I drew my cell phone from my pocket, snapped it back and saw no missed calls. *He still hasn't called me.* I knew dealing with his mother's funeral and all of the arrangements had him busy. But it isn't that hard to make a call—touch base with one little call. My mind wandered back to a different time, a time when I had a choice, a time before I was totally hooked on this man.

*   *   *

"Be careful, those oleanders are poisonous." Bradley walked over to me as I hung around the wall of shrubbery. He was taller than me, dressed in a short-sleeved collared shirt and khakis. His shoes had a shine to them. I liked his short hair. His bangs fell along his forehead, keeping him youthful, like the twenty-two-year- old he was, rather than the thirty-year-old his clothes would suggest.

"Oleanders are only poisonous if you eat them." I picked a flower off the large plant and pretended to put it in my mouth.

"I hope you aren't really planning to eat that?" He tilted his head and smiled.

"Would you have something else you'd rather I put in my mouth?" I wagged my brow in a flirtatious way.

"I need to talk to you about that." He turned and stepped over to a bench alongside the pink, red and white flowered wall. He waved me on. "Sit with me?" He sat and patted the wood plank seat beside him.

I was enjoying my quiet time, but he was cute, very nice, and he had an interest in me, especially after the hand job I gave him in the bathroom a week ago. I wasn't certain that was a first for him, I mean having another man hold his penis, but I was certain he hadn't done it before while on his *church mission* to Miracle House.

I remember that day in the bathroom, kissing him on the mouth while he nervously kissed me back. The two of us, locked in the men's room at Miracle House. This day, when he called for me, I noticed a serious side of him. Instinctively I resorted to my coyness as I slowly swayed over to the bench and sat beside him.

"I want to talk to you about what happened last week." He shifted his body and folded his hands in his lap. "I've never done anything like that before."

"That's what they all say, counselor." I could see he wanted an out. Suddenly I was being nonchalant about an event I hadn't been able to get out of my head since it happened.

"Please, don't make fun of me, and don't play down the feelings between us. I take pride in being a youth counselor for my father's ministry. I am telling you the truth, Ethan. I've never been with another guy before. When I say that was a first for me, I meant it." He stared down at his hands, pressing them on his knees. It looked like he was forcing his legs to the ground. His fingers tapped nervously.

"Oh, so you're a virgin? That would be a first for me." I playfully tossed my head.

"Please, Ethan, don't make fun of what I'm telling you. I know what I did was wrong. I'm sorry for that. I'm older than you and I'm in a position of authority. I should have known better." He shifted his body and leaned over his knees, furiously tying his hands in a knot.

"Bradley, give yourself a break. You're five years older than me. You still live at home with your parents. You've never had sex. Something tells me we aren't too far apart in maturity."

"It's not about maturity, Ethan, it's about responsibility. I have responsibilities to the church, my family, and Miracle House. I owe you more than that. I owe everyone better." He crossed his leg and twisted his body away from me.

"Are you trying to say you didn't like what happened with us?" I kicked my shoe into his foot, causing the reaction I was looking for.

He looked directly into my face. "I should tell you that I didn't like it, and we shouldn't do it again, but I can't tell you that, Ethan. I know what I'm supposed to do, but it is very different from what I want to do. I enjoyed being with you. I enjoy you, Ethan. You make me feel alive. You make me smile. Whenever I'm around you I feel like I can be myself. I can just be Bradley Bennett, young man trying to make it in the world. Not the preacher's son, the youth minister, the only child, the impostor." He rocked back and forth in a moment of blankness, neither of us able to find the words to say.

Me, without words—that was rare. This conversation was totally unexpected. My mouth was as dry as a nun's crotch. I wanted to be with Bradley again. A swirl of emotions released in me. I wanted him, and it seemed he, too, wanted me. It was obvious he was afraid, unsure of what came next. I knew he wouldn't take the first step. It would be up to me to find a way to make it work.

Thinking back about Bradley, all those years ago, I found it exhilarating, frightening, and exciting. At the same time, it was a disappointment. I realized it never really did work out the way I had hoped it would. I was reminded of his family, his sense of duty to them, his commitment to them— especially as an only child. Something I would probably never be able to compete with, dead or alive.

* * *

My landlord was surveying the complex, trailing me, as he often did. Mr. Faranghi yelled out with his gruff voice and jumbled speech. "Hey 103, I saw you come in late last night. What, you working two jobs? Nobody goes out on a Monday night." He chuckled and drew hard on his cigarette. Raising his bushy eyebrows snoopily, he then exhaled a large plume of smoke while staring over at me, waiting for my response.

I hated the way he called me by my unit number. It wasn't any of his business where I was, yet I answered him anyway, with a lie. "No, no second job. I went to meet a few friends. Some of us go out when we are invited, regardless of what day of the week it is." I kept walking and barely looked his way. I was already a few minutes behind schedule. I certainly wasn't going to stop and chat to tell him I went out to meet a stranger, we fucked, and I came right home afterward. And, yes... it was rather late.

"It's too bad about 203." His thick Middle-Eastern accent cut through the air and tapped me on the back of the head. "I used to see you two talking all the time. It's too bad to hear she was murdered."

I stopped and turned around. "Too bad? It is a tragic, despicable act someone committed killing that girl. She was a very nice person." Without thought, my hand perched on my hip. "I can't image what kind of pig would have killed her. I can only hope she didn't suffer." Again I pictured her dead body propped up against the dumpster, her throat slit from ear to ear. I didn't even want to imagine what led up to that type of end.

"Hey Pretty Boy, did you hear they found another dead body last night? Maybe this morning, I'm not really sure." I could hear his slippers dragging on the cement path. "The TV news said the body had been there a while, perhaps dumped even before your little friend was killed." He seemed excited to tell me this new information, and somewhat annoyed with my relationship with Nasreen. Some people just liked knowing more than others; no matter what it was they knew. He was one of those. But I never knew whether to believe him or not. It seemed lying was simply a part of his nature, like under-tipping, or being cruel to animals.

I spun back around on the sidewalk and took a giant step back toward him just in time to watch him choke out a cough and then grotesquely spit something into the bushes beside him.

"Where? Who?" I didn't go any closer to him. Instead I stayed my distance.

He pulled a pack of cigarettes out of his pocket and lit another. "Not too far from here, down by that dirty Mexican food place on the corner. I guess the body was found in the ditch that runs behind the place." He made a sweeping gesture with his arm, smoke trailed his hand. "I hope it's not another one of my tenants. I hate it when people don't give a 30-day notice." His sinful laugh crept along my spine. "You better be careful going out so late. You never know who is lurking around the corner." He stood there clucking his tongue.

I wasn't yearning for a cigarette any longer. I twisted back and headed forward on my path, yelling to him over my shoulder. "Bye, Mr. Faranghi." I couldn't stand the idea of his mocking eyes on me. I felt dirty around him. And it didn't help that I'd already felt dirty. I never liked the morning after one of my rendezvous. In fact, I hated myself afterwards. Yet, against my best judgment, I'd always managed to tilt to that behavior.

I snaked through the apartment buildings, and out the front entrance of my complex. I was shocked to hear my landlord say someone else had been found murdered. I rarely watched TV so I was the last to know anything. The fact that someone in my complex was found murdered, and now someone else down the street had been found dead, it was all becoming a bit eerie. As much as I hated to admit it, my disgusting landlord had a point. I should probably be a little more vigilant, perhaps even on guard. Just the fact that I was a flamboyant gay put me at risk. A lesson I've already learned the hard way. My hand automatically went to the scar on my head. The raised piece of flesh was a true reminder of just how vicious, cruel, and nasty people could be.

I only had to walk half a block to Van Buren Street. I approached the busy street; morning traffic buzzed by. The draft from a bus just about blew me over. Fumes filled my lungs. I stood thinking about the news I'd just received. I glanced up and down the road for a safe crossing. In the distance I could see the Mexican food place down on the corner, the one he was talking about.

I caught a break in traffic and jogged across the street and into the parking lot of Last Chance. I passed by a few leathery faces of the needy who began to gather around the entrance. A few were familiar regulars. They sat on the parking curbs, the sidewalk, over near the dumpster, and a few leaned on the metal pillars under the covered parking spots. They had unkempt hair. They wore sweaters with frayed sleeves, ragged pants, with rear ends worn down to strings, coats patched with duct tape, and shoes with little sole. All of them waited for a handout, but few of them were willing to enter the actual building to get it. Unfortunately, that required a seventy-two hour commitment. Something many of these people where incapable of giving. They had to also give assurances—no drug use, no drinking— and they had to be willing to be placed in a halfway house, or potentially even a psychiatric facility.

The co-worker I was supposed to relieve after working the nightshift leaned out the back door. Staring annoyingly, he tapped on the face of his wrist watch and hurried me along. I knew I was a few minutes late, so I apologetically stepped it up. He had every right to be upset. I didn't like to be forced into overtime either, especially if I had places to go and people to see. I rarely had, but no one else needed to know that.

"Sorry." I ran past him.

I realized I hadn't seen Willie outside. That was unusual, and Samantha wasn't in the office yet either. There had been no sign of her car. People were already lined up inside, some waiting to be checked in, and I knew there were many inside who were waiting to be checked out. I had to hit the ground running, no time to even have a cup of coffee. No time to call Bradley.

I would have called him. I always called him when I walked to work in the morning. It was the start to my day, almost every day. He would tell me how he missed me, and he'd make promises of being with me someday. "Just us," he'd say. I liked to hear of his upcoming plans: where he was going, who he was seeing, what he was doing. But this weekend, with his mom's death and all, I was giving him time, time for his family. And now, since he hadn't called me, I didn't feel like calling him. Besides, today I was not myself. Today I was still staggered by Nasreen's death. I was trying not to be so consumed with Bradley. That was a first. I had not even wondered what his wife Amber, might have made him for dinner last night, or if they fucked for the first time. Or so he says.

* * *

The next few hours flew by before I popped my head around the corner and noticed Samantha had snuck in without saying hello. I could see her working to do a placement for a client who sat across her desk. That was what we called them, clients. It gave them more self-worth than the word victim, homeless person, or drug addict. Because the program provided services to victims, Samantha made special arrangements to help with placement once they left our facility. This was a part of her job she took very seriously. Once they were gone, their best chance for success would be their next stop.

Samantha looked up. Our eyes met. Her smile was oddly strained. I smiled back. Her look signaled we needed to chat, but there was no time, not yet. I could see she was stressed about something. Her usual bright glow was rather dull. Her hair hadn't been combed. It was thrown up in a messy lump on her head. Her clothes looked like she pulled them out of the dirty clothes hamper in a hurry to get out the door.

No one else would sense the stress that caused a certain tightness in her face. But I did. I knew this upcoming birthday was bothering her. But it now appeared even more than I thought it would. Not much caused Samantha to be off balance. But no matter what was going on in her life, Samantha didn't allow it to affect her job. Her compassion never wavered.

The only time I ever even saw her slightly freak out was when she did an intake for a mother and daughter who needed to get away from the mother's boyfriend. He had repeatedly sexually abused the young girl. The mother was screaming furiously, begging to be placed in a safe home, admitting she had to run away to keep from killing him for what he had done to her little girl—something Samantha knew would have kept her mother alive.

Samantha would go out of her way to make use of all the local services at her disposal in order to assure her clients had the best chance at escaping their demons, whatever they were. She often said our facility should have been called *Best Chance* rather than *Last Chance*. In order to break multi-generational cycles of homelessness and domestic violence, Samantha knew the value of building relationships. Just like the one she and Ms. Beth had. She knew all too well—the right person and the right place could change the path of a person.

I danced around the front counter, doing a few last-minute things before heading out for my lunch, hoping to give Samantha enough time to wrap it up. I could hear her arranging transportation for the clients who nervously awaited Samantha's instructions. She also assisted them in arranging continued counseling. Whether it was for drugs, alcohol abuse, rape, domestic violence, or homelessness, Samantha wanted everyone to have the benefit of a counselor. She believed everyone should have their own private shrink on staff. Me personally, I'd rather keep all my shit to myself. I never liked opening up to a complete stranger. I just like fucking them.

"Ethan, I'll be right with you." Samantha spoke in her work voice. She stapled some papers, slid them into a file folder and stood up. Then she walked around her desk and nicely extended her hand to draw the tall woman out of the chair. She handed the lady the folder, wrapped her arms around the overly thin, frizzy red-haired woman and bid her a heartfelt farewell as they walked toward me. Samantha hugged everyone. Often carrying on about how the human touch was essential to survival.

"Thanks, Miss Green. No one has ever been as kind to me as you. Thank you for treating me like a real person." The woman drew Samantha's hand toward her face and began to kiss it. She had eyes that sunk so far into her head they almost disappeared. "Thank you so much." Her high, over-gaunt cheekbones appeared hollow to me. She smiled softly, revealing her toothless gums.

"Come on now." Samantha moved to the exit, her arm wrapped the female as she pulled her along. I could always hear the jingle of Samantha's bracelets when she moved about the office. "You'll be fine. I'm always here if you need me." She gave the woman one last hug.

I watched Samantha say goodbye. Then she twisted back and looked right at me.

"Don't you need a cigarette or something?" She removed her long sweater, slung it over the back of her chair, fussed with her wrinkled blouse, and then came over next to me. "I am so ready for a break. Oh, wait one second." She turned back and trotted to her desk and grabbed the small box that sat beside a framed picture of her, Madison and me, back at Miracle House, eons ago.

"Since when do you want to go with me on a cigarette break?" I held the door open and followed her outside.

"Shows you how desperate I am for conversation." She leaned in and pecked my check as she glided through the door.

The sun was high in the sky, it was bright, and the weather was already warm for April in Arizona. I flipped my sunglasses on, tapped a cigarette out of the pack, lit it, and followed Samantha to a table in the employee courtyard. "Now talk to me. What on earth is wrong with you today?" We moved toward a large, branchy mesquite tree that cast a nice shadow. "You are definitely not yourself. I know when you reach out for that special little box of yours something isn't sitting right with you." I arched my brow and stared at her. "And I want to know why you weren't answering your phone last night? Your roommate, Ms. Happy called me in a tizzy."

I drew hard on my cigarette, my other hand on my hip I paused and waited for her to answer.

She stopped and whirled around. "Turns out my not answering the phone had little to do with Madison's tizzy. Apparently you haven't seen the news?" She wasn't wearing sunglasses so she squinted as she stared at me.

I stepped past her. "Okay, so what's new besides another murder? Just down the street by the way. You know I never watch the news, not if I can help it. It's always bad news anyway." We took a seat in the corner, away from the two other groups of people on break. "Is that it, the murder? Is that what you're talking about?" I watched Samantha take her seat opposite me and open her precious box.

"Well, that's part of it. There is so much to tell you really, I'm not even sure where to start." Samantha fanned the smoke that lingered around her face. She took the colorful cloth out of the container and spread it on the table between us.

I waved my cigarette in an attempt to divert the smoke from going in Samantha's face. "You can start by telling me where you were last night. And why weren't you answering your phone? I even tried you a few times." I decided it was easier to smash out my cigarette. "What time did you leave work last night?"

"I left soon after you. I walked out to my car, and oh my God! Willie came screaming out of nowhere and scared the crap out of me. He was back to thinking he was Jesus Christ, ready to die for the people, he said. Shouting loudly about death and dying, screaming kill me, kill me. He really freaked me out, Ethan. He was waving around that pocket knife of his. I'm really worried about him. I was going to try to talk to him but he started to screech 'Get out of here! Get out of here.' He was swatting at the air with the knife. Willie didn't even know it was me, Ethan. He looked at me with an intensity I haven't seen in him before. I couldn't recognize the person behind his eyes." She tossed the magic stones from their box out onto the cloth. "He shouldn't have a knife."

"I have told you when you leave work, especially after dark, you need security to walk you out to your car. What the fuck were you thinking?" My face flushed as I thought of the terrible things that could have happened to Samantha. She was my closet friend, my sounding board, and my family. Samantha was one of the few people in my life who I could always count on. She loved me, for me. I couldn't imagine life without her.

"Ethan, chill!" she snapped. "So many things in my life, with Madison, with work, and now Willie, just haven't been right." She stared ominously at the stones, the colors, and their placement on and off the cloth. "And now I can see why," she says convincingly while she analyzed the stones.

To some, my best friend may have seemed a little eccentric at times, especially to those who didn't know her. But for me, that was one of the things I loved most about her—her difference. I didn't have to believe those stones could predict her future, but I could support the fact that she did.

"I could sense he wouldn't hurt me, Ethan. Willie would never hurt me."

I could see Samantha wasn't totally convinced by her own words. She closed her eyes and fell into a moment of complete concentration as she waved her hands over her forewarning stones and breathed in deeply. She didn't care other people were around. She was in a trance.

I lit another smoke. "I know you have a sixth sense and all, but I'm telling you, Samantha, it isn't safe to trust Willie. I think you better listen to my senses for a change." I stared down at the stones, which to me predicted absolutely nothing. "Willie's never been right, Samantha. For all we know, he's the crazy fucking murderer running around the downtown area, slicing throats with that pocket knife of his." Her eyes snapped open with that statement.

"Bite your tongue, Ethan." Her tone was loud enough the other employees outside in the break area looked over in our direction. "God, Ethan—how can you even say that? You've known him longer than I have. You know Willie isn't capable of murder." Sam's distressed pitch was not reassuring, especially as she stared at the small stack of black stones.

I choked out a large plume of cigarette smoke. "You can't be sure of that." I stared at the stones that oddly teetered on each other, right next to the inside edge of the cloth nearest Samantha.

"Willie is no murderer. He's more likely to harm himself than anyone else." She fixated on the stones.

I was sitting downwind from a guy eating a tuna sandwich for lunch. When I caught a whiff, my stomach began to growl. "Are you going to tell me what you're looking at in those stones, or not?" I tilted my head and gave her my best bitch look. Her green eyes were sharp. Her cheeks were flushed. Samantha's full lips had a natural rosy hue to them. I gazed at her while she studied the stones. The emerald pebble closest to her reminded me of her approaching twenty-fifth birthday. "Doesn't that represent *green-backs*? And because it is closest to you, doesn't that mean it is coming soon?" I never knew if her magic was real, or coincidental. But she was often *right on the money.*

Samantha looked up at me and rolled her eyes. "I wish I wasn't getting his stupid money. I should just give it away."

"I'll take it if you don't want it." I smiled and held out my hand. "You need to get over it, Girl. It's not every day someone leaves you that kind of money. You deserve it. I'm sure your mother would want that for you." I wondered what mother wouldn't want her daughter to be wealthy, even if the money did come from an abusive stepfather. Startled, I jerked at the sound of a loud motorcycle that sped down the street in front of our building.

Samantha ignored the noise. Her stare remained locked on her precious stones. The heat from the sun seeped through the branches and warmed my neck. I looked at her and noticed what a pretty person she had grown into. Not just the shape of her face: her kind eyes, thick lashes and button nose. It was her person. Samantha's character is what was so attractive. She wasn't after money or possessions, and she really did want to make a positive difference in the world. But while I noticed her good traits, I also witnessed sadness. There were signs of worry all over her face. If I were coming into a few million bucks, the last thing I'd be was worried.

"Tell me what it is I can't see in those stones of yours." I watched her methodically study them. The colors, the shapes, their position, she looked at them as if they told an uncertain story.

"There is so much, really, and very little of it appears to be positive. Let's just say, if this was a reading for someone else, this is where I would begin to bend the truth." She smiled out of the side of her mouth. "It is hard to see if it directly affects me, or has a dire effect on someone close to me, maybe even multiple people in my life somehow. That's what makes this so challenging." She nervously tugged at her ponytail band, freeing her hair for a moment before combing it back up with her fingers and returning it to the messy pony.

"The stones are making my point. Yet another reason for you to be careful, follow procedure." My voice hitched, almost as high as my eyebrows. "Jesus, Samantha, Nasreen was killed blocks from here, and somebody else's body was just found down the street next to the canal."

I wondered if her stones had anything to do with me. Was I going to be one of her black-colored pebbles of doom?

"Oh damn. See, there is so much to tell you. That's the other thing that is so upsetting to me, Ethan. You remember the transvestite, Derrick Johns? He was here in the facility about six months ago. Stayed the full seventy-two hours and then left without being formally discharged."

"Yeah, I remember him." I curiously leaned in on my elbows. "He was the one who said he couldn't survive in a halfway house or any other place that forced him to follow rules, so he didn't take your placement referral and he left."

"It is so sad, really." She scooped up the stones from the outer edges of the cloth and tossed them back into the box. Perspiration began to build on her upper lip.

"What! You don't mean Tequila Mockingbird? It wasn't her that was found dead, was it?" I cut off my breath as I waited for Samantha's response.

"It was him, and her. I mean, he was in drag when he was found." Samantha's face remained especially sympathetic.

My heart stopped for yet another dead person I knew, but didn't really know. "How'd you find out?"

"I saw Ms. Beth this morning at the courthouse. She told me he'd had his throat cut, just like the other victims. He might have been dead, lying down the street from us for several days." She swung her arm in a gesture toward the canal behind the Mexican food place. "They aren't releasing all the details to the public. You know—the transvestite thing. Ms. Beth says the evidence showed he put up a good fight. He had typical defensive wounds that said he didn't take it lying down."

"It was only a matter of time before they found that queen dead."

"Ethan!"

"What, it's true. You know what Tequila Mockingbird did for a living." I felt bad for saying it, but it was too late, that dog was already out of the gate. "Ms. Beth? Why did you see her this morning?" I glanced down at my cell phone. Bradley would usually call me around lunchtime. There was no missed call, and no voice mail, either.

Samantha threw up her hands and grabbed her head. "Oh my God, Ethan! That was the other thing I wanted to tell you. I'm telling you, my aura is off, my energy is totally messed up." She swept her hands over her chest and shoulders, her arms, and her lap, brushing herself, as if to ward off bad. "Ms. Beth and I met down at the courthouse this morning. She was working with an officer on a case in the downtown precinct. That's how she found out all the info on Derrick Johns. She said they had the TV on down at the station when she saw Madison on the screen. I guess we both sensed the need to be with Madison after her little episode with the vultures."

"Madison? What is it you were going to tell me about Madison? What vultures? Why was she on TV?" I was surprised she hadn't mentioned this earlier in our conversation.

"That is what I am getting to." Samantha twisted her legs around and kicked off her sandals, and then began peeling off her socks. "I don't know what I was thinking when I put these socks on this morning."

"Hello! I'm waiting!" I watched her roll her socks into a ball.

"Madison was pummeled by the media going into the courthouse this morning. After fourteen years, New Mexico caved on the death penalty and decided to put her cousin's murderer to death by lethal injection. I guess they're still trying to determine the date, but they think it will happen within the next thirty days." Samantha's hands rested on the top of the table. She was still studying the stones that, for her, forecasted the forthcoming events. "I just feel so discombobulated. My visions, my thoughts, my stones, everything is so stirred up. I thought the stones could clear it up for me, but as it appears, they're predicting a lot of turmoil ahead for all of us."

Us, I thought. What would I have to do with her predictions? This was *her* reading. I watched her make great effort to make sense of her magical stones.

I reached across the table and took Samantha's hands. "You're the one who always says peace comes from within, so don't look for it without. Isn't that what you always tell me?" I didn't really expect a response. "And if you want my opinion, it's about fucking time they kill that child-raping bastard." I leaned back and snatched another Marlboro from the pack in my pocket. Pressing it in between my lips, I lit up. Smoke swirled up my nose and into my eyes, causing tears to overtake my vision.

"Ethan! Nobody deserves to die." I saw her glance back down at the stack of dark stones, before scooping them back into the box. "Nobody!" Her tone was merciful.

I wiped my eyes. "Don't be so naïve, Samantha. I'm sorry, sugar, but some people just don't deserve to live."

Crossroads

Chapter Seventeen

Samantha 'Sam' Green

Today seemed like one of the longest days of my life. After showing up at the courthouse, in the morning, I only spoke to Madison once, very late in the day, just as she was leaving work. She told me she had to sneak out through the special entrance where the sheriff brought litigants to the court from the jailhouse downtown. I could hear the weariness in her voice. My day was equally grueling. It was just past eight o'clock, long past the end of my shift, and I was clearing my desk. I would have liked to grab a yoga class tonight, but the last one was at 7:30. Instead I decided to run by my grandmother's house. I was sure Gram could help recharge me. I gave her a quick call and told her I was headed her way.

I gathered my belongings, and with my knee, I nudged my chair into its proper slot behind my desk, then called out for security to escort me to my car. I figured I should do as Ethan had said. That was a rarity, for sure. He lived much closer to the edge than I cared to be.

Todd was the security guard on duty. He was a tall guy, big, broad-shouldered, very tough appearance, but really a teddy bear once you got to know him. He carried a night stick and mace, adding to the hard-hitting persona.

Todd opened the door to the outside, glanced around, and then signaled for me. He then led the way out to my car. I looked around the dark parking lot, lit only by a few tall lamps. The moon was moving toward full, but still remained low in the eastern sky. The stars were coming out and beginning to twinkle at a distance.

A cool blast of air circled my body, and chill bumps rose to the surface. My eyes nervously shot around the parking lot, to near the dumpster. Over toward the far corner opposite us, my vision narrowed in on the shadows, behind the bushes near the building. There was no sign of Willie, or anyone else for that matter. I felt foolish having Todd watch my back. I flung my purse across the front seat and pulled my sweater on before climbing into the driver's seat. I thanked Todd and let him shut me in my vehicle.

While moving through the busy streets of Downtown, I couldn't help but look for Willie. There were drifters, beggars, prostitutes, and homeless people always wandering the streets of Phoenix, especially in the area closest to my job. As I moved through the city, streetside coffee shops, trendy wine bars and eateries lined the road. While I drove to Gram's house, my mind was still back at work. To be precise, my thoughts had never left the results of my stone reading from earlier in the day.

It was the green stone, particularly the way it had almost fallen off the cloth and into my lap, a prediction most people would see as divine. Me, I had a shooting pain in my gut at the idea. It couldn't have been made any clearer to me if the money-stone would have ended up in my pocket. I was soon to be a millionaire, all at the cost of losing my mother. The money left to me by my stepfather was nothing more than a reminder of what I had lost. My mother's husband was a man who had only become my father through adoption.

Even now, I wish I had never said anything to my mother about what he did to me. Especially now, I yearned to have her here with me. I wanted my mother to see the young woman I had become. That stupid money was a miserable reminder of how it was really my fault my mother was dead.

I sat at the traffic light, my foot pressed hard onto the brake, my mind in a fog. I was just around the corner from my grandmother's. Waiting for the light to turn green, I realized just how fast life could change. I was still shaken by the information I had gathered in the way all the other stones fell. Yet I was blurry on exactly who, what, where, and when, but I was certain danger lurked. Death was imminent, waiting for the right time to strike.

While I waited for the traffic light, I momentarily closed my eyes, desperately hoping to hone in on a clearer image of what was to come. In split seconds, the person in the car behind me laid on the horn, startling me into hitting the gas pedal and lunging forward. I hadn't even noticed all the other cars around me had moved through the crowded intersection.

When I pulled to the curb in front of Gram's house, the curtains were still open in her front room; her table light cast a glow on the front yard. I saw her head pop up, and in just a few moments she was greeting me on the front porch. I put on a happy face, sucked in a big breath, and pretended as always that I was coping with my life. I strolled up the walkway lined with blooming roses. The front yard was a perfectly manicured green lawn, with yard art splashed about. A sandstone angel marked the bottom step to the covered entrance. The divine being had been sitting on the edge of the grass for so long I'd seen the bottom of her dainty toe weather away over time. There was a large chunk of petrified wood displayed on the corner of the patio, beneath the hummingbird feeder that dangled off the porch overhang. It was a total find on one of our outings up north.

"Hi honey." Gram held the screen door open for me. There she stood, already dressed in her favorite raggedy, old housecoat and slippers, generally in bed by 9:00 these days.

"Hi Gram." I leaned in for a hug and kiss, remaining bonded at the cheek for a few seconds. Her skin was warm and smooth, comforting. Her scent was the familiar night cream she regularly used after washing her face. The fragrance, for me, was a calming odor, refreshing; it was my grandmother.

"Come in, Sam. I have a plate on the stove for you." She was insistent.

I followed her as she shuffled crookedly on the shag carpet, through the living room, to the hallway, and then into her kitchen. Immediately I could smell jasmine incense. A thin trail of smoke rose from the brass burner on the entry hall table. Her TV room was at the front of the house, near the entryway. A worn brown leather chair, with a multicolored knit blanket tossed over the back was her favorite place to hang out. The day's newspaper was spread across the ottoman next to the front of the overstuffed chair. A TV tray sat beside her throne, a box of tissue, the TV guide, a few books, a pair of eyeglasses, the remote control, and her weekly pill container took up the space. An end table on the opposite side of her chair accommodated a reading lamp, a telephone, a round sandstone coaster, a few more books, a small bowl of peanuts, and a bag of chocolate kisses, with some empty wrappers tossed to the side.

Like a passage of memories, the walls of the hallway were lined with family photographs. First was a highly crafted oval wood frame that held a picture of my grandparents on their wedding day. My grandmother was beautiful as a young bride. Her eyes were my mother's eyes. The same green eyes I'd always see in the mirror looking back at me. Alongside the wedding photo was a picture of my grandfather in the military. Beside that was another one of him as a ranger. He was handsome in both his uniforms. Next to that was a photograph of my mother when she was a teenager, around fourteen; she was in a group hug with both of her parents. They were all so happy back then. Again, I could see the resemblance, the way she stood, her smile, her hair, those green eyes. They were on a family vacation at the Grand Canyon. They posed near the edge of the deep gorge. Gram always joked about how the stranger who took the photo for them kept insisting they take one more step back.

Next in the procession of framed faces was my high school graduation picture, a cap-and-gown shot. I hated that picture. I had a big zit on my cheek, just beneath my eye, and the cover-up job I did made it look even worse. But I knew my grandmother loved the picture, so I kept my negative comments to myself. She was so proud of me. My favorite photo was next, the one of me and my mom standing in front of a gigantic ocotillo cactus at the Botanical Gardens. Its spiny arms dwarfed us. The red flowers that tipped the arms resembled bright, flickering flames. That was what my mom had said when she stared at her favorite desert plant. We were locked in a grip. Our smiles were wide, our eyes happy, as Gram coaxed us with the word, *cheese*.

"Why are you looking at all those pictures like you've never seen them before?" Gram turned back from the kitchen and watched me stand in the hallway, staring at the past.

"It's just nice to see, that's all." I lifted my gaze and moved into the kitchen. "It smells good, Gram. I've had a long day, and I barely remember eating anything. Right now, food of any kind sounds absolutely wonderful." I draped my sweater over the back of the kitchen chair and went to the sink to wash my hands. The dish that held the purplish clump of glycerin soap was one of my ceramic creations from seventh grade art class. Plant clippings and aged, dirty water filled an old jar that sat on the kitchen window sill before me. I drained the brown water and refilled it from the tap. A variety of bread products were spread out on the countertop. "What's all this?" I pointed to the items, assuming it might be something for the party.

"Oh, I stopped by the day-old bakery store today and picked up some extra muffins and bread for you and Madison. You can't beat the price, and today was 2-for-1. I can't eat all that, and I have no more room in my freezer." She pulled a paper sack from the slot between the fridge and the end of the cabinet and put the items into it. "I want you to take it home, along with this for Madison, the poor dear." She tapped the plastic container that sat on the countertop. Gram was of the opinion food could ease most pain. "You know she called me today and thanked me for the meatloaf I sent home with you last night." Her eyes gleamed proud.

"That's nice." I was glad Madison called her. I know how much my grandma liked her.

"She took it in for lunch today. I can't believe she thought to call me." She reached in the drawer for some silverware and grabbed my plate. "Especially with all she had happening today." Her head shook in pity.

"Gram, you don't have to serve me. You go sit down. Let me do this." I lightly pressed her shoulder, hoping to coax her into the kitchen chair.

"Oh please, Sam, I want to do this. Now don't sass your old grandma, go and sit. You need to eat something, Samantha Green. Besides, you don't seem yourself tonight. Your aura is a little dim and your energy seems extremely low. I'm gonna grab you a glass of ice tea with your dinner. I know how much you like tea." She twisted back to the refrigerator and pulled out a jar of sun tea.

"I sat here all day and watched Madison's story on TV. My goodness Sam, she was so young to have gone through all that. It was a huge affair in New Mexico back then. The Governor and everyone came out for the search. Hundreds of people looked for that poor little girl, her cousin, Lisa. All along, the murderer lived right across the street. Killed her right there in his house and even offered up his help to the family in the search." Her head wobbled with sympathy for Madison's past. "What that man did was downright shameful, Sam, horrific. Some people, you can't even believe what they are capable of." She dropped some ice cubes in a tall glass and continued. "I saw lots of clips of Madison from back then, as a child. What cute little girl she was. She went by the name

Matty. That was what they constantly referred to her as, Matty." She poured tea into the glass.

"Her dad still calls her Matty." I picked at the food in front of me. I felt bad that the worst part of Madison's life was going to be flashed before her eyes on the twenty-four hour news cycle. I couldn't even imagine how this would affect her. An uncontrollable, whiney voice rang out in my head saying selfish things like: *What about me? Poor me, I have no parents. I was a child who saw a bloody tragedy before my very eyes. I was a kid when I was expected to grow up.* The tone changed to critical. *But it was all my fault.* The voice in my head went from a sharp bleat to a loud, high-pitched screech. *Oh my God! Someone I know could die soon. Get over yourself.* I began to shake, my fork clanged the plate. It would kill me if Gram were one of my black stones.

Gram kept going on about things of the past, unaware I was tormented about what the future held. "Matty, the young Madison, was interviewed saying the killer had talked to her and her little cousin the very same day that he climbed into that bedroom window. I can't even stand to think about it." Shaking her head, Gram scrunched her features. "Matty's cute little voice in those interviews, she was such a strong little girl." She stirred the sweetener into my tea.

"Stop thinking about it Gram." I hated that annoyance came across in my tone. Gram seemed to grab onto worries easier these days than in the past. Besides, I already knew all the gory details of Madison's earlier life. I don't think there was anything at all about that event that Madison hadn't shared with me over the years.

"Here you go." Gram slid the tea in front of me.

"This pot roast is delicious." I felt bad for snapping the way I had. I took a sip of tea, as I pushed food around on my plate. "Thank you, Gram. Now sit." I leaned out and pushed back a chair for her, an inviting smile tugged at the corners of my mouth.

"I'm gonna get me some sweets before I sit. You know me—I'd almost give up my dinner for my goodies. I probably should give up my dinner." She grabbed hold of her midsection and jiggled it some. "I figured since you were coming over so late, I'd have my dessert with you."

I watched her slice a piece of angel food cake from a loaf she had wrapped in foil on the counter. She scooped some strawberries on top of her cake, plucked out a can of whipped topping and generously sprayed it, before returning the can to the fridge.

Gram had lost a little height over the years. Mild osteoporosis had begun to compress her spinal column in tiny increments. I was told it was a painful disease. I hated the idea of her suffering any discomfort. You would never know she was in constant pain. At seventy-eight years old she was so different than most other folks I'd met that age, many of whom often complained about all their different ailments. Gram rarely complained about anything. She dropped into her chair and finally parked herself. Joyfully, she dug into her strawberry shortcake.

Gram stared into my face as she hummed with delight over the flavor of her dessert. I could see her eyes searching mine. The way Gram held her fork and licked her lips reminded me of my mother. In fact, so many things about her, about her house, were all reminiscent of my mom. The kitchen was painted bright yellow, just as it was at our house when I was younger. It even had the border of flowered wallpaper lining the wall near the ceiling. My mother loved yellow, and flowered anything would work for her. My mom kept the sugar on a decorative tray with creamer, a crystal dish with spoons and a container of teabags, just like her mother does, still.

I stood and walked my dirty dishes to the sink, where Gram had a small bowl of soapy water that held her kitchen cloth. The bowl remained in the sink, always. My mother had done the same, swearing the soapy water kept the cloth from taking on a mildewy smell. My mom hated a stinky washcloth. I quickly tossed the remainder of my dinner down the disposal and washed up my dishes so Gram wouldn't see how much I wasted of her good cooking.

"Are you finished?" I reached out to take Gram's dessert plate.

"I think I'd have to lick it if I were gonna get it any cleaner." She looked at me as if she were trying to get my attention.

I giggled slightly.

"Samantha! Where exactly are your thoughts tonight? I can see that mind of yours running like an old sewing machine." She gripped her plate, not letting go of it until she captured my attention.

My mind wasn't really in this particular moment, which I knew was wrong, and the guilt of it all caused me to snap back to the conversation with my grandmother.

"I'm sorry, Gram." I twisted around to the sink with her dish in my hand.

"Why are you so down? It's not like you to be this melancholy." She stood and walked over to the sink beside me, her hand on my shoulder. I could feel the genuine concern. "You're not the only one who is intuitive." She lightheartedly raised her brow. "Where do you think you got it from?" She turned off the water and gently guided me back around to see my face. Our eyes met. Every time I glanced into her eyes, I noticed them getting smaller. "You need to tell me what is running through that head of yours." Her voice took on a commanding tone, but her touch remained soft as she pulled me into her bosom, gripping me tightly with her loving arms.

I wrapped my arms around her, my wet hands clung to her robe, and the flood gates opened. I felt her grip me even tighter as my body shook. "I don't want the money, Grandma. I don't deserve to have it. It's blood money. They're dead because of me." I felt her push back, again our eyes met. The money wasn't the only thing weighing on me. Nor was it the only cause for the tears that flowed down my cheeks. Fear of the unknown was also weighing on me.

"I'm not gonna have you talk like that, Samantha. You are not responsible for the death of your mother. Carolyn was not right mentally. She always had difficulty accepting reality. Your mother had a breakdown, plain and simple. Neither of you can be blamed for the deaths. There is no one to blame, sweetie. Not you, not your mother, not even Karl can be blamed for what happened. I never want to hear you talk like that again. Their deaths were not your fault!" Her voice hitched insistently. "That is your inheritance Samantha, and you deserve every damn penny of it. The divine Spirit has a plan. You're in it, Sam, and it's fantastic. You need to realize that."

My eyes flowed over with tears as I saw her desperate attempt to make me feel better about being an orphan with money. I couldn't find the words, nor could I find the motivation to tell her of my dismal prediction.

Her hands cupped my face. "Oh, honey, that money has nothing to do with the way they died. Karl and your mother wanted you to be taken care of in the event they were no longer around, plain and simple. For whatever the reason! The trust fund that was set up for you has been providing for our needs for years. Your old Gram couldn't have done for you what that money has done for you. I could have never bought you a car or sent you to college." She drew me back and once again firmly took me into her embrace. "This money will give you opportunities, Samantha. It won't make your life better, but it may make it easier. You can go back to school full-time and get your psychology degree, just like you've always wanted. You won't have to worry about your bills, the rent, car insurance, gas."

I pulled out of the loving hold Gram had on me, twisted back to the sink, grabbed a hand towel and began drying the few dishes in the drainer. "I'm going to finish these, run the vacuum, and then get home. I'm just really tired, Gram. I don't know why I'm being such a crybaby tonight." My eyes were still tearing. The thought crossed my mind that maybe it was close to being that time of the month, but it wasn't.

"Now I know there is something wrong when you want to run the vacuum at nine o'clock at night," she said as she reached into the cupboard for a couple of mugs. "This calls for a nightcap. There will be no vacuuming tonight."

Gram opened the fridge and began to fill the cups from a wine box that sat on the top shelf.

"Samantha, you are not going to clean my house any longer. After this weekend, you're gonna hire someone to do it for me," she laughed aloud. "Take this." She handed me a full coffee mug of Pinot Grigio, and then continued filling one for her. "Now then, you go on out to the Arizona room and I'll be there in a minute. We're going to get to the bottom of what's bothering you, even if it means we have to get to the bottom of this box of wine to do it." She smiled, her eyes gleamed, the wrinkles on her face gathered when she winked. She spoke over her shoulder, directing me to the back patio with a head nod.

Gram's Arizona room was a semi-outdoor room off the kitchen. Once a patio, she had it partially closed in, still giving her an outdoor feeling. The room bordered the back yard of her house and was one of her favorite places to be, day or night. It faced east so the area remained cooler in the summertime than other parts of the house. I set my wine on the iron table beside the glider and stepped over to the bench that held a Hindu statue of Shiva, next to a large white candle and a burnt, banded bundle of sage lying in a dish of ash.

I bent over and lit a candle, and then put the match to a fresh stick of incense. My face felt bloated from sadness, my eyes stung from the salt of my tears. I called on Shiva for strength, asking the Hindu God to help ease my mind. My hands in prayer position, I placed them at my heart and quietly said the prayer of intention that my grandmother had taught me.

Asatoma sadagamaya (Lead me from the unreal to the real); Tamasoma jyotir gamaya (Lead me from darkness to light); Mrityorma amritam gamaya (Lead me from time-bound consciousness to the timeless state of being).

Draping the statue was a set of Indian prayer beads Gram had received as a gift years back from one of her yoga instructors. Gram had a collection of polished stone carvings on one shelf, the windowsills and the half-wall all held a smattering of gems and special mementos used for protection, warding off evil, and bringing positive forces back into your life. For Gram, these sacred guardians each had special meaning. Many of them had wonderful healing powers. Many rare, unusual, and fascinating quartz crystals and tumbled stones lined the room, promising to align balance and empower chakras.

I tossed the burnt match into an ashtray full of burnt matches. Beside the decorative dish lay a hefty piece of pyrite, which was a jagged mineral, with a metallic, brass-yellow hue, earning it the nickname fool's gold. Well aware pyrite was a stone of intellect and protection, I picked up the stone. It enhanced intelligence, mental stability, logic, analysis, creativity, memory, and psychic development. I desperately needed something, anything, to increase my own mental abilities. Pyrite was a powerful protection stone, very grounding. Additionally, it was a stone that brought good luck and good fortune—something I was praying for.

Just off the porch, on the other side of the half-wall leading out to the grassy area of the yard was a chiming water fountain. I turned back to the glider and took a seat. Sipping my cup of wine, I listened to the flowing babbling brook sounds. The beautiful, deep tones of chimes and bells were mesmerizing. In the moonlight I could see the water bubble up through the two center bells, and then spill over into a pool of water held in a copper basin. Over the years, I had seen the durable basin go from its bright fiery copper color to the aged greenish patina look that it now had. A small, solar yard light cast a glow around the fountain, illuminating a bronze statuette of a fairy leaning out toward her dainty finger, and kissing a butterfly on its tip. The base of the figure was surrounded by green ground cover with petite white flowers.

The fragrance of Gram's backyard was a mixture of so many different blooming plants. She had a naturally green thumb. Nature was her greatest source of energy, she'd always say. Ceramic pots, hanging baskets, and basically anything that held potting soil, became home to a plant. She even had an old pair of grandpa's boots turned into a habitat for some of her beloved clippings.

A slight breeze brushed my neck. Light tinkles of brass clinking together carried through the air as I watched one of Gram's dainty wind chimes sway. The sweet aroma of the gardenias from across the yard overwhelmed my senses. My mother loved gardenias. She used to cut the delicate white flowers and float them in a crystal bowl of water in the middle of the coffee table in our living room. The fragrance filled our house. I closed my eyes and inhaled a deep breath through my nose while I spun the silver band on my thumb, every rotation I silently chanted: *Please mother, help me! Please mother, help me! Please mother, help me!* The desperation in my noisy mind rose with each sequence. I'd never felt as afraid of the future as I did right then.

I heard my grandmother's slippers dragging through the kitchen as she headed toward the back patio. She was humming a song. I listened to her distant, off-beat drone, trying to name that tune, when I recognized the Beatles' number as: *All You Need Is Love.*

After my mother's death, for several years, Gram and I regularly pulled out mom's favorite music and listened to the albums she'd collected over the years. The only records my mom ever felt were worthy of hanging onto were her favorites, which made them that much more special. Gram still had all the albums and the very old turntable my mother used as well. Similar words from the memorable song began to pound at my psyche.

Nothing I could know that wasn't known.

Nothing I could see that wasn't shown.
No one I could save that couldn't be saved.

I felt Gram's soft touch on my shoulder, so I turned back, only to find her standing across the room, still in the doorway off the kitchen. I was drawn to place my hand on my shoulder. The energy of the touch radiated through me, the trueness was remarkable. If it hadn't regularly happened I might think of it as unbelievable, perhaps even far-fetched. But this was nothing new. Yet it always caught me off guard when my mother showed up.

"Do you feel her?" She looked at me as if she already knew. "You smell those gardenias? She has to be here with us tonight. Besides, I don't think she's ever missed one of your birthdays." Gram smiled cheerfully, as if she'd just seen the daughter who's been gone for over a decade. "We're going to have a wonderful night for your birthday, right here in this backyard." She gazed about, clearly planning ahead. I could see she was placing tables and chairs, coolers; perhaps counting the cups, plates and napkins, making a list of the food she'd need to buy and make, and the beverages she would serve. She always made everything perfect.

I felt a chill run the length of my spine. I took in a deep breath. *I did feel my mother.* I loved that she was never more than a breath or two below my consciousness.

"Here," Gram handed me her cup of wine, "hold this." She pressed it into my hand.

I grasped the mugs and elevated my arms high overhead, moving our wine out of harm's way. She threw a blanket over my lap and slowly lowered herself into the glider next to me, then spread the knit cover over our legs.

"Okay, I'll take that back." She held her hands wide and cradled her cup, and taking it to her lips, she sipped her wine. "Now tell your grandma what's going on with you, or don't, it's up to you. There has to be more to it then you've let on. I haven't seen your aura this dim since you were a child." She rested her cup on the arm of the glider and we began to rock in unison. "Remember Sam, what I always say about worrying; it's interest paid on trouble before it's due. Not to mention, in every life we have some trouble, when you worry you make it double. So don't worry, be happy." Behind her smile, her voice took on a singing quality.

We sat in silence. I said nothing for a few minutes. I hesitated telling her about the reading I did. I found it ironic, when I read for people, I generally preferred to keep it positive, direct, and to the point—offer no false hopes. Yet here I was, contemplating offering my grandmother vague, false hope about my ominous vision. My most trustworthy confidant would be misled.

"Honey, I'm retired." She tapped her fingers against her mug. "I've got all night. Besides, it's beautiful out here. Look at the stars." She sipped her wine and tilted her head back. "What a beautiful moon. We're lucky you know—to have a night like this, clear and crisp. I heard a storm was coming toward the end of the week."

"That's what I'm afraid of." I couldn't help the words that slipped through my lips.

"What did you say? You're gonna have to speak louder for this old woman to hear you." She cupped her ear my direction.

"Nothing, Gram. I didn't say anything." Her expectation weighed on me. I sipped my wine, leaned back and tried to relax.

"Remember when you were younger, we'd sit out in the backyard and just listen to the sounds in our heads, in the garden, the universe, and all around?" Her hand reached for mine, we held on to each other and rocked, both of us staring off into the brilliance of the night.

"As I recall, you referred to it as honing my senses." I squeezed her hand and smiled mischievously. I could feel the thinness of her skin, the bones of her hand, her deformed, aged fingers and swollen knuckles.

"Oh, yeah—and what's wrong with that?" She elbowed me in a teasing way. "Close your eyes," she dared me, "and let's see what you've learned after all those years."

I watched her close her eyelids, I too closed mine; I was onto her. I indulged her, wholeheartedly, just as I always had. Once again, I unreservedly let go and let my mind and my senses wander.

The smell of the neighbor's Japanese honeysuckle overtook my nostrils. I drew my grandmother's hand to my face, eyes closed. I sniffed the back of her hand and her wrist, overdramatizing the sniff I hoped to tickle her skin with air from my nose. "Ginger Soufflé," I said, a grin crossed my face. I knew this was the lotion that she kept beside her bathroom sink.

She jerked her hand away and playfully slapped my shoulder. "You're so funny."

"I'm kidding." I kept my eyes closed and we quieted, falling back into stride with the glider.

Our sluggish swaying was rhythmically putting me in a trance. Nature's orchestra created the background music. The crickets chirped, birds stirred in the surrounding trees, and bugs crawled around, rustling in the bushes. I heard the sounds of traffic in the distance. But it was the distressed voices, the arguing, and the high-pitched screaming in my head that I was trying to distinguish. I squeezed my eyes shut, as if the pictures in my mind, of who, what, or where, would be plastered to the insides of my lids. I searched every corner of my mind and found nothing that got me any closer to understanding my omen. Then out of the shadows of my psyche came an explosive gun shot. I lurched in my seat. Fear rushed in like a gust of wind blowing a door open. I felt an excruciating pain in my gut.

"Are you all right?" My grandmother gripped my hand. "What is it, Sam? Tell me, what are you looking at? Samantha!" she screamed.

My eyes remained clamped together for fear that I would lose the vision. The intoxicating fragrance of gardenia once again engulfed me. My mother had a way of reassuring me she was always there. My hands began to get warm, the image was scarlet red, not just dripping, but gushing, tears were pouring from my eyes. Then another loud, piercing sound burst in my skull. It was the screaming cry of a man, a man who was a stranger to me. I opened my eyes to the piercing stare of my grandmother.

My sixth sense, or my gift, or whatever you wanted to call it, was sometimes not such a gift. The premonitions I every so often had were not always easy to read, sometimes difficult to see, and even tougher to share, especially when it pertained to me, or potentially someone else I knew. I was never really sure how accurate the visions were. Unfortunately, hindsight can sometimes be painfully clear. And sometimes that is too late.

Chapter Eighteen

Madison Morgan

It was no coincidence a few reporters followed me when I left the courthouse. They blasted me with questions. I ignored them and launched myself onto the northbound Park Central bus just before the driver swung the door shut. I was certain they weren't prepared to take the ride with me to law school. Unfortunately the bus was my regular transportation to night class. The buses still went places the newer Light Rail didn't yet travel.

I sat back and waited for my stop, pondering my day. I exhaled while staring out at the descending sun. Having a person like Sam in my life for so many years actually caused me to think differently. I no longer believed in coincidence. Sam believed as Einstein had, "coincidence is God's way of remaining anonymous." Me, I was more the type to trust that coincidence was nothing more than a carefully planned event. The blur in the line became trying to figure out who was doing all the planning.

The crowded bus braked hard before coming to a stop. I popped up, pushed through the people, headed to the exit, and bounced out onto the curb in front of the law school. I was relieved to walk into the protective hall that housed my evening class. No reporters, no blaring memories of my childhood, no one pushing me to discuss death, killings, and murder.

225

I flipped my backpack to the floor and chucked my briefcase up on the table. Out of it I plucked a legal pad, a pen, my voice recorder, and a Power Bar. I then tucked my briefcase under the table, right beside my pack, so as not to infringe on my neighbors space. Peeling my jacket off, I hung it over the back of my chair before taking my seat.

I looked around at the other law students; no one seemed thrilled to be here. Most often, night class appealed to the person like me who had just worked a full day, or perhaps a student cramming to get in the class as a requirement, forced into the odd hours. Taking a deep breath, I picked up my pen and flipped through my pad of paper until I found the next empty page. In the upper left corner I wrote the date, my name just below. In the far right corner I scribbled my teacher's name, and the title of the class just beneath. I sorted my notes later, and it was important for me to be precise. It made studying for my tests much easier.

Professor Berkley, my criminal law instructor, began to talk, opening tonight's discussion on a recent deterrence study done by the DPIC. He started out with his usual caveat about research and how it is read and reported—not always trustworthy, and often subjective, slanted one way or another to coincide with a particular group's viewpoint. People clicked their pens and shuffled papers, while the late arrivals scrambled to get into their seats. I was still trying to figure out what DPIC stood for.

"There have been many studies on deterrence over the years. Although some have claimed a deterrent effect, experts have raised questions about the methodologies used in these studies. Measuring why people do not commit crimes is very difficult and the studies have been inconclusive at best." His voice carried well.

Professor Berkley was a tall, angular man, his posture straight as a board. Blue eyes shone vividly from his middle-aged face. He used his hands and arms to speak, flailing them wildly with each expression.

I wasn't in the mood to sit through this class tonight. My mind was wandering, hardly able to pay attention to the voice of my teacher—a teacher I really liked. Then I heard the conversation taking an unexpected turn.

"A recent study published in the *Journal of Criminal Law and Criminology* reported that eighty-eight percent of the country's top criminologists surveyed do not believe the death penalty acts as a deterrent to homicide." He was looking down at his paperwork as he read aloud.

I already knew this. I shrunk in my seat. I was sure a few people turned and gawked at me. As it turned out, DPIC was the acronym for *Death Penalty Information Center*. My first absolutely ridiculous thought was that Sam must have called Professor Berkley and given him a heads-up. This was exactly what she and I talked about earlier in my chaotic day.

As he spoke, he walked around the expansive lecture hall. "Eighty-seven percent of them think that the abolition of the death penalty would not have a significant effect on murder rates. Seventy-seven percent believe that debates about the death penalty distract Congress and state legislatures from focusing on real solutions to crime problems. This is what they think—I want to know what you think." His eyes shot past me, all around me, yet never stopped to focus directly on me. But I was sure he wanted to.

Then the shouting started.

"An eye for an eye!" Someone in the next aisle voiced his opinion.

"Kill and be killed." Another person in the back of the room yelled out.

"No one has the right to take another's life! Why should we feed them and educate them for the remainder of their life?" This man appeared sophisticated, his hair perfectly placed, his face clean shaven, his suit expensive. He was possibly a late bloomer in law school, probably in his forties. But he was arguing both sides, calling for death at the same time suggesting no one had the right to kill.

"Besides, life in prison doesn't really mean life," he continued. "Until it does, we're not ready to do away with the death penalty." His face turned bright red.

"Bad people kill, not civilized ones." A small, studious female let out a few words in a tiny, high-pitched squeak.

To borrow an old expression, opinions were like assholes, everyone had one, and they all wanted their views to be heard. I hated waiting for this class to end. I felt like a defendant about to hear a verdict, and the waiting was torture. Professor Berkley had to calm the impassioned class, harnessing the fury. In a firm, but very diplomatic way, he recommended one person speak at a time. I couldn't help but think of most of them as hostile. Yet these have long been my same thoughts, comments, and hopes.

"Go ahead Ms. Dahl." He extended his arm and gestured for her to join the debate. "What is your argument? Please stand. Speak out so the rest of the class can hear you."

A young woman in the far corner of the class, a peace sign covering the front of her tee-shirt, pushed back from the table, stood, tugged at her jeans, and turned toward the other students. "I oppose the death penalty, in general. Not because I'm such a good person, but because I think that it is a terrible power to entrust to anyone. I believe this because death is a penalty for which no compensation can be offered if it was carried out in error, and because I'd rather not live in a country where the government feels empowered to kill people." She humbly returned to her seat, fidgeting with the thick yellow rubber bracelet that wrapped her wrist. She reminded me of Samantha. I think I've heard those exact words come out of her mouth.

I knew that bastard killed my cousin. He so much as admitted it. This argument wouldn't pertain to him. He was not wrongly accused. Lisa's body was found in his yard, his semen was found.

His fucking sperm! My gut began to churn at the miserable thoughts. I was beginning to feel like I should have skipped all this and gone straight to the gym, understanding time had not blunted those sharp memories. I was in the mood to pound on something. I wanted to hit something, very hard.

"Mr. Lopez, please stand to speak." Like a conductor, Professor Berkley encouraged the man to rise.

His hair, short and brown, stood on his scalp like needles in a pin cushion. The bright lights of the classroom lit up his scalp. "Another reason to oppose the death penalty is because of the problems in the criminal justice system. In short, if you are wealthy you will not get the death penalty, but if you are poor, and often a minority, your chances are much higher." He quickly sat back down in his chair.

I fluffed my short dark hair and looked down at the muddy color of the skin on the back of my hands. I appeared to be more Mexican than I did white. I knew all too well what he was talking about. I remember being afraid to speak Spanish to my mother in public for fear someone would think we didn't have papers. Unfortunately many people lumped all brown-skinned people together, considering them illegal.

"Capital punishment! I think if someone kills a cop, they most definitely should…" A clean shaven guy, around twenty-five or thirty, full suit and tie, still in his jacket, jumped out of his chair to talk—only to be shut down by the teacher.

"Please! Mr. Kyle, there is no need for outbursts. This is a civilized discussion. Now then, feel free to address the entire classroom." My teacher made a grandiose gesture.

"All I was going to say was if someone murders a police officer, I think they should suffer death by execution." He gazed in the eyes of many and adjusted his tie. I could smell his heavy cologne from across the room. The florescent lights made his skin look gray. He spoke with authority, the kind of guy who wanted everyone to know he was summa cum laude. "If we don't set an example, and protect our officers of the law, we are all going to be in danger."

"Thank you Mr. Kyle. You may now take your seat." Professor Berkley paused and waited for the class to refocus on him. "Is a police officer's life any more significant than the life of a mother? What about a sister who is brutally murdered—should her murderer be treated any differently than that of the policeman? If a father were protecting his family when killed, does that change the way the killer should be punished?" These were rhetorical questions trying to get us to think, which is what this teacher was so good at.

Walking over to his podium, front and center, he looked back at his notes and began to read. "Since Mr. Kyle brought it up," he smiled, "another study I have here focused on whether the death penalty deterred the murder of police officers." I heard my stomach growl as he read off the facts. I had been reading up on facts like this for years. "The study concluded that there was no consistent evidence that capital punishment influenced police killings. Police do not appear to have been afforded an added measure of protection against homicide because of capital punishment." He turned away and began to wander the classroom again. "We have heard the personal views, how about the constitutional ones?" Shrugging his shoulders, he challenged: "I'm surprised no one has mentioned the financial comparisons of life in prison versus death?"

The class went on for two more hours debating this subject back and forth. I heard many other arguments. "It is barbaric and violates the cruel and unusual clause in the Bill of Rights." "The endless appeals and required additional procedures clog our court system." "It is useless in that it doesn't bring the victim back to life."

"The death penalty gives closure to the victim's families who have suffered so much," a middle-aged woman, whose face always looked sad, meekly added. I studied the woman's poignant fidgeting. She seemed to agonize over each word. "Life in prison just means the criminal is still around to haunt the victim. A death sentence brings finality to a horrible chapter in the lives of family members." One might get the impression she was speaking from experience and still lacking closure. Perhaps she had been a victim of some violent act? By the vacant stare she carried, it was likely she was a survivor, possibly losing someone she loved to an act of violence.

After that, the class went on to talk about almost everything I'd been through. How family members of crime victims may take years, or even decades to recover from the shock and loss of a loved one. Some may never recover.

My body tensed and I felt a sharp jab to my heart for that woman. The thought of never getting over Lisa's murder sickened me. The nightmares, the haunting sound of his voice, the trial, his sweaty face, his devious eyes—all of it—was never ending punishment. So, I had to question, was there ever really true closure? Many people had the idea that the basis of recovery was to achieve some kind of closure. I'm supposed to believe the death of Lisa's killer offered that. But I wasn't really sure that would shut the door on my past. I just wasn't totally convinced ending his life would end my nightmares.

As the clock approached 9:00, arms started stretching high above heads and the contagious yawning began. People began to fidget in their seats and look toward the door at the front corner of the room. Before Professor Berkley released the class, he offered what seemed to be his personal view on the subject of the death penalty.

He removed his glasses and held them in one hand as he spoke. "For centuries the death penalty, often accompanied by barbarous refinements, has been trying to hold crime in check; yet crime persists. Sister Helen Prejean, a leading American advocate for the abolition of the death penalty, said it best when she said 'The profound moral question is not do they deserve to die? But, do we deserve to kill them?' I will see you all next Tuesday night." He set his glasses on the podium at the front of the room and began to fold his notes into a large binder.

Pushing back from the table, I reached down and grabbed my briefcase, pulled it to my lap and started to put my pad and pen away. Standing, I pulled my jacket on, bent over and tossed my backpack up onto my shoulder, grabbed my briefcase and turned for the door when suddenly I found Professor Berkley by my side.

"Madison—I just wanted to tell you I'm sorry about the timing of this subject and all." His eyes were kind. He dipped his head, pushing his words with compassion. "I saw you on the news today. You did a great job holding your own with the media." He rested his hand on my shoulder. "What you went through as a child must have been extremely difficult. You should be very proud of where you are today. You have lots of promise as an attorney." He smiled. "My course outline was set months back. But, I hope you got something you can use, should you be bombarded again by the press." He smiled and winked. "You understand—there are no coincidences."

"Thanks, Mr. B. Anything will help. But what I'm really counting on is being able to run faster than those reporters." I gave him a head nod and pivoted toward the door. By now, he and I were the only ones left in the hollow classroom. "See you next week, Professor."

*   *   *

It was dark. The bus was dimly lit. Three other people occupied the hard, plastic seats. I stared out of the windows. The downtown streets were slow, and work traffic was gone. Foot traffic was almost nonexistent, like most Tuesday nights past 9:00. The tall office buildings were freckled with lights. The moon, not yet high in the sky, every so often shone through the passing buildings. City offices and apartment buildings lined the avenue. I decided there was no way I was going straight home tonight.

I was hyper, worked up after class. My mind was racing and I had energy to burn—bad energy. The boxing gym was open till midnight. I would take Sam's advice and get rid of some of my negative energy. It doesn't serve you, she would say, it doesn't serve anyone when you carry that around.

She often tried to convince me it was negative energy that attracted negative things, and I was asking for trouble with the chip I carried on my shoulder. She saw thing others didn't—except she wasn't the first to accuse me of having a chip on my shoulder. Ms. Beth one time referred to it as a block on my shoulder. She meant it to be funny, but I know how she candy-coated the truth.

It was my stop. The doors flew open and I jumped to the curb and began to walk. The noisy bus pulled away. I was left to hear my own breathing as I hoofed it a few blocks, en route to the gym. I turned off the main drag and headed through the inner-city residential neighborhood that flanked the boxing club. The streets were dark, lit only by moonlight and the occasional porch light. Sounds of laughter and loud voices came from a few houses I passed.

Mexican music blared from a car parked at the end of the street. I saw the cherry of a lit cigarette on a dark porch across the road, just before smelling its smoke. Most front yards consisted of compacted dirt, mostly because they were being used as parking areas. Two ferocious barking dogs banged against a chain- link fence as I strode by. When I heard a deep voice yell out from the house, "Shut up!" I impulsively picked up my pace, whispering "good dogs" under my breath as I moved passed them. I felt sorry for the poor pit bulls. They did a hell of a job protecting a yard full of crap, nothing more than piles of junk. I'm certain they were rarely rewarded for their vigilance.

Turning off that street, I headed down a back alley, before cutting across a vacant lot. The moonlight revealed a field of shiny broken shards of glass, a stack of old tires, clumps of palm fronds that didn't make it to the dump, and in the distance, what looked to be an old refrigerator turned over on its side.

When I neared the edge of the open lot the graffiti on the rear wall of the gym came into sight. A large, dim light attached to the building illuminated the gang symbols that covered the concrete wall. Aged, probably built in around 1940, the old brick building was originally the home of some sort of manufacturing company. Later it became home to a major beer distributor, before finally becoming the Central Boxing Gym.

Stars were beginning to break through the glare of the city. As I made my final trek across the dark parking lot I looked up at all the twinkles, way off in the far distance, each one of them beginning to push their way through the obscurity.

My thoughts quickly went to my small cousin. I wondered what she would be doing with her life, had she lived to be a young woman. As I approached the building, my nostrils were quickly offended by the stench coming from the overflowing commercial dumpster at the corner of the building.

I passed the large metal container. Startled, I jerked my head back, when suddenly I heard the loud scream of a cat. It was a peculiar growl. My heart began beating at a rapid pace. Frightened by the screeching noise, my eyes, already adjusted to the night, took only seconds to zoom in on the activity. Out from behind the container a cat with a mouse wriggling in his mouth leapt toward the vacant lot. My heart still racing, I watched the animal scurry away with his tasty treat, looking for a heap to hide behind.

It reminded me of a time when Lisa's cat, Sylvester, which became my baby boy after her death, trapped a mouse in the pantry, right off the kitchen near the back of Lisa's house. The incident happened the very day before she went missing. Devoid of any consideration whatsoever, Lisa picked up the dust mop and began to smack it toward Sylvester's head until he dropped the helpless creature.

We both screamed and yelled at the top of our lungs as Sylvester chased the scared mouse around a case of bottled water that had been left on the floor beside the backdoor. Then he had the little fellow trapped over near the water heater. Finally, Lisa held Sylvester back just long enough for the mouse to escape into the cupboard where the pots and pans were stored. Lisa propped the dust mop back up in the corner of the pantry. She stooped down and picked up Sylvester, his large body dangled from her skinny arms, his mouth made an odd clicking noise. We went outside and plopped onto a green patch in the middle of the backyard— Sylvester was still in Lisa's arms.

"Why did you want to save that mouse?" I asked her as we both patted Sylvester's dusted-up fur. "I thought Uncle Joe said it's good for Sylvester to kill the mice." I reminded her.

"My daddy isn't always right." She said so matter-of-factly. Her eyes looked over at me and she smiled. She was missing one of her front teeth. I could still see Lisa's innocent smile, her compassionate eyes.

Now looking back on that moment, as I watched the cat in the shadows pull apart the small prey, I realized how fine a line there was between life and death. One minute you are on the search for dinner, the next minute you are dinner.

I wheeled back around toward the entrance of the gym. There he was. Never even able to take a step, I ran right into him. Chest to chest we faced each other. I heard a gasp escape my lips. His strong arms wrapped completely around me, trapping my arms to the side of my body. Dangling from my ensnared hand was my briefcase. I had no time to react. I was locked in his grasp. My lungs were just about empty as he squeezed the air out of me.

"Let me go!" I screamed in his face.

He held me tight. The smell of alcohol emanated from him . I couldn't swing my arms, our bodies so close I could barely move my legs. I could have hit him hard, a knee, right where it counted—if he hadn't caught me off-guard. Trying to break the grip, I hitched my chest forward. His eyes were smiling. He laughed loud, finding joy in the scare he had put in me.

"There is a murderer on the loose, Matty. Haven't you been paying attention?" He relaxed his grip. He must have seen the anger in my eyes. "I'm sorry. I really didn't mean to scare you." My dad's rough, hard working hand gently grazed my cheek.

"I hate it when you do that, Dad. It isn't funny." Pushing past him I made my way up the sidewalk toward the entrance of the gym. "It's so late. I'm surprised to see you here." I spoke over my shoulder as he followed closely behind, tapping my backpack.

"Wait up!" He reached for my arm and grabbed me. "I left you a message, but you didn't return my call."

I realized I hadn't even looked at my cell phone since leaving class. "Sorry, I didn't get your message."

"Your mom told me to get out from in front of the TV. She says I'm driving her crazy flipping through the channels and watching the nightmare of our past come back to life." He put his arm around me, slowing my pace. We sauntered toward the entrance to the gym. "Once your mother started mumbling at me in Spanish, I knew I'd better get out of the house for a while." He chuckled. "I looked at the clock and took the chance you might come here after school tonight. I thought maybe we could get in a workout together." He gripped my hand and drew me around to look at him. I leaned on the old brick building just outside the entrance, my pack smashed into my back. "Are you all right, Matty?" He cupped my chin and tilted my head so my eyes couldn't look anywhere but into his.

236

"Yeah, Dad, I'm okay," I lied, then pushed him back slightly and made a move for the door. I was trying to get away from my thoughts, not hash them over.

"Wait!" His forearm held me in place. "I saw you on TV today." His light eyes were bloodshot. Etched lines spread like fans on their outer edges. The circles beneath them carried an ominous shadow. I knew he had his own issues when it came to the past.

"I know." I said nonchalantly. "The reporters accosted me going into the courthouse this morning." I was proud, happy with how I handled myself on television while under assault.

"That isn't what I'm talking about, Matty." His voice began to quiver.

A distressed look I hadn't seen in years overtook him. My legs got weak. My heart softened.

He cleared his throat. "Today, on TV, I saw you back then. Back when your cousin was murdered. Back when you were a small child and I wasn't there for you. Back when you were being questioned and interviewed by strangers and I wasn't with you." He pulled me into his chest and wrapped his arms around my shoulders. I could feel the warmth of his body through my clothes. In my ear he whispered, "I'm sorry, baby. I should have been there."

"You were there, Dad." I was puzzled by his sensitivity. "Uncle Joe needed you, I needed you. You were there. I don't understand." I picked up one of his hands and gripped it between both of mine.

"Oh Matty. I was there. I was with the police, I was with my brother. I was handling all of the details instead of comforting you. I see that now. It broke my heart today, to see so many shots of you, alone, gripping that cat of Lisa's. Sylvester proved to be the one friend you could trust." His lips curved into a feeble smile. "No wonder you loved that cat so much. All the people interviewed back then said what a big girl you were, so brave, so strong, so very lucky to be alive. You were all of those things, Matty. All of those things and so much more." The desperate look in his eyes, his slouched posture, the pleading grip he held on me—it was all a little much.

"What are you talking about, Dad? You were by my side. Once you heard about Lisa's disappearance you immediately flew to Albuquerque to be with Uncle Joe and me. I don't remember it any other way."

I quickly thought back to that time and I mostly remembered him coming to my rescue. But his persistent comments were dredging up my memories of being alone—alone to cope with Lisa's kidnapping, and then her murder, while he comforted the fear, anger, and horror my uncle faced.

"Madison, you haven't been home watching our history unfold as I have." He squeezed me so tight I gasped to get a breath. It was a breath worth struggling for. "I love you, Matty."

Perspiration seeped through his cotton t-shirt. The brawny smell of his cologne made me feel like a child, vulnerable yet invincible as I rested my face along his neckline. My throat knotted, I was rendered speechless.

"You are still my baby girl. No matter how old you get, you are still my baby." His arms encircled me. "I hope you understood back then how much my brother needed me," he whispered.

I felt my legs get weak. My eyes began to pool up. My backpack pressed hard into the block of the building and into my spine. The briefcase at the end of my arm began to feel like it weighed a hundred pounds. "It's okay Dad, really." I felt him exhale as he released me and pulled away.

Still toe-to-toe, he said, "That's my girl. Now let's go practice that left jab of yours. Gym closes at midnight. That only gives us a few hours." He faked a jab to my chin. "Lord knows you need it. You were way too easy to ambush." He turned toward the entrance to the gym.

I took a deep breath, held my chin out nice and strong, wiped the water from my eyes, and followed my father inside.

Chapter Nineteen

Jason Magnus

One cell over, as if on stage, there was a preacher man who stood beneath the bright florescent light, claiming to be Jesus. He bellowed Bible verses over the crowd. I couldn't help but stare at his ungainly appearance. He was a thin, long-limbed, small-headed man with crater scars that pitted his cheeks, and a few missing front teeth. He looked as if he'd found God in a back alley somewhere, just after realizing he'd been mugged, beaten, raped, and left for dead.

The groaning shriek of metal signaled 10:30 p.m. as the hour of darkness once again fell upon the chamber and the cell doors came to a screeching halt. However, obscurity didn't stop the sermon. I tried to block out the voices that rattled around the corridor, but I couldn't. My head hummed with the chatter. As if the theater lights had never gone off, Mr. Holy Man was still standing in the center of his cell churning out John 3:16.

"For God so loved the world that he gave his only begotten Son!" His voice pitched on those words. "That whosoever believeth in him should not perish, but have everlasting *fucking* life. That is eternity, man. God loves us all, brothers."

The heckling crowd mocked him, yet he repeated the passage over and over, along with many other verses. With boos and hisses he continued his sermon in the dark, spurred on by the occasional amen.

My eyes began to adjust to the night. I could hear a couple of losers becoming increasingly belligerent with one another. My body jerked and twitched, continuing to withdraw from the drugs that had sustained me for the past three weeks. These other guys, many of them, were struggling with the same types of demons—demons that persist in haunting us with our own deeds. Demons who don't let up, especially in this shithole. Jail is a perfect place for them to fester, until mere reflection feels worse than being gutted. I totally understood that when you packed this many cranky son-of-a-bitches into tight fucking quarters anything was bound to happen. This was my third straight night, and not one person had left my cell, yet three more men had been added to the small space.

The odors that engulfed the county jail were horrendous. Everything around me was steeped in urine. The foul air smelled of unwashed feet and sweaty bodies. I glanced around the darkness and observed the moving shadows; floor pacers, bodies curled up on concrete, and blanketed bulges everywhere. The blanket was sometimes the only privacy found. Some of the guys seemed comfortable in this environment, while others seemed to be deteriorating mentally and just plain freaking out with every passing minute. A few of the inmates remained very stiff, afraid to move, afraid to touch anyone, afraid to talk, while others were up in your space and face, and they wouldn't shut the fuck up.

I arched my head back and leaned into the wall, trying hard to block out the noise. Inching my body down farther onto my mat, I noticed I was sweating profusely, yet I was not hot. My skin was seeping three weeks' worth of drinking and drugging. Pushing my legs into the crowded space, I couldn't get comfortable. Similar to a nest of snakes, I was in the middle, cramped into this little fucking space, tangled up on soiled mats, each of us trying to get out of our heads, and out of this reality. At the same time, we all fought to claim legroom.

Seven men filled the cell, a cell that was designed for no more than two. I mean there was no fucking room to move, and I was stuck beside the disgusting toilet that brimmed with filth. Weekend busts and seventy-two-hour stays were considered new arrivals. Some guys were in and out of here so fast they let them in lockup still dressed in their street clothes. If you were sentenced to any more than seventy-two hours you were sent out to Tent City. Some of these guys were awaiting that transfer to hell. It was a move to more permanent quarters. This was the Hilton compared to Tent City. Been there, done that. Not going back.

"Shut the fuck up!" shouted Donald Trump, tired of the preaching. He was at the opposite corner of my cramped cell, sandwiched between the drag queen and the guy who'd be more suited for juvenile detention, the picker, who was on day two of relentlessly scratching off his skin.

"Man, you better get used to it." Another man said as he rolled away from the clatter.

You're in the county fucking jail—what do you expect? There are people in here who may never fucking shut up. All night long you'll hear the whining... "I am supposed to be provided with my own bed and a proper cell." "I should not be treated this way." "You must let me out of here. This is a human rights violation." My favorite one was "I was falsely arrested." Like there was anyone who really listened to that crap, much less someone who really gave a shit!

Some of these luckier bastards were still dozing in a narcotic haze. They really weren't even here in this shit-hole. I turned on my side and curled into a ball, my back to the toilet. Ignoring the intense growl of my stomach, I closed my eyes and tried to sleep through the stomach cramps that were beginning to wrench my gut. I began to doze to the Bible thumper's aimless rambling. Then I heard it. It was my mother's favorite passage.

"The Lord is my shepherd. I shall not want. He makes me lie down in green pastures. He leads me beside quiet waters. He restores my soul. He guides me in paths of righteousness for his name's sake. Even though I walk through the valley of the shadow of death, I will fear no evil, for you are with me; your rod and your staff, they comfort me." The man took a long breath and continued. *"You prepare a table before me in the presence of my enemies. You anoint my head with oil; my cup overflows. Surely goodness and love will follow me all the days of my life, and I will dwell in the house of the Lord forever."*

My mother always called this a prayer of confidence, self-assurance. The purpose of the message, she said, was to ease stress and help us more clearly calm the soul. I wasn't feeling calm, so I began to chant the prayer in my head. Soon I heard her voice recite the prayer along with mine, just as we had done together when I was a young boy.

My mother's sweet voice continued to awaken my senses as she told me stories about King David. She always reminded me I, too, would be a great man some day. I was dozing and chanting the prayer, her prayer, in and out of consciousness, barely awake, slightly aware, my body relaxed.

I saw her face. Just as she was before she died. Her image wasn't clear—rather sheer, kind of translucent—yet it was like she was there. Just her and me at our dining room table, having a chat, like we always did. Only now I was the one who was different. I was a grown man.

"Jason," she said as she stroked my stubbled cheek. "You can't keep this lifestyle up. It will kill you. You are not acting like the man I knew you'd become. You are better than this. I love you my son." I felt her touch. "I'm sorry I left you. But Jason, this wasn't your father's fault. Your father loves you. He has done the best he can for you. You're better than this, Jason! You have much more potential." I felt a jolt in my chest. "You're better than this! You're better than this!" Her voice was high pitched. Her soft, loving touch was gone. My eyes sprang open.

I shot up on my mat. My dank, detention center jumpsuit clung to my skin. I looked around my cell as if I would find my mother sitting there beside me, somewhere, anywhere. The only part of her that remained in my cell was the sting of her words. She was right. I am better than this. She was also right about my father. None of this was his fault.

Again, I glanced around, fucking dazed, I was shaken. After all these years it took my mother's own voice to make me realize what a fool I truly was. My mother's scolding words were oddly familiar. My best friend, the person who cared most about me, had said the same things to me over and over again.

"You're better than this" was the common phase that regularly left Amber's lips. Her beautiful lips, her green eyes, her words, her hugs, her kisses—I missed them all. I knew I resented my father because he had moved on and I hadn't. Plain and simple, these were my demons, not his. All the years of counseling, treatment programs, and drug and alcohol meetings had taught me this. Only now I could actually see it was true.

The silence was deafening. Finally everyone was asleep. I leaned into the wall, pulled my knees into my chest, and I began to cry. A slumbered hum floated over all the bodies as I fell apart. I wrapped my arms tighter around my legs, squeezing them, gritting my teeth, my blood boiling. The rage beneath my fury could only be directed one way: inward. I was a total failure. I hated myself. My mother was right. My father was right. Amber was right.

There was no way to keep up this lifestyle and live. I didn't have to look around to know this wasn't living.

I couldn't help but wonder if I'd been hallucinating or if my mother had actually come to me in my sleep. I wished in some way to evoke her spirit—or whatever it was—to reappear. I closed my eyes. My mind only conjured misery, once again.

*　　*　　*

Months after my sixteenth birthday, I had another vandalism issue. This time it ended up in the courts. According to the professionals, I had anger management problems. Testing positive for methamphetamines, the courts ordered rehab. Amber tried convincing me this would be God's way of protecting me—helping me to find a better path. She was always so sure God was on my side.

That was the first time my father footed the bill for a thirty-day drug treatment program.

It became the first of many visits to rehab. This was when they tried to convince me that my self-centered behaviors were substitutes and masks for my real feelings. Amber used to accuse me of the same thing, and she was only fifteen and had never had any kind of counseling.

I had counselors who were sure they had me figured out, telling me things like: my so-called need to dominate and control was directly proportionate to my perception of myself as powerless, fearful, and entirely inadequate. My constant fear of being seen as weak, for suffering, and grieving, created a panic that manifested through my ego, anger, and arrogance. Even if I agreed with the diagnosis, it didn't mean I could cure the disease.

It was so clearly obvious to me now, even with all the opportunities, all the love and support, I chose the wrong path. I was a drug addict, not an idiot. I was able to avoid being seen as emotionally weak, and instead settled for being seen as a total loser. I was pushing thirty and I was unimportant to anyone. I have nothing and I've done nothing, except to create a lonely, lonely existence for myself.

Unfortunately, this run did not end when I was sixteen. I evidently wasn't ready to turn my life over to a higher power. The only higher power I wanted was escape, something to take me out of this world. Oftentimes, the anniversary date of my mother's death, her birthday, or mother's day were triggers for my behavior. I was young, naïve. It didn't occur to me that alcohol and drugs might be exactly what caused me to become totally unhinged. The loss and the emptiness were enough to disrupt my clear thinking.

After that first treatment program I really thought I had a grip. I had faced the sudden loss. I had forgiven myself for not being the perfect son. I did have conversations with God. And they were good ones, honest ones.

Amber and I were hanging out a lot after school. We started acting more like boyfriend and girlfriend rather than just friends. When we were together she'd hold my hand, doodle on my thigh, play with my hair, kiss my neck, and sometimes even my lips. We went to first base regularly, but no further.

Her parents warned her about me. Saying I was trouble, with a "Capital T." Even though we grew up together, they knew me since I was a baby, knew all I'd been through, they still advised her she could do better.

I hated the way they always pushed her to hang out with Bradley, certain a preacher's son would be a much better influence than a kid without a mother. Little did they know, Bradley was often our alibi, as we, too, were often his. Amber always laughed at the insinuation Bradley would be interested in her *that* way, teasing it would be more likely he would be interested in me.

I suppose she was wrong, considering they are now married with a kid. Or so I hear. As we all got a bit older, Bradley had friends Amber and I didn't know. He became somewhat secretive, even guarded, when we asked what he was doing. I was pretty certain I wasn't the only one living two lives. Yet Amber's parents constantly pushed him, over me, to be Amber's boyfriend. They constantly reminded her I was the kind of guy she should forget about. They were thrilled Amber and I were enrolled in different schools. Turns out they were right.

*   *   *

I couldn't sleep. Tears were beginning to dry on my face, causing my bristled skin to feel stretched. The thumping, swollen, infected scrape on my neck itched. The intolerable snoring of inmates droned in my head, the loudest of them was mere inches from me. It's no wonder he was happily snoring, he had a fucking bed.

Soft, steady moonlight pushed through the small jail cell window, giving the space a glow. I could see the man beside me lying in a fetal position on top of the thin mat, the he-she's jet- black hair tossed over his arm where he rested his head, lines of old mascara lining his face. Then I saw the whites of his eyes. They were intently looking right at me.

He spoke softly, "Don't be so hard on yourself." His voice sounded like that of a woman.

I didn't realize the shame I was feeling was visible. A gracious nod was my only response. Feelings of unworthiness began to gobble me up. I was a terrible son. My father bailed me out many different times, only to be slapped back by my continued failures. Letting him down and letting everyone else down was what I excelled at. I wasn't being hard on myself, I was being honest—for the first time.

Looking back, I could see that my father was there for me, his wallet open to anyone who could help. It was too bad it was often his heart he kept closed. The second time I was arrested for shoplifting my dad never told anyone. Not even his wife. He understood when I was suspended from school for fighting. Said if someone had spit on him he would have had to break the guy's nose, too.

When I was seventeen, the bag of weed that he pulled out of my backpack was returned to me with a warning. Whenever his wife hollered about what a loser I was, he never disagreed, yet he'd explain to her how adversely affected I was by the losses in my life. He respected my privacy, rarely looked in my bedroom, never after 10:00 p.m. That is what made it so easy for me to get out. Many nights my life didn't begin until *normal* people were sleeping. The fact that I had a separate entrance made it that much easier to come and go undetected. *Why didn't he see that? Perhaps he did.*

The final straw for my father was the night I decided to take his car, a bottle of his booze, and money out of his wallet. I ended up getting hammered and driving down to the South Side of Phoenix to look for drugs. There, I could always find what I was looking for. On my way home, just before sunrise, I ended up getting popped for a DUI. His car was towed, and right before my eighteenth birthday I was in for another thirty-day treatment program. This time I was sent to a rehab house in Utah referred to as *A Simple Path*. Only the path wasn't so simple. My father sternly threatened me. He wanted to make sure I understood this would be the last time he'd pay for me.

"You are soon to be a man," he said. "It is time for you to grow up and take responsibility for your own life. No more, Jason. No more! You can live with me until you finish high school, but that's it, Jason. I swear on your mother's grave, that is it.'

I heeded the warning. Returning from Utah, from rehab, I was filled with hope for the future, I was clean, and I was sober for thirty-eight days. I got back just in time for the beginning of my senior year. Amber and I started up again, in a much better place than where we were when I had left. Rather than make amends and destroy Amber with the truth of who I really was, I promised myself that from that day forward I would no longer keep things from her. I lied. I lied to her and to myself. I could never live up to that kind of honesty. I wasn't ready, then.

The start of my senior year, everything was not everyone else's fault. I was truly taking life one day at a time. And I kind of liked it that way. Amber and I fell into a comfortable place. Working fulltime with his father's ministry, Bradley could no longer be an excuse for getting Amber out of the house. I spent time doing things for Amber's parents, hoping to get them to like me more. I helped them around the house, helped her dad rebuild the motor on his car, put up a block fence. We laid tile in their main bathroom, and I put a pan rack together and hung it in the kitchen for her mother. All that, and they still never really extended the trust I was looking for. Amber had to become somewhat rebellious to spend more time with me, using each of her girlfriends as her way out of the house —even lying to extend our evenings together.

Because of the DUI, I couldn't drive for six months. Amber had a car so she always drove, often picking me up in the morning and giving me a ride to school, even though her school was in the opposite direction. She said I was the brightness she needed to start her day. I had to wonder if I wasn't the only liar in the relationship. I regret never telling her she was the brightness of mine. She had been the brilliance and optimism, the unfailing good humor, and support that had sustained me. Always a smile on her face, a cheerful and lively manner, Amber was beautiful, pure, and genuinely kind.

Our time in the morning, before school, was short. Just long enough to hear about four songs on the radio. We had a special song we considered to be our very own, and when it rang out she'd blast it, sing, and then look at me with adoring eyes. We'd talk about our future together, getting jobs, having kids, and buying a home and fixing it up. We even talked about the types of flowers we were going to plant. Amber actually made me believe all those things were possible, as long we were together. When we weren't together, addiction slipped in.

For a while my sobriety wasn't really an issue. Amber and I spent a lot of time alone. Amber's father was a city employee, always bringing home passes to this or that. The zoo quickly became our favorite place to spend Tuesday afternoons. It was the Phoenix Zoo on Tuesdays and the park downtown on Thursdays—habits I knew Amber was hoping I would adopt. Productive hobbies to keep me busy and out of trouble.

One of the highlights at the Zoo was Monkey Village. It was basically an aviary filled with squirrel monkeys. There were no real fences between us and them. Rather, it was a half wall and a manmade ravine that separated the playful, yet wild animals.

Amber and I both loved watching the monkeys. We sat for hours in front of their enclosure, watching them leap from branch to branch, swinging from rope to rope, like trapeze artists. We laughed aloud at the funny things they did, the way they interacted. I often wondered if they enjoyed watching us the way we did them. I would run up to the edge of the enclosure and clap my hands. The monkeys would clap, too. I made funny faces. The monkeys also made funny faces. I acted like a monkey and swing my arms, turning back to Amber, overpowering her with my gangling grip before pretending to separate the hair on her scalp and act as if I were eating the bugs that came from her head, then breaking out in hysterical laughter.

The park on Thursdays was just as much fun, only more private. It was a small park in the center of the city. Mostly business people frequented the square. She'd help me work on homework while we lay on our bellies, resting on a blanket we'd spread across the grass. She would read to me, and tutor me, always reminding me of my intelligence. I'd play with her long hair, sweeping it back out of her face. Her skin was soft and pale. Small freckles tipped her button nose. I tried to seem interested in school, history, math, and English literature, but it all seemed so useless.

Eventually I would beg her to stop the studying. I'd wrestle her over onto her back, my body, much larger than hers, and I would naughtily press her into the ground beneath us. The playful gesture always led to her arms wrapped around me and my lips locked with hers. My hormones raged. Her self-control became tiresome. Amber and I had worked into heavy petting at this point in our relationship. But she had her stopping point, always. "No Jason," she'd say, before pushing back. I respected that, keeping my hardness tucked down. I constantly fought off the urge to take her. To show her I was a man in every way.

As the holidays approached, the party invites were harder and harder to refuse. By Thanksgiving, with months into my sobriety, I finally decided I had the strength. Amber took me to a party with a bunch of her school friends. In the beginning, it was a great time. Lots of music, crazy kids acting up on the dance floor, which was the center of someone's living room. I smelled the pot. No biggie. I saw the chugging going on. That was cool.

It was what I didn't see that had me jonesing. The stuff I considered my mischievous demon went on behind closed doors. My mind began to play with me. Even it knew I was nothing more than an addict.

I began to assume the drugs were there, at the party. I abruptly got up from the sunken couch, searched out my girlfriend, grabbed her by the arm and pulled her out of there. Amber seemed to understand. And then I smelled alcohol on her breath. I knew even she had betrayed me that night. If I couldn't drink, she shouldn't drink. That was my thought process.

I instructed her to drive us away from the party. I was silently feeling hurt and betrayed. I was angry, and I wanted to get high, which made me even more agitated. Getting high was suddenly a thought I couldn't escape. I knew I was supposed to call my sponsor, but right then, I didn't feel like being talked off of the edge. What I wanted was to get high.

"Right here!" I flew my arm in front of her face. She turned into the dark side of Encanto Park. It was past 10:00, so the lights to the tennis court were off. "Come on," I said, as I jumped out of the car and opened the back door. I gestured for her to get out of the car and go for a walk. My energy was high. I was anxious.

Amber obliged. She jumped out with a free spirit and bolted for the water. Encanto Park was one of the few places in downtown where there was a lake.

"Come on you," she invited, with a mischievous smile. She jogged over to a large pine tree, where she held up, breathless.

I followed her. "How's this?" I pressed her into the tree.

She seemed a little timid at first, but after I latched on to her rum-soaked lips she let loose. More aggressively than usual, I pulled her blouse up and began kissing her nipple with my tongue. That was a first for us. I had touched them plenty, just never with my mouth. Just before I was going to press through the band of her pants, I stopped.

"You've been drinking?" I stepped back and stared her directly in the face. "How could you? How could you drink when you know I am fighting to stay sober?" I pressed the guilt on her.

Amber stood dumbfounded. "You're kidding me, right? I am not the one with the drug and alcohol problem, Jason, you are." She tapped her finger on my chest while staring back into my face.

I moved back away from her and paced with phony anger. I stomped back and forth. It was almost Thanksgiving, the weather was chilly, and my thoughts seemed even colder. Being around my family and anyone else who loved me was too intense. Amber was suddenly my reason to check out, run off and go back to my mindless existence.

There wasn't much of a moon on this dark night. All the park lights began to shut down simultaneously with loud humming clicks. No other cars were around. No other people. I didn't want to leave her near the lake alone. But I wanted to leave. My mind was made up. I needed Amber to go. Chrystal meth had won. She was the other woman calling me to her.

"Jesus Christ, Amber! Where is the goddamn support?" Those were especially bad words. I waved my arms in the air. She hated for me to use *God's name in vain*.

"Jason!" she cried. "I will not allow you to talk to me like that." Falling right into the addict's plan, Amber began walking back to the car. "You are totally overreacting."

As she approached the driver's side, I grabbed her arm and turned her back to face me. "I don't know what you want, Amber. What about living a *clean life?*" I pushed her back, pressed her against the car with my body, feeling the tremor between us. Her eyes began to fill with water. "Since when do you drink? What about my sobriety, Amber? Didn't you think of that?" I was a master when it came to guilt. I especially hated this part of myself. "I guess not." I slapped the top of her car and stepped back away from her, and then shoved my hands in my pockets.

"I can't believe you are freaking out like this. I took one sip of Renee's drink. One sip, Jason!" She had a scowl on her face I'd never seen before. Tears dripped off her cheeks. "You owe me an apology." This forceful Amber hadn't shown herself like this before.

"I'm sorry. I'm sorry, Amber. I'm sorry I'm a fuck up. I'm sorry I can't be normal like you." What I was really thinking was *I'm sorry I have no fucking control over my desires.* I felt every muscle in my body tensing when I raised my voice. I slammed my fist into the palm of my other hand and abruptly turned away. The fist pounding anger was not meant for Amber, but rather, it was intended for me. I was disgusted with myself. I was a failure, and I was accepting it. "I'm going to walk home from here." I looked her in the eye and lied. My body shook uncontrollably. "Get in the car and go home, Amber."

"Why Jason? Why do you do this? You are so predictable. Go ahead and go. Go be with your prostitutes. Go suck down a bottle of booze, puff or snort your drugs, or whatever it is you do." Suspicion was a sharp thread in her voice. "Go on! Go and get it all out of your system." Through piercing sobs, she screamed. "But Jason, whether you want to believe it or not, you are better than this. You are so much better than this!"

Shocked by her complete knowledge of my crippling cravings, I tromped off, yelling over my shoulder. "I'm sorry, Amber. I'm really sorry." The sound of her pain crushed me.

*　*　*

"I'm sorry, I'm sorry, I'm sorry!" My eyes popped open to find the ink-black stare of the man with the mascara-stained face. I was sweating profusely, my body shook violently, and my stomach twisted fiercely with retching cramps. No matter how hard I squeezed my eyes shut I couldn't sleep, and I couldn't stop thinking of all my fuckups.

"Sometimes the words *I'm sorry* just aren't enough." His voice was silky-smooth. "I suppose if it were enough you wouldn't be here in this jail cell right now." The moonlight illuminated his sympathetic gaze. "Actions speak volumes," he says. "You have to become the change you want to see." He was sitting up cross-legged on his mat. A flicker of hard-won wisdom sparked in his eyes. His long hair was tossed over to one side of his shoulder, a blanket thrown over his lap. Eyes wide, he obviously hadn't fallen asleep, and it appeared he had no intention of trying.

I gave no response, but I agreed with everything he said. I put my head down to avoid the mysterious stare of my cellmate. A tidal wave of raging grief welled up and threatened to spill over. I no longer had to wonder why I've slowly died inside. I should have never left Amber in the park that night. I should have called my AA sponsor. I should have never started drinking again. But mostly, I should have never gone back to the pipe. Regrettably, I've spent my whole life getting it wrong. I wanted badly to get it right. I just wasn't sure where to start. I closed my eyes and made a desperate attempt at a new beginning. I began to pray. I prayed to a God who hadn't heard from me in quite some time.

Chapter Twenty

Ethan Price

I didn't care that it was almost midnight when he knocked on my door. I had long forgotten about him not calling me, or including me in his grief in any way. All I wanted was to have Bradley with me. When he arrived, weary, lost, and whipped, drained of every bit of energy, I knew just what he needed. Bradley needed something only I could provide. Something I was good at. One of the only things I was really good at. I wasn't expecting Bradley to be so needy. But it was even more unexpected to realize I was even needier.

I pushed back into his hardness, his hands gripped onto my prominent hipbones. With a strong thrust, we were one. Our bodies bucked back and forth together. His hands roamed my body, I groaned with pleasure. He led the rhythm that caused a wave of pleasure to wash through my body. He electrified me, sparked a new and painful desire, reminding me how much I loved this man, how I wanted him so badly to be mine.

Exhausted and breathless, at precisely the same moment, we both collapsed to the bed. The meshing of our bodies had created a hot, slick wetness. The orgasmic aftershocks nipped at my body. We both rolled over onto our backs. We were breathing as if we'd just run a marathon. His energy radiated liberation, a releasing of emotion and pent-up spirit. I leaned on my side and pressed my head into his bare chest. His strong arm wrapped my shoulder, his hand dangled into the ticklish crevice of my neckline, petting me lightly. He was attentive. Finally he was here, right next to me. I could hear the beating of his heart, his heavy breaths, yet his mind was elsewhere. Someplace I knew I'd never fit in.

This brief moment of silence spoke volumes. Bradley had been through so much. I snuggled close and pressed my ear to his bare skin, as if my closeness could penetrate his thoughts. I could smell my scent on him, the lingering aroma of lovemaking, along with the tang of heartache. I was afraid his mother's death would impact him in ways he might find difficult to deal with. I felt bad for him, at the same time, I hated to admit it, but I was glad she was finally gone. I could never compete with her. Over ten years of loving Bradley and now, now I finally had a chance. I knew he'd never be mine so long as she was alive. I gripped onto him even tighter.

I followed his blank stare across my bedroom and noticed the paint chipping in the upper corner of the wall, just beneath Nasreen's upstairs apartment. I hadn't even told Bradley. I felt an aching wound of remembrance. I knew her belongings were still there, even though she wasn't. I felt bad for the thoughts running through my mind. I knew Bradley loved his mother almost as much as he loved life. But I also knew he would have never come out of the closet and told his mother about me. He always said it was senseless.

"All she will do is worry about my soul making it to heaven," he would chuckle. "It is the knowledge of sharing eternity with the people she loves that makes her life gratifying. I will never take that from her, Ethan."

There is no comeback for that type of thinking.

His love for his mother was always evident. His mother meant everything to him. I loved and hated that about Bradley. I loved my mother, even after she watched me walk out her front door, never so much at an attempt to stop me, nor an effort to reconnect with me. But I never knew any kind of love that carried with it a commitment like the dedication Bradley had to his parents.

For a brief moment, my thoughts drifted to my own family. It had been so long. I wondered if any of them had died, become successful, homeless, sick, or even gay. I couldn't help but see the irony of this situation. In the name of God, both Bradley and I had a life not of our choosing. I was forced onto my path, Bradley was held back from his.

I couldn't take the quietness. "Bradley, I'm really sorry about your mother." I gently trailed my hand across his chest, down his tight abdomen, over the curve of his hip, and back up again. My fluffy pillow curved around his head. The flicker of candlelight danced across the ceiling.

"Thanks. I'm really sorry, too. I'm just glad there was no suffering." He kissed me on the forehead.

"I didn't know she had a bad heart." My hand rested over Bradley's heart.

"None of us ever knew she had a heart problem." A sigh of disappointment leaked from his mouth. "But Ethan, this marks the beginning of a new chapter. I can finally be myself." He sat up slightly. A smile played at the edges of his lips. His eyes shimmered with hopefulness.

"What about Amber?" I was hesitant to bring it up so quickly, but Bradley was the one who started talking about *new beginnings*, so why not be clear about what I am to expect?

"Amber really loved my mother. She took it very hard. And Jacob, it was really his first experience with death, the poor little guy. But he handled it like a champ." His gaze wandered the small bedroom of my apartment, probably imagining how awful it would be to live here.

"How is Amber going to feel about getting on with a new life— a life that doesn't include you as her husband?" I raised my gaze to see the response in his telling eyes.

"She feels just fine." He cupped my chin and drew me in. Our lips met. "I'm sure she is relieved. Now she can continue her Tuesdays at the zoo and her Thursday rendezvous at the park without the cover of lies," his voice fell. He flopped back onto his back and drew the bed sheet up over the lower half of his body.

"Amber is having an affair?" Shocked by this new information, I needed to reaffirm what Bradley was telling me.

"It is hard to really call it an affair with our open marriage. But I suppose if you'd consider a past-life ghost an affair, then yes." Bradley's condescending tone was something I rarely heard. "He was her high school sweetheart. A great guy, until he wasn't."

"Are you joking? I mean—if you're going to try and be funny after all these years, please let me know when to laugh." I didn't want Bradley to know how taken aback I was. He'd never been this honest. I cuddled my head onto his shoulder, removing my gaze from his.

"I'm not trying to be funny, Ethan." His tone took a turn.

"If your marriage has been open, why would she lie to you about meeting him?" I lightly brushed over his nipple with the backside of my hand and waited for him to fill me in.

Bradley was a thinker. He kept his thoughts in—tended to analyze everything before speaking. As I stroked him, his skin appeared pale next to mine, and mine always seemed pale next to most. The hair on his chest was sparse. I found myself softly plucking at each wispy strand as I waited for him to speak.

"She knows I wouldn't approve of her wasting years waiting for someone who wouldn't be there. He was never there when he should have been. He turned out to be a big loser."

I felt the rise of his chest as he took in a deep breath.

"Amber and I have silently lived a lie," he spit out the words, "a lie that has been convenient to both of us. No more! She needs to move on, find real happiness, and so do I. Now it is our time, Ethan." Once again he turned on his side to face me. "You have been loyal, very committed to me over the years. It is time for us, Ethan. We can finally be together." He leaned in and pressed his mouth onto mine. Wet and deep, it was a kiss that I wished would last forever. The kind of kiss I would never forget. It was a passionate reminder of the overwhelming guilt I felt from my secret betrayals. I knew I hadn't always been so loyal to Bradley. But I *had* waited for him. I had always been his, should he have wanted me.

"Why hadn't you ever told me this before now?" Even with my own deceit, I felt slighted by his.

"What? Tell you what, Ethan?" He pulled away and again rolled onto his back. He raised his arms and folded his hands under his head. "You wanted me to tell you Amber is still in love with her high school sweetheart. You have known our marriage was a pretense. But it was built on friendship and love just as any other marriage, Ethan. It was built on loyalty." His tone hardened. "I will never stop loving Amber, and I will never stop caring about what happens to her, but our marriage is over." His eyes were glued back on the chipping paint. "Amber and I were best friends before we were husband and wife. That isn't going to change. We will always be a part of each other's life. We share a son." He said this with less conviction.

"You were both living a lie?" I could understand his lie, but I couldn't understand hers. *Why would she have stayed? It isn't his son.* Even I knew that.

"There is so much more to the story, Ethan." He pushed his body up and leaned on the headboard.

"You've had ten fucking years to fill me in on the story, Bradley." I was upset, hurt by this.

"I'm telling you now, Ethan!"

259

I threw my legs over the side of the bed and sat up. He reached out and tried to grab my arm before I swung out of the bed.

"You always made it seem as though you had to get home to your dutiful wife, Bradley." I flipped the bedside lamp on and stared down at him.

"Amber had been just as committed to my betrayal as I have all these years. It was the part I was playing. If nothing else, Ethan, I owed her my respect as her husband. We have lived our lives for others and I had the starring role." His features scrunched, as they often did when he was upset.

There was nothing I could say to follow that. Why had I never heard of Amber's flaws? All these years I'd seen her as perfection. The wife I wanted to be. Yet, she too, had suffered a life of desire, tinged with sadness. She was more like me than I knew. I said nothing, turned around and sat back down on the bed, grabbed a cigarette out of the pack on the nightstand, pulled the ashtray out of the drawer, and lit up. I rarely smoked cigarettes in my house. Even I hated the stale odors of old smoke. My naked back to Bradley, I took in a long drag and watched the smoke rings puff out, up into the still air, they floated across the room. I've been a skeleton in Bradley's closet for so long, he was trying to figure the best way of letting me out.

"Ethan—come on. I'm here with you now. Let's start over. Let's begin again." His hand pressed into the flesh of my naked hip. Appling pressure, he tried turning my body to face him. "Come on—don't be so sensitive. I've never made you think I wanted to be with Amber more than you. Those were always *your* hang-ups. I've always been honest about my real feelings."

"It just would have been nice to know her feelings all these years." I snuffed out my cigarette and flopped back into his arms.

All the years Bradley remained in hiding it was as if he'd thrown me in the closet with him. I never felt like our being together was wrong, just deceitful. Yet I was never ashamed of our relationship.

Nevertheless, I was the one left to feel like the dirty little secret. I knew he loved me, yet I was never really sure he really wanted to be with me more than his wife and family. He never understood how it affected me every time he went home to her. There is a very fine line between loving someone and being in love with someone.

I felt Bradley's lips on my neck, and then the warmth of his mouth was on my nipples. His tongue trailed the distance of my torso, stopping only when he found my little friend, hard and waiting. His mouth warm and wet, he almost completely covered me. I laid back and pressed my head into the pillow while massaging Bradley's head and moaning in ecstasy.

A blowjob wasn't one of Bradley's favorite things to do, but at that moment, I couldn't tell. Shivers of pleasure swept through my blood as I swelled in his mouth. He finished the job quite nicely and threw his body over mine. I felt the hardness of him. I could see the desire he held. My legs went high over his shoulders, giving him the space he needed. This time it was pure, raw, emotion as he thrust himself in and out of me. This time it was his skin on mine, no rubber tainted the moment.

Bradley had never been able to repress his attraction to me. I know he really tried to ignore it at first, especially when I wasn't quite eighteen. I am sure he thought his behavior and his feelings toward me would change, but they didn't. Married or not, son of a preacher, Bradley had always been gay. He wasn't effeminate in any way, well, not compared to me, and he didn't flounce around limp-wristed. He just can't refuse me. As he passionately made love to me, I could tell he'd finally shut off all thinking. I could tell he was only feeling pleasure, no guilt.

*　　*　　*

My head was jarred, slightly rolling off the pillow as Bradley tried discreetly sliding out of the bed, waking me from a peaceful, contented sleep. Bradley's naked body moved through the darkness of my bedroom and into the bathroom, quietly closing the door behind him. A glow of light seeped into the room from under the door. I heard the toilet flush and the faucet run. I pictured him rinsing his mouth and spitting into the sink before splashing his face with water, then running his wet fingers through his short, dark brown hair. I was right. When he returned, the light from the bathroom illuminated the water droplets that still clung to his face. His hair was damp and slicked back. His thick eyebrows and eyelashes were moist.

"I need to get home." He stepped into his pants. "I can't believe we fell asleep. It's already three o'clock in the morning." He poked his arms through his long sleeves.

"Why are you leaving?" Even I could hear the whiny tone of my voice. "I thought we were starting our new life." I stared at him dressing in the slice of light coming from the bathroom.

"Not everything at once, Ethan. Soon, though." He tucked in his shirt and did up his pants and belt and walked over to my side of the bed and knelt beside me. His lips pressed into mine. "Soon we will sleep together through the whole night." He moved over to the chair in the corner of the room and began to put his socks and shoes on.

I rolled out of bed, grabbed my jeans and walked into the bathroom to piss. I called to him over my shoulder. "When will I see you again?" This one question always made me feel so needy. I flushed and stepped into my jeans.

"I hope soon. I'll call you this afternoon. Maybe I'll come back again tonight, who knows." His manner was playful. "Would you like to go on a date or something this week?" He rose and grabbed me as I came out of the bathroom. While I was wrapped tightly in his grip, I stared into his brilliant blue eyes. The stubble on his face made him look manly, a characteristic I found irresistible. "Maybe I shouldn't assume you have time for me." Bradley pulled my eyes into his.

The physical strength in his grip was such a turn on. But his wavering commitment wasn't. "I don't know what I'll be doing tonight for sure." I playfully batted my eyes. I knew I'd be waiting for his call. That, I knew for sure.

He pulled away. "Well, I'll check in with you later and see. If we can get together great, if not, I have lots to do with clearing out my mother's house, her things, and going through the details of her estate. Hopefully that is where you and I will live someday. Once I get out the old, I can make it nice, with room for the new." He threw on his jacket and coolly stuffed his tie in the side pocket, as if he didn't just say what I think he said.

"You and me, live in your family home?" We began walking through the apartment. I switched on the kitchen light and rubbed my eyes in the brightness.

"It's not like I'm going to kick Amber and Jacob to the curb. I'm going to give her the house. She deserves it. She is the one who has put so much of herself into that home. My mother and father's home is in the heart of the city. A few renovations inside, hardly any change to the outdoors, and we will have a nice home in the historic district. Isn't that where all the gays live?" He smiled sideways.

"Oh, sure, living in the *gayborhood* sounds great. We've just never had this conversation, that's all." I was smiling deep down inside, afraid I was dreaming, afraid none of this would actually come true.

"I never felt free to have it until now." He kissed me on the forehead. "I'm trying to tell you life is going to be different, Ethan. You need to begin to believe me for a change. But for now, I need to get home. I don't want Jacob waking up to me not being there. He doesn't know yet how much his life is going to change." He turned and headed for the front door.

I grabbed my cigarettes and lighter off the breakfast bar and followed him. His slacks caressed his body, his shirt was custom made. His slip-on loafers had a shine I could see myself in. We stood in the open doorway of my apartment. I flipped off the porch light as we said our last goodbyes.

"Don't forget to call me." I placed my hand on his face and drew him in. "I really like this idea of beginning a new chapter, and so far the first few pages have been very intriguing." Our mouths pressed passionately together. I can't remember ever kissing Bradley this much.

"I'll not only call you, but count on seeing me again tomorrow night." His intense stare penetrated my heart. His strong arm wrapped my lower back while his piercing blue eyes held my gaze. "I promise." One more quick, wet smack on the mouth and he turned and left across the courtyard.

He had a determined walk as he strode down the path to the parking area. My heart aflutter, I lit a cigarette and watched him leave. This Bradley was a different man. He was eager, willing. He was bolder than I'd ever seen him. Last week, he'd have never kissed me in an open doorway, even if we were under the cloak of darkness.

Bradley stopped just before rounding the corner, looked back at me and waved, before moving out of my sight. I leaned in the doorway and finished off my cigarette, never remembering a time I was smiling this much. I always knew the death of his mother would have a great impact on him. But I had never realized how her death would have had such a great impact on *me*.

I pitched my cigarette into the dirt planter bed beneath the stairwell. And just as I turned to go back into my apartment, I caught a glimpse of the bright, red-hot tip of a burning cigarette. There my nosy landlord stood, propping his fat body against the edge of my building. His dark stare was on me. I caught his eyes, yet he didn't turn his ominous gaze. *Was he there all along? What did he hear? What did he see?*

"What the fuck are you staring at?" I mumbled under my breath, making sure he didn't hear. Without another thought, I shut the door, locked it, and went back to bed. I was alone, and yet for the first time, I didn't feel lonely.

I was filled with excitement, giddy. My mind was active, hard to shut off. For the first time I truly felt like I did have a future with Bradley. A house, a yard, a man—it was the closest thing to family I would ever know. I want a dog. A small dog I could hold on my lap. I want a swing on the porch. I want pots with flowers, lots of colorful flowers. I want to entertain friends. *I want Samantha to like Bradley.* I couldn't wait to share my good news with my best friend.

Chapter Twenty-One

Samantha 'Sam' Green

Sleep never came to me last night. I awoke even before the sun did. My hair, my pillow, my bedroom—everything smelled of burnt sage. I swung my legs out from under the covers, flipped my lamp on, and sat on the edge of my bed. The stuffed bear gifted to me by Ms. Beth years ago, meant to be a consoling friend on the night I was orphaned, sat atop my dresser, his button eyes stared right at me. Strangely, my little friend didn't calm me now as he did all those years ago. In fact, I leaned forward and twisted his wooly body, causing his dark glossy eyes to look somewhere other than at me.

After my horrifying vision, Grams insisted on smudging me before I left her house. She lit the end of her braid of sage, took the burnt, smoking herb in one hand and created a cleansing smoke bath as she lightly waved it around my body. I smelled as though I was still immersed in the cloud. She started with the bottoms of my feet and then worked the smoke up around my body, to my head and my crown chakra. The effect of the smoke was to banish negative energies. I hope it worked. I was still feeling riddled with anxiety, so I wasn't holding out much hope.

Gram really believed this would purify my thoughts, drive out bad spirits, terrible feelings and influences, and somehow protect me from my own premonition.

"Fate cannot be sidestepped or outrun,"she had said. "But, we can certainly do our best to guide the bad energy elsewhere."

Last night I could hear the worry in Gram's voice. It was almost as if she were trying to convince herself this ritual would work, rather than convincing me. But there was no need to influence me. I knew smudging, done correctly, could bring on physical, spiritual, and emotional transformation. I just wasn't feeling it this morning. Not sleeping last night had a lot to do with my negative energy. I closed my eyes and breathed in optimism, hoping to envelope a positive mindset.

I quietly chanted the affirmations that had become my familiar friends over the years. "My mind is calm. I am calm and relaxed in every situation. My thoughts are under my control. I radiate love and happiness. I am surrounded by love." Then I repeated the chant in my head.

I do believe that the future can be changed. Visions are only a warning of how things will be if nobody does anything about them. The problem is this: most people don't notice visions as warnings, and they let fate take its course. It can be frustrating to watch my predictions play out. I see things happening that I can't stop. Even with my warning, some people are just set on letting fate take its course, rather than trying to alter it.

I first learned I had contact with the spiritual world when my mom died. I felt her spirit almost immediately. I saw her in my dreams. Then I became aware I had actually been seeing other people all along, I just never realized they were dead people. Typically I heard, rather than saw things, voices, chatter mostly. But with great concentration, I might catch a glimpse of something—scenery, maybe a personal feature; it varied.

The majority of the time I couldn't make it out, so I blocked it out. That is until Gram started to notice my psychic ability. Gram was very interested in trying to talk to my mom and my grandpa. She had a lot of unanswered questions. Questions she gingerly asked through me. Consequently every chance she got we'd sit in with her friends and challenge my skills. They'd all ask me questions about the dearly departed and I'd answer them the best I could. Sometimes I'd get a gasp, mostly a lot of head nodding. I didn't always hear the answers, but often gave them anyway. It seemed to comfort the old gals. Oftentimes I had already known what they wanted to hear, so I was just satisfying them.

In my teen years, Gram noticed I was more accurate with my information. That was when she began to take me to study with a group of local psychics. We'd get together monthly, usually on the third Thursday. These were strangers to me at first. I was not comfortable telling people that I had psychic ability. Most people were skeptical of my abilities, so I didn't push myself on them. I was still not comfortable with my skills, but I'd be damned if I was going to deny them either.

Over the years, most of the outside energies had been protective. I could remember how, at a very young age, I had heard a man's voice scream, *Freeze!* just as I was about to walk by a TV that sat atop an old wood stand in Gram's living room. Within seconds the TV crashed to the floor. Another time, I was playing in a tree-swing in Gram's backyard when the same voice urged me to run inside the house, just before lightening torched the tree limb I had been playing beneath. As I grew older, I came to recognize that voice as my grandfather's.

Another time, just before high school graduation, I was just about to pull away from a green light, just as an incredibly intense force of some sort caused me to press my brakes rather than my gas pedal. I immediately knew it was my mother, even before my car took on the fragrance of her perfume. My mother's sudden warning alerted me to stay put. And just as I hit the brakes, someone barreled through the red light. The impact of that speeding car would have killed me. My visions had always offered me answers and given me direction. Why now did I feel so lost?

I was still settled on the side of my bed when I noticed a light streaming down the hall from the living room. The clock read 5:32 a.m. I stepped into my slippers and walked out into the front room to find Madison on the couch, her stocking feet propped up on the coffee table, a laptop computer on her lap, and a cup of coffee in one hand. Her free hand was petting Charlie, who was flipped up on his back beside her, blissfully relishing the belly rub.

"What are you doing up so early?" I shuffled over to the couch and sat beside her and pat Charlie on the belly.

"I couldn't sleep. I decided I might as well get my homework done." Madison shut her computer and looked up. "Wow! Why are your eyes so swollen? And what is that smell?" Her features scrunched up as she stared into my face.

"'Tis the season for allergies," I lied. I wasn't about to tell her I cried buckets last night. I just wasn't in the mood to go through it, not with her. "And the smell, well, let's just say I sat in on one of Gram's ceremonies." I stood and sauntered into the kitchen for a cup of hot tea.

"What kind of ceremony?" Her interest seemed genuine.

I spoke over my shoulder. "Oh, you know. She wanted to bless the yard and the house for my birthday party, so she lit up her sage stick and I became smoke drenched."

The microwave beeped. I grabbed my steaming cup, poured in my yummies, dipped in my bag, and rejoined Madison back on the couch. "I can't believe it is already Wednesday. This week is flying by. You must have been out late last night. You weren't here when I came home." I blew into my hot cup.

"I went to the gym after school and stayed until closing. I ran into my dad." Madison moved her computer to the coffee table in front of us. "I got in a pretty good workout last night. I know you can't relate, but sometimes it just feels good to beat the shit out of something, and that is just what I did." She cocked her neck to one side and stretched her arm out as if to work out a few tight muscles.

"How'd you get over to the gym?"

"I took the bus to Monroe and walked through the backside of the neighborhood. Why?"

"Are you crazy? You're asking for trouble walking through that area at night." My voice went high.

"Don't worry. I didn't walk—I ran like hell." She laughed and took a big swig of her coffee.

I slapped her on the leg. "Don't do that. It isn't funny, Madison. You don't even follow your own rules. You are not even the least bit cautious. Do you have a death wish or something?" All I could think about was my grim forewarning, my very unclear grim warning.

"Oh, nice play-on-words, Sam—*death wish*. Are you fixated on death or what? Are we back to the death wish I have for my cousin's sick, twisted killer? You are so sure I wish him dead, aren't you?" Madison was more suspicious than usual, rather snappy.

"Boy, you are way off." I couldn't dare tell her of the unclear images that kept flashing in my mind. She was skeptical on a good day, and I could see this wasn't going to be a good day. "I'm just saying, Madison—if you don't want to get blown up in a minefield, don't walk into the minefield. I'm sorry for caring." I picked up Charlie and cradled him in my arms.

Madison reached out and touched my arm. "I'm sorry. I'm just feeling a little uptight. This whole death penalty thing, all the news, the reporting, hell we're all over the Internet; me, Lisa, my uncle, and my father. The story, it's everywhere, Sam. I can't get away from it. It just stirs me inside. It fucks with my head. I never thought I'd be so disturbed by it." Madison was torn. Perhaps she hadn't ever felt the emotion that was suddenly tugging at her now.

I put my hand over hers. "I am always here for you, Madison."

She looked into the bottom of her cup. "I wish I could forgive him." Her voice fell flat.

"Forgive who?" I never heard Madison actually say those words.

"The killer, Sam. Lisa's killer. I wish I didn't hate him with my whole being. I wish I didn't pray for him to die. I just wish I didn't ever even have to think about him again." Madison shot up off the couch and went to the kitchen.

"Forgiveness is a very large undertaking, Madison. But I've always told you the payoff is tremendous." I yelled out, hoping she was still listening. Madison had a way of shutting me out after she was done with hearing what she wanted, more often saying what she needed.

"I'm sorry. You were saying something about a payoff." She appeared in the doorway between the kitchen and the living room, a fresh, steaming cup of coffee to her lips.

"I think it was Gandhi who said, 'The weak can never forgive. Forgiveness is the attribute of the strong,' and I know you to be a strong person, Madison. To not forgive this man allows him to have power over you. It allows him to steal your energy." Damn, I didn't want to use the words *power* or *energy*. She gets freaky about stuff she can't totally wrap her brain around.

"I can't forget what he did, Sam. How am I supposed to excuse murdering a small, helpless child?" Madison was burdened. "I still picture my little cousin being hurt and violated by that pig. Now I envision someone hurting him, torturing him, and causing him pain. The kind of pain my uncle felt, just before taking his own life. I want him to burn in hell." Her teeth clinched with every word. "Whenever I imagine that vile man frightened, anxious, and hurting, I get a rise of satisfaction, a contented feeling of retribution. Does that make me a bad person?" Her eyes searched for acceptance.

"Forgiveness is not about forgetting or pardoning him, or even excusing what happened. Forgiveness is, first and foremost, an internal process, Madison. It is primarily for you." I was shocked she was standing through this. She was actually being honest with her feelings. She was listening for a change. "And Madison, hell is not the devil's home, or a place that burns evil. Hell is the doom we suffer on earth. Hell is our karma. Hell is living out your life in prison."

"Do you think my cousin Lisa has forgiven me for not waking up that night? Could it be I am living my karma for not screaming, for not being the one to actually save her from that savage bastard? You think she has forgotten about all that and pardoned me?" She briskly crossed the room. Turning into the bathroom, she shut the door behind her.

I yelled after her. "Oh, Madison—Lisa knows there was nothing to forgive. She released you long ago." I set Charlie on the couch and moved toward the closed door, a door meant at shutting me out, in a way I didn't take personally. "And if you would just open your spirit-mind and listen, Lisa would probably make damn sure you knew that." I leaned into the bathroom door. "She would tell you to stop blaming yourself, Madison. She would also tell you to forgive him and forgive yourself." I knew these things because Lisa had told me. This guilt Madison carried was nothing new, but the idea of forgiveness was.

She flung the door open. "I'm so glad I live with a physic. Could you please tell me what kind of day I'm going to have?"

I raised my voice. "Not a very good one if you don't change your attitude. What have I always told you? Bad things happen to people with bad attitudes." I noticed I was uncharacteristically pointing my finger at her. "You might want to change that." I said to Madison, but could have just as easily been telling myself those words.

Madison shut the door, again closing off her feelings. Sometimes she just knew how to push my buttons. One minute I'm ready to feel sorry for her and wrap my arms around her, sharing every ounce of positivity I have, the next I don't even want to share the same air.

I returned to the couch, sipped my tea, and basked in the silence for a few moments, before the sound of running water flowed into the room. For years now, Lisa had communicated with Madison, through me. But it had been subtle little things, all unknown to my disbelieving roommate. Lisa came to me about her cat, what became of Madison's cat, Sylvester, after her death, and she told me he was going to die, before he actually did die. Lisa felt bad for Madison. She was the one who encouraged me to get Charlie for her. Lisa knew she was going to get the job as the judge's assistant all along, wanting me to convince Madison it was the best thing for her future. Lisa told me Madison's brother was going to break his leg, and her father was still drinking too much. I tried to weave this information into our conversations in helpful ways.

I looked over to the clock on the cable box. Since I had a late start-time at work today, I decided to catch the seven o'clock yoga class. It wasn't often I was up early enough for that one. Charlie had made himself comfortable right in the middle of my lap. I felt guilty tossing him off as I rose. I was suddenly imagining the anguish of Lisa's father, learning his little girl had been abducted, raped repeatedly, and suffocated to death. I could see how he couldn't live with that nightmare.

Chapter Twenty-Two

Jason Magnus

If God and faith were to be found inside the jail, pain and suffering probably had something to do with it. Sick to my stomach most of the night, I woke early with my abdominal muscles clenching and churning. I had no choice but to use the small, unconcealed, metal toilet in my cell. My gut wrenched with diarrhea craps, I buckled over in pain praying for God to get me out of here. I prayed for God to give me strength to never return to this fucked up place. And I prayed for the ability to free myself from addiction, failure, and stupidity. But mostly, I prayed for a chance to reunite with Amber. I knew I needed to apologize to her before I ever had a chance at recovery. That is what I spent most of my prayers on, Amber. I needed her forgiveness to move forward in my life.

Like clockwork, at 6:30 a.m. the cell door screeched back. Without hesitation, I flew through the corridor to the bathroom for privacy. Sitting on that cold, tiny stainless steel shitter, in the small cell, begging God, with all the other inmates listening in, was probably as low as I've ever been. Now, as I sat in the privacy of a bathroom stall, it might have even been slightly worse. All my fuck-ups bombarded my mind. While I sat clenching my gut, I realized there had been so many low times, too many. It was difficult to think of all the times I had promised myself there would be no more—yet there I sat. *I'm done with this,* I said to myself, again. I had finally lost every ounce of dignity. I had to be done. This was my time. *Be strong, Jason—be strong!*

All this sadness in such a small space, I was happy as hell to be leaving today. No more being jammed under the bed or next to the waste of others all night long. My stomach cramps finally subsided somewhat. I stepped out of the stall, determined to feel better. I pulled the collar of the orange jumpsuit up over my nose and took in a lot of slow, deep breaths through my nose.

The smell of a jail-cell bathroom was disgusting. I couldn't seem to get enough fresh air into my lungs. I went to the sink to clean up—as best as I could without a toothbrush or a razor. My whiskers were thick, filling in the crevice of the dimple that marked my chin. The blue part of my eyes seemed to be fading, yet the whites were brilliant white. It was a sign of a clearer head.

"This is crazy man. I don't know how they get away with havin' us sleep in these conditions." An older fellow walked in the bathroom and moved rather slowly toward a stall, showing how the stiffness of the concrete floor had affected his body.

"It's not right," a dark skinned man protested, stretching his stiff body. His eyebrows were bushy. A hairy mole sat atop his lip. When he talked it sounded like gargling, like he had water in his lungs. "It's inhumane in every regard," he said, with some sort of a Middle Eastern accent. I suspected he was probably some rich doctor in here for a DUI, or maybe beating his wife into submission. He looked Iranian, Iraqi, Saudi, or something. He reminded me of my landlord. Mean, cat-kicking bastard. I'll never forget the time I watched him punt a tenant's cat after it shit in the bushes near his front door. And he never noticed me watching him. I never told him what I witnessed.

Speaking of him, I had to face that asshole today when I went back to my apartment. This last time I checked out of my life I had owed him rent money. I was currently down for the month, still with about a week left. I was hoping to cut him a deal and work like hell to make it up. I sold most of what I had that was worth anything to buy drugs. When I got out of here, my first calls would be to my sponsor and my boss. I needed to stay clean and sober, and I needed money: in that order.

By the time I walked out of the restroom they were slinging the morning chow. People were already arguing over the television channel, and minister man was back to being Jesus, blessing the food and shouting the Lord's Prayer. Donald Trump was still telling us all he wasn't a drunk. I robotically trudged through the routine, biding my time. And it wasn't long. Just after finishing my disgusting food ration my name was called, along with nine others.

Officer Brown lined us up in the center of the floor near the large steel door.

"Come on girls. It's your chance to leave this place. I'd step it up if I were you." He clapped his hands together.

I chugged down my milk, took my food tray to the trash, smacked it on the side a few times, and then set it down on the table before joining the other inmates who awaited their departure from hell. I stood and spied a row of men on the other side of the thick glass window, who would walk in, just as we walked out.

Officer Brown took a wide stance and glanced around. "Just these nine, all you others, back! Ready—open!" he yelled.

The locks clicked loud, the door slid wide and we walked forward, into the control of two other officers. With a loud clang, we were trapped in yet another small space, a cube-like room, with two doors and one long window with a view back into the misery, misfortune and despair I was finally departing. My drag queen cellmate, who unknowingly turned out to be my sounding board and advisor, was staring at me through the glass. I raised my gaze until our eyes met. My look intently on him, he slowly and methodically moved his hand to his head, then to his heart. Again, he repeated the exaggerated movement over and over. His fingers pointed to his heart, then to his head—his heart, his head. The message he was sending became clear. *Think with my heart, not my head.* I tapped my heart with two fingers and threw him a piece sign, along with a nod.

The door behind me opened. I turned and marched through. We trailed one detention officer as another followed the pack of inmates through a long, brightly lit hallway. The uniform in front led us to a holding cell. One by one we would be called and processed out. My experience told me this was going to be another long, drawn-out process before finally being released. We were all put into a small room with block walls, two long concrete benches, and a steel door with a small window. Once in the room, they instructed us to listen for our names over the loudspeaker. I knew once they called my name, it was about a half hour before they came to pick me up.

The officers left us. Much of the bench space was already taken by the other inmates in the room before us. I found a piece of the wall to lean on. Grabbing his feet, a guy was using a portion of the bench as a bed swinging him off and knocking him to the ground, had crossed my mind. But then, I thought better of it, recalling my cellmate's advice. Instead, I tipped my body into the cold concrete wall, took in a large breath, and prayed for my name to be called soon. The fact that I decided not to knock his ass on the floor actually caused me to take pause. *I could change my course. I do have the power.*

"Cracker, move your fucking legs and make some room for some other mother-fuckers to sit their ass down." A big black man, twice the size of any normal human being stood beside the napping inmate. He didn't touch the man. He just towered over him in a very intimidating stance.

Suddenly the young man was sitting straight up, his back pinned against the wall. He stared anywhere but at the linebacker who hovered over him. I couldn't help but laugh inside, realizing this new me was going to need some time to adjust to the suggestion that all thought comes through the heart rather than the head.

*   *   *

There was no clock on the wall. I had no idea what time it was, but I knew hours had passed. People had come, and people had gone. Yet the room was still crowded, and my stomach was beginning to wrench again. *Please no. Please no.* I couldn't take the humiliation. I already watched some other dude take the plunge, only to hear the jabs from his audience: "Courtesy flush" and "Put some water on it."

I stared at the small toilet in the corner. On one side a drinking fountain with a sink next to it, on the other was a half wall. It was just big enough to cover one's ass, but not quite big enough to give any privacy. The steel door opened, two guys stood and walked to the exit.

"What time is it?" I was getting antsy.

"It's two o'clock," the guard announced as he escorted the two inmates away and shut the door.

"How much fucking longer do I have to wait? Christ, I've been in here since 8:00." I was starting to sweat. Staking claim to a spot on the bench hours ago, I rested my elbows on my knees and dropped my face into my hands. My skin was beginning to boil.

Everybody added their two cents about how fucked up the system was. And then they all went back to their own little worlds. The room felt as though it was closing in on me. To keep my mind in check, I had to talk myself off the ledge. I wasn't feeling good. I was hungry. And I was still coming down from drugs, and being in a holding tank with a bunch of stinky guys wasn't helping anything.

Finally, I heard my name over the intercom. I felt like a child. Quickly the excitement of leaving this place filled me. Energy rushed through my body. My anger disappeared. I took in a deep gulp of air, and as unpleasant as the odors were, I still felt a liveliness that lifted my spirits. I rose and paced the small space and waited for the door to swing back.

Soon I was being escorted through the unit's heavy steel doors and into the jail's main artery. An officer helped me to retrieve the clothes I was wearing on the day I was arrested. I pulled the filthy jeans and the ragged long-sleeved, pullover out of the bag. The horrible stench that followed about knocked me over. I reached into the bag and pulled out a pair of torn, stained boxers and a pair of tube socks that were as dirty as if I'd worn them without shoes. I glanced up and saw the officer point over to a few big cardboard bins in the back of the room.

"Go ahead. If you find something you can use, take it. If there is anything in that bag of yours that you don't want, you can toss it in that other round can in the back." His arm swung toward the trashcan.

I exchanged my orange jumpsuit for a wrinkled, green polo shirt and a pair of khakis that were just a tad too short. I wore my tattered tennis shoes. I looked down and could see my ankles. But it didn't matter—I was dressed and ready. It was impossible to stop smiling, high-waters and all. I came from behind the privacy wall, tossed my trash, and followed the officer through the next set of locked doors.

"Good luck, guy." The officer took me over to a tall counter. "I hope I don't see you in here again." He probably said that to everyone. He turned and went back through the steel door.

I signed lots of papers, then waited as they retrieved one more packet filled with my belongings. The woman brought back a large manila envelope with my name on it.

She set it on the counter in front of me. "This was everything you had on you when they brought you in. Sign here and it is all yours." Her eyes remained on my face. "Boy that is some scratch you have there, on your neck. You might want to get some antibiotic ointment on that when you get a chance." Her motherly tone was comforting.

"Thanks." I lightly trailed my finger across the raised flesh. I had almost forgotten it was there. Now that I touched the wound, it began to itch.

I signed the paper and retrieved the package. I was fairly fucked up by the time I ended up in jail. No sleep for days, besides mental exhaustion I had been physically exhausted, not to mention high on drugs and alcohol. I hardly knew what to expect would be in the envelope. This was like opening a gift. I prayed my keepsakes were all still there.

I spilled the contents out on the stainless steel counter. The first thing to slide across the countertop was the cross I made for my mother. Clanking directly afterwards was my grandpa's knife, followed by a single key on a ring that doubled as a bottle opener. I breathed a sigh of relief, kissed the cross keepsake and stashed it away. As I went for the knife, I noticed there was a dark crusty substance on the steel. Upon further observation, it appeared to be dried blood. I quickly tucked it into the front pocket of my new pants. I had no idea where the blood could have come from.

I went through my wallet, counted six dollars, found some loose change, my driver's license, my boss's business card, and another card I had carried for many years. I drew the aged card from the concealed pocket of my frayed wallet and read it to myself. *Elizabeth Hanson—Child Protective Services.* I flipped the card over to find -*Miracle House Volunteer—A Place Where Everyone Gets a Chance to Start Over.*

That sounded like a good place to be right now. I couldn't help but wonder if Elizabeth Hanson was still around. I'd carried this card for over a decade. I honestly didn't know why I never threw it out. I didn't even know if Miracle House even still existed. *Maybe it was time I found out.*

I tucked the card back into its special spot in my wallet. I poked my face into the manila envelope to make sure there was nothing else I was missing.

"It looks empty to me," the nice woman behind the counter declared. "Are you missing anything?"

"My cell phone." I was pretty sure the phone was some sort of final trade-out for drugs. It always was. But I thought I'd ask anyway.

"It's not written on this piece of paper, so I'm certain it was not on you when you were booked in." She held up the inventory list— a list that bared my sloppy signature.

"That's okay, I remember now, I didn't have it with me." I stuffed my wallet into my back pocket.

"You are free to go, Mr. Magnus." She lifted her hand and pointed to the door leading to the outside.

"Thanks." I turned and followed the loud buzzing noise.

One strong push and I was walking out the front door of the county jail. The afternoon sun was bright, warm. "Ah man, fresh air," I whispered to myself. I hesitated, not sure what to do next. I needed to find a way home. With the sun at my back, I walked up 35th Avenue toward Van Buren Street. I could catch a bus a few blocks away that would take me almost all of the way to my apartment complex. As I walked, I could think of only one person: Amber.

* * *

Years ago, that night of the party, after stomping off and leaving Amber in the park, I went off and did what I did best. A few days went by before Amber called me, apologizing. *Sorry for what?*—I didn't know. Thanksgiving was around the corner and she wanted me to know just how thankful she was to have me in her life—a statement that totally baffled me. I was the one who was grateful, yet I never knew how to really show it. I was the asshole, the one who didn't deserve to be appreciated. I knew it was never intentional, but she had a way of making me feel worse by her acceptance. It was so much to live up to.

After the holiday weekend, Amber and I talked regularly, but our visits were becoming more infrequent. The last few months of the year became too difficult for her to give me a ride to school. It was our senior year, she was busy with her studies, and her classmates, plus, Amber had a job. Me, I was busy trying to conceal my misery, hoping to somehow make it to graduation, still skating on my dad's buck.

That year, Christmas came and went. Amber and I exchanged small gifts, shared a meal, but for the most part, she did things with her family and friends, and I did things with me. My hidden drug use and my drinking all began to escalate again. I didn't like spending the holiday with my dad and his new family, so if I couldn't get out, I would hole up in my room. They never so much as checked on me. Christmas break ended and it was back to school for my final semester. Staying up late and sleeping in all day was about to come to an end.

My dad started really coming down on me about getting a job, reminding me my time under his roof was about to run out. He forced me to meet up with one of his pals who owned a construction company. It was probably one of the best things my dad ever did for me. Max, that was his name. He was the one my dad's friend hooked me up with. I worked every day from 3:30 until 6:30. I loaded trucks and inventoried materials needed for the different jobs. I washed and fueled and oiled the equipment.

On Saturdays I actually worked with Max learning the contractor trade. He did a little bit of everything, so my skills became well rounded. Jack of all trades, master of none. I learned how to use a tape measure and a table saw. Max taught me to lay tile, build a patio, and roof a house. I actually tiled a shower, painted a bathroom, and installed kitchen cabinets. Max always said I was a great helper. *Fast study,* he'd say. Little did he know I worked better with a little bump of speed. And before long, I didn't need my dad for cash. Max started paying me by the job.

Amber and I still managed to see each other, just not as much. It wasn't the zoo and the park anymore—no time. But when we did see each other, we had returned to a comfortable place. Even after knowing I'd broken my pledge of celibacy, Amber was still my girl. But she wasn't really a girl any longer. She was a beautiful young woman. Her body was full. Her hips shapely, her breasts were plump. She had matured into a very sexy woman. Sexier than any of the women I had ever had.

Amber held to the promise she made to herself, to God, and to her parents to remain a virgin until marriage. Even though I wanted her so badly, it got to where I stopped trying. It was just an understanding we had silently come to. It bruised my ego too badly for her to continually reject my advances. My hands never got very far with her. I often found myself shivering with desire when we kissed. So all I could do was imagine doing with Amber what I had done with other women.

* * *

I reached up and grabbed the rope overhead to alert the bus driver we were approaching my stop. I could see my apartment complex in the near distance. Jumping to the curb, I bound down the sidewalk home. I turned off the main street and cut through the wall of oleanders. I snaked through the buildings, landing on the back path toward my unit. That was when I saw him coming my way. He was angry. He was yelling. He was loud.

Chapter Twenty-Three

Madison Morgan

I packed my items into my backpack and headed through the courthouse. I was thrilled to have this day behind me. Desperately in need of fresh air, I picked up my pace. With a full docket today, I had struggled to stay awake through the last few cases. Last night my dreams were suffused with the moaning death of Lisa's killer, making it difficult to get any sleep. I was exhausted, and my body was a little sore from the workout I had put myself through. I stood in front of the elevator doors and stretched my waist from one side to the other.

For a moment, I flashed on my father, his apology, his warmth, his remorse—all unexpected. I stepped into the crowed elevator, turned my back on the people staring at me, and faced the closing doors. What I had expected from my father was the anger he so often expressed for a killer who was now a dead man walking.

Exiting the elevator, I marched across the corridor and pushed through the doors. Finally, I was out into the early evening air, like being out of prison. I felt free. My mind had trapped me in a place that was so confining I might as well have been in prison.

Last night I laid awake most of the night thinking about death. Samantha was right. Maybe I really did have a death wish. I wished to see Lisa's killer dead. And according to my dreams last night, I wanted to witness his death.

Jumping off the high curb, I bolted across the street and waited for the approaching train. My thoughts melted in with the sounds of the city at rush hour. Every other kind of capital punishment went through my mind even though I knew Lisa's killer would die by lethal injection.

The first method of execution my psyche played out was a hanging. I pictured the large sandbag dropping. His head at the other end of the rope snapped. I remember reading once that if the rope was too long, the inmate could be decapitated, and if it was too short, the strangulation could take as long as 45 minutes. I'm not sure which I preferred. I was startled awake.

The light rail quietly pulled away from the platform. I took a seat in the back corner, where I leaned into the cool window. Totally vegging-out, I stared at the passing cars. Last night, once I returned to a deep sleep, I went back to the demise of a killer. My nightmare shifted to the electric chair. I envisioned him shaved and strapped to a chair with belts that crossed his chest, groin, legs, and arms. A metal, skullcap-shaped electrode was attached to his scalp and forehead over a wet dripping sponge. I watched as he was blindfolded and the warden signaled the executioner, who pulled the handle.

Lisa's killer gripped the chair. His body turned bright red. His flesh swelled. His skin stretched to the point of breaking. The jolt I felt shook me out of my sleep, but the sickly sweet scent of burning flesh had already permeated my nostrils.

My body swayed to the motion of the train car as it came to a stop. The doors slid back and I stared at the people who stepped on and off, hoping to somehow get my mind off the nightmares of last night. Miracle House was still a ways off. I leaned back and closed my eyes for a few minutes. I was exhausted. My nightmares had won the battle last night. Like Ebenezer Scrooge, who had received three ghosts about living, I met three haunting nightmares of death.

Last night, the final time I drifted off to sleep, I dreamt of a firing squad. I was one of five shooters armed with a rifle pointed at the person who had been a part of my nightmares for years. In an enclosed space, about 20 feet away, sandbags stacked high around a chair that confined the strapped-in body of my cousin's killer. His eyes were scared. His stare invaded my sleep until a black hood was pulled over his head. A doctor located the heart with a stethoscope and pinned a circular white cloth target over it. I was hoping to be the shooter given live rounds. The earsplitting noise from my rifle jerked me awake. That is when I decided it was time to get out of bed.

It wasn't quite 5:00 a.m. when I finally decided to give up trying to sleep. I figured I'd get a head-start on my day and catch up on homework or something. Instead, I jumped on my computer and looked up lethal injection. As it turned out, lethal injection was now virtually the universal method of execution in the United States. And as a consequence of my research, I found out that during the course of the execution, Lisa's killer would feel a burning sensation running the course of his veins. There was a chance he may experience severe pain, especially if a second dose of potassium chloride was needed to stop his heart.

I couldn't believe my father would have me think this was some sort of mercy killing or euthanasia of some sort. When I thought about my father, his exasperating anger, and my uncle and the bitter resentment that was ultimately the cause of his death, I could see the value in forgiveness. Sam's words had not fallen on deaf ears. I wasn't sure I could ever forgive that murdering pig for what he did to Lisa, but the thought of finally forgiving myself, now that was intriguing.

*   *   *

I jumped off the train three blocks away from Miracle House. After a sleepless night plagued by capital punishment, and the week from hell, there was only one place I could go to ground myself. Miracle House had a way of helping me to stay focused on what was important in life.

The air was cooling as night began to fall. Had it not been for the group counseling, and the specialized therapies, and meeting my best friend, I know I never would have come this far in my life. Samantha has been preaching forgiveness from the very moment I met her. But really, this morning was the first time it ever really registered with me.

I glided through the front door of the complex and up to the thick, protective glass window.

"Hi, I'm Madison Morgan. I'm a volunteer with the women's unit." The girl behind the counter was someone I hadn't seen before.

She looked up and smiled. "How can I help you?" her voice carried through a loud speaker that was built into the glass.

I poked a hand into my bag and pulled out my volunteer badge, reassuring her I was who I said I was. Due to domestic violence issues they were extra protective of this unit. The door buzzed and I entered the safe haven. Walking around the main counter I headed straight back to the nursery. It wasn't quite six o'clock, so I knew there would be plenty of babies left from the day. The mothers had to retrieve their little ones by eight.

"Hi Madison, long time no see." Cheryl, the childcare coordinator, was grabbing her items and heading through the door just as I was coming in.

I held the door for her. "Hello. Yeah, I've been crazy busy." I grabbed at the jacket she was struggling with and helped her get it around her shoulders. "I've been really busy with work and school, but I needed my baby fix, so here I am." I watched her spin through the threshold, fumbling her personal items.

"Lord knows we need you. Jessica is in charge tonight. She can put you to work. Thanks for showing up. We really need the volunteers." She smiled and moved on.

I turned into the room. Smells of baby powder, lotion and formula overwhelmed my senses, and so did the smell of urine and dirty diapers. The area was cordoned off into sections. There was a play space for bigger kids, toddler to kindergarten, and there was a separate room for infants—an area that could be seen through a enormous picture window off the large play room. Changing tables, feeding stations, rocking chairs, and cribs filled the smaller space. There were a stove, sink, and refrigerator in the far corner. Lots of small children bounced around. Others sat quietly at a table playing with toys. A few lay on a big round rug in front of a television set over in the corner. One little boy wheeled a toy car up and over the furniture, across the floor, the length of the wall, all along the counter and back to the furniture again.

I entered the room with the infants, tossed my belongings into a special nook, splash my hands with sanitizer, and picked up the loudest crying baby. Within seconds, a staffer pressed a warm bottle into my hands. It just so happened I knew this child's story—a very sad story, indeed. I took a seat in the rocking chair on the far end. Despite my anger at the stupid ass, meth-head teenage mother who birthed this poor baby, I lovingly held the tiny, writhing body, nothing but affection in my heart.

Her face was purple from the exertion of her screams. Her eyes were angry slits in her head. Her little fists were like pink roses thrashing about in the wind. I tried to gently force the soft nipple of the warm bottle into her quivering lips. Finally, she took it. Her cries, for now, were diminishing. Her body squirmed in my arms. I could feel my heart beating rapidly. I rocked her back and forth. The strength of my arms held her tightly against my body, reassuring her

I was there. Someone was there for her. It made me feel incredible to be that person.

I sat and rocked, tilting the bottle of formula in her lips. I watched as parents came and went. I couldn't help but wonder what problems they must have had, causing them to live in the protected ward of a halfway house. Any time I had problems in my life, coming here, spending time with the babies seemed to make all my worries fall away. Even if the best I could do was clean the nursery, it still made me feel better. Death penalties, murder trials, traumatic experiences, work, school, all of my guilt—everything—took a back seat to this small infant I held in my arms.

As I looked down, her tiny wet eyes opened. A smacking noise rose from her lips. The bottle was empty. I stood and gently shifted her little body to the top of my shoulder, where a small blanket covered my upper arm and chest. I flipped her onto her belly and lightly patted between her small shoulder blades until I heard a slight burping gurgle. While I swayed about the room, my thoughts wandered.

Over the years, Sam and I had spent many hours, right here, rocking babies and discussing life. Life had dealt us maturity at a young age. As we rocked in our chairs, we were like two old souls trapped in the body of teenagers. I talked about my family, the books I'd read, the classes I was taking, my grades. Sam went on about the crazy things she and her gram would do to conjure up spirits. I told her of my plans for college, my aspirations to someday be an attorney, maybe even the District Attorney, conceivably even a judge. Sam talked about how much she missed her mother. Then Sam shared the difficulty she experienced forgiving her mother for killing herself. I talked about the trials, the testimony and the depositions I was periodically called on to give. Sam admitted that the thought of her stepfather stealing her virginity constantly gnawed at her. She said it was harder to forgive him for the pain he caused her mother than it was to pardon him for the pain he caused her.

As I sat there and thought about the maddening resentment Sam had worked through in order to move forward in her life, I realized just how intense her shocking ordeal had been. Yet she had moved ahead in her life. Sometimes I still felt like that eleven-year-old child trapped on the floor next to my cousin's empty bed. I hadn't yet moved out of that place, a place where a little girl called out for me and I was not there to hear her plea.

Little Desiree cried out. She started thrashing about in my arms. I rolled her over on her back again, wrapped her in a thin blanket and began to cuddle her close to my body. Only a few moments, and I could tell I was familiar to her. Could she remember my smell? Perhaps the roughness of my hands? Maybe she even noticed I had one green eye and one brown one? Within minutes her lids began to get heavy. While she dozed, her moist lips puckered. Her face and body gradually relaxed under my caress.

I carefully sat back in my chair and rocked gently, watching as mothers came in to retrieve their children after being either in private therapy, a group counseling session, AA meetings or one of the other many drug abuse programs offered at Miracle House. And if they weren't doing that, they were returning from a job off the campus. Those were the only conditions for which the House would step in as a child care center. They were very strict. Anyone who lived on campus also had to submit to regular drug and alcohol testing, assuring the House they were *clean*.

When I went to lay Desiree in a crib, I couldn't help but hear Sam's voice telling me, "The weak can never forgive. Forgiveness is the attribute of the strong." Up to now, I had always thought of myself as strong. But it was some of her other words that continued to rattle in my head. "To not forgive this man allows him to have power over you. It allows him to steal your energy." Today, if no other day, I could see how that was so true. The thoughts of this man had drained every ounce of energy in my being. I hardly had the energy to hate him anymore. But what I truly hated, even more than I hated him, was the idea that he still had power over me by the mere fact that I hadn't forgiven not only him, but myself, for the death of my cousin.

Chapter Twenty-Four

Ethan Price

I lumbered along the path to my apartment, two bags of groceries in one hand, some wine and flowers in the other. As I approached my door I heard loud voices in the distance. Fumbling with my things, I turned back to see a man in pursuit of my landlord. Barking obscenities, he followed him across the dirt lawn toward his apartment. The voice seemed familiar to me. Pretending not to gawk, I knelt at my entryway as if to gather my things. I couldn't help but watch the two argue. It was easy for me to cheer for the man who spoke out against my disgusting landlord. Just before reaching his doorway, Mr. Faranghi abruptly stopped.

The cranky Iranian turned and faced his menacing follower. "I already told you—I am not letting you in your apartment until you give me the rent you owe. I've been chasing you for three weeks." Even though the other man was taller and stood over him in the doorway of his apartment, Mr. Faranghi was wide enough to stand his ground.

The long-limbed man began waving his arms and screaming loudly. "You can't just lock me out of my apartment like this. What about my clothes, my belongings, my tools? Please. Please! I promise I'll get you the rent. One week, I beg you. That's all I need, just one more week and I'll pay you what I owe." His pleading tone sounded sincere.

Mr. Faranghi stepped up to the man and puffed his chest. "I've heard that before. You don't fool me. It wouldn't surprise me if you just got out of jail." My landlord's mocking voice carried through the complex. "Now go," he waved his arms as if he were shooing dogs off his porch, "before I call the cops on you." He slammed the door on the desperate man's face.

"You fucking asshole! One fucking break—that's all I need." The man in the high-water khakis didn't give up. He smashed his body into the door, his face pressed into the wood, "Please Mr. Faranghi, one more chance. I promise this time will be different." He softened and continued to plead with the landlord, to no avail. The door remained closed.

There was something about his voice that was familiar to me. For a moment, his words stuck in my gut. I recognized that voice from somewhere. *But where?* My neck craned back to watch him. He wasn't wearing socks with his short pants. He appeared to be in need of much more than rent money. He abruptly switched from his praying temperament and began to violently kick and punch at the door, before finally retreating. His back still to me, he tromped down the path, toward the rear of the complex. Then he unexpectedly turned around, causing me to spin around and begin to nervously rattle my keys. When I slowly turned back, he had disappeared from my view. I was disappointed I never got the chance to see his face. I was most certain I knew him from somewhere.

With the setting sun, and the coolness of night almost upon us, I couldn't help but feel sorry for the guy. He was definitely right though, Mr. Faranghi could be a real asshole. It was apparent this man was desperate and in a very bad way. Yet he received absolutely no sympathy from the fat Iranian. For a moment, there was a part of me that wanted to chase after the stranger, extend a helping hand to the poor soul. *Samantha must be rubbing off on me.* But, the part of me that was selfish and wanted to go into my apartment and prepare for my special night with Bradley won out.

Finally stumbling across the threshold with all my bags in tote, I kicked the door shut behind me. *Ahh, there's no place like home*—even if it was a small, stuffy apartment. At least my rent was paid.

I tossed my dinner groceries up on the counter, along with the bottle of wine. First I pulled the only vase in the house out of the cabinet above the sink, filled it with water, and stuffed in the beautiful floral bouquet I had just bought. I danced the arrangement across the room and placed it right in the middle of the kitchen table.

Even though at that moment I was feeling miserable, I found myself humming some silly song. Now I kind of understood the expression Samantha often used. "Every day may not be good, but there is something good in every day." She'd use this on me when I complained about my life, my day, my job, and anything else that was bugging me at the time.

Samantha started work late today, so she was still at the office dealing with the crazies when I left. I can't say I felt sorry for her, though. I was there early this morning, slaving for hours, doing all kinds of shit long before she arrived. However, I did feel bad about leaving her alone to deal with Willie. He was someone I had known longer than her.

When I bolted out of work, they were loading Willie into an ambulance and running him over to the hospital. Right before I was ready to leave he showed up at the center covered in blood again. His injuries seemed superficial, but still Samantha insisted on getting him off the streets, if only for a night. That was always her motive when dealing with the homeless. I'm almost convinced the blood wasn't even his, but I wasn't going to tell her that. There were times it was just better to let her have her way.

She was going on and on about his aura, her visions, and something about someone being in danger. And all along, as Willie was going *psycho*, all I could think was we might be the ones in danger. As much as I loved that girl, some of that crazy voodoo stuff, her visions, the voices, the various auras she sees, and those stones—her so-called pebbles of power, I sometimes have to just let it all go in one ear and out the other. Who am I to rain on her psychic parade? If she wanted to believe a midnight phone caller who hung up on her was a call from heaven, or random feathers were signs from above, and discarded pennies were connections to the deceased, I was going to let her have her certainty.

I really was feeling just a bit guilty for leaving her. But I couldn't take the way Willie was hollering my name. His pleading tone was like an animal in distress, begging me to release it from a trap, just before having to resort to gnawing off a limb. As much as I wanted to help Willie, the problem with getting him to the hospital was he wasn't so willing to go. I hated to see the distress it caused him. That is what sometimes made it so difficult to help mentally ill people like Willie. Some people were just psychologically incapable of even knowing when we were doing what was best for them. Willie, by far, was one of those.

By the time I snuck out, Samantha had calmed him, and had convinced him that the hospital was a friendly place, a place that would help him and then let him go—which was wrong in it of itself. I wanted so badly to tell Samantha why I was excited about going home, but I never had the chance. The day got away from us before I could tell her that Bradley and I were going to move into his mother's house.

Once again, I heard myself humming while I retrieved two place mats and two settings, then I rolled a fork and knife into a paper towel for each of us and set the table. I reached into the cabinet and pulled out two gold, tapered candles and a pair of crystal candlesticks. I dug in my pocket for my lighter and set the ambiance.

Samantha's grandmother had given me the candlesticks a few years ago. She said everyone needed a little something classy in the cupboard to pull out on special occasions, telling me how these candlesticks had served her well over the years. I had always wanted the occasion to use them, and tonight, with Bradley coming over for a real date, sort of a celebration of the beginning of our new life together, I'd say this was the right occasion. I set out the plates, utensils, and the wine glasses, and I began to prepare a few steaks.

Once the meat was seasoned and marinating, my potatoes wrapped and ready for the oven, I bounced over to the sofa, dropped to my knees and drew the tray of marijuana from beneath the furniture. I rose, turned, then plopped back onto the sunken piece of antiquated crap I called my couch, and proceeded to get high. Kicking back, I leaned my head into the wall, then closed my eyes and let the smoke slowly seep from my lips.

My phone began to ring, startling me slightly. I dug it out of my pocket. Bradley's number lit up on the face. Enthusiastically, I answered. "Are you on your way?" I felt a smile spread across my face. My heartbeat raced with excitement.

His response wasn't what I had expected. I listened to him go on about taking things slow. He gave an obligatory apology and reminded me this was a school night for Jacob. He said we could go out on Friday night instead. *Like I'm going to take him to Samantha's birthday party!* But of course he didn't ask me if I had plans for Friday. Nor did he ask if I'd already gone through any fucking trouble for our supposed date tonight.

Bradley went on and on about how he needed to talk to his son, help him cope with the death of his grandmother, lend a hand with homework, and slowly introduce the idea that he and his mother would be separating. I barely listened. My heart fell, not for the kid. I tried to be supportive. I didn't want to sound needy or put-out, even though that was just how I felt. I couldn't help that I let Bradley know that I always felt like I took a backseat to everything and everyone in his life. It just came out that way.

We hung up. I took another hit off my pipe and flipped open my laptop. While I waited for it to come on, I went over to the table and poured myself a glass of wine, blew out the candles, and walked back over to the sofa. The smell of burnt wax filled the air. I plopped the computer back onto my lap and surfed my favorite sites until I hit on someone interesting.

This guy answered my request quickly. As much as I was interested in staying home and eating steak, I was now equally as interested in this aged beef I was looking at. He was searching for a hook-up, something Midtown, immediately, easy to get to, hard to pass up, no ties, no names. I agreed to the rendezvous, shut my computer, slugged back my wine, took one more hit of pot, tucked my phone into my pocket, grabbed my pack of smokes, and walked out the front door.

Smoke bellowed from his enormous mouth like a chimney. The judgmental eyes of my landlord followed me as I walked through the complex. His stomach sagged over his belt, and his shirt was wrinkled and sloppy. From across the courtyard I could see his sinister stare was on me from the moment I stepped out of the door. I didn't let him know I saw him. The last thing I wanted to do was talk to him, so I picked up my pace, almost to a jog, as if I had somewhere to get to in a hurry—which was actually the truth.

The night air was chilled, but calm—no breeze. While I walked, I thought about the man who earlier had been yelling at my landlord. His voice was pinging in my head. His brilliant blue eyes were becoming haunting. Eyes I barely caught a glimpse of. Eyes I would never forget. Eyes that were suddenly crystal-clear in my mind. His strong chin, his mannerisms, his pleading tone, all of it I had seen before. It was years ago, my life on the streets, a dark alley—an alley where we rescued each other.

I told myself that couldn't have been Jason Magnus. It had been many years since I'd seen him. How could he live in the same complex as me, yet we never ran into each other? His family was well off, lived in a great house, a nice area. This was way out of his neighborhood.

My mind wandered back to the night when I saw him in that alley. No matter what he was doing in between those old buildings, or what he has done with his life since then, I felt a debt of gratitude for Jason. He really didn't even know me when he offered to take me home, feed and clothe me. I was nothing more than a stranger, yet he took me in. Sure, we'd seen each other once or twice. Nonetheless, Jason didn't have to be kind to me that night, but he was.

I stood on Van Buren and waited for a break in traffic. Now I was totally feeling guilty for not reaching out. Especially because Jason was someone I felt I owed. Yet, in reality, he was a stranger to me now. After all these years he could be a completely different person. He may *have* just gotten out of jail. For all I know, he could even be the murderer people are looking for. I quickly recalled Jason as a young man, the nice guy who had helped me out. I can still recall the words he had said to me that night when I questioned his generosity.

"My mother, when she was alive told me, 'No one should ever be without food, water, and shelter.' So, I'm doing this for my mother." He convinced me to go with him. "This is America, after all," he added. "We have more money than God. And God has everything, including my mother. The least you should have is a fucking place to sleep." As we walked to his house, I could tell her death had been a crushing blow to him.

I darted across the street and jumped up onto the train platform, and waited for the next Metro. I felt sad for Jason. He must have carried that sadness all these years. Who knows what else had been on his path over the past ten years. Something has led him to his current dilemma. While I waited to catch the train, I couldn't help but look around, down to the other people on the platform, and in a way I was hoping to see Jason, someone I think I once knew.

Chapter Twenty-Five

Jason Magnus

Before leaving jail, like a fool, I had convinced myself I was done with being on the streets. Yet here I was, walking along Van Buren, looking for a familiar face, someone, anyone that could put me up for the night. Sundown was upon me and the air took on a gloomy chill. My gut churned with anxiety as I wandered the stomping grounds of an addict. The people I saw, the ones who were familiar to me, they were the last people I needed to see. I was certain life would be better without them, without the drugs.

The best part of staying clean would be not spending all my time thinking about drugs, looking for drugs, and wanting to get my hands on drugs. Having a family, people who loved me, someone who would look forward to seeing me at the end of every day—that was what I wanted for myself.

I viewed a crowd up ahead and decided I'd best go a different direction. I could tell by looking at them they were up to no good. They were the people I would have walked up to before tonight. I just wanted to be a normal person. I wanted a normal life. But there was nothing normal about being a drug addict. Even though I had just stepped out of detox-hell, I still wanted to get high. My mind screamed at me to give it drugs.

I reached into my pocked and pulled out my old wallet. I thumbed through it as if more money had somehow appeared since the last time I had checked. It hadn't. I was still about as broke as a person could get. When I glanced down at myself, like a punch to my gut, I was reminded I was wearing someone else's clothes, I had nowhere to sleep, no one to call, and a buck left to my name. Everything I owned was out of my reach. Everyone I loved was too.

Without a doubt, at that very moment, all I wanted to do was keep walking into the crowd of familiar faces and proceed to get buzzed out of my head. But instead, as if some energy force had stopped me, I remained paused on the sidewalk, my wallet open to the street lamp overhead. The aged card I had carried for so many years was between my fingers, the light was exposing the words, *Miracle House—A Place Where Everyone Gets a Chance to Start Over.* It was the moment of truth I needed to remind me I wanted something more than drugs, something more than the streets, and something much more than a life of regrets.

I cut across the street, jumped over the tracks and headed back toward my apartment complex. I was sure I could find a place to pull up for the night, under a bush, behind a trash can, or on the sidewalk at the all-night store. Tomorrow morning I'd make my way to Miracle House. I know I'd promised myself many times before to do that very thing, but this time I would stick to it. More than anything else, I wanted to change. I wanted to be a sincere and honorable man. It felt good just saying those words in my mind. *Sincere* and *honorable* were words Amber had once used to describe two of her favorite traits in a person.

While I trudged along, my mind churned with thoughts—back and forth it went—tossing around all the reasons to not take drugs. But quickly, and without warning, my mind battered me with all the reasons why I couldn't stop using them.

The brutal mind-fucking continued as I stomped my way back toward the 24-hour store that was adjacent to my apartment, back on the other side of the road. Once again, I darted through traffic. At a distance, I caught a glimpse of a friend of mine; she leaned on the back edge of the store, a cigarette hung from the corner of her mouth. She had been off drugs for a long while, yet the poor woman just couldn't get off the streets, in a different sense, with prostitution and all. She was a person I'd really like to see get a fucking break in life. Some people just seemed destined for despair. She was one of them. I was beginning to wonder if I was one of them, too.

"Hey Raven," I yelled out and waved my arm while trotting her direction. Had life not been so hard on her, she'd be a beautiful woman. Her skin was dark, more chocolate than black, shiny, glittery from some cream or something she had rubbed on it. Raven's real hair was short. Her wig—this one she had on—was a gigantic curly afro that rested on her shoulders.

"Hey Baby." She leaned in and gave me a kiss on the side of my face. Her big loop earring lightly brushed my cheek. "Where ya been, Jason? I've been worrying about all my people since they found that young girl, back over there, dead." Raven's head turned, her eyes shot to the backside of the building. She made a striking gesture at her jugular. "I'm glad to see you, Sugar." She drew in deep, her cigarette tip turned bright red. Her eyes stared into mine while smoke bubbled out of her mouth.

"You didn't answer me—where ya been?" She tossed her cigarette to the ground.

I rolled my shoulders. "Let's just say I've been changing my ways, cleaning up for a few days." I leaned back into the cool block wall, right beside her, and stared at the discarded cigarette, watching as it slowly burned out. Raven's lips were big with bright orange lipstick, half of which was left on the end of her cigarette.

"You got popped, huh?" she chided. "At least while you're in that jail cell you're not off doing them nasty-ass drugs." She did a head nodding gesture that reminded me of my mother. Her eyes narrowed in on me, even as I tried to divert my gaze.

"Who was the woman?" I pointed toward the same spot in back. "I'd heard about the murder on the news. Was it anyone we knew?" I hated to hear of death. It made me think of the poor family members and loved ones who were left behind to sort through their misery.

"I guess she was a tenant in our complex, college age, real pretty young girl according to the store clerk. That's all I know." Raven shook her arms overhead. Jingles from her bracelets rang out. "She lived in one of the buildings at the front of the complex, near everyone's *favorite* landlord. Omid told her he spoke to the cops when they searched her apartment. They told him she suffered a brutal death. Her throat was slit, she'd been raped, her panties were missing, yet her purse had all its contents, ruling out robbery." Raven shook her head, her afro moved wildly.

"Omid told you all that, huh? Since when do you call him Omid? He insists on everyone else calling him Mr. Faranghi."

"I guess I am special." Her blank stare said something else.

"Her panties were taken? Why would he know that?" I guess it was a rhetorical question because Raven's stare was unbroken.

I couldn't believe she wasn't even the slightest bit more nervous. She stood around and waited for Johns to proposition her. Any one of them could be the killer.

"It sounds like a freaky pervert is out killing people. I can't believe they would inform the victim's landlord of such details. It is still an open murder investigation. Isn't it?" I stared at her. She was still off in her thought, not answering my question. Just hearing her say his name made my stomach queasy. "You got another one of those?" Raven already had a new cigarette hanging from her plump lips.

"That man has his ways of getting information." She reached back into her well endowed bosom, pulling from it a pack of cigs.

304

She lit mine off hers, and then stuck the cigarette in my mouth. "He usually gets what he wants." She drew hard on her cigarette, while her eyes blankly stared at something.

"Thank you, darling." To draw her eyes in, I touched her arm softly, noticing a few bruises on the underside of her bicep. I said nothing. But the look I conveyed while taking the cigarette was one of sympathy. Also of gratitude, the cigarette tasted awesome.

Her hand went to my cheek. "You've always treated me with respect. I like that about you, Jason." She turned her gaze back toward her money-making corner. "I need to get back to work. A girl has got to make a livin'.'" Her smile was crooked. She tugged at her short, very tight skirt, shoved her breasts even further up and out of the top of her blouse and then leaned in for a peck on my cheek. "Jason, you handsome thing, I'll see ya 'round." She went to spin around when I stopped her.

"Raven, wait!" I reached for her hand and held it in mine. Her long fingernails curled over my skin. "I wouldn't ask you if I wasn't so fucking desperate." She had to have heard the tone of weakness in my voice.

She flipped her big floppy hair back off her face, and looked at me through her long, thick, fake eyelashes. "One night, Sugar— that's all. I can't do anymore than that. The couch is all yours 'til morning. And you got to wait a few more hours 'til Mama makes some money before we go back to the apartment." She winked and strutted over to the street.

I yelled after her. "I'm right here. I'm keeping an eye on you, girl. I'll wait all night if I have to." I took in a drag of smoke, savoring the taste of willpower, feeling as though I'd jumped the first major hurdle of escaping my addiction. Having a place to go was crucial. "Thanks Raven!" I loudly called out. Then I heard myself repeating the words in a whisper. *"Thanks Raven, Thanks Raven, Thanks Raven."*

I spied a car slow along the curb. Raven leaned in the passenger window. The door swung open. She dropped inside the front seat. Away they went. I leaned back into the wall of the convenience store and slid to my seat on the sidewalk where I was able to spy a dude I knew selling dime-bags of crack on the opposite side of the street.

Raven referred to herself as Mama even though she really wasn't much older, and probably was never anyone's actual mother. I suppose it was because she had had so much life behind her in such little time that she seemed so mature, older. She was what they'd call, *wise beyond her years*. She lived in the same complex just one building over from mine. She had the grueling task of fucking fat-ass men to pay her rent and keep food on her table. That was what she knew.

The multitude of cars pulled in and out of the store. Some came for gas, others for milk and bread, and plenty of people came to this store for beer. Countless twelve-packs went out the front doors while I waited for Raven to return. Pacing along the sidewalk bordering the store, I desperately needed to figure out a way to get my things—my tools and all my stuff—out of my apartment. I was useless without my tools. I couldn't earn money—legally that is.

Each time the thought of responsibility and commitment arose, or even the idea of actually doing what I said I would do, the drug cravings began to eat away at my confidence. I gawked at the drug dealer standing on the corner, across the street in front of the pawn shop. His victims kept coming and going, pumping his pockets full of money and his black book full of promises.

Memories of my ghastly acts and all my past crimes began to bombard me. It was the pain of those memories that I wanted to escape, and meth allowed me to do that. Unfortunately, as a sober, clear-headed person, the bombardment never stopped. It was like a photo album in my head. The pictures were clear, 3-D, and very fucking real. That had always been my problem. I'd never learned to cope with the constant remembrance of so many things that went wrong in my life, most of which were brought on by my own foolish behavior. I knew I needed to learn to cope. I also knew that they were a permanent part of my past. *But knowing doesn't make it so.* That was something my dad always said, right after he'd mockingly say, "You think you're so damn smart."

* * *

Hours had passed and all I could do was wait for Raven. I milled around the front of the convenient store, the parking lot, the gas pumps, the ice machine, and the trash cans watching Raven come and go with clients. First was an old four-door Oldsmobile, then a Chevy, a Jeep, then a Ford truck, even a little Mini Cooper swung in for some drive-up sex. I knew she did some of her tricks in the car, so I couldn't help but get a laugh at the dude in the Mini Cooper. I could picture Raven and her wide behind backing up on him in the tight quarters of his little ride.

When a black Hummer pulled to the curb, I watched nervously as Raven proceeded to get into the vehicle with three men. Those two hours she was gone were an eternity. But when Raven returned, the skip in her step when she moved toward me indicated she had made her quota for the night.

She waved me to follow her. Soon we were approaching the door to her apartment. "Why are we running to get home?" Raven was walking so quick I had to hustle to keep up.

"It's Wednesday night." She flipped her cigarette into the gravel. "I never know if he's going to drop in. But Wednesday nights seem to be a favorite. He gets mad if I'm not around." She moved a flowerpot beside her door and grabbed a key that was hidden beneath.

"It is almost one o'clock in the morning!" *Who is he?* I wondered who it was that had that much control over her. "I thought you were on your own, you know, no boss, no man, if you know what I mean." I stood back and looked around while waiting for Raven to open the door.

The apartment complex looked a hell of a lot better at night. Darkness covered the worst of its flaws. And Raven's entrance was the nicest around—with flower pots, a small painted bench, with a door decoration, one that might give the impression someone religious lived here.

"I don't have a pimp, if that's what you mean. No one controls me. I do this man because it benefits me. It makes my life easier." She opened the door wide and gestured for me to enter. "All I am gonna say is, if he comes in that front door, you better be asleep."

"I thought you had a rule about paying customers in your house." I held the door and forced her to go in first. This way she had to look me in the eye when she answered.

"He's not a john, he's the landlord." She didn't blink an eye.

I was left speechless. The guy was sickening. Now I felt even sorrier for Raven than ever before. How could I stay there knowing he would eventually come? The minute the door swung shut, she kicked off her high platform heals, peeled off her wig, and slung it to the chair in the corner of the living room. She began to vigorously rub her head while moaning about her sore feet. She walked over to a closet, drew out a pair of sheets and a pillow, returned across the room to the couch in the far corner, and took a few minutes to make it into my bed for the night.

Raven's house smelled of vanilla. Everything was clean and in its place. Family photos were on her wall, magazines were spread across the ottoman, and wrapped candies were in a bowl in the middle of the dining room table. Raven went to the kitchen and prepared a pot of coffee. I watched as she lay out a paper towel underneath two cups, a spoon, sugar, sweetener, and a container of dry creamer. No one would ever think the person who lived in this apartment was a street walking hooker.

"I set the timer on this to pop on at 8:00 a.m. We can share a cup of coffee together before you get an early start." That was her nice way of telling me I'd be hitting the road early in the morning.

A newspaper sat atop the kitchen bar, opened to the want ads. I wondered what kind of job Raven might be qualified for. I saw the highlighter next to the paper, but noticed nothing was marked. I felt sad—for Raven and for me. I watched her carefully remove a dainty gold chain from her neck, which could barely be seen through the other layers of larger, much flashier beaded necklaces. She took the chain and pendant over to a small dish on the kitchen window sill where she carefully placed it.

"Raven, why the half heart?" The adorned piece was one part of a broken heart. "Who has the other half?" It was easy to see the feelings the keepsake evoked.

"Do you really want to know?" She leaned on the kitchen bar and tilted onto her elbows, her face directly in front of mine.

"I really want to know." I could see a slight embarrassment in the way she hesitated.

"No one has the other half, I threw it away. This half," she turned and picked up the jagged heart, "for me, this half represents the best part of me. Once I got rid of my demons, and kicked that bitch *Crystal Meth* to the curb, honey, I knew my life would change. I was a good hearted person before all that shit, and this heart reminds me of that."

She kissed the piece of precious metal and placed it back in its safe spot. "One of these days, and I mean soon, this girl ain't gonna be doin' no more street walkin'." She was hopeful. I don't know why, but I believed her. She always made it seem like tomorrow was going to be okay. Tonight was no different.

I walked around the breakfast bar. "Thanks again, Raven. I'm out of here first thing in the morning. I promise. I really appreciate this." I wrapped my arms around her and awkwardly kissed her on the side of the head. "Thanks for everything," I whispered in her ear and gave her an extra long squeeze. "You're a good person. I really owe you one—a really, really big one." Her short, tight curls scratched my nose.

"Stay off drugs!" she snapped. "That alone would be payment enough. You are much better than that. It is time you started to see your potential, Mister. Now get some sleep. Mamma's gonna put a razor in the bathroom for ya. Maybe you ought to think about using it in the morning. It always makes me feel better when I look better."

"Yes, Mamma," I playfully responded.

"Just 'cause you been in jail don't mean you gotta look like it. Besides, I kinda like that baby face of yours, and that sexy dimple on your chin." She lightly stroked my bristled face before walking away. She turned off the lights, leaving a dim nightlight on in the hallway before walking into her bedroom and shutting the door.

I strolled over to the sofa. Raising my arms high above my head, I took a deep breath into my lungs, an inhalation of relief— relief I was off the streets for this one night. A slice of moonlight pressed though the front room curtains casting my stretching shadow upon the couch and the wall behind. I twisted around and kicked out of my shoes. Retrieving the items from my pant pockets, I laid them out on the coffee table in front of the sofa. My pockets empty, I dropped my slacks to the floor and stepped out of them while pulling my shirt over my head. Rolling my shirt in a knot, I knelt down, grabbed my pants off the floor, folded them, and set the clothes on top of my shoes, before dropping my long body onto the couch.

I was extremely tired. I stretched out and instantly realized the sofa was too short for my long legs. I smashed my head deep into the fluffy pillow Raven had set out for me, pulled my knees in a bit and began to melt into the sofa. The smell of fresh, clean sheets was especially nice after the stench of that jail cell. I could barely hold my eyes open, yet I was uneasy about falling asleep. My mind raced with the things I needed to do.

My gaze fell to the items I'd left on the table beside the couch. My old wallet, my grandfather's knife, a few coins, and the cross I'd made for my mother, along with a half-smoked cigarette and a pack of matches. I realized if I couldn't get back into my apartment, all of my worldly possessions could be held in the front pocket of a pair of pants. I closed my eyes and prayed to all of my angels, and to God, to please help give me strength. Strength to stay sober, strength to be a better man, and strength to have the courage to find Amber and apologize for what I did to her all those years ago.

My insides stirred and rolled. My mind was agitated—not only at the thoughts of my past, but at the idea that my landlord could walk through the door at any moment to take advantage of this very nice, giving and kind individual in the other room.

I heard the shower running, and the sound of a television blaring in the background. Both were sounds, which for me, had a relaxing quality. My body twitched, my eyes began to droop, and my face muscles relaxed. I was comfortable, peaceful, my mind, my body, came to rest, finally.

Crossroads

Chapter Twenty-Six

Samantha 'Sam' Green

I woke early this morning, way earlier than I was used to, hoping to get to work and catch up on the things I had neglected before leaving last night. I longed for sleep, but my mind battered me with images and emotions, visualizations I needed to receive while conscious rather than slumbering.

This morning there would be no time for meditative affirmations to prepare me for my day. I walked out of my bedroom and heard Madison stirring. She was already awake, just like yesterday, drinking coffee and doing school work. This time she was sitting at the kitchen table.

Immediately upon seeing me, she began chattering. "Good morning. How's your week going?

"Fine," I lied, while rubbing the sleep out of my eyes.

"Have you seen your grandmother? She's been working awfully hard to make tomorrow special. All she can think about is your birthday. I just love that woman. I've talked to her more in the past few days than I have in all the years I've know her." She kicked back on the wood chair, balancing on the back two legs, making me a nervous wreck, her gaze followed me around the kitchen.

"Yeah, I've seen Gram, and I've talked to her several times. I am glad she is having so much fun planning my party." I stretched my arms overhead. "I'm sure it will be great fun." I didn't want to be a total bummer. I dragged my feet across the kitchen to the cabinets.

"What are your plans for tonight? Can you feed Charlie later, scoop his poop? I'll be in late." Besides the usual morning conversation, it seemed Madison was unusually eager to converse— probably because I was in a hurry and had little time for the exchange. She stood, walked over to me, and put her hand on my shoulder. "You okay?

"Yeah, I'm all right, just been really busy, and I am in a bit of a hurry this morning, that's all." I leaned into the countertop.

"Your grandmother seemed to think you had a lot on your mind. 'Too much,' she said. But she wouldn't elaborate. She said something about 'talking of it might give it legs,' whatever that means."

It was too early in the morning to have so many questions launched my way. I yawned, not overly eager to engage. "You know Gram, if she didn't have something to worry about, she'd make it up." I opened the cabinet and took out my tea mug.

Madison's softer side had appeared, out of the blue, as it frequently did, always unexpected. Her sincerity, earnest as it was, often caught me off guard. She must have noticed that I was a little melancholy, so she prepared my cup of tea and followed me through the house talking. She even offered to iron my top and slacks, something I never took the time to do. I brushed my teeth while she talked about her week, her homework, the birthday party, and all she was going to do to help my grandmother with the gathering. I thought it odd she totally avoided the whole media attack and death penalty case.

While I slid into my clothes, Madison stood in the hallway and let me know her father was taking some tables, chairs, and coolers over to Gram's for the festivities. And her mother was bringing some of her Mexican specialties, which was great because I loved spicy food, especially hers. My gram's friends were all going to be bringing something to eat, as well. Usually it would be some kind of casserole, maybe a veggie platter, and a few salads. And Ms. Beth insisted on supplying the cake and ice cream.

While I stepped into my shoes and pulled my hair up, we cleared up the plans for Madison to use my car tomorrow. She wanted to take me to my office, work half a day at the courts, help out Gram with the last minute party preparations, and then pick me up from work, come home, change clothes, and deliver me to the celebration. Madison's smile and the brightness in her eyes all said she was happy with her role. I followed her back to the kitchen and watched her feed and give water to Charlie as his furry body crisscrossed her ankles.

One more day until my birthday—my twenty-fifth birthday—a special one by most accounts, especially for anyone who was inheriting a large sum of money, yet I was not excited about the leading up to this significant milestone in my life. Instead of the guessing game I usually played with myself, mischievously trying to figure out what imaginative gift my gram would conjure up, I was delving into depressing thoughts, unclear intentions, and the presence of something dark in my very near future. The uncommonly cheery tone in Madison's voice wasn't helping me feel any better.

"What is going on with you? You seem lighter, more at ease. Considering what you've been through in the last few days, this isn't what I would expect." I used both hands to grip my cup of tea as I slurped and stared at Madison.

"I've been thinking about everything in my life, and you're right, Sam, I do have a negative edge to my personality. At times, it's a sharp, bitter one, an edge that I want to lose. One that is often misunderstood. I've thought about it, and I don't want to be angry anymore. I want to be more engaging. I want, like you say, 'to rise up and greet life every day.'" Madison returned to the kitchen table and flipped open her computer. "I've got homework to finish for class tonight." It was obvious she was uncomfortable with the emotional truth she had just shared.

"Why the sudden change of heart?" I waited for her to look up and then I stared right between her eyes, just above her nose, directly at Madison's brow chakra. Gram always called that the third eye, the eye of wisdom. I noticed a hazy orange halo of color around her head. Her aura was signaling signs of power, inspiration, and encouragement.

She did look up, bringing my gaze into hers. "I went to Miracle House last night, spent some time with little Desiree. Something about being in that nursery makes me see life in a different way. It forces me to remember everyone was a child once. And going there last night helped me to see that we don't all have choices of what happens in our lives—especially our very young lives."

She paused and tipped back her huge coffee mug, her swallow was loud. The house was particularly quiet. The morning sun was beginning to push through the blinds. "*Forgiveness*—isn't that what you said?" Madison stared at my face. "'To err is human, to forgive is divine.' I've decided I'm really going to work on it. Just saying the words to myself and firmly placing the idea in my head makes me feel better already." Madison smiled wide, then jumped out of her chair and darted to Charlie's water bowl, where she rescued a small moth that had just mistakenly splashed in.

I watched her gently carry the wet insect to the back door, where she carefully released it, onto a plant on the back porch. She then returned to the table and back to our conversation. When Madison spoke of forgiveness, especially to the point of quoting Alexander Pope, I honestly couldn't tell if she was mocking me or being sincere.

"I'm proud of you, Madison. If you can forgive that man for what he did to Lisa, your life will move on in the most positive way. I promise. Being conscious is the first place to start." I turned and set my empty tea cup in the sink, wheeled back around and grabbed my bag off the back of the chair that was now acting as a cradle for the cat.

"Oh no, I can't forgive him for what he did to my little cousin." Madison's tone was suddenly imposing. "I am finally certain of that, Sam. What I want to know is that that murdering bastard is dead, and the sooner the better. It's too bad they can't make him suffer in fear like he did Lisa, or anguish, like my poor Uncle Joe. I'm sorry, Sam, but I am surer than ever about my feelings. I know once he is gone from this earth, and punished for his crime, I will finally begin to forgive myself for not waking to save Lisa."

I was dumbfounded—speechless. I wondered if my face told Madison the real truth of what I was feeling. Stunned! Her hateful words, even though they were of a hateful man, shocked me deeply. A sentiment I felt the need to turn away from. I could not find any words. I wrapped myself in my sweater and slung the strap of my purse over my shoulder and stared down at her. dumbfounded, I tried to unearth any positive thing to say. I just watched her save an insect from a certain doom. Yet there she was—a total contradiction.

I had to remind myself Madison was a work in progress. Forgiveness was a giant step for her, kind of like being outside the gates of prison for the first time after many years of captivity—her own mental prison, but a prison nonetheless. However from my point of view, there was another set of gates that kept Madison enslaved.

Madison set her empty coffee cup on the table and began nervously pecking at her computer keys. My gaze went to her throat, then to her heart chakras, where I could see a shady dull band, brown in color. Madison was unsettled, distracted, and unclear with her thoughts. These couldn't be her true feelings. It all made sense to me now. I could see these comments coming from her father, but not from her.

I took in a deep breath and carefully contemplated my words before speaking. "Forgiving *yourself* is a start, Madison. A choice that isn't always clear in our heads." I stood beside her until she looked me in the face. "Nevertheless, we need to make the forgiveness crystal clear to our hearts or the transformation won't be complete. The connection of the head to the heart is essential."

I knew that in her heart Madison was still unsure how to move forward. I choked out the words in a reverent tone. The murky aura that was present around Madison's heart center wasn't uncommon. But, for today, I decided, I had bigger issues.

"Have a nice day, Madison." I tapped her shoulder, my hand lingered with the expectation my energy, bad as it was today, was still better than hers. I hoped that our connection would somehow jumpstart her morning. Instead, it was her energy that shot back through my body. Like an erupting volcano, it was like hot lava burning through my veins, right up to the moment I released my grip. *Happy birthday week to me,* I thought.

* * *

A gut-wrenching angst carried me out of the house, and all the way to work. By the premonitions I'd been receiving, I was certain the palpable warning was of some future event. Now I wondered if Madison could have something to do with it. The sensations of uneasiness—of disquiet I was feeling—suggested the impending disaster was soon to be upon me. I hated to use the term "gut feeling" because so many people who have absolutely zero intuition often use the phrase to express a hunch, in most cases, a guess. But the sensations that were pulsating through my body tended to occur just prior to disasters, accidents, deaths and other traumatic and emotionally charged events. Still, the details weren't coming to me easily, so I figured I had time—time to figure it all out, and time to try and protect the ones I loved.

As I came through the entrance to my job, I couldn't help but pause and glance at my reflection in the mirror in the foyer of Last Chance. Why anyone would ever want the victims of so much pain to have to look at themselves first, I'll never know.

The bright light in the vestibule wasn't very welcoming. It caused me to squint as I stared at my mirror image. Since my stone reading had indicated I was part of the premonition, if not right in the middle of whatever was to come, I found myself regularly looking for color changes in my own aura.

Usually, my aura was generally colorful bands, kind of like hula hoops, often cleaner and brighter than others I came in contact with. According to experts with, whom I've studied over the years, the vivid clear aura represents openness and spirituality. As I gazed at my color bands, they were typically brilliant, but the brightness I'd become accustomed to glimpsing in the mirror was now muted. If it were to become white, that was when I'd really begin to freak out. Several hours before death, the aura becomes white and greatly increases with intensity. Just like Willie's aura was yesterday, just before I put him in an ambulance and sent him to the hospital. That incident still had me shaking inside.

I buzzed myself through the security access. It was quiet, earlier than the normal shift change. Few people were around. I walked past the admittance area to my office and went to my desk. There I began going through my note pad and to-do list, when I heard my muffled phone ringing. I dug it out of my purse and answered. It was Gram. We spent a few minutes talking, we said our "I love you's" and we hung up. This week, for some reason, or many reasons, my grandmother had been calling me more often than usual. Asking me silly questions about this or that, teasing me about getting old, all along slipping in a little lawyer talk about trusts, insurance, and investments, all before ever getting to the real reason for her call—my well being.

I placed my cell phone on the desk and then stood and peeled my sweater off, wrapping it on the back of my chair. As Gram aged, if she didn't have something to worry about, she would dig it up out of nowhere. This time, no digging was necessary. I really hated the fact that she witnessed me totally freak out at her house the other night. I know it didn't help her anxiety. She wouldn't say, but perhaps she, too, was an eyewitness to my future. Maybe she, herself, had seen something chilling in my path. Maybe that was why her fretting was turned up a notch.

*   *   *

Lost, completely immersed in my work, I finally lifted my gaze across the office to the clock on the wall. It was past nine and Ethan hadn't shown up for work yet. I stood and walked around the facility and asked everyone about him. No one had heard from him. My suspicious mind went into a panic. *My vision!* Of course my thoughts were going to run in a crazy direction when one of my best friends was an hour late for work, especially when he was rarely ever late at all. I mean, as irresponsible as I might think Ethan was, he never missed work.

I rushed back to my desk and grabbed my cell phone. I'd missed a call from Gram. I wasn't sure if that was before or after I had talked to her. I dialed Ethan, only to hear his voicemail. I snapped my phone shut. I leaned into my desk, my throat tightened, Ethan's face flashed in my psyche. Then Bradley was suddenly at the forefront of my mind—I couldn't totally make out the images. They were together, they seemed happy, laughing, playful, when suddenly, arguing—blood, screaming and crying became vivid imagery in my head.

My phone rang out, startling me back to reality. "Ethan! Where are you?" My emotion poured into my phone.

"Sweetheart, it's just me again. Your grandmother. Samantha, Honey, I felt a sudden urge to call you." She had a curious quality to her voice. "Are you okay? Is everything alright?"

"Gram, I can't talk. Someone here at work needs me. I'll call you later." I hung up. Something told me she already had an idea of what I might be struggling with.

I redialed Ethan, and still there was no answer.

Crossroads

Chapter Twenty-Seven

Ethan Price

I was dressed and ready for work when I opened the door to find him standing in the threshold. Startled and surprised, I couldn't budge. He grinned broadly before covering my mouth with his palm, silencing my cries. He leaned in quickly and grabbed me around the waist, thrusting our bodies back into the house before kicking the front door shut behind him. His strength was overwhelming. Who was this man overpowering me, stripping off my clothes? This was not the Bradley I knew.

As we tussled about in the front room of my apartment, an animal magnetism had taken over Bradley. He pulled my snug tee-shirt over the top of my head, undid my belt and took my pants down to my knees. His mouth felt like fire against mine. Our tongues moved inside of our mouths with vigor. He nipped gently at my lower lip while dropping his pants to the ground. Then he sensually sucked my lip between his as our kiss grew deeper. His arm reached around my body, gripping me tightly. He spun my body around to face the countertop at the end of my kitchen bar.

His wet mouth glided across my exposed skin like a flame lighting a trail of fire. He nuzzled my neck, my back. I felt his hand push my upper body to lie across the flat bar. His touch was hot and insistent. I was feeling warmer and warmer as his hardness pressed

323

against me. I shivered beneath his touch. I hadn't questioned his appearance, not yet. While I was bent over on the bar, with his foot, he gently spread my ankles apart, and then he pressed his body firmly against mine.

His hand locked to my hips. I clung to the cabinet, gasping for air. He pushed harder and harder, causing me to feel pain and pleasure all at once. Just when I thought I could not take anymore, Bradley erupted. He held his arm tightly around my waste as I slowly relaxed my muscles. He hugged me up close to him, slowly swiveling my body back around. We were now eye to eye. My naked ass pressed into the cool kitchen cabinet. Our pants remained on the floor.

"I want you to know you don't take a backseat to anyone." He cupped my chin in his hand. "Now do you believe me?" He forced our eyes together. "I'm telling you, Ethan, I want to be with you. But I do have other pressing things in my life. And because I have those responsibilities doesn't mean I wouldn't rather be here, with you." He looked around. "Okay, maybe not here," he chuckled, then pulled his pants back up around his waist and fastened them.

I dressed myself. I felt full of life, easily forgetting all about being stood-up for dinner last night. "I can't tell you how surprised I am." I tenderly ran my hand against his face. Our eyes playfully fixed on each other while we gathered ourselves.

"Sure you can," he said, smiling out of the side of his mouth as he fixed his tie. "It's easy. All you need to say is, 'Bradley, I am so surprised to see you. Thanks for taking the time for me this morning.'" He used a mocking tone, pretending to speak like me. He leaned in and kissed me on the neck while I tucked my shirt back into my jeans. "Do you think those pants could be any tighter?" he teased, pulling at my belt loop.

"Oh, so this is how it's going to be? You give me a little time and you think you can tell me how to dress." I straightened the collar of his shirt, and fixed his jacket, then playfully bit at his lip.

My phone was ringing. I didn't answer it. I was sure it was work. What was I going to say? *Oh, sorry I'm running late. My lover dropped in for a quickie this morning. It couldn't be helped. I'll be in just as soon as I regain my strength after the orgasm he gave me.*

"I need to get going." Bradley moved toward the door.

"Yeah, me too."

"I'm glad I caught you before you left."

"Yeah, me too."

"I tried calling, but you didn't answer my call." He reached around and used my belt loop to pull me in. "So, I just took a chance and dropped in on you."

"I'm really glad you did." I kissed him hard on the mouth, thinking to myself—*maybe I should avoid more of his calls.* I took my hand and placed it over his crotch. His pants could not conceal the hardness. "I know someone else who is glad you did, too. When will I see you again? I mean, really *see* you again. Like a date?"

"How about tomorrow?" He leaned against my front door and waited for my response.

"That's Friday. Its Samantha's twenty-fifth birthday. Her grandmother is throwing her a big party. I wouldn't miss it. And since you aren't her favorite person, it might not make for a good date night. " I nudged him and smiled.

So?" Bradley held his ground and held my gaze. "I'm finally coming out of the closet, I'm giving up my family, and we are planning to live together, the least Samantha can do is trust that I love you. Eventually she is going to have to give in because I'm not going anywhere. I thought she was your most accepting, non-judgmental, forgiving friend? " He raised his brow and turned away from me while moving toward the front door. A manly smell of cologne trailed him.

"Are you saying you want to come with me to her party?" I followed him, surprised by his interest to not only be with me, but to do it around other people.

His stopped and turned back. "There has to come a time when we let people know about our relationship. I've told my wife, I suppose you can tell *your* wife. Assuming you haven't already." Again, he pulled at my waist until our bodies pressed tightly together. He was the same man I'd known for years, yet he was so unlike himself. He was very different, changed. I liked this guy even more. I didn't know that was possible.

"If I wanted to have you be my date at Samantha's party, she would absolutely want you to be there." I called his bluff. "My wife likes to keep me happy, after all." I played his game.

"What time shall I pick you up?" He awaited my response. His leg brushed against mine, so casually that it might have been nothing, except for the fact that my adrenaline level soared.

"You can come by around 6:30." I opened my front door and watched him walk out. My heart pounded rapidly—him being here, both of us starting out our day together—I loved it. To think that this could be my future firmly planted a big smile on my face.

Bradley agreed to pick me up and go to Samantha's birthday party. I knew once I told Samantha everything, she would be good with him. At least I'd hoped she would be. She always said she wanted me to be happy. I know she hated that Bradley stayed committed to his wife while keeping me on the side for all these years. But Samantha didn't ever know the whole story. Hell I never knew the whole story.

I backed out of the entrance to my apartment, locked the door, and then strode onto the path toward the front of the complex. That is when I heard it. A bloodcurdling scream echoed through the cluster of buildings in my complex. The deep, spine-chilling screech was so loud I was sure some father had just discovered his wife had drowned all four of their children in the tub. Late for work already, I ignored the man's cry and ran toward Van Buren Street.

Chapter Twenty-Eight

Jason Magnus

I woke to a light beeping noise coming from across the room. Soon the aroma of coffee began to engulf my senses. My sleepy gaze wandered the small space. It took me a moment to realize where I was. But when I caught a glimpse of Raven's bushy wig on the chair in the corner, I quickly remembered I was homeless and sleeping on the couch of a prostitute, a prostitute who just happened to be a friend of mine. I slowly sat up and swung my crinkled legs over the edge of the sofa. My body felt like a twisted pretzel that had been crunched into the bottom of the bag. Apparently I hadn't moved since falling asleep. Exhausted, I basically fell on Raven's couch last night and became comatose.

Remaining on the couch, I sat in the pleasant aroma and allowed myself to fully awake. I yawned and stretched my arms overhead while basking in the scent. For me, the smell of coffee totally evoked a happy feeling. Even though I was homeless, without all of my things, my tools, a job, and my apartment, I was smiling. The tremors of my addiction were gone. Happy that I didn't wake up in jail today, I felt as though I was rising from the ashes, beginning to find my wings. Sleeping in my own bed would have been nice, but Raven's couch was better than jail or the streets any day or night. I felt a rush of gratitude flow through me.

I leaned over and drew my pile of clothes near and began to dress. I wanted to be quiet since I hadn't heard Raven stirring just yet. I was certain she would soon swing open the door and join me for that cup of coffee. But I knew how nice the last few minutes of sleep could be, and I didn't want to be the one to rob her of that.

Slivers of sunlight pressed through the curtains. I slid my shirt over my head. The morning air was chilly in the apartment. I stood and pulled the high-water khakis over my hips and buttoned them. The fact that they were too short didn't bother me today.

With light footsteps, I made my way to the bathroom. Raven had left a razor and a can of shaving cream with a fresh towel next to the sink. By the curly black hairs in the blades, I was certain this wasn't the first time it had been used. While washing up, shaving, splashing my face, rinsing my mouth, I looked with determination at the reflection staring back at me. Combing my hair with my wet hands, I again committed to staying sober. I promised myself I would finally go to Miracle House and take that first, very difficult step toward recovery.

I rehearsed the conversation with my landlord, over and over again in my head; my begging him nicely to give me my tools, convincing him this was the only way for me to make money and pay him back. I would pack up and leave my apartment immediately after retrieving my personal belongings. I leaned in close to the mirror, looked into my eyes, brighter blue today than they had been in months. My hand traced the outline of my chin, the dimple. My face felt clean, smooth, for the first time in a long time. It was nice—very nice. It took a few years off my street-worn look. Although I had a rough appearance, fortunately, I was still young enough to try to dispose of it.

As I wiped up my mess and finished my business in the bathroom, I mentally mapped out a walking route to Miracle House. I reviewed what I would say when I arrived. I wanted to convince them I knew I had hit bottom, and I was ready to turn my life over to a higher power. This time I would really mean it. I wanted them to understand I could earn my own keep with the trades I had taught myself over the years. I would contribute to the house in some way and work outside if needed. I stared into my reflection and tried to persuade myself I had something I could offer to someone.

When I came out of the bathroom there was still no noise coming from Raven's room. I went back over to the sofa and neatly folded my bedding, then sat and put on my socks and shoes. If I wanted to see Raven before I left, which I did, it was time to start making some racket. I was ready to have that cup of coffee with her before getting a start to my new life. But more than anything, I needed the pep-talk Raven was always so good at giving. The words of encouragement she often saved for others.

"Wake up sleeping beauty." I hollered toward her room from the kitchen as I poured two large mugs of coffee. I felt the heat from the steam that rose to my chin. I stood at the kitchen bar and read through the want ads for a moment before playfully raising my voice. "If you don't get out here I'm gonna drink all of your coffee." I intentionally loudly smacked my lips as I gulped from the hot mug.

I heard a loud bang, and thought it was Raven coming out of her room. I turned back from the kitchen and glared at her bedroom door. It remained still, slightly ajar. A door slammed, just before the rumble of feet on stairs could be heard rolling down just outside Raven's apartment. I peeked out the blinds over the kitchen sink, realizing all the noise had come from the neighbor who lived above. My stare followed the person as he hit the path and disappeared around the corner of the building.

I was disappointed Raven hadn't yet appeared. I walked over and leaned into the opening of her room.

"Come on, Raven," I playfully called to her. Don't forget, you put me on a time limit." My shoulder lightly brushed the door causing it to push back just enough to see Raven's blank stare.

On impulse, I let out a scream that could be heard around the world. A lightning bolt of shock went through my body. Instinctively, I snapped the door shut. Then I stood shaking, fearful and unsure of what to do next. I looked at the phone on the wall near the breakfast bar and thought about calling for help, but I was frozen in place.

My hand still gripped the doorknob. I had seen eyes like that once before. They were the eyes that belonged to a dead woman, someone who had probably overdosed, lying in a dark corner of a crack-house. Because I did nothing then, because I left her lying there, her eyes still haunted me today.

Upon taking a deep breath and saying a small prayer, begging God for strength, and then pleading for Raven to be alive, I opened the bedroom door and found Raven's naked body splayed across her bed. My heart was in my throat, pumping like a freight train. She was only partially covered by her tussled sheets, exposing parts of her cocoa skin, and a wisp of black pubic hair shaved into a thin line. I saw bruises on her legs and other parts of her body.

On impulse, I snatched at the sheet to cover her private parts. Raven's head was twisted awkwardly to one side. Then I saw the blood. It was all over her neck, the pillows, the bed—it was everywhere.

I fell back on my heels, stunned, I just stared, shooting pains stabbed at my chest. I was unable to wrap my fucking head around the horror scene. Raven's mouth lie gaping open, blood spilling from a deep slash on her neck, spreading out onto the bedding. Her throat was so badly cut her head seemed almost severed, propped on her pillow.

I turned away. I felt sick, queasy, dizzy. Bile rushed into my throat. I tried not to vomit. My thoughts were suddenly like a loud motorcycle racing through my mind. I had been sleeping in the next room. I couldn't understand how something like this could have happened. Then sadness overtook me. Poor Raven. My hands gripped my head.

I heard a strange voice. Then I realized it came from me. With little awareness, I had begun to sink to the floor, to pull on my hair, to cry. Once I regained myself and my nerve, I stood, turned, and took another look. I couldn't stop looking at Raven's face. *This poor woman.* She was the kind of person who got used to taking what was given to her and being grateful for it. And to now end up murdered like this seemed so unfair. She never was able to experience the life she deserved.

I used the heel of my hand to wipe away my tears. Then I stepped closer to the bed. One of Raven's arms rested out to her side, the other at the top of her head lying across the blood-soaked pillow. My chest ached from the effort of reining in my emotion. I stared at her hand covered in dried blood. I could see she was holding something shiny. Upon closer observation I about fell to the floor again when I noticed the item in Raven's hand was my grandfather's pocket knife.

I had just been slammed in the sternum by a fucking sledge hammer. All of a sudden my criminal mind took over and, without hesitation, I felt the need to cover up the crime. And it wasn't even my crime. On my mother's life, I couldn't figure out how my knife ended up in Raven's dead hand. I delicately reached between Raven's stiff fingers and slid the knife into my grasp. It was hard for me to believe my little knife caused that large slice. My heart was beating out of my chest. My mouth was dry and it was all I could do to keep from barfing everywhere.

Even as I held the cold keepsake in my hand, I still couldn't believe it was mine. I ran to the coffee table in the living room with the bloody item in my grip. Remembering I'd left my knife along with my mother's cross there before passing out last night, I approached the table, hoping to find my memento. But it wasn't there, and neither was my mother's cross.

I felt my legs wobble beneath me. I could see my wallet, the coins, and the half-smoked cigarette I felt the need to save. My grandfather's knife and the cross I had made for my mother were both missing. I knew I hadn't misplaced them, yet I found myself glancing around the room. I went to the bathroom and cleaned my knife with soap and water. In the medicine cabinet I found some alcohol and cotton swabs and used them to vigorously wipe the knife another time. I went into the kitchen and found a plastic grocery sack, grabbed the washcloth from Raven's sink, and began to use it as a protective glove.

I touched nothing else as I went around the apartment and wiped everything I could remember coming in contact with. *Like I could somehow trick the experts.* I returned all the bedding to the closet, folded it all as if it had never been used. The way Raven's one bedroom unit was positioned in the complex, the morning light flooded through all the slivers of space in the blinds and curtains. This added to my paranoia.

As I methodically retraced my every movement, I found I was muttering to myself, to Raven, apologizing for leaving her like this. Telling her I was sorry for not protecting her. Previously coming to the decision I would be disposing of a few things, I bagged the pillowcase I slept on, proving I had watched way too much TV. More evidence of that came when I grabbed the towel and razor I had recently used. Even worse, I poured the bleach I found on top of the washing machine down all the drains I had that could bare my DNA. I cleaned things better than I'm sure they had been in a long time, and Raven kept a clean home.

My eyes burned from the bleach. I whispered my regrets for disappointing her memory—both Raven's and my mother's. I returned to the kitchen for a final washing of my hands when I noticed the little dish on the window sill was empty. The broken heart that had been so carefully placed there last night was no longer in the dish. I was pissed.

Clear as all the mistakes I had ever made in my whole, in my entire, fucking life, I could remember Raven putting that necklace in that dish, just like I can recall leaving my knife and cross on the table next to the couch. Somebody came in and took them. Someone walked right in and slit Raven's throat—in the room right next to me as I slept on her couch. And now whoever it was wanted people to think it was me who had done it. Suddenly numbing my mind seemed like a good idea.

I know I didn't do this, but proving I didn't do it was another story. I might be a loser and an addict, but I was no killer. My mind pushed away the thought of running to drugs. It would be easy to run back to the streets, to the mindlessness the drugs offered, back to a place where my troubles and cares would never find me. But that was the story of my life, always doing what I thought was easy. I had always made the wrong decision. Being on drugs had never made my life easy. It just allowed me to escape the moments that were so difficult to bear. I knew there was no escaping this.

I knew I needed a *miracle* to get me out of the mess I was in. Yet, taking refuge at Miracle House no longer seemed like the best idea. I didn't know for sure where I was going, or what I was going to do, I only knew I needed to leave Raven's apartment. Now.

I made one last sweep of the apartment with my eyes, I grabbed the items I was taking with me, used the corner of the pillowcase to turn the doorknob, and I let myself out of the apartment. Looking first to make sure no one was in the area, I left Raven's for the last time. I hurriedly made my way off the grounds and away from the complex.

* * *

After leaving Raven's apartment, I probably went two miles into the morning sun before looking back. I stomped past the liquor store, two taco stands, the tire repair garage, and the auto body shop before I realized I was crying. I wanted to leave this life behind, yet I could feel it nipping at my heels. Picking up my maddening pace, I wanted badly to find a place where troubles would no longer find me. Unfortunately, I was fairly certain that place didn't exist, no matter how fast I was trying to get there.

In my grip, as if it were a bag of dirty laundry, was the pillowcase stuffed with everything I thought might bear my DNA. It was slung over my right shoulder pounding my backside with each step.

I roamed around to the rear of an exotic dance club that was set back off Washington Street. The parking lot was vacant, no cars and no people around that I could see. I lifted the lid of the big dumpster and tossed in the items I had taken from Raven's.

I quickly made my way back around to the front of the building and back out onto the Washington. I jogged across the street and began to head the opposite direction when I heard someone yelling my name.

The sudden jolt of fear and paranoia made me feel like I was going to throw up. I craned my head toward the cackling sound, recognizing the junkies on the corner, I decided to avoid them. I waved them off and kept walking briskly away from them. The coolness of the spring air brushed over my sweaty face.

No matter the weather or the time of year, there was always a certain smell on the streets. It was a smell I had begun to associate with drugs, poverty, pain, and now murder. I passed a hundred phone booths, each time my thought was to pick up the phone and dial 911, and each time I kept walking. All day I hid in the shadows, tensed at every noise, certain the cops would pull up to the curb any minute, jump out of their squad car, cuff me, and then arrest me and throw me back into that shithole for something I didn't do.

After hours of roaming, I finally found myself in Patriots Park downtown, where I rested on the lawn beneath a large pine tree— the same pine tree Amber and I had sat under so many years ago, most often on Thursdays. Today being Thursday, I realized it was no coincidence I was here. This park had been a place that for years had brought me comfort. It was a place that brought my thoughts to Amber, my past, and my future.

I much preferred watching people rather than being watched. People came and went as they strolled through the park. Some stopped to eat lunch; others took a break for a smoke, perhaps a phone call or two, and many were simply intent on hanging out in the slivers of sunshine offered through the canopy of trees. Even as I tried to sort my thoughts, they were still muddled with dread and apprehension.

I couldn't get Raven's dead stare of out of my mind. At this point I was unsure of what to do. My mother always said, "If you are unsure of what to do, it is often better to do nothing." So in this case, I took my mother's advice, while refusing to hear the voice in my head that sounded more like my father saying, *"Call the fucking police."*

When the spring afternoon warmed and the sun shone directly on me, I moved over to a shady spot on the other side of the park. Taking up a city block in the middle of town, the park wasn't really considered big, but it was spacious. There was no playground or dog area, yet kids and dogs often played here. It was mostly brick pathways meandering through the grass and trees, and seat-border planter beds, offering pedestrians shortcuts to a parking garage beneath the park, and skateboarders and bicyclists a trail to blaze.

I sat on a ledge of stone that held back a small mound holding a huge desert tree, and I gazed around the square. As the day ticked on, there was much more activity now than there had been earlier. Joggers were lapping the park. Mindless pedestrians enthralled with their cell phones strolled through. Business people were huddled on benches along the park's edges, and the occasional dog sniffed out his territory for doing his business.

Hungry, exhausted, and still extremely paranoid, I decided to move over toward a small brick building that housed the public restrooms. This was a more concealed place—less conspicuous than sitting in plain sight. There were also two big trash cans, and I noticed a few people had tossed their unfinished lunch, not to mention a few drinks that weren't quite empty. I'd been quite thirsty and the fountain water wasn't doing it for me. That is when I saw her.

There was a woman who resembled Amber. She was walking away from me, a small child in tow. Yelling out her name, saying I'm sorry for the world to hear, was the first thing that came to mind, before I caught myself. I couldn't believe it was Amber. Was it? I knew it was her. I'd know her anywhere.

I turned and began to follow her. Then I looked down at my clothes, the high-water pants, dirty shirt and old shoes. I realized only moments ago I was reaching into a garbage can, not to mention I was on the run from a murder scene. I stopped dead in my tracks.

Chasing her down wasn't an option. So instead I stood stunned and staring. I never knew she had a child with Bradley. My eyes followed her every move. I watched her hand move to her face to adjust her sunglasses. I noticed the way she clutched her purse under her left arm. Her hair flew back lightly as she walked out of my life, again.

The questions began to pound my mind, rapid fire starting with: Bradley, really? Who was the young boy? Could it be her son? Was he a nephew, some friend's kid?

Amber's ambling gait was the same as when we were kids; the smooth sway of her hips, her slow stride drew me in back then, and it attracted me still. She looked beautiful. She had hardly changed. The years had been good to her—much better than I had been. She was still graceful, her pale skin looked perfect; her body was youthful in the spring dress that clung gracefully to her.

I watched her stand at the corner waiting for the traffic light to change. Even now, as she lovingly stroked the child beside her, and then squeezed him close while crossing the busy street, I could see the gentleness that she carried with her to adulthood. She had a tenderness I desperately missed.

When they hit the curb on the other side of the street the young boy abruptly swung his gaze in my direction. When I spied his face a lump the size of my fist crawled down my throat. It was the dimple right at the point of his chin that caused my knees to buckle. I gasped for air, once more I wanted to call to Amber, but I didn't. I returned to the small brick building in the middle of the park, where I knelt and then sat on the ground. Once again defeated, I'd been slapped with the reality of what once was, and what could have been. Bradley had married my Amber and they had a son, a son who resembled me. *How could it be?* I put my head in my hands and began to cry. I didn't care that people thought I was the crazy man in the park. It didn't matter to me that strangers were witnessing a loser hit bottom.

*   *   *

The agonizing minutes turned to excruciating hours. Then it was rush-hour, and the people were like ants crawling through the park, along the city streets, the shops and restaurants. The entire area was bustling. I had finally begun to gather myself after seeing Amber.

I looked up and saw the woman from court coming toward me. When she made an obvious attempt not to catch my eye, I knew she had not only seen me, but recognized me. It was time for me to get on the move. I watched her enter the coffee shop across the street from the park before I took off. To where—I didn't have a clue. The sun was setting over the city as I began to walk into the maze of high-rises, the tangled web of prostitution, crack-houses and drug-infested back alleys. These were the familiar stomping grounds that had been my doom.

Chapter Twenty-Nine

Madison Morgan

I sat on the bus as it rambled past each block, headed toward my Thursday night law class. My mind raced back through the day. It was another grueling one. Knowing I was taking half a day off tomorrow in order to help Sam's grandmother get ready for the party, I basically had to do twice the work in half the time. Court business didn't stop for anyone, especially the clerk. But it could be rearranged, and that was the advantage to running the courtroom and controlling the calendar.

My body rocked forward and then back with each start and stop of the bus. People flooded in and out. There was standing room only, and I was sitting, feeling a bit caged in.

Since leaving the house this morning, Samantha had been on my mind. I spoke to her twice today, each time she was over-stressed about all the crazy visions she had been having. And it didn't help when first thing this morning she couldn't reach Ethan. Thank God he walked into the office while I was on the phone with her.

But unfortunately it proved her vision wrong, leaving her to mentally scramble for the meaning to her images. I hated to minimize her predictions because I have seen so many of them come true. But I couldn't stand to see Sam put so much weight behind forecasting future events, especially when they involved people she knew. I didn't like seeing her under that kind of pressure, especially when she should be happy to be turning twenty-five, and thrilled to never have to worry about money again.

We zoomed past the beautiful Central Library, with its mix of steel, aluminum, concrete, and glass which was reflecting the setting sunlight. The sight of the Phoenix Art Museum and Park Central Mall indicated my stop was upcoming. I clutched my personal things and braced myself on the edge of my seat, nudging the guy in front of me to let him know I would be standing. I glanced at my watch, happy to know I had a few extra minutes to pop into one of my favorite coffee shops adjacent to the law school.

The bus slogged to a stop and the doors slid open. I heard my stomach growl as I pushed through the oncoming crowd to exit. Sweat and cigarette smoke jolted my senses as I pushed through the pack of people. I heard myself mumble something about the second-hand smoke, the smell, and how it would kill others. *People were so inconsiderate.*

I quickstepped down the sidewalk. My plan was to cut through the park to get to the coffee shop sooner. I bolted across the street to beat an oncoming car. I relaxed my stride when I hit the meandering brick walk through the park. Right as I passed the concrete building that held the public restrooms I noticed him. The man who had been in my courtroom only days ago was leaning into the wall. It wasn't uncommon for me to see defendants I recognized, mostly because I lived in the inner-city and used public transportation much of the time. He looked different without the jailhouse orange jumpsuit and the scraggly, whiskered face. But his eyes—his intense blue eyes—were unforgettable, currently looking sad rather than irritated and angry.

We both turned away from each other just as our eyes met. It seemed he, too, recognized me. This was a downtown park. Homeless people found refuge here. City dwellers jogged in

Patriot's Park. Business folks would eat their lunch in the park, and mothers brought their children to play in this park.

The area was bustling with activity. I stood at the curb and waited for a break in traffic before darting across the street. This time I took the crosswalk. The last of the day's shadows filtered through the tall buildings of downtown. I strolled into the coffee shop, whiffed the aroma that immediately gave me comfort, and I plopped into a small booth in the corner, facing the large flat-screen television on the wall.

The waitress must have seen me glance at my watch. She came right over and quickly took my order of an iced coffee and a club sandwich. I didn't have much time, but I had enough to have a bite to eat. I exhaled absolutely all the air from my lungs, and then I leaned back and waited for my dinner. When I glanced up to the TV on the wall, the national news anchor had just tossed it off to another reporter in a courtroom drama that was playing out on the other side of the country.

It was the sentencing trial of a serial killer. Not the best dinnertime TV, unless one were a courtroom junkie, like me. He was to receive eight consecutive life terms for the murders of four women and three young girls. I watched with great interest as the report highlighted bits and pieces of the victims' families' impact statements—something I was all too familiar with. I knew just how difficult it was to put into words the impact the murder of a loved one had.

The restaurant noise was almost deafening. I really had to focus in on the television to hear what they were saying. One at a time, as these victims of violence approached the podium, their tearful statements were all consistent with: "I hope you rot in hell, you son of a bitch," and "You are not God." "Why my daughter?" "Why my wife?" "It was not your right to decide who lived and who died."

The murdering defendant sat stoic and hard, unfazed by their words or their grief, his eyes narrowed, seemingly full of hate. The camera hovered on his heartless expression. Hatred bubbled in my throat. The waitress brought my iced coffee to the table, set it down, and left.

Glued to the TV, I stirred sweetener into the Styrofoam cup and watched the real life drama unfold. It wasn't until a small woman, the mother of a twelve-year-old murder victim, stood and faced the killer and spoke that something inside of me softened. There she was, this tearful woman talking to a handcuffed defendant in the courtroom. She explained how her life was changed forever when he kidnapped her beautiful twelve-year-old daughter from her father's rural home. After a three-day statewide search for her—a search that included hundreds of volunteers, state, local, federal law enforcement, *and* the killer—only to have him later confess to the FBI that he had taken the young child, along with so many other victims.

I heard myself shushing the people clanging around me as this woman told a story very similar to mine. I leaned in.

She went on. "You are sick," the woman said, with a softness to her tone. "I wanted to hate you for what you did to my daughter. I have come to believe I will never know why you chose to rape and strangle her."

I could see the woman fight to keep her composure. She paused and drew a tissue from the podium she was speaking from, and she composed herself before continuing.

"When I found out what you had done to my baby, I wanted to die with her. I have never experienced such great pain emotionally or physically." She looked down at her hands and twisted the Kleenex.

The fragile woman briefly stopped. It seemed she was struggling to gather herself. She then lifted her gaze and faced the killer with a newfound strength. It was a force that was visible to the viewing audience.

The mother looked straight at her child's killer and said, "Mr. Limbaugh, there are people here who hate you. I'm not one of them. I forgive you for what you've done. You've made it difficult to live up to what I believe. God says to forgive. He doesn't say to forgive just certain people, he says forgive all. So, Mr. Limbaugh, I forgive you." She began to weep.

The camera zoomed into the face of wickedness. The killer's features softened and his pursed lips began to quiver. Then he started to cry. Not a single other person made him cry. At that precise moment, I realized that the only way I would be able to live a good life was to stop hating Lisa's killer. I had to do what this courageous woman had done. I had to let go of the hate. Samantha was right. This poor woman was right. I needed to forgive that vile man so Lisa could rest in peace—so I could live in peace.

The waitress delivered my sandwich. As I picked at the turkey that overlapped the toasted bread, I could see how I had been consumed with hate. My heart and soul had been filled with blackness and it had shaped the person I had become. Just by her words, it became obvious how that woman had taken back the power from her daughter's killer. He no longer controlled her. She wasn't going to allow it. My stomach turned at this new revelation. Suddenly eating wasn't something I wanted to do. I wrapped my sandwich in a napkin and placed it in my back pack. I tossed some money on the table, grabbed my belongings, my cup of coffee, and I headed out the door and down the sidewalk.

The streets were busy, traffic was thick, and so were the smells of gasoline and diesel. I reached into my pocket for a few bucks and handed it to a young lady on the corner who had her hand out, with a most pitiful look. I could tell she was on drugs, and most times I would have kept on walking, perhaps even thinking, *get a life, get a job*. But tonight, tonight I felt sorry for her. I placed the money in her hand and told her to buy a meal and skip the drugs. I picked up the pace in order to make it to school on time.

I stopped and stood at the crowded corner and waited for the signal. The sun was descending in the desert beyond the buildings. The air took on a slight chill, and the city streetlamps began to pop on. I couldn't believe there were so many gas-guzzling vehicles still flooding the streets. It was no wonder so many noxious fumes were trapped in the downtown corridor. The light changed and I crossed with all the others. There were only a few more blocks between me and my classroom.

While I walked at a steady pace, my mind raced through everything I had just heard on TV. And then I began to go over all that was said about Lisa's killer at trial—the sentencing phase, and then the death penalty hearings. I remembered there was little relief when the jurors found him guilty of first-degree, capital murder. But when the words *death penalty* were tagged on, I felt a sudden release, followed by what seemed like endless tears. And for a time, this had seemed to pacify my rage and hate for him.

Nevertheless, at this moment, I unexpectedly wanted the chance to say to him what that woman had said to her daughter's killer. I craved the chance to see him break—watch him cry, with the simplest of words, "I forgive you for what you've done." But that would never happen, and I knew it. I wish I had taken my power back then, when I gave my own victim impact statement all those years ago. But I hadn't.

My phone began to vibrate in the front pocket of my backpack. I struggled to get to it as I kept up my pace to class. When I noticed it was Samantha calling, I answered.

"Hello." My breath was a bit heavy.

It was Sam. "Hi Madison. I was headed over to Gram's house to help her with a few more things for the party tomorrow and thought I would check in."

"I'm headed to class." I stepped off a curb and crossed at a light.

She was going on about her visions again, certain her grandmother was worried about her and just using tomorrow's party as an excuse to get her over to her house tonight. I slowed my stride as I approached my law class.

"I am sure your grandmother just doesn't like to see you stress out unnecessarily." I watched the students begin to pour into the room. I wanted to tell Sam about what I saw on TV, but knew I was running out of time. And it was apparent something else was on her mind.

"My grandmother always said, 'Clairvoyance is the art of *seeing* beyond the five senses' yet when that sixth sense gives me angst, or ominous visions, she is the first to tell me I am 'over thinking things.'"

"She just doesn't want you freaking out over useless information."

"My visions aren't pointless, Madison."

"No, that isn't what I meant. It's just, you don't have all the details, and without all the facts that just leaves you to fill in the blanks. And that is just too many what-ifs, Sam. I am sure that is where you grandmother is going with that." I leaned back on the building. I was never good at saying the right thing.

"My gram is the person I inherited this ability from, Madison. She is the one who taught me to connect and communicate with spirits and see things others can't. Gram is the person who gave me the confidence to consider my predictions as real possibilities. And now she is trying to convince me I am transferring my stress to my insight."

"Okay, now you've lost me," I admitted.

"My grandmother thinks I am freaking out about my twenty-fifth birthday and the inheritance," Sam said unconvinced.

"Well, aren't you?" I looked at my watch and began kicking my heel against the wall.

"Gram is convinced the dark visions I am projecting are coming from my own psyche. Put there by the fact that I haven't forgiven myself, my mother, or my stepfather." Sam's voice lowered. She seemed to be confessing something to me.

"Forgiveness, huh—seems to be the topic of the day." I watched my teacher shut the doors to the classroom. I knew I needed to hang up at a time when Samantha probably really needed to talk.

"What do you mean, 'the topic of the day'?"

"Oh, nothing. Listen, I am really sorry, but I have to get going to class. I am already late. You need to practice what you preach, Sam."

"What do you mean?"

"Remember what you told me this morning about forgiveness. 'When we forgive, we need to make it crystal clear to our hearts or the transformation won't be complete.' Isn't that what you said? Why don't you take your own advice?" I was loving, but firm. I also understood I was having difficulty applying the same counsel.

We said goodbye. I turned off my phone and entered the building. I found the timing of her call odd, but knew when it came to Samantha, there were no coincidences. After hearing me tell Sam to forgive her rapist-stepfather, I knew it was also time for me to begin to consider doing the same for Lisa's killer.

Chapter Thirty

Samantha 'Sam' Green

When I bumped up to the curb in front of Gram's house, I turned off my car and sat in the silence, an opportunity I rarely found these past few days. Gram's front porch light illuminated the cozy entrance. She had added more colorful flowers to the pots that lined the step. I needed a moment to clear my energy so Gram would stop worrying. Ill-fated visions, depressing thoughts, unclear intentions, and the presence of darkness are all of the things that followed me around today. Each one nipped at my mind, at my thoughts and my beliefs. I couldn't allow this harmful force into Gram's house, again.

I watched as a cat scurried across the road in front of me. I cringed at the idea of it being a black cat. But upon a second look, I recognized it as the neighbor's cat, the one Gram always complained crapped in her flower beds, and it wasn't black. I was confused by these ominous thoughts I'd been having. It was so uncharacteristic of the person I was—the person I wanted to be. This typically wasn't the way I used my sixth sense. Yet over the past week I had become overwhelmed with negative energies, auras, and bad thoughts.

I sat in the driver's seat of my car meditating in front of my grandmother's house. I squeezed my eyes shut and did my best to change the images that were going through my head. I couldn't even think of a Beatles tune to hum, which always worked to get me out of any funk. My energy was so bad my deceased mother didn't even want to hang around me. *It wasn't the first time she hadn't stuck around.* A hostile reflection just spilled into my psyche. I was conscious enough to recognize it was a powerful wave of anger at... my mother.

Most people believed it was my stepfather who hurt me the most. My grandmother was certain it was the years of sexual abuse that had held me back from fulfilling my truth. But really, it was my mother who hurt me worse. She was the one who left me without a mother. She was the one who cut short a life I was so dependent upon. It was my mother whom I needed to forgive. For some reason I have held onto this pain. It was weird that it was coming up for me now. Gram could be right. Madison, too.

This resentment toward my mother that suddenly bubbled in my chest might be exactly what would keep my visions from being genuine. From the very moment my mother walked into the room that night with the gun dangling from her grip, the nagging question, *why* has continued to haunt me. *Why did she kill him? Why did she kill herself? Why did she do it in front of me? Why did she leave me alone?* And then the why questions always seemed to come back to me. *Why hadn't I said no to him? Why did I ever even tell my mother about him? Why couldn't I have stopped her? Why had I just sat there and watched?* I felt tears dripping down my face. This wasn't good. I knew this wasn't good. I gripped my steering wheel and screamed inside of myself.

I needed to stop blaming myself for my mother's death. It wasn't my fault her husband was a child molester. My mother just snapped that night. I could not have foreseen that, at least not then. It was at that moment that I realized, like Madison, I, too, needed to forgive myself. Yet I still found it ironic, the idea of Madison coaching me on forgiveness.

I leaned back into my seat, relaxed my grip on the wheel, and I tried pushing all thoughts out of my head. What I began to hear was my grandmother's voice telling me, "If you absorb the energy of the person you are trying to heal, it's because you haven't been able to heal your own heart."

Maybe Gram was right about my visions. Maybe I was bringing them on myself. I fervently whispered my prayer of protection.

The Light of God surrounds me. The Love of God enfolds me. The Power of God protects me, and the Presence of God watches over me. Wherever I am, God is!

I wiped the tears from my face. I hoped Gram wouldn't notice I'd been crying. I popped out of the car, filled with a new vigor. I wanted to put a little pep in my step. But I was tired, plain old worn out from work and the emotion that seemed to latch onto me as I approached my twenty-fifth birthday.

While stepping along the concrete path to Gram's front door, I noticed I was humming, singing in my head. *It's been the hardest day's night, and I been working like a frickin' dog. I really deserve to be sleepin' like a log.* I couldn't help but smile. I knew my mother was with me. I was certain she forgave me.

* * *

When I strolled into Gram's house it was dark, no lights were on, and I couldn't find her. I fumbled around with a few lamps as I walked through the living room. Flipping switches, I hit her bedroom and bathroom before the kitchen. The light overhead buzzed before snapping on and brightening the kitchen. She had a stack of store-bought, fresh-cut flowers lying on the counter that needed to be put in water. That wasn't like her to leave flowers out of water.

The hunt for my elderly grandmother always made my heart drop, and at her age, my mind often went to the wrong place. And tonight, with the dark cloud that had followed me today, morbid thoughts continued to taunt me. I suddenly envisioned her fragile body in a heap in the backyard, passed out in her flower bed. I hurried through the house and out onto the back patio. That is when I saw her. She was struggling to line the backyard with tiki torches.

"Gram!" I hollered as I traipsed across the grass toward her. "I told you I was coming by to help you tonight." I grabbed the torch from her grip and stuck it hard in the ground.

"Well, hello there, birthday girl." Gram leaned over, giving me room to kiss her on the cheek. "You've been crying." Her compassionate gaze lingered on mine. "You remember Evelyn, don't you?" Gram made a gesture toward the smaller, older woman on the other side of the yard, struggling in the dark, trying to drive a torch into the garden soil.

"I'm so sorry. I didn't see you over there. Sure, I remember you, Evelyn." I flew over to her. "Let me do this one for you." I reached for the stick that was in her grip.

"It is nice to see you, honey." She handed me the wooden torch and wrapped her arms around me. Strangely she held on, as if she knew I needed a hug. "I haven't seen you since you were a small child. I don't know why your grandmother thinks you should remember me."

She was so small my chin rested on the top of her head. Evelyn held me tight, her ear pressed to my chest. It was as if she was listening for my heartbeat. I could smell stale hairspray.

Turning from our embrace, I pushed the stick into the ground. "I didn't know you had company, Gram. How'd you get here, Evelyn? I didn't see a car out front." I fetched another torch. There were a handful of them left on the patio that still needed to be placed.

"She drove," Gram interrupted. "I had her park next door in the Peterson's drive because they are out of town. No sense in her parking on the street." She snickered. "I figure if their cat can use my flower beds I can use their driveway."

"You two shouldn't be out here like this in the dark," I reprimanded. "Gram, why is it so dark in the house, anyway?"

"Oh, that lamp on the timer in the front room blew a bulb when it popped on earlier. I meant to change it. I must have gotten sidetracked." She smiled wide as she went around the patio and lit a few candles. "That's what happens when you get old. Besides, Evelyn and I got to doing things out here, chit chatting and catching up, and the next thing you know it was dark." She waved out the flame of the stick match she held between her fingers. She always said a match was easier on her old hands than a lighter.

"Evelyn recently lost her husband, Ed." Gram blurted out. Then she walked over and turned on the backyard fountain. Almost simultaneously, the automatic timer on her yard lights clicked, illuminating the backyard, highlighting the heartache in Evelyn eyes.

I moved back over beside Evelyn. "Oh, I am so sorry your husband is no longer with you." I put my hand on her shoulder.

"Oh, honey, he is with me. My Ed is here all the time," she purred fondly. "We were married sixty-one years." Her crooked smile lit up. "He is not only here, but he is no longer suffering. He knows who I am again. Ed remembers everything, just like when we were young." She spoke with pride.

In that moment, I could see she was right. He was there. And he was a talkative fellow. She was like me. I was like her. Glimpsing Gram's face, I knew this was not a coincidence.

"Evelyn, have a seat." Gram motioned her to the patio and turned to me and winked. "I'm going to refill your iced tea, unless anyone wants something stronger?" She stood with her hands on her hips and awaited a response.

"Do you want help, Gram? When I came through the kitchen I noticed all the flowers on the counter. What are your plans for those?" I stood at the edge of the patio and yard while watching Evelyn slowly lower herself into the glider.

"Oh darn! That is something else I forgot about. Your old grandmother needs you to reach up in the spare bedroom closet and get me that box of vases. We'll set those out for your party."

"I'll get them for you now." I moved toward the door.

"You just sit down and rest for a minute," she said with authority. This time there was no wink. "By the looks of you, a little rest is just what you need." Her eyes went right to mine, which were probably still red and swollen.

Both Evelyn and I agreed to the tea.

"Go on, you visit with Evelyn, and I'll be right back out with some tea." Gram gave me the eye, the one that said: go sit.

I watched her turn and hobble off, pausing with her hands at prayer position to momentarily pay respect to her Shiva statue before going into the kitchen.

Gram's body had all the signs of someone who had worked way too hard for the day. I could see the party preparations were taking a physical toll on her. I strolled around the half wall and went to sit on the wood bench catty-corner from Evelyn. Evelyn patted the open space beside her and insisted I sit next to her on the glider. I couldn't help but notice her hands; they seemed large for her petite size. Then I sat and noticed her ears and nose, both proportionate to her hands.

Evelyn stared at the fountain. "I have always loved the sound of water." Her words came out slow. Her voice was smooth.

I listened to the faux babbling brook, the deep tones of chimes and bells that floated in the water. The evening air was fresh, comfortable, and the sweet smells of spring were fabulous. Gram's place had a way of grounding me, bringing me home to what was good in the world and in my life.

I felt Evelyn's hand reaching for mine. "Is your mother always with you, honey?" Evelyn's question threw me.

"Not in the way I wish she was." I couldn't help that it came out rather snarky. I nervously adjusted my body on the glider.

"She is sorry for that, Samantha. She wants me to make sure you know she's sorry." Her grip on my hand grew tighter. It was warm, soft. Her skin was covered in liver spots and her fingernails were painted bright red, almost as red as her lipstick.

"I know." I felt sick to my stomach with guilt for the anger I harbored toward my mother.

She tapped me on the leg. "It's okay to miss her, and it is quite all right to want her here with you. We cannot always control our thoughts. Anger is one of the most difficult of the emotions to keep intact. But it does not serve you, Samantha. You must work on letting it go."

We sat silent for several moments before Evelyn began to talk again.

"The first time for me was when I was seventeen. I'd had a dream my older brother got into a bad car accident. He was nineteen and away at college. I didn't say anything to anyone. I had lots of dreams, nightmares, daydreams, whatever you want to call them. Vivid ones, ones so real I had to pinch myself at times to come back to reality. Two weeks later someone in a truck hit him, head on. He lived. He was lucky. Back then the cars were big and heavy." She smiled and stared into the night sky.

My mouth was beginning to get dry. This wasn't making me feel any better. I gazed blankly over the backyard while listening to Evelyn.

She continued. "After that, I really started paying attention to my dreams. I began writing them down and predicting all sorts of things, things that never really happened. At least not the way I thought they would, so I stopped forecasting the future. That's when the voices started. Back then, you tell someone about those kinds of voices, they'd lock you in a room and throw away the key." Her free hand swung out over the lawn, throwing a key.

Gram brought out two fresh glasses of tea, then immediately retreated back into the house. Knowing her, she was probably listening through the kitchen door. I gripped onto the cool glass and took a few large gulps. Crying always made me thirsty.

Evelyn took a short sip. "Where was I, dear?"

"Voices, you began hearing voices."

"Oh yes. Anyway, I'd begun to not only have visions, but I often would hear the muddled speech of strangers." She set her tea on the little side table. "And it had been years since my brother's accident. A spirit, a voice, a ghost, my own damn mind, people called it all sorts of things. Then, this powerful force told me my sister's kid was going to drown in the pool. I didn't listen. I refused to hear it." Her hands twisted the napkin nervously as she spoke.

I set my tea down and turned my body on the glider so to face Evelyn.

"Samantha, I knew from the moment I met you as a small child that you possessed this power. Your grandmother wanted me to come here and persuade you to stop carrying the darkness of others. She hoped I could help you increase your clarity, perhaps convince you this was about something other than your foresight." Her wrinkled face twisted at the idea of letting down my grandmother.

"What about your sister's child? The drowning, did it really happen?"

"Yes, it did. Just like I had saw it would." Her face drooped. Sadness overtook her features.

The minute I had asked I wished I could have taken back the question.

"I can see something is weighing very heavy on you, child. You know, it is possible this *something* comes from both inside and outside of you, Samantha." Evelyn turned and gripped both of my hands and closed her eyes. She began to chant. "Divine Goddess, Goddess Divine, Divine God, God Divine, banish all the forces of

354

evil, destroy them, vanquish them, so that Samantha can be healthy and do good deeds. Heal the pain of her memories, so that nothing that has happened to her will cause her to remain in anguish, filled with anxiety. Look to those inner sores that make her unable to forgive. You who comes to forgive the afflicted of heart, please, heal Samantha's heart." She opened her eyes and caught my shocked stare.

She had hit the nail on the head. Only moments ago I had convinced myself my ominous vision was planted there by unresolved grief. Now I was convinced it was both, grief and certainty.

"Visualize a triple circle of purplish light around your body and repeat after me, Samantha." She closed her eyes again. "I am protected by your might."

I closed my eyes. Feeling the energy of this elder envelop me, I did as I was instructed. Word for word, I followed along. Softly and precisely, I repeated the words. "I am protected by your might. O gracious Goddess, day and night—Thrice around the circle's bound, evil sink into the ground." My heart began to beat out of my chest. This small, old, woman was confirming my blackness. I felt my knees begin to get weak. I nervously looked back at the doorway for Gram. She wasn't there. I didn't want her to see this. I don't want her to be scared.

"Samantha, I don't want your grandmother to worry either." Evelyn smiled. "Ed talks a lot. He tells me many things. Beneath our perceptions are layers of beliefs, choices and energy which become the foundation of what shows up for us and then becomes our reality. Samantha, it is these beliefs that manifest as what works and what doesn't work in our life. You cannot change the course of things. You can only change how you accept them." She reached up and held my face in her hands and stared me square in the eye. "Just remember that. Nothing predicted or unpredicted is ever your fault."

I watched as water filled her eyes. She then stood, pulled me up to her and hugged me close. I leaned over as she whispered in my ear.

"You will get through this, Samantha. It might not feel like it, but you will." Her voice took on a reassuring tone—with a hint of pity. "Always remember, those who loved you who left this earth before you, they are always with you." Her lips pressed onto my cheek and she said goodbye before turning and heading inside of the house.

I fell back on the glider, unsure of what just happened. I was left to fumble through forgiveness, my voices, my ghosts, and my ominous forecasts. I was pretty sure that was the opposite of what my grandmother had intended when she arranged this meeting. I was also pretty sure there were no accidents.

Chapter Thirty-One

Ethan Price

Buying gifts for other people was never easy. First, it was always difficult for me not to buy for myself. And then, I often went through the list of things I thought someone would need rather than what they might want. And in Samantha's case, that was clothes, a new purse, and some decent shoes. I have always wanted to give her a makeover. She was already very pretty in a natural way, without all the extras, but it was with the necessities that she needed some coaching. She was always in baggy clothes, never showing off the real body she had underneath all the excess material. And those shoes she wore were like water-skis. Maybe when she cashes in on her trust fund she'll make me her personal shopper. One can only hope.

Here it was going on ten o'clock at night and I still wasn't home. It was a nice evening to walk. And somehow the noise of the city soothed me. The moon was high in the sky and behind the glare of city lights, the stars shined bright. My future shined bright. I could see beyond the coming weekend. Today I had actually looked beyond my job, my apartment, and my compulsions. Today, I hadn't even thought of having sex with a stranger. I can't say I didn't notice a few guys cruising me at the mall, but I didn't want them fucking me. I was still smiling inside from my rendezvous with

Bradley. That was all I could think about. It felt good to be this happy.

After wandering through Park Central Mall and perusing several shops downtown, I finally decided on a simple leather necklace with a crystal pendent for my best friend. It wasn't easy, but I let go of my wants and bought something I knew Samantha would appreciate. I found out crystal was the universal stone. It has a pure and powerful energy source, which I knew was important to Samantha. The necklace was supposed to receive, activate, store, transmit, and amplify energy. These were all things that fit perfectly into Samantha's world. But what ultimately sold me was when the salesperson said the stone was believed to bring harmony to the soul, open the crown chakra and all that other stuff I don't understand. But Samantha understood, and after seeing her at work today, wound up tighter than a drag queen in an evening gown, I thought a little harmony for the soul was just what she needed.

I squeezed out the doors of the train just before they slid shut. I stood on the Light Rail platform and caught my breath. Whores and homeless people didn't scare me, but the meth heads did. To avoid them, I jumped off the curb and darted across traffic to get to the other side of Van Buren. The cool air swept past my face and ears as I trotted across the street. I was uncomfortable walking through the junkies on the corner. Those people were unpredictable, just like Samantha had been lately. She totally overreacted to my being late this morning, acting as if I'd been shot or killed. She was totally pissed I didn't take her call. I didn't tell her it was because Bradley was fucking my brains out. Instead I made up some lame excuse about oversleeping, which was worse, because then she looked at me like I was a liar.

Throughout the rest of the day she went on about her unclear visions and how they were haunting her. I could see they were bothering her without her ever even mentioning them. I attempted to ease her mind, reminding her this birthday brought with it a lot of bad memories, but also a lot of good fortune. I couldn't help the play-on-words. She didn't laugh. For some reason I think the whole trust fund thing was really weighing on her. She had an edge I wasn't used to. I tried to convince her to let go of the guilt of receiving something good out of something so bad. I'd been around enough counseling to offer her that. Then she decided to tell me Bradley and I kept coming up in her mind, and it wasn't good. Okay, then she had my attention. I hadn't yet told her Bradley had finally committed himself to me.

I rounded the corner near my place and up ahead I saw red flashing lights. Police cars were lined up at the curb, right in front of my apartment complex. My stomach sank, my thoughts went to Nasreen. *They caught her killer,* I thought. *It's someone in the complex.* I cut across the dirt entrance and headed along the meandering path to my building. I was rubbernecking my way through the maze of structures when I came upon a cluster of people standing under the large lamp that lit the path.

From a distance I heard the boisterous voice of my landlord before making out his portly silhouette in the shadows. Two uniformed police officers stood next to him along with the nice detective from the other night. The detective stood with his notebook in hand. That was not a good sign. That meant he was still gathering information. Since they were on the path, rather than cut across the dead lawn, I decided to stay my ground and walk through the commotion.

"Mr. Price." The detective turned to face me. He'd played right into my hands.

"Ethan," I corrected him. "Did you find out what happened to Nasreen?"

"No Sir. Nothing yet." He turned back to the other two officers, and with a simple head nod they disappeared.

"*Now it's Sir, huh?*" I clutched Samantha's gift bag under my arm, drew a cigarette from my pocket and lit it. "So what's going on here?"

"You got another cigarette?" Mr. Faranghi reached his hand out and stared into my face, assuming I was going to hand him a smoke.

He was right. When he slithered his sweaty hand across mine in the exchange, my skin crawled. I was glad he had his own lighter. I watched him draw in almost half the cigarette in one long drag, leaving a one-inch red tip burning bright, so bright it grossly displayed his long, grimy fingernails. I watched my landlord pace the sidewalk with the cigarette.

"Anyway, Detective, tell me what's going on. What brings you to my neck of the woods, again?" I tossed my cigarette to the ground. I'd lost the desire to smoke after watching my landlord inhale a cigarette in two hits.

"We had an anonymous caller report a murder in the complex. You didn't see or hear anything strange last night did you?"

"Last night? No!"

"What about today? Did you see or hear anything strange today?" He had out his pad and pen, as if what I was going to say would be important.

"Strange? Everyone around this place is strange," I began to whisper, "especially that guy." I slyly eyed the landlord. Mr. Faranghi's back was to us, yet I was still nervous he might spin around.

"This is a serious situation, Mr. Price." He was annoyed.

"I am being serious, detective." I spoke with a muddled tone. "He is always lurking around every corner. If anyone saw anything it would be him." I smiled nervously when I saw the dark eyes of the Iranian staring at me.

"I'm the property manager. With all the convicts in this place it's like being the warden of a fucking prison. I can't take my eyes off of anyone." He stood very close to me. Too close. "You got a problem with that, Pretty Boy?" He clucked his tongue, the way he often did. His voice was intimidating.

I turned my back on him and faced the detective. "Well, anyway, I did hear a blood curdling scream come from the back of the complex this morning." I searched my memory banks for anything else that might help, but the minute my mind went back to the morning, all I could think about was Bradley.

"Mr. Price, excuse me, Ethan, what time was that?"

"I was running later than usual. I didn't look at my watch, but it must have been somewhere around 9:30 a.m. It was a man's voice, strong and deep, startled would be the way I'd describe it." I watched the detective scribble on his pad. My creepy landlord was breathing heavy while looking over the detective's shoulder. "Why? What did the police find?" I pried the detective for more information.

"Thanks to the 911 caller, we received information that led us to the body of a female victim." His features turned grim. "It appears she died within the past twenty-four hours. The caller led us right to the victim without giving us any other details of the homicide."

"I'm glad someone called. Imagine the smell if she had been in there much longer." Mr. Faranghi was twisting the forbidden trinket around his neck and mumbling in his language. "For all we know she's been in there too long already. And what about the money to repair and paint to rid that odor? Who pays for that?" he asked.

The detective seemed to ignore the comment but he also wrote down what my landlord said. Then he turned back to me. "According to Mr. Faranghi the victim was a tenant in the complex."

"Who was it?" I was shocked.

"I am sorry, Ethan, but we have to make all the proper identifications before releasing any names." He snapped his notebook shut. "If I have any other questions I will call you." He no longer looked comfortable talking about things.

"You have my number. I am certainly willing to help. I sure hate the idea of having a murderer in my apartment building."

"We have an enormous team of people working this scene. We are still not sure if there is a connection between the two deaths." The detective returned his pen to his pocket. "If you think of anything else Mr. Price—huh, huh, I mean, Ethan, sorry. Please, take my number." He pressed his card into my palm. "Don't hesitate to give me a call." The detective quietly gave the impression he wanted me to call, no matter what.

"How much longer you gonna need me tonight?" Mr. Faranghi stepped back into the light. His black and grey flecked hair was as thick as his accent, and he was dripping wet with sweat. The mole that sat atop his right nostril shimmered with moisture, as did his brow.

"Good luck," I said. "Don't let me keep you from solving a crime." I extended my hand to the detective, and tossed a head nod to my disgusting landlord, before retreating to my apartment. Anyone that had to deal with that insensitive bastard needed all the help they could get.

Instinctively I pulled my cell phone out of my pocket and looked at the time. It was 10:45 p.m. and Bradley hadn't called to say goodnight. I turned and walked away from the two men. I gave a generous swish of my hips with each stride, mostly because I could feel them both watching me. This time I decided to cut across the flattened grass. I glanced up ahead, toward the back of the complex, and noticed a few police officers stringing yellow crime-scene tape. I stepped into my apartment, turned back and shut the door, latched the security chain, and twisted the locks on both the deadbolt and the doorknob. It was the one time I was glad not to have any windows in my cheap-ass place.

I know it's been only women who have been killed in my complex, but Tequila Mockingbird was no woman. Someone may have thought he was, but nonetheless, he was dead. And that was right down the fucking street from here. Now that I finally had a future I wanted to be a part of I wasn't taking any chances. I reached for the chair in the kitchen and walked it back to the door and tilted it into the handle, wedging it tight against the front door.

I felt the vibration of my phone. It was Bradley finally calling to say goodnight. We talked about my day, then about his. I lit the candle on my kitchen bar and grabbed a bottle of water from the fridge. I wondered if he could feel me smiling over the phone. I'd melted into the conversation so much I'd forgotten all about the potential intruder. While I drifted around getting undressed, Bradley told me that he and Amber started going through his mother's things. He revealed to me they ordered a slew of death certificates, and opened separate accounts. He mentioned something about Jacob's school teacher. Everything suddenly seemed so honest between us.

I didn't even have to remind him about Samantha's party. He was the first one to bring it up. He said he had already told Amber he was going out with me on Friday night and likely wouldn't be making it home. I finished my conversation with Bradley, but not before hearing him joke about being excited about our coming-out party—glad Samantha was gracious enough to have him. I didn't tell him that I never mentioned to Samantha he would be my date for her birthday bash. I didn't lie, I just avoided the truth.

Chapter Thirty-Two

Jason Magnus

The streets were dark and nearly silent. The late-night sky was sprinkled with stars, and the moon was a big round globe, high above the city. Waking to find Raven murdered, seeing Amber and the boy she embraced, it all fucking rocked my world. It was a shockwave to my system. I didn't even know how to begin to process the events of the day. I had staggered about for hours, starting with the warehouse district, then restaurant row, I trekked by the US Airways Center, home of the Phoenix Suns. The stadium glowed. The roof had a light-purple hue illuminating the night sky. Next on my path was the Diamondback's Stadium, St. Vincent de Paul's, several bars, and at least seven churches, none of which were open for a loser like me to find refuge.

The city sidewalks were filthy, dirtier than the grimy streets. They were littered with smashed ketchup packets, sticky soda stains, old gum, as well as candy wrappers and cigarette butts. I passed a large hall with a live band. People inside danced and sang to blaring Spanish music. A crowd of folks outside smoked. I bummed a cigarette as I strolled through the horde that gathered by the front door. They talked loud and they laughed loud. They seemed to be having fun. Lucky them. I put my head down and kept walking. Over a hundred other places I passed, Miracle House wasn't among them. What I needed more than anything was a miracle, yet I hadn't taken a step in that direction. Amber had always said, "Don't believe in miracles—depend on them." I was certainly depending on one now.

All the miles I'd put on these old shoes tonight, and here I was, back at the park, exactly where I started. Back to where I saw Amber for the first time since it happened—for the first time since I was the worst kind of man there was to a woman.

I took a seat on a bench just off the path. My gut churned at the hammering thoughts of my past. My life, my relationship with Amber. We had dreams, we had promise. I'd fucked it all up. I always fucked everything up. Amber constantly said we were destined to be together. Unfortunately our destiny didn't pan out. These were the thoughts that had punished me for the past ten years. And once again they were bombarding me, on what was already one of the worst days of my life.

A rush of people no longer crawled through the park, and all the shops and restaurants that bordered the area were closed. The public transportation shut down at twelve, so it was basically deserted downtown—a few other lonely suckers and I roamed the streets. I perused the scene from the bench I was resting on. Once spotting a good location, one that was away from the overhead lights and not too close to the sidewalk or the street, I rose and headed that way. Finally hitting upon the site I would be calling my home for the night, I plopped my butt to the ground under a big tree. It was the perfect place if you had to sleep in public. The bathroom was close by. The tree I rested beneath was beside a retainer wall I could lean on or sleep against. It was hard to watch your back while sleeping out in the open.

When I glanced up, on a bench about twenty yards away under a park lamp, there was a young Asian dude watching me from a safe distance, just as I kept an eye on him. He fiddled with something in his hands. His left leg pumped like a piston. Fear sizzled from his body. He must be a newbie to homelessness. I watched him nervously stand and pace. Then he'd sit back down and pump his leg some more. Up, down, up, down. It was becoming rather hypnotic. My mind began to slow, finally.

I pulled my arms into the short sleeves of my shirt and lay them across my body for warmth. A loud growling noise came from my stomach. I knew if I didn't think about it my hunger would subside.

It was hard not to wonder what the scene at Raven's was like. I didn't want her laying there any longer. I was certain with the information I had left with the 911 operator, a CSI team was probably at her apartment right now, tearing it apart. They weren't going to find the murder weapon, and I was pretty sure they wouldn't find my fingerprints.

I told the female operator I was a homeless person, which I currently was. I also informed her I had witnessed a large man enter the house, right after midnight, even though I hadn't. When asked to describe him, the only thing that came to mind was his big gut, dark hair, and the mole on his face, and then I hung up the phone and used my shirt to wipe off my prints before hurrying away from the booth.

It took me all fucking day to do the right thing. I just couldn't stroll by another phone without picking it up, particularly after seeing Amber, more precisely, Amber and the little boy who resembled me. *Was it wrong of me to think he could be mine?* I didn't deserve for him to be mine. But I hoped he was.

I slid my body down further onto the ground, with the hope that the wall would shield me from the incoming breeze. I was almost laying down, using the concrete wall as my head rest. I was very weary, yet sleep wasn't coming easy. Before I knew it, morning would be upon us and the sunlight would once again illuminate my flaws. I dozed in and out. My mind could not get away from the reflections of my past. The site of Amber brought the worst parts all back. Everything, as if it were yesterday. How it happened, and why I now had so much regret.

* * *

Amber stayed loyal to me through our high school years. And when time allowed we still did things together. Even though my drinking and drugging was beginning to peak, again, I actually made it to my graduation. Not because of hard work: just good luck, or perhaps even dumb luck. Graduation night, Amber and I both had separate events, separate schools, separate commencement ceremonies. We had both agreed we'd meet up later. I would join her with her friends. Considering most of my friends had already decided I was a loser, there was no argument on my part.

It was a huge party up in South Mountain Park. Everyone was there. High school kids from a variety of schools were out celebrating at the big mountaintop bonfire. It was an annual event for seniors. Often when I was outside of my own element, I had my usual—*I'm all that*—attitude, you know the kind. My mannerisms were always Mr. Stud muffin, smooth talking with the girls, my stance was habitually macho, and my mouth was regularly vulgar. I could converse with the guys about sports, and with the girls I could talk about feelings.

The drugs I was on that night had me amped up, pretty major. Apparently the pint of Jack I'd jugged before meeting up with Amber didn't take much of the edge off the meth I'd snorted.

When I drove up to the party I saw Amber in my headlights. Off with her friends, she was sitting on a concrete picnic table under the large Ramada on the hillside. I stepped out of the car and wandered around for a few minutes, hoping to shake off a little bit of my buzz before approaching her. As I came closer, I paused and watched her from a short distance.

It was rare for me to see Amber drink, but from where I was standing, Amber seemed more uninhibited than usual. The colorful, spring, flowered dress she was wearing was just above her knees, with thin straps over her shoulders. It showed more of her chest than I was used to seeing. She was hugging her girlfriends and giggling loudly. Her hair swished back and forth along the tops of her shoulders. She was playful in a way that she never was without alcohol.

Amber twisted back and spied me at the edge of the parking lot. I saw a big smile stretch across her face and she began to wave me over. I pulled my shirt out of my jeans, stuffed my hands in my pockets, and reluctantly headed into the crowd of her friends.

"Well hello, Graduate." She wrapped her arms around me and gave me a big hug. "A tie? What a nice surprise. I haven't seen you in one of these in a while." She slipped the tie off over my head and slid it over hers.

I liked the look of my tie on her. "You look great," I said, kissing her on the mouth. "You taste pretty good, too." I licked my lips. "Margaritas, huh?" I smiled.

"Skinny Margaritas," Amber corrected me. "It's the new drink for ladies."

"Oh, I get it. You're a lady now, so that makes you think you can drink?" I kissed her deeper, much longer than the first kiss. I had a prickly feeling people were watching us. "What have I told you about drinking—haven't you learned anything from my mistakes?" My tone was playful, but my words had real meaning. I know they fell on others' ears.

"Mr. Magnus," she sucked my bottom lip into her mouth, "I don't need your permission to party and have fun." She gave a flirty giggle. "I am a graduate. I am all grown up now." And then she sauntered off, back to a circle of girls who all screamed with excitement upon her return to their clique.

I guess everyone was as happy as I was to be getting out of high school. I decided to give Amber time to relish the accomplishment of graduating with her girlfriends. So I walked over to a bunch of dudes perched next to a large boulder on the other side of the bonfire. They were doing the usual whooping and hollering, chest-bumping and high-fiving. I strolled up to the crowd of jocks, and with my normal attitude, I boldly readjusted my balls before puffing out my chest. I was a tall guy, broad shouldered, not intimidated by too many people, physically.

"Hey, what's up?" I looked at the circle of people, not really giving a shit what any of them said.

A few head-nods, fist-bumps and handshakes, and I was in the gang of partying graduates. I hung out for a while, trying to give Amber some space before I snatched her away from this crowded place. I stood shooting the shit, razzin' the girls I knew, saying hi and bye to others I had met here and there, and I knew I would probably never see again. Amber took time to check in with me on occasion, give me a kiss, and reassure me we would only be at this party a little longer. I took a few hits off the occasional joint that went by, and I drank a couple of beers that were handed to me, along with doing a few swigs off the tequila bottle that was going around.

After a few hours, I headed back over to my father's car. When I shut the door it took a minute for the inside light to go off, concealing me in the darkness I sought. I was then able to reach under the seat for the other pint of Jack. I slugged back some before anyone knew the difference. Then I poked my hand into my pocket, reaching for the little bullet I carried, something used to make it easy to get a quick shot of crystal meth up the nose. I did my business and stepped back out of the car to pee. While I stood at the trunk of the vehicle and let out all the liquid in my bladder, I searched the crowd for Amber.

I traveled back up the short path to Amber's crowd of friends. Chilled by the night air, Amber strolled up to me and snuggled in. She rested her head on my chest. I wrapped my arms around her and held her tight. I quickly became paranoid, thinking she might hear the speed I had just snorted pumping through my heart. Amber began rubbing her body on mine, more physical than ever before. Her hands were crawling across my shoulders, my back, and then my butt, just before she tightly pulled me into her, our bellies pressed firmly together, and so did a few other things. I pulled back, uncomfortable in case others might be watching. I was right. They were. Amber always had a few friends who thought I was good for nothing, and they were eyeballing this situation. By the look in their eyes, they weren't happy.

It was starting to get late. Everyone was getting pretty hammered, starting to separate off into little groups of two, everywhere, with a handful of the solo guys over here, and a handful of single girls over there. I led Amber over closer to the fire, and for a few moments we stood arm-in-arm, staring into the blaze, her once again telling me we were *destined to be together*. Then Amber moved her body in front of mine, again, this time her back to my front, and we continued to stare into the fire. While I stood behind her, Amber tenderly took my arms and wrapped them around her waist, squeezing us tightly together. I rested my chin on her shoulder and lightly kissed her neck while staring into the dwindling flame.

My body began to convulse with desire. I lightly stroked the soft skin on her arms to warm her. Amber began to sway her hips to the rhythm of the blaring music. I felt her ass moving against me. It felt good. She felt good. The brilliant fire had burned down to a low glow.

"Babe," I whispered in her ear as I turned her to face me. I could feel my penis getting hard. I wanted her. I wanted her, badly.

"Let's go to the car." We kissed, mouths wide, our tongues were in a tangled dance.

Suddenly Amber was the one tugging on *me* to follow *her*. We were trudging the terrain in the dark when I heard Amber squeak and stumble in her heels. I swung her into my arms and we laughed playfully while we went the rest of the way down the steps and to the parking lot. I set her to the ground gently, then opened the back door to the car. She climbed in willingly, almost anxiously—at least that is what I have always told myself. I leaned in and kissed her. Slyly, not shyly, Amber slipped the tie she'd stolen from me earlier in the night over her head, and then she roped my neck with it.

"I'm a big girl now, Mr. Magnus," she said, as she coaxed me to lay my body on top of hers.

I climbed in the backseat. My body exploded with hunger for her. I kissed her face, her neck, her chest. It was obvious by her easiness Amber was a little more loaded than I had realized. My adrenaline was pumping more than usual. Meth did that to me. I moved the thin straps off her shoulders and tugged down at the top of Amber's dress. Then I pulled her bra up over her breasts, never taking the time to work the snap underneath her body. I licked her tits, both of them, before I sucked her nipples, making them hard with desire. Knowingly or unknowingly, Amber began to gyrate her hips, rubbing her pubic bone on my cock through my slacks— something she hadn't ever done in the past. I was already hard, pulsing for her. I took her hand and guided it down my pants. Then I began to work at getting her panties off.

All I could hear through my bliss was her moans of pleasure. I pulled her panties down around her knees and spreading her legs with mine. I reached for her moist lips. My fingers went inside her, for the first time. Her body bucked against my hand. My long legs kicked at the door. I pressed the full weight of my body onto hers as I struggled to get my pants down to my knees. Since becoming a teenager, I'd waited for this moment with Amber. My mouth over hers, my fingers inside of her, Amber's moans were louder, more intense.

"No," she whispered as we rustled around in the backseat of my father's car.

I ignored her and continued to press. When I touched myself to her wetness, I heard the faint whimper of a virgin. I felt her legs squeeze tightly around me.

"No Jason. Not yet. Not like this," she said in a tone that was unconvincing.

I pushed my hardness into her and began strongly pumping, pressing myself harder and harder into her. Then I could feel her squirming, moving her body in a crazy way.

"Jason, no - I said stop!" She dug her fingernails into my skin.

This time her voice, her tone, and her actions were very persuasive. There was no ignoring her now, her *NO* was no longer a yes, maybe. I felt the pain in my back when she tore through my skin. Her forearm was now between us.

"Stop! Please Jason, stop!" she cried. "How many times are you going to make me ask you," she pleaded, desperately trying to get me off the top of her.

Yet, I felt like this was the first time I heard the word *Stop!* in the *true meaning*. I immediately pulled out when I realized she was no longer enjoying it.

"Why did you have to be so rough?" she cried, as she grabbed her panties and pulled them back up around her waist. She began kicking at me to get off of her. "Let me out of here!" Her voice caught with tears as she pushed past me.

"I'm sorry, Amber!" I followed her out the door while pulling my pants back up around my waist. In as sincere a voice as I could possibly muster, I repeated myself. "Amber, I'm sorry."

I wasn't sure if she heard me. I watched her run back up the hill crying to all of her girlfriends, where I saw them all circle around her. I combed my hands through my hair and tried to figure a way out of this. In some way, I had convinced myself she would calm down in a few minutes, forget I had forced myself on her, and come back down to the parking lot and leave with me. And like any other night out, I would take her home, walk her to the front door, kiss her goodnight, and then I would go out and get a prostitute to satisfy my needs.

I don't know why I didn't just stay at the car and wait for her. I should have given her time. Instead, I made the mistake of pursuing her.

"Amber!" I yelled. I began to stomp up the hill toward her. "I love you, Amber." I decided if I publically declared my feelings for her it would somehow numb her to what had just happened. Unexpectedly, I saw several big bodies coming my way.

These bodies, some of them, were the same guys who I had just spent half the night partying with. Amber's friends saw to it that I was punished for my dirty deeds. In the three minutes that had passed these people had already held court and found me guilty.

* * *

The next time I opened my eyes I was in a hospital bed. Bradley was in a chair in the corner of the room. He stood and walked over to my bedside, pressed the button to lift my upper body, and told me what a waste it was to end up in the hospital on graduation night. He held up a mirror and showed me my two black eyes and the wounds to my face. Even though I felt the pain pulsating from every single one of my injuries, Bradley went into detail about each one of them, anyway. I had a broken nose and stitches in my eyebrow. My injuries were nowhere near as bad as my bruised ego. And not even close to the guilt I felt from the pain I had caused to Amber.

Bradley conveyed his delight at my awakening, right before he ripped into me, sharing his disappointment, like any *good* friend would, about my drunkenness and the drug use I had fallen victim to, again. He told me they kept me in the hospital because I was knocked out and wouldn't come to. He insinuated it was the drunkenness not the beating that kept me down. He always hated the drugs, he and Amber both. That is why I hid my meth use from them, always.

But truthfully, Bradley's real reason for being at the hospital was to tear into me for taking advantage of Amber. When I asked him where she was, why hadn't she come to the hospital, why wasn't she in the chair instead of him, he unloaded on me.

"She wanted to be here. That is how crazy she is about you. Everyone talked her out of punishing herself. They damn near had to tie her down to keep her from rushing to your side. No one wants to see her waste any more time on you. But she loves you, Jason. You are her drug. Even though you are bad for her, she cannot stop you." The vein in his temple pulsed. I had never seen him that way.

"Can I say anything?" My head was pounding.

"No! I am done listening. You hurt her, Jason. Amber has lots of friends who want to see you out of her life. And that is before they all know exactly what you have done. You really hurt her. You have hurt us all, Jason."

Bradley paced around the room, yet most times he managed to keep his stare on me. "Since we were kids, Amber and I, both, have tirelessly been there for you. We've been like brothers, you and I." He tapped his chest and pointed to mine. "Everyone loves you, Jason. Why can't you see that? Amber has been devoted to you. And your father, no matter what you think, he's put up with more than enough from you." He turned his back on me.

I was not able to talk. I had no comeback. No response. Everything Bradley was saying was true.

Bradley twisted back and looked me in my swollen eyes. "We've tried to fight this addiction with you, Jason, all of us. But this obsession you continue to have with sabotaging your own life, well, we can't stick around for it any longer. Lord knows we have all tried. But you don't make it easy, Jason. You have to be a part of your own recovery. We can't do it for you. You have friends, a girlfriend, and a father who loves you. You are smart and good looking. It isn't like you have to hide who you really are." Bradley spoke passionately, but he was very naïve if he didn't think as an addict I wasn't always hiding who I was.

I couldn't apologize. It was as if my mouth had been wired shut. I couldn't open my fucking mouth to express the regret I was feeling. Everything was a moaning-mumble. Besides, I knew he wasn't open to hearing any more of my excuses. We had been best friends for far too long. The Three Musketeers, that's what we sometimes had called ourselves.

"I know there is something good in you, Jason. I just wish you'd work harder at bringing that side of you out. You are the one who needs to come out of the closet, my friend, not me. And I don't mean the gay closet, either." He forged a phony smile. He knew I was one of the few people he was honest with when it came to his sexuality. "You blew it. You had the perfect girl in Amber, and you blew it. If I didn't like men I'd marry her myself. Lord knows my parents would love that. We are done, Jason. Done! I've gotta go. You owe her, Jason. You owe Amber something much more than false regret. Until you can offer something further, she doesn't want to see you." He turned and stormed out. He was right when he said I had the perfect girl. He was also right when he said I blew it.

My father and Bradley brushed shoulders in the doorway of my hospital room. My dad walked in just as Bradley walked out. He was carrying a large suitcase. The air in the room took an even colder chill. My father informed me I had been mysteriously left in the backseat of his car, and parked at the emergency entrance of the hospital. The whole ordeal brought me little sympathy from my dad, especially when he found out Amber no longer wanted to see me. Since we were kids that had never happened. Amber didn't ever abandon me. All the shit I did to her over the years, my dad knew Amber had always been in my corner, my *defender*, he called her. I always knew her girlfriends hated me, all of them. They finally got to her.

"You must have really fucked up, son," he said, looking into my swollen face as I lay in a hospital bed. "They found your drug vial and the liquor bottles in my car. I don't know what you did to Amber, but her father called and warned he'd alert the police if you ever showed up on their doorstep again." Sweat gathered at his temples. Disappointment dripped from his words. "Even with the support of your family, and Amber's love, you've managed to slide back into your old behaviors. I am disappointed in you, Jason. Your mother would be crushed." My father knew how to hurt me. Bringing my mother into it was a sure way to reach into my chest and rip out my heart.

Only a few days ago my father was telling me how proud he was of me. He acknowledged the efforts I had made to work, graduate high school, and to kick some of my bad habits. He had hope in me. Or so it seemed. Yet when he spoke with such confidence in me, *I* knew I was still drinking and drugging. I knew I was a phony. I had just become better at it, that's all. I also knew it was by luck not effort that I had graduated, and out of need not preference that I worked. I guess the joke was on me.

"Tough love, Jason..." My father put his hand on my arm and paused. "I can only apologize so much. Son, I never meant to abandon you. I have always been here when you needed me. I had to grieve, too, Jason." While he leaned over me I saw tears begin to fill his eyes. "I also loved your mother. Bertie and I were best friends, Jason, not just husband and wife." His stare was intense.

I could see he loved her, maybe even still. At that very moment I felt sincere sympathy, and for a change, it was not for me, but for my father. I had let him down, I knew that. I had let everyone down.

"They call it tough love, Jason, mostly because it is tough on everyone involved. Son, listen to me. This is the toughest thing I have ever had to do." He briefly halted and swallowed hard, his gaze went to the large suitcase he carried into the room. "I don't want you coming back home. The doctors said when you woke up you would be discharged. So, when you get out of here you need to go somewhere else." He turned away and began to pace around the small space of my hospital room.

"I'm sorry," I whispered. "I am really sorry."

"I heard that before. Over the years I've tried everything to help you. Everything! It hasn't worked. This is your doing, Jason. I am not going to have a drug addict around my family any longer. You are a loose cannon." He returned to standing beside my bed. His tone suddenly took on that of a stranger's, talking of his family as if I weren't a part of it. "You go out there and get yourself a life, a family. Then you'll know exactly what I am talking about." He looked directly into my face.

"Grow up, Jason. Get sober. Learn to care about someone besides yourself." He leaned over me and gently kissed my forehead. "I will always love you. You will forever be my one and only son. But right now, Jason, I don't like you. When you become a man I can like, come home. You will be welcomed." He turned and walked out of my room.

This time I couldn't chase my father. It was too late to beg and plead. I didn't bother to call after him. He'd obviously been there, done that, and was now finished. My father had witnessed my coming in and out of sobriety. Sixty-six days—forty-five, twenty-four, seventeen days.

You get the picture. I had always picked right back up where I had left off. Each time I broke sobriety I started drinking and drugging at a higher rate. The alcohol got stronger and so did the drugs. My dad must have seen this. I could glimpse it in his eyes; he was tired of trying.

This had been a punch in my gut, far worse than the ones that had left me lying in a hospital bed all alone and lonely. I had no one, and I had nowhere to go. I wanted my Dad to lecture me. I needed him to tell me my conduct was deplorable and restrict my use of his car. I desperately needed the hope for the future that he sometimes offered in his discipline, telling me it was never too late to change. And I needed Amber to inspire me.

Crossroads

Chapter Thirty-Three

Madison Morgan

I bounced out of bed before my normal time this morning. I took my shower and cleared out of the bathroom. I knew Sam would be a whirlwind in there today. We'd need to leave early this morning because we would be commuting together today. I slipped into my clothes and followed the exquisite aroma of coffee. I popped a cup of water in the microwave for my roomy. Then I blasted the Beatles birthday song through the iPod and served up a nice warm cup of tea to the birthday girl.

Every time I entered Sam's room it reminded me of a young girl's bedroom, the way it burst of color, among other things. She had a vibrant pink comforter with colorful blossoms in purple, blue, and green. The sheets matched. So did the drapes. Samantha's collection of dolls took up a bookcase, and a stuffed teddy bear, one I realized had special meaning, sat on top of her dresser. The window sill was loaded with special stones, feathers, and some random pennies she'd found by chance laying heads-up. All these items were mementos she'd gathered over the years. She was certain some beloved spirit had left them in her path.

The few things in the room that reflected her maturing style were the chair in the corner draped with a few day's worth of clothes, the overflowing laundry basket next to the closet, and a brass incense burner on the desk, loaded with a mound of ash. Her room always smelled of sandalwood, lavender, and jasmine.

When I went to put Sam's tea on the bedside table, I had to move her laptop. I couldn't help but notice it was open to an internet page with the topic—*Is Suicide Forgivable?* And the subtext read: *How to get over losing a parent to suicide.*

I heard Sam's breathing change before noticing any movement. Then the covers rustled. I snapped the computer screen down and placed the tea saucer on top of it. Sam slowly rolled over. She looked up at me with surprise. I gave her a wide grin, and in my tone-deaf voice I began to sing along with the Beatles. Even though I was smiling on the outside, my heart was suddenly aching. She scratched out a soft *thank you* with her morning voice. I backed out of the room, wished her a happy twenty-fifth birthday, and I silently wished for so much more.

I gave Sam a chance to slowly rise. Birthday or not, she wasn't an early bird. The last few days had been rare, extremely uncommon. I didn't hear her come in last night, so I'm sure she was late. While she was getting dressed I heard her Gram's ring tone go off on Sam's phone. Then I could hear Sam humming happy birthday, probably as her grandmother sang.

Last night I was so tired I was already in bed when she came in. I decided to skip the gym after class and come straight home to cuddle with Charlie. He and I hit the sack early. That cat of mine would sleep anytime, all the time.

Sam darted into the bathroom. The shower began to run. Three minutes late she was fanning the door to get air to clear the mirror. There was little chance to chitchat as we both flew through the house to get out the door on time. I learned that she stayed at her grandmother's house past 11:00. From the sounds of it, they had dinner together, arranged a bunch of flowers, and talked about Samantha's future.

Sam fumbled through the door with an armload and a wet head. I hated the fact that she was forced to leave earlier than was necessary in order for me to use her car. I know she much preferred mulling around before jetting off, especially on her birthday. But it wasn't happening, not today. With good public transportation, I rarely saw the need to have my own car. This was one of those times. But in order to help Sam's grandmother the way I needed to, using Sam's car was the only alternative. I was keyed up, eager for the party tonight. I was only working half a day. I actually seemed more excited than Sam, and the party was in her honor. After seeing the computer screen this morning, I had an idea what might be on her mind.

*   *   *

While riding in the car together, and sitting in silence for several minutes, I decided to gently push Sam for information. "What's wrong? You don't seem your normal, chipper self." I hated when someone asked me that. I especially hated it when they were right.

Sam said nothing. Staring blankly forward she pressed the gas pedal and sped through a yellow light just turning red. I couldn't be sure she was still trying to make sense of her mother's suicide or if she had been studying the site for work purposes. Sam was always trying to learn new ways to help her clients cope with their own issues.

"How was class last night?" Diversion, now that was more like Sam. Never one to talk about herself, she always made it about others. She looked out of the corner of her eye in my direction while fluffing her long, damp hair, as if the cool morning air would somehow dry it. Another reason I loved my short hair. "Class was fine." I could tell she didn't feel much like talking. It was her birthday so I backed off.

The traffic was heavy in the downtown area, especially in the morning, and it was easy to zone out as you waited in the line of cars trying to get through each light. I leaned over and turned on the stereo. Meditative flute music emerged from the speakers. Seeing the irony, I couldn't help but chuckle. Sam had no response. Her gloomy sadness enveloped the car. *She had no room to talk to me about energy.* I thought.

"Twenty-five can't be all that bad." I spun the dream-catcher that hung from her rearview mirror.

"How do you know?" Sam waved her hand, fluttering the feathers on the handmade woven net object, stopping it from spinning.

"Well, for starters, your grandmother is going through a whole lot of trouble to make sure it's the best damn night of your twenty-five years." I suddenly had a tone, like, *come on cry baby. And I hadn't even brought up the inheritance.* And really, I knew I had no right to say anything at all. Sam was rarely a crybaby. After my mind caught up with my mouth, I wanted to take it back, but it was too late. It had already escaped my lips.

"You're right. I'm sure it will be great. I have no doubt my gram is doing everything in her power to make it so. And you, Madison. I know everyone is helping. Thanks." She anxiously played with an old-fashioned pendant that hung from her neck. "What I doubt," she paused and gripped the steering wheel even tighter, "I doubt actually making it there." She mumbled softly, but not soft enough.

"I heard that. What on earth do you mean? Of course you will make it to your own birthday party! I am picking you up. I'm not that bad of a driver." I was insistent. "Why do you say things like that, Sam?" I already knew she wasn't going to answer that. "I've never seen this side of you." I reached across the front seat and lightly touched her hand, making her present to her nervous tendency to fiddle with her necklace.

"Where did this come from? I haven't seen you wear it before."
I lightly touched the pendant.

"It was my mother's. And before that it was Gram's. I know it
was special to both of them. I never wear it, for fear something
might happen to it. But today is special, for all sorts of reasons. So, I
decided to put it on." She glanced to the rearview mirror and
adjusted it.

"I like it." I smiled at her. "I'm sure your mother is thrilled you
wore it. And I'm certain your grandmother will light up when she
sees that you have it on."

"Good, I want everyone to be happy." She turned the wheel
and pulled up into the parking lot and around to the backside of the
building where she parked.

I ignored the comment and pressed my cup of coffee into the
center console, stepped out of the vehicle, and walked around to the
driver's side of the car. I was totally confused by Samantha's
sarcasm. I mean, I knew she had a lot on her plate, but coming into
a bunch of money seems like it would ease some of her problems,
not create more. But it was early in the morning. I had to keep
reminding myself she wasn't an early bird.

"Pick me up over here, at this door." Sam pointed to an
employee entrance as she gathered her items from the backseat of
the car.

"Right, I know. I will check in with you later, but I'm thinking I
will be here at this door around 6:30, probably not sooner. I am sure
I will have a full day, birthday or not." I climbed in the car and
adjusted the seat, moving it back to give me some leg room. "Your
grandmother is counting on me having you at her house by 7:00.
You better be ready before then." I drew the seatbelt across my
body. Sam would never consider leaving a client in need—in
particular if it were on the occasion of celebrating herself.

"I'll be ready. I brought all my clothes in with me." When she fumbled with the bag to get it to her shoulder, a book popped out and hit the pavement.

I unclipped my seatbelt and spun down to the ground to pick it up for her. "*Angel of Dark Intentions*, huh? I never knew you to read fiction." I handed her the book.

"It isn't fiction." She snatched the book from my fingers. "Thanks." She stuffed it back into her bag. "Anyway, I was saying, this way you won't need to take me home first. We can go directly to the party from here." She slapped her bag, as if to say she had everything she needed inside.

"Great!" I lied. I couldn't imagine the change of clothes that could be stuffed into that small bag. Nothing I could envision would constitute a birthday party outfit. Not that I was a fashion icon, but she was the celebrated honoree. Her grandmother had invited a ton of people. People Samantha didn't even know were coming. "Surprises," was how her Gram had put it. "It isn't no fun without surprises."

I decided I would give her my gift before we arrived at the party. It was a beautiful embroidered tunic decorated with blue sequins and magenta and gold beads. Something I wouldn't be caught dead in. But it was something I knew Samantha would appreciate, especially for a special occasion. Too bad I didn't have it now.

I shut the door and adjusted the mirrors on the car. This place always made me anxious. The kind of people that came and went—the people Sam liked helping, they were the ones that made me nervous. No wonder they called this place Last Chance. Everyone else had already washed their hands of these poor people. I watched Sam spin her hair up on her head and clip it before she entered the building. I waited until the door closed behind her. Then I pulled away and headed over to the courthouse.

* * *

Sam was definitely not herself today. And by the looks of what she was reading she had a lot more on her mind than I knew. I had been so into my own crap this week that I had missed all the difficulties my best friend was experiencing. My phone rang. I picked it up.

"Hello, Dad." I fumbled with my cup of coffee, the steering wheel, and the phone.

"Hi, baby. Did you hear?" There was a certain jubilance in his voice.

"Hear what?" The only thing I could hear was a flute, wind, and a faux babbling brook. I quickly turned the car stereo down.

"A federal judge in New Mexico has scheduled the execution. That bastard dies next week. The judge did not grant the stay. He will die on a Thursday, just like Lisa."

"Wow, Dad. That's unexpected news." I was stunned. My first thought was, that gave me a week to get to New Mexico. I had to see him. I wanted to watch his face, his eyes; I wanted to be in front of him when I told him that I was going to forgive him. "What about his attorneys?" I asked. "Can they file another motion?"

"No! That's it, Madison. No more chances for him. The execution has already gone through the federal appeal. He's toast. Pack your bags. We're going to New Mexico."

"Daddy! Stop that kind of talk. I can't take it anymore. Don't you see what this has done to me? To you?" I nervously swerved into the parking garage adjacent to my building. "I can't do this any longer. I'm tired of hating him." I reached out and pressed the big green button for my parking ticket and watched the arm lift before I pulled forward.

"You won't have to do this any longer, Madison. Don't you get it? He's going to die."

"No Dad, you are the one who is not getting it. Don't you understand? If we continue to hate him, if what we share is our hate for him, Dad, he never dies." I swung into a parking spot and shut off the car. "I've gotta go, Dad. Don't forget, you're bringing tables and chairs to Sam's party. We will talk later. Goodbye." Suddenly I could see the real value in forgiveness, and it had little to do with seeing Lisa's killer brought to tears.

Just before I hung up, I heard him say, "Wait!"

I pressed the little red phone on my key pad. Even though I had said goodbye, I still felt as though I had just hung up on my father, and I didn't like the way it felt.

Chapter Thirty-Four

Ethan Price

When I stepped out of my apartment this morning to head off to work, the police officers still sprinkled the premises, crime scene tape remained, and my creepy landlord, who regularly lurked across the courtyard, was nowhere in sight. While I walked toward the front exit, inquisitive, nosy, meddlesome, whatever you want to call it, I craned my neck toward the back of the complex, only to see a few uniformed police officers guarding the yellow tape barriers. When I turned back and straightened my gaze I was abruptly stopped by the strong arm of my landlord.

"Hey, Pretty Boy!" His voice startled me. But it was the grip he had on my arm that frightened me most. "I heard you talking about me. What else did you say to that detective?" His bushy hair looked as if it hadn't been combed in days. The front of his wife-beater tee bore the stains of a few days worth of sweat, food, and liquid beverages.

I jerked my arm from his tight clench. By the throbbing pain I felt, I already knew a bruise would follow. "I don't know what you are talking about!" My eyes darted side to side and I stepped around him on the wide concrete path, and kept walking.

"I'm watching you, Price." His accent was thick, his words were intense.

My heart was pounding in my chest. *No shit*, I thought. That was what always creeped me out—his watching me. I waved back at him just so he'd know I knew his stare followed me. A chill rose along my spine. I lengthened my stride and picked up the pace. Besides being scared shitless, I definitely didn't want to be late for work. Not again.

*   *   *

Once I arrived at work, the first thing I wanted to do was wish Samantha a happy birthday. When I found her, she was bent forward at her desk, her gaze intent on the cloth of rocks laid out in front of her. It was obvious whatever it revealed was holding her attention.

"Hey birthday girl." I walked around her desk, leaned over and kissed her on the cheek. "What are you seeing in those precious little stones of yours?" She quickly scooped her pebbles into the cloth.

She finally looked up. "Hi, Honey." Her eyes were tired looking. "Oh, this is nothing." She placed the stones back into their box. "You know me. I'm just giving myself a little birthday reading." Her smile was forced.

"Yes, I do know you." I knew she was not taking this birthday very well. Too bad. I was really hoping she'd be back to her usual self today. Now I was leery to bring up Bradley. But I knew there was no other way than to just get it out there. "Are you excited about the party tonight?" I moved back around her desk and sat in front of her.

"Truthfully, I am excited to see everyone. I am also looking forward to seeing Gram so happy, but mostly I am eager to get it all over with." Her hand glided over a picture on the corner of her desk. It was a picture of her mother. She was pretty. Samantha resembled her. It was a photo that had been in the same spot on her desk since moving into this office, and Samantha was studying it as if seeing it for the first time. I was beginning to think we were talking of two different things.

"It's going to be great seeing a bunch of old friends, huh? People you haven't seen in awhile." I was trying to work up the nerve to spill the beans. "I know your grandmother called me for a few names and numbers." I smiled, trying to get her attention.

She seemed totally preoccupied, shuffling her files, jotting down notes. "Gram is very excited for tonight. I didn't get home until midnight last night. I stayed at her house, had dinner, and worked on all the flower vases she wanted for the tables. Then I filled candy dishes and set out a few bowls of nuts. I also peeled and chopped while Gram cooked, cooked, and cooked some more." She beamed when she spoke of her grandmother. Samantha was beginning to loosen up. "It will be nice to see friends. It is probably just what I need." She looked up. Her hands wove together on top of the open file. Her face softened and our eyes locked, finally. "Now, tell me what you bought me for my birthday." She leaned on her elbows. A genuine smile crossed her face.

"That's my girl. I got you something very special. But that has to wait until the party." I tilted my head to the side. "There is something else very special I wanted to tell you, though." I reached over and held her hands. "It's Bradley, Samantha. We can finally be together." I watched her eyes widen. I began to talk a mile a minute. "He and his wife are no longer together. He's finally able to be honest. Well truthfully, Bradley says his wife has always known, and he has been honest. It was really always his family that kept him from being real." I took in a long breath and leaned forward on her desk. "I want to bring him to your party, Samantha." I raised only one brow and puffed my lip, and then stared directly in her face, awaiting her approval.

"Oh my God, Ethan!" She put her head in her hands.

It wasn't the response I had expected. "Samantha?" I questioned the drama. This type of theatrics was so unlike her. "Samantha! Answer me." She acted as if she had gone off into some sort of a trance. I finally reached across the desk and grabbed her by the forearm. "Sam, what the fuck is wrong with you." I wanted to shake the blankness from her eyes.

"Oh, Ethan—you can't be with Bradley. Not now. Not yet." She looked terrified. Her face was colorless.

"What are you saying?" I leaned in some more and tried to see into her thoughts. "Why are you telling me this, Samantha?

"Your aura," she said, "my visions, none of it is good, Ethan." Samantha looked into the deep darkness of something that seemed to be punishing her.

"Samantha, what is it you've seen?" When it came to my future, I was always willing to listen. If it was about my past, I was so over it. Samantha had always been dead-on when it came to predictions. But I had never seen her hand out dire warnings before.

"I'm sorry, Ethan. I don't even know why I am saying anything. I've been having crazy thoughts, Ethan, bad dreams—wild and extreme visions. I don't know what to think anymore. My head is so messed up. Gram wants to blame it on stress, my birthday, and all the money I am about to collect. Gram thinks that I am still chastising myself over being molested by my mother's husband. And through all of this, I have finally convinced myself that I do hold resentment." She stared down at her fingers as she traced a large scratch in the wood grain of her desk. "I have figured out I have a lot of feelings I need to let go of, Ethan. I am ashamed to say it, but, I've realized the pain that grips me is the resentment I hold for my mother. She loved me, I know that. Everything she ever did she did for me. Rather than carrying anger for the stepfather who raped me, I have been carrying ill feelings for my mother who killed herself. That is messed up." Her eyes began to well up. "I am actually still pissed she did it. I am pissed my mother left me when I was young. I am crazy mad she isn't going to be here to celebrate my twenty-fifth birthday. How do I tell Gram that?" Tears streamed down her face.

I went around the desk, leaned down on one knee, and hugged Samantha. She was shaken. I hated that it took all these years for her to finally feel her pain. She had always helped others feel theirs, including me. I held her for a moment. Back when we used to go to group she never showed anger for her mother. She never really showed any anger at all, for anyone, or anything.

"You can't be with Bradley, Ethan." She pushed back on my shoulders and looked me directly in the eyes. "I am clear on one thing, something about you, him, and a stranger. I don't like it, Ethan." She was overwrought. "I mean, I never want to stand in the way of your happiness, you know that. But I can't seem to shake these bad visions."

I stood up beside her. "Oh, sugar—me, Bradley, and a stranger—sounds like it could be kind of fun." I was trying to lighten things.

"I am not kidding, Ethan. I see a stranger, someone, I can't fully picture. It's not good, Ethan." Samantha had a muddled look on her face.

Now she was really starting to stress me out. Samantha looked over my shoulder to her 9:30 appointment. She held up her hand, gesturing for one more minute, and then she leaned in and whispered to the side of my face.

"You know I love you, Ethan. That is the only reason I am sharing this. I am not going to stop you from bringing Bradley to the party. Even though I am sure it is not a good idea." Her eyes were loving, kind, fearful, and uncertain. "It's your call. I can't be responsible for all things. That is something else I am trying to come to terms with." She planted a kiss on my cheek. "Now go." She shooed me out of her office.

I turned to see an older woman standing in the doorway, probably homeless, maybe a drug addict, almost surely an alcoholic. She looked like she needed the guidance, and the gifted, loving support of Samantha, almost as much as I did. I turned back to Samantha. We had a silent exchange, communicating to each other that we knew this conversation was unfinished. I left her to do her job, and I went to do mine.

A good psychic knows the truth. I'm not talking about the palm-readers on the corner, the gypsies at a fair, or the telepathic folks on late night cable TV. Over the years I'd seen too many of Samantha's premonitions come true. I had witnessed people being shocked by Samantha's validations. I had heard the calls from people telling Samantha what she told them actually happened. I knew better than to disregard any of her insights.

Chapter Thirty-Five

Jason Magnus

Friends can be found when you least expected it. Before totaling passing out in the park last night, I invited the young Asian dude over to hang out. It was impossible to fall asleep with him staring in my direction. Besides, his nervous pacing back and forth made me a nervous, fucking wreck. And once I figured out he was basically a young kid, I invited him over to share the small spot I'd secured for the night. I'd guessed he was somewhere around sixteen, he swore he was eighteen. Turns out he was a homeless, gay kid. Seems I came across gays fairly often. I never had anything against 'em, especially the homeless ones. He reminded me of someone else I met years ago, someone else who was young and totally out of his element.

At first light, when my eyes popped open, I was spooning with another new friend I had made in the middle of the night. A stray dog, small, shorthaired, long, pointy ears, found his way into the curve of my body as I slept on the hard, cold, ground of the park, smack-dab in the center of the city. I rolled over onto my back and stretched my body, feeling the pains of camping without a cot, sleeping bag, or a campfire.

I blinked into the brightness of the morning sun. My hand rested on the little bristly fellow. He rolled over on his back at the same time, kicking his legs, as if to ask for a belly rub. I obliged. My mouth tasted like someone shit in it.

Through the tree branches above, I stared up at the blue Arizona sky and I tried to get my bearings. I didn't need a compass to tell me I was at the bottom of a barrel. My mother always said, "The fruit at the bottom of a barrel is likely to be bruised from the weight of the other fruit." Boy was she right. She also said, "That weight can sometimes make the fruit ripen, juicy, and just perfect."

A wave of pleasure swept through me as I remembered my mother coming to me in a dream this morning, hugging me, holding me, and comforting me. But mostly she reassured me. That was what she did. My mother's spirit restored confidence in her son. She always told me angels came in our dreams. That was before she knew she'd be my angel.

For a moment, I just hung out there and collected my thoughts. There were many. Like an apple in a barrel, I saw how I had let the weight of my life bruise me. It reshaped me, damaged me, it left me changed for good. My dreams and my nightmares were always filled with vivid imagery of my fuck-ups. The recollection of the past, the dreaded what-ifs, the would-ofs, and should-ofs of my life, all of it was just another part of coming off the drugs. Yet seeing Amber sent me into a different tailspin of reflection, every restless second of last night was like wearing a straightjacket. The thoughts of her had taken hold of me, reminding me, with glaring clarity, of all the mistakes I had made in my life. And the possibility that Amber may now have a kid, well, that just reminded me of all the missed opportunities.

While I continued to wake, and take in my surroundings, our eyes met. My new Asian buddy plopped on the concrete wall behind me.

"Good morning." He was American, yet he spoke with a thick Asian accent. He reached out and handed me a cup of coffee.

I rolled to my knees and reached up. "Where did this come from?" I gratefully took hold of the steaming cup and began to slurp on it.

"I walked to the coffee shop. They open very early." He smiled and pointed across the street.

Morning business traffic was well underway. Clusters of people were beginning to travel the sidewalks. Screeching cars, the whizzing sound of speed, and blaring horns began to fill the silence that had once surrounded the park.

"Thanks." I stepped up, pat him on the shoulder, and sat atop the wall beside him. The sun was already bright.

"I'm homeless, not broke." He smirked slyly and looked down at the little dog. "So, I guess you have a knack for attracting strangers." He looked refreshed. Not like someone who stayed up in the city park fretting all night.

"I guess." I knelt down and picked up the little Chihuahua-mix that stared up at me. I set the little guy on my lap while I sipped my coffee and watched as my day was set in motion.

Last night, after hours of talking, I finally convinced my new friend to go someplace where he could receive some real help. A place he could go to get off the streets. I pulled the tattered card of the CPS officer from my wallet, flipped it over to read the back, and together we mapped his route from the park, through the city, and to Miracle House. I assured him living on the streets was no kind of life. And even though the card was ragged and the ink faded, I convinced him the place still existed.

I encouraged him to make up with his family, go home eventually, or at least call home. I told him to forgive them, now. Don't wait. I wanted him to try to understand them. I let him know they probably just didn't understand him. And more than anything else, I made him realize just how very lonely life could be if you didn't spend it with the ones you loved. The counsel I had time and again heard myself actually giving to others sounded like it made a lot of sense. Advice, so often, I should have taken for myself, yet never had.

We parted ways. I watched him trot off, cross the busy street, and jog over to the next block to catch the Metro. As I glanced up the street I noticed an old man in a sweat-stained ball cap, a jacket that was two sizes too big, wearing a pair of baggy jeans. He was conducting an invisible orchestra, creating havoc on the crowded sidewalk. I dragged myself to the brick building that housed the public restrooms in the middle of the park. My little friend followed me, lifting his leg on every tree along the way.

The toilets had no doors. I hated that about public park bathroom stalls. I felt fortunate there was toilet paper. I proceeded to clean up. As much as one could in a sink with cold water, no towel or washcloth, not even any soap. I splashed my face with the cold water and slicked my hair back with my wet hands.

Like jail, there were no real mirrors, just some metal shit that gave back a murky reflection. The stubble on my chin seemed like more than a day's worth, but it was hard to tell. I rinsed my mouth and spit in the sink. I looked down at my grass-stained, dirt-stained, and blood-stained pants. I was shocked to find a splotch of dark brown blood on the knee of my khakis. It could easily be mistaken for dirt or oil. But I was pretty sure it was blood, which brought me right back to my reality.

When I stepped out of the little building, the small dog was gone. Not that I wanted a dog. Not that I could care for a dog. But I was suddenly upset the little guy was no longer around. My eyes wandered the park, one end and then the other. He was nowhere to be found. I guess even he figured out I wouldn't be able to take care of him. My mom always said "a dog can be the best judge of character." By habit, I reached into my pocket to stroke my mother's cross. I was reminded I no longer had the keepsake. Slouching with disappointment, I trudged toward the coffee shop across the street.

The smell of bacon and syrup floated in the air. When I approached the restaurant, while I stood at the edge of the outside eating area, I could see the television inside on the wall. I casually leaned into the decorative barricade while hoping to catch the morning news. This busy breakfast hour brought in a bunch of men in suits and women wearing business attire heading to work. I knew I wasn't clean, but I was cleaned up. I didn't think I appeared to be a homeless person. Some sort of a vagrant they might chase off the premises just for trying to watch TV. Yet I wasn't comfortable going into the restaurant and taking a seat. Nor was I comfortable with the way people looked at me as they passed.

I just wanted to get back to my apartment, get my tools, my things, and move on. I wanted the police to arrest someone for Raven's murder—someone besides me. The news anchor's voice caught my attention when he mentioned the name of my apartment complex. This was what I was hoping to catch. I turned my gaze to the large screen on the wall. It was shocking to hear there had been multiple homicides in the area, two women in my own complex. It was even more shocking to hear they hadn't arrested anyone for Raven's murder.

My blood began to rise in my body. The 911 call I had made and there were still no arrests. I was puzzled. Certainly the cops checked him out, ran a background, and searched his apartment. I must have been wrong about my landlord. There was a murderer, someone besides him. Maybe it was one of Raven's clients who followed us back to her place? Maybe it was someone else who had stalked her? Maybe it was just some crazy-ass coincidence and Raven was a random victim? I didn't fucking know. I felt sick. I came back to I *needed to get my stuff.* I wanted to get my shit from my apartment. This was what began to pound at my psyche.

The foot traffic in front of the restaurant was busy. The food smelled good. It looked real good, too. I stuck around for a few minutes and mentally collected myself. I decided I was going to go back to my apartment complex. I was going to return to the scene of the crime. I wasn't about to wander the streets all day, again. And I damn sure wasn't sleeping in Patriots Park tonight. Hide in plain sight. It worked for Osama Bin Laden. Well, it worked until it didn't. Last night, really this morning, in the wee hours, I'd come to the decision there would be no more hiding. I had done nothing wrong. Well, besides sleeping through the attack and then anonymously reporting the crime, rather than manning-up and calling the cops immediately. I should be blamed for all that.

Of course that was part of my problem. My first reaction was always the wrong one. I stepped away from the coffee shop and head down the sidewalk, realizing I had made bad decisions my entire life. I should have called the cops the minute I found Raven. I knew that then, and I know that now. Doing nothing was something I did real well. But at the time it was a choice I made. It was the wrong choice—again, always. No more doing nothing. No more wrong choices. This time I made a plan. I decided to go back to the apartment and talk to Mr. Faranghi. I might be stupid to go back to that place. It may possibly be another wrong decision on my part, but it was what I was going to do.

It had to be crawling with police. My stomach swirled with anxiety. I took in a deep breath, a breath tinged with sadness. I knew cops never cared much about the death of a prostitute, especially a black one. I can't believe they would still be there. Hopefully for Raven, the other victim was a pretty, white female, and then maybe the murders will get the proper attention.

With great intention and a strong point of reference, I ignored the hunger pains I was suffering and continued to put one foot in front of the other while I headed toward my apartment. The sun was inching up in the sky. It was a clear, nice day, if only my life didn't suck. As I thought about things, I decided to use the police to my advantage should any of them be left in the complex. I knew that asshole landlord of mine wasn't supposed to lock me out of my place. But in the heat of arguing with him I never so much as brought that up. Half of what he did to his tenants wasn't legal, but he often got away with it because of his clientele.

I sprinted across the street, jetting between a few slow moving cars. Mr. Faranghi used intimidation, blackmail, and pure brute fear as a management technique. But his tactics regularly won out because I was just like so many of his other tenants, and couldn't afford any run-ins with the law, nor could I afford the court costs of eviction. But today would be different. I would reverse the treatment and threaten to report him for his misguided management style.

I figured once I had Mr. Faranghi's attention, I would promise to pay him every penny plus late fees and I'd get a key to my locked apartment, today. It had worked before. I needed to "man up to responsibility!" This was the advice of a stranger. The Asian kid who was taking my advice gave me that in return. And I listened. This time when I approached my landlord, I would keep my temper in check, no kicking his door, or screaming into his face. This time I'd get my apartment back. I'd get my tools. I'd get a job. And I'd get in touch with my father. I hoped my sobriety would speak volumes. It always did. I would show them. I'd apologize for being a bad son, and maybe, just maybe, I could become a part of the family, again. I cut behind a commercial building and traveled through a vacant lot.

But first, first I needed to apologize to Amber. I needed to see her. That was the first step in forgiving myself. It was a giant first step toward healing. And for an addict, healing meant recovery. Another thing I knew and did nothing about. But more important than the apology, more important than falling to my knees and begging her forgiveness, I was finally ready to listen to Amber. Finally, I was ready to face the shame of her scorn. I was ready for her to tell me how I hurt her, how I took advantage of her, and how

I had let her down. I was finally prepared to man up. That was plan A. Plan B, there was no plan B. I needed plan A to work.

Chapter Thirty-Six

Samantha 'Sam' Green

As my day went on, the ominous visions began to diminish somewhat, but they were still there. I had just decided to move them to the back of my mind, even if only for a day, my birthday. I was trying to take Evelyn's advice about perception and beliefs. The old gal told me to do everything possible to change my thoughts, and try not to take responsibility for what was out of my control. That was exactly what I was trying to do. Even I knew the law of manifestation. But sometimes it took a stranger to knock me back onto my path. My grandmother's friend Evelyn had done that for me.

It was true what they say—*big things are merely a bunch of small things*. She reminded me of that. As a person thinks and believes in something, that something will undoubtedly become a reality. I also knew that both attraction and manifestation go hand in hand, and the last thing I wanted to do was attract something bad through my feelings, my thoughts, or my visions. So I worked extra hard all day at changing them. Every time they came up, I acknowledged them, and then I let them go. But really, it was just easier to stay busy, which is what I did. Back-to-back clients all day long. I had barely allowed time for lunch, and I ate that from the top drawer of my desk—in between the appointments I had with clients.

I had heard it was sunny, bright, and beautiful outside, something I wouldn't know. I was way past the halfway mark in my day and I hadn't so much as made it over to the window. With the minute I now had between clients, I leaned back on my chair, stretched my arms overhead, took in a deep breath, and contemplated the day I had had up to now. The florescent lights above hummed. The noise of fax machines, telephones, and copy machines hummed louder. Loud voices came from the intake counter. And soft music floated over the office.

I had several files moved to the completed box, and only a few clients remained. I needed to get through just a little bit of extra paperwork before leaving tonight. Fridays were always busy because we tried extra hard at getting people placed before the weekend. This would clear space in the facility for some other needy person who would inevitably come in through the doors on a Saturday or Sunday, looking for refuge from their demons. But I was doing pretty well with time, which made me happy.

Unexpectedly, I sniffed the aroma of my mother's fragrance. The last several hours had exhausted me. Hearing about the ill-treatment of others, and worse, the ones who committed those cruelties upon themselves was also very wearing. Today was uncommonly stacked with mothers who were tormented by the abuses to their daughters, unprotected by them, from their boyfriends and husbands, leading them down the dark path of regret, sometimes alcoholism, and drug abuse. An all too familiar story. And today, oddly, it was extremely significant.

When I finally looked up at the clock again and realized it was going on 4:00, I could hardly believe how fast the day had gone. As I went through the last few bits of paperwork on my desk in the temporary silence, I flashed on the sadness I had witnessed in Ethan's face this morning. I know my reaction to his declaration of love for Bradley wasn't the one he was looking for. The guilt of that response was weighing heavily on my mind.

Both of us had been too busy today to even share a break together. I hadn't even had a chance to take back my response. For so many years I had heard him talk about how Bradley was going to leave his wife. Bradley and he were going to live together someday. Bradley was an honorable man. He did it out of friendship. Time and again none of these things had proven to be true. And each broken promise turned into hurt feelings for Ethan.

I guess with the recent visions I've had, the fear of something happening to Ethan, Bradley being a part of my mental picture and all, it all caused me to somewhat overreact. I was feeling badly. I've always been there to counsel him when Bradley let him down. And that has been over a period of many years. As hard as I have tried not to build resentment toward Bradley, I couldn't help it. I still harbored anger towards him for keeping Ethan trapped in a life of waiting for love. Yet, as Ethan's best friend, I knew that was all he's ever wanted, Bradley: I really wish I had responded more enthusiastically to Ethan's announcement early today. But I hadn't.

My quiet moment was broken by the voices in the corridor, suddenly louder than usual. Todd, our security guard, bolted around the corner with his billy-club in hand. The screaming was loud. *Ethan!* My mind reacted. I was choked with worry. The phones were ringing non-stop, and a Beatles' tune, *Strawberry Fields Forever*, in the muzak version, began to play from the radio that sat on top of the filing cabinet in the corner of my office. It immediately calmed me.

As it turned out, Ethan was fine. One of our clients had freaked out in the client area and stabbed another client in the eye with a pencil. I called the proper authorities and waited in the lobby, watching the ruckus until they came. Our staff was great, very efficient, immediately jumping into action to attend to the needs of the injured. Todd had secured the attacker with what looked like a plastic zip-tie around the wrists. Ethan was still at my side. His arm was wrapped tightly around me. He knew I was shaken by violence.

As we stood around waiting, Ethan reassured me everything was okay between us. He didn't blame me for feeling the way I did about Bradley. Then, without hesitation, Ethan jumped at the chance to associate this incident to my ominous visions. He was convinced I was accurate about something bad happening, but he was certain I'd been misled by my own mind. He might be right. That is just how unclear I had been over the past several days. The dread I had put myself and everyone else through had been such a bummer. With that, I apologized for my reaction about Bradley, and I invited him to bring his longtime lover to my birthday party at Gram's. He hugged me hard. Ethan clapped his hands together and giggled like a school girl, before darting home to get ready for the party. It was refreshing to see the happiness on Ethan's face. A well deserved joy.

I went back to my desk to clean things up a bit before going to get ready for a birthday party: mine. I could feel myself smiling. I had hoped Ethan was right. I wanted this to be the end of my ill-omened vision, although a pencil had never been part of any of my images.

I leaned back in my chair, under the hum of the lights, and I took a moment to myself. Years of my grandmother's wisdom began to flood into my thoughts. *People come into our lives for a reason.* And unfortunately many of us stroll through our existence not recognizing the twists of fate, or the flukes that link us. Spirit has a funny way of manifesting itself, of guiding us by the events in a day, a week, a month, or a lifetime. *But we only benefit if we are aware.* This she pounded into my head. I knew it could be in a fragrance that captured our attention, or as simple as a song that comes on the radio at just the right time to be connected to a thought. Spirit has even bumped me, literally, with an unexplainable instinct that caused me to brake the car at a green light, while watching a vehicle run through the red light.

Today, what suddenly became crystal clear was that Spirit came to me in the form of desperate souls. As odd as it seemed, it was commonplace for me to find my path through the pain of others. It was easier for me to remove myself from the hurt I was suffering when I could comfort the hurt of others. I more or less knew that about myself. But today, that became obvious. What was also obvious was that the spirit of my mother unmistakably had something to do with it. And she especially picked today, my twenty-fifth birthday, to make me finally understand. Now I can forgive her.

Crossroads

Chapter Thirty-Seven

Madison Morgan

While I stood in Samantha's grandmother's backyard, finishing up with the last-minute details for the party, I took a moment to watch the sun setting in the west. The pollution of the inner-city softened the sky's colors. Scattered particles of varying sizes created reddish-brown waves in the skyscape. Off in the distance I gazed out at the bright reds and oranges of the setting sun that filtered through the city. I took another look around the backyard, put away the fuel for the tiki-torches, put a trash bag in the large can, topped off the coolers with ice, and then walked through the patio adjusting furniture before ending up in the kitchen.

Every single thing was perfect. Samantha's birthday party was going to be awesome. Regardless of Sam's recent omens, I was finally confident it would be going off without a hitch. Her grandmother had outdone herself. I stood briefly in the doorway of the kitchen and I watched Sam's Gram put the final touches on a few food platters. I listened to the artificial chirps of crickets and frogs, as music sounding like a late night at the river's edge lightly played in the background.

It was obvious the day's chores had taken their toll on Sam's grandmother, yet she smiled and hummed as she prepared for the festivities. The short sleeves of her flowered day-dress frayed at the

409

ends. Her apron gripped her bulge, her nylons sagged around her ankles, and her hair was rolled tight around a number of pink curlers.

Mouthwatering smells began to fill the room. I took in a deep whiff of a casserole baking in the oven.

"Yum, it smells really good in here." I wanted to make my presence known.

She turned and looked back at me. "It was real nice of your father to bring all those tables and chairs over to the house. And that big cooler will come in real handy tonight." She wiped her hands on her apron. "And you, Madison." She shuffled over and wrapped her arms around me. "You were wonderful this afternoon. I couldn't have done all this without you." She squeezed me. "Thanks. I know you've been goin' through your own troubles, you and your family."

"Of course." I looked her in the eye. "Samantha is my best friend. I want this to be a special night as well. It is all part of her gift." I winked and stepped up and clenched her hand in mine. "And don't you worry. I'll be here for the clean-up, too." I smiled.

I looked at the clock on the wall and realized I needed to hurry along, so I said my goodbyes. I made sure Sam's Gram knew how special she was. I told her how much Sam admired her—loved her and looked up to her. I wanted to make sure she knew how much her granddaughter adored her, and what a nice thing she was doing by throwing her a party. I offered my help one last time. Before leaving I grabbed the overflowing trash from the kitchen, changed out the bag, and headed to the car. I dropped the garbage in the can on the way.

* * *

I was driving home to change clothes before picking up Sam from work. It was just past six o'clock and I knew I couldn't reach her on the business line, so I dialed her cell. There was no answer. Real quick, I dialed her back. I took a chance her phone was buried in the bottom of her purse and she couldn't get to it quick enough. I got her voicemail again. This time I left a message and let her know I was headed to the house before coming to get her. Just in case she needed something. *Like an outfit that had been ironed.*

It was odd to be driving a car. But I liked the liberty of being on my own schedule. And not having a stranger sitting beside me was nice as well. I had only spoken to Sam once during the day. At that time, she was busy, but seemed much better. Sam told me Ethan wanted to bring Bradley to the party. I could care less, really. Bradley was never my favorite person. I never liked fakes. At least Ethan was real. "But, hey, everybody changes, right? That was all those years ago." Those were Sam's words. She was always willing to give someone a chance.

Why Ethan was so in love with Bradley, I'll never know. Back when we were spending all our time at Miracle House, Bradley always seemed like the boring, churchy guy. He was nice, did some really good things for the center—it's just he never seemed Ethan's type. Even though Ethan was the younger of the two he had a maturity I don't think Bradley had yet experienced. It has been so long ago, I tried to think back. I guess Bradley was okay looking, a decent build. He just had that clean-cut look, pressed khakis and a white shirt, and tie, always. He often looked as though he was going to whip out a Bible, or maybe a free bookmarker with something like John 3:16 printed on it. But once I found out he was having Ethan blow him in the bathroom, I lost faith in Bradley. But then, I knew Ethan. Really, now that I look back on it, Bradley probably fell prey to Ethan, rather than the other way around.

Traffic was typical Friday, after-work, before-weekend, crazy traffic. I had to breathe in and talk myself into relaxing. As I drove home, out of the passenger window I could see the sunset leaving a spectacular glow in its parting. And from the driver's side I could see a beautiful full moon rising. Big and brilliant it made its way up into the sky. I estimated the time it would take to press my red shirt and the new jeans I bought for the occasion. Charlie would need to be fed and his box cleaned.

I realized time was short. I also knew it wouldn't be the end of the world to be late. *In fact, it might even be better,* I thought. This way everyone has a chance to get there. Even though it wasn't a surprise party, I thought it would be nice for Sam to be one of the last to arrive, instead of waiting for people to show up for the party. Besides, this way I didn't have to wait for Sam and get huffy with her on her birthday, since I knew she'd be late at the office because she always was. While sitting at a red light, I spun the dream catcher hanging from the rearview mirror. I felt myself smiling for Samantha. This would be a great night for her. I was excited for her, even if she wasn't thrilled.

I only had a few blocks to go before getting home. My thoughts went to my father. He and I worked together setting up the tables and chairs for the party. We sat out on the patio and put air in twenty-five balloons and tied string to each one. He had experience with helium; I did not. He made a comment about marijuana, smiling, whispering about Gram being the way she was because she smoked the "wacky-tobacky." I assured him the odor he was sniffing was burnt sage.

My dad went to the Buddha statue in the corner of the patio and playfully rubbed his big belly and made a wish for a successful party for Sam. He was sweeter than usual. The edge that had so often been there wasn't. He never said anything about me more or less hanging up on him, which was a relief. We talked about Mom's green chili enchiladas and how we were both craving them—how we were excited to eat them, later. He asked me about school. We talked about the gym, work, and my brothers.

Finally, he did ask me why I was having the sudden soft heart. He seemed genuine. It was weird. So I actually told him my real feelings. Something I didn't always do. There was something suddenly comfortable between us—something I'd longed for, something I didn't know I needed until I had it. I tried explaining to him some of the things Sam and I had been talking about. Unfortunately, when it came to enlightening him about forgiveness, I didn't have the same finesse as Sam. So, I put it in terms my father could understand. I told him I'd come to the conclusion Lisa's killer would suffer more if he knew he could no longer hurt us. We agreed to forget about it for now and have a nice night. He promised not to talk about the death penalty with anyone at the party. I promised him we would go to New Mexico next week for the execution. Each of us with different agendas.

Crossroads

Chapter Thirty-Eight

Jason Magnus

By the time I walked all the way back to my apartment a blister had formed on my right heel. The big toenail on my left foot was throbbing and felt like it was going to pop off any second now. My legs were exhausted, tight and cramping. It was almost dark, I was worn-out, hungry, and I was not prepared to hear no for an answer. All I wanted to do was get my apartment back, take a hot shower, change my clothes, eat something, and start my life over.

I pushed through the rusty gate at the front entrance. The gate had never been shut up to now. It creaked open. I looked around the complex, no police cars, no CSI vans, TV cameras, no nothing. A small piece of yellow crime tape draped from the second story banister of one unit. And as I glanced to the back of the complex, toward Raven's apartment, a large X of crime tape crossed her doorway.

I looked over toward the manager's unit, and there he was, Mr. Faranghi, standing on the front porch of his apartment; his head tipped back, his lips rounded as he blew smoke rings that resembled tiny nooses. He twisted the golden pendant that hung from his neck. He saw me coming and grinned. Tapping his ashes off his cigarette, he leaned his large body into his front door. His sweat-stained work shirt was unbuttoned and untucked, exposing the front of his food-stained tee. I felt sick. A flash of white noise rushed through my head. Hunger was taking hold. *Holy fuck*, I thought. I paused near the bank of mailboxes in the middle of the courtyard and smoothed my wrinkled, worn clothes. I bolstered my strength and my courage with a big, deep breath and stuffed my shaking, nervous hands into my pockets, realizing once again my mother's cross was missing.

I stepped out from behind the wall of mail slots, moved back onto the meandering concrete path, and headed to my sneering landlord. The muscle in my jaw began to twitch. The large overhead lamp cracked on, casting a large circle of light onto the pathway. A woman pushing a grocery cart, with two kids in tow, cut across the concrete walk and parked her basket on the front patio of a nearby unit. My head down, I slowed my stride toward Mr. Faranghi.

When I lifted my gaze, our eyes met. He made a tsk-tsk sound with his tongue, then he wagged his finger at me. Thick hair puffed out of his shirt collar, front and back. He tossed his cigarette to the ground, turned and opened his apartment, and with a wide stance, he stood in the entrance.

"Thought you'd give it another try, huh?" He barked with bitter laughter. His bushy eyebrows wiggled in a creepy way, his tongue played with wisps of his mustache.

"Mr. Faranghi, please," I reached out for a handshake, "hear me out." I held my hand out and awaited his grip. Nothing. Instead he gripped the door trim and stared at me. I returned my hand to my pocket. "Okay, fine."

"You going to kick my door and start screaming at me, again?" His accent was thick as ever, his voice was louder than usual. His right hand disappeared behind the wall. He seemed more uptight than necessary.

"I'm cool Mr. Faranghi." I held both my hands up, as if to show him I was here in peace. "I just want to work something out with you. Anything—whatever you want. I just need to get into my apartment. I can't make any money without my tools. I need clothes, you know, I need my things. Please, Mr. Faranghi! Please let me in." I put my hands to my heart in a praying manner, and tipped my head toward him.

His right hand still hidden behind the wall, he seemed to relax somewhat, allowing the door of his apartment to crack open, further. He clicked his tongue again. "If I were to consider it, it will cost you." He stepped forward, his left hand went up to door jam, spreading across the entrance, like I was going to try to force my way in or something. "You are already about a month behind." He was cold and indifferent. "How will you ever get caught up?"

"I will, I promise. I will work hard. I have a job," I lied. "I'll do things around here, too. I can do anything. I'll be caught up in no time. You'll see. I can even clean your vacancies." I looked past him into his apartment. A single tapestry hung on the wall inside, with the sewn-in beads forming the word "Allah-u-Akbar." I had no idea what it meant.

"I might just have a few vacancies you can freshen up. How are you at cleaning up blood?" He had a jackal's grin. "We've got a murderer in the complex." His smile was dangerous and insinuating.

My heart began to tap as fast as a scared bunny. I held my hand over my chest to keep him from hearing it. "I can do anything," I said, trying desperately to keep my voice even and strong.

The big Iranian was unmoving, his shoulders curled up. Holding his ground he seemed to consider my offer. While I awaited his arrangement, I peered through the crack in the door to the table beneath the religious wall-hanging. That was when I saw it. A beaded pattern I was very familiar with. It was my mother's cross. How could it be on the table in his apartment? My empty stomach turned to water and I felt the urge to throw up. My face flushed. I wanted to say something, but my mouth was glued shut. I could hear him hem-and-haw about what a loser I was, and how it would be a huge mistake to let me back in. Then my eyes landed on another trinket I was all too familiar with. It was Raven's necklace.

It was absolutely silent for one long minute before the screaming began. And before I had time to think about my actions, my foot was firmly planted in his apartment, keeping him from shutting the door and locking me out.

"Why the fuck do you have Raven's necklace and my mother's cross?" I pushed past him, toward the table that held some sort of samurai sword, a few burning candles, some incense, and a book appearing to be a bible, lay open and on display. I reached for the cross and necklace.

"You shouldn't have come in!" The crazed Iranian slammed the front door shut. In his right hand was a revolver. And it was pointed directly at my face.

I threw myself at him as hard as I could. One hand gripped at the gun, the other hit, pulled, pinched, and gouged at his eyes. I did everything I could to get him to drop the weapon, but he didn't. We twirled around his living room, dragging along the walls and tripping over a chair before finally toppling over the coffee table and falling to the floor.

"You are going down for the murder." Faranghi jumped on top of me, driving his fist into my face. "It was the perfect set-up!" He smashed my face with the butt of his gun.

I felt cartilage give way to the thrust. I could taste the blood as my own tooth went through my lip. Breathing was difficult under his heaviness. I could feel something stabbing into my spine. *I was not going to be blamed for killing anyone.* Both of my hands grasped the pistol still held tightly by my landlord. His large body straddled mine. He tried desperately to regain control of his weapon. I knew I was fighting for my life. With all of my strength, I clinched the barrel of the gun. I turned it back on him and began to buck and kick my way out from under his fat body. My voice frenzied, I yelled loud, so shrill it made my teeth ache. Then I heard a noise louder than my screams. It was the sound of a gunshot. For a moment I wasn't sure where the bullet went. Then I saw his eyes go wide, then blank. With a thud, Mr. Faranghi's lifeless body fell to the floor beside me. He remained still and limp.

Time suddenly slowed to a nauseating crawl. I rolled to my knees and surveyed the situation. My heart moved slowly into my throat. I could feel it pounding there, choking me.

He was dead. I reached for the gun, still clutched in the death grip of my landlord, his finger still on the trigger. I shifted the gun to the crook of my arm and rose. I couldn't achieve a firm stance. My legs frantically wobbled beneath me. I stepped over to the table and grabbed my mother's cross and Raven's necklace and put them in my pocket. Glancing down, I noticed there were other personal items spread across the table. I couldn't help thinking this was a shrine of sorts for the murdered victims—his murder victims.

My body was violently shaking. I knew I needed to get out of here. The cops would never believe my story. If they had, this man would have already been arrested. Anyone on the outside looking in, might think I attacked my landlord and killed him because he locked me out of my apartment and wouldn't let me back in. I glared down at his dead body, through a mist of rage, I weighed my options, and they boiled down to this: I had no fucking options.

Crossroads

Chapter Thirty-Nine

Ethan Price

By the time I left the office tonight Samantha was finally acting more like herself. She was getting excited about her birthday party and everything. You would think the whole pencil in the eye would have thrown her for a loop, but instead it set her at ease. I think she was finally convinced that all the crazy thoughts and premonitions she'd been having leading up to her party were somehow connected to the incident, or maybe she just came to terms with her stress that had led to the visions. Either way, it seemed *my* Samantha was back.

I questioned the Bradley factor, the bleak warning about him and me getting together. Samantha had admitted to being fuzzy. I sloughed it off. As the ambulance pulled out of the parking lot of our facility, carrying crazy pencil guy, Samantha nudged me, put her arm around me tightly and said she was happy for me and Bradley. She reminded me that all she ever wanted for me was my happiness. It made me feel good to have my best friend back. It seemed the dark cloud that had followed her for the past week was gone.

I pretty much had to jog home from the office to get there in time to change and be ready for Bradley. He was picking me up at seven o'clock. And he reminded me of his punctuality when we spoke earlier. He was nervous about tonight. I was nervous about tonight, and I never got nervous, not like this. The butterflies were running rampant in my belly. The thought of an actual date with the man I loved was beginning to fill me, my heart, my spirit. All the times I wanted to go out with him in public, introduce him to friends, be with him at a party, and it was finally happening. I was smiling.

Just before I shut the door to my apartment, I heard a loud shriek come from somewhere in the complex. I was absolutely silent for one long minute to see if I could hear where the screaming had come from. I felt a wave of fear weaken my knees. I closed the door, locked it, and leaned against it for a minute, recalling the violence that had surrounded me over the past few days. I couldn't help but think about all the dread Samantha had earlier in the day. I took a deep breath, reassuring myself it was all nonsense, and I had nothing to worry about. I stepped back, grabbed the chair, and once again propped it up under the doorknob. There had always been racket in the complex, just never dead bodies.

I took time to smoke a few hits of pot while I stripped down and traipsed through the apartment. Then I flew around to get ready. I changed into my favorite jeans—the tight ones, the kind you had to suck in a deep breath in order to get them buttoned. The collared shirt I picked out was a beautiful teal, crisp-cotton, button-down that Samantha had bought me for my birthday last year. I looked damn good in it. I twirled in front of the bathroom mirror, put the finishing touches on my hair, then I brushed my teeth, before splashing on too much of my cologne and walking back out to the kitchen.

I leaned into the countertop and took another hit off my pipe while I waited for Bradley to call. I looked over at the clock on the wall. It was just now 7:00. My phone rang. It was Bradley. I was smiling again. The sound of his voice, the anticipation of the evening, everything was making me happy, almost giddy. I agreed to meet him at the front of the complex, right at the main entrance in ten minutes. I stuffed my phone and cash into my pocket, picked Samantha's gift off the counter, fixed the bow, signed her card, and headed out the front door. Bradley said he picked up a bottle of wine, so I left the one I bought on the counter. Who knows, maybe my date and I would have it when we came home? It really felt good saying that.

When I stepped out of my apartment I took a minute to light a cigarette and look around. Then I locked my door and headed along the sidewalk. I heard loud laughter coming from the bank of mailboxes. Maybe that was what I had heard earlier—*hilarity*. Someone with a hearty laugh can sometimes resemble a frightful scream. I took in a long drag, hoping to finish my smoke before getting to Bradley's vehicle. He never liked that I smoked.

From a distance I could see Bradley's car was already parallel to the curb. I tossed the cigarette to the ground, lengthened my stride then dashed through the gate toward the car.

When I opened the passenger door to hop in, the light popped on, and I noticed he was on his cell talking to someone. I placed Samantha's gift on the front seat. A look of distress was on his face when he looked up at me. His finger went to his lips, as if to shush me. Rather than jumping into the car, I stood at the curb with the door swung open.

The scent of Bradley's cologne wafted my direction. It was nice, a pleasant smell, very clean. I leaned on the car and waited for him to hang up. The traffic out on the Van Buren was loud, yet by Bradley' tone, I could tell something was wrong on the other end of that call. Suddenly the butterflies that were dancing in my stomach earlier now seemed more like insects crawling on my insides.

"Ethan! That was Amber." His voice was high with anxiety. "It's Jacob, he fell. It's his arm! Amber thinks it's broken. She is going to run him over to the hospital. I need to go and be with them." He leaned across the front seat to talk to me. "They're going to the hospital just down the street from here."

I dipped my head down into the car. Our eyes met. "Of course, I understand," I lied. "You go." I leaned in and grabbed Samantha gift bag. Suddenly I was jealous again. Envious of a little boy's broken arm.

"Get out of the car!" A tall man jumped out of the shadows, startling us, he slammed something against the hood of the car that made a loud clanging noise. "Get out of the fucking car!" He was beside the driver's door yelling at Bradley. Within seconds he had opened the car door and heaved Bradley to his feet.

"Jason?" Bradley questioned the man.

"Jason!" I screamed from the passenger's side of the car. I recognized his face.

"Bradley? Ethan?" His dimpled chin dropped, the creases in his forehead deepened.

All three of us looked at each other trying to figure out the connection. However, time did not slow long enough for introductions. It was the kid I had known from high school, no longer a kid, but a grown man. It seemed he was a desperate man. His eyes were wild, his lip was cut, bleeding badly, his eyes were puffed, his nose was crooked, a large knot shot out over his left eyebrow, and blood covered the front of his clothes. But it was the gun that he gripped in his right hand that held my attention. *Had there been a crime committed? Was he running from another murder scene in the complex?* I remembered seeing someone the other day in the complex that resembled Jason. *Could he be the murderer everyone was looking for?* My mind started screaming a million things at once.

"Bradley, he has a gun!" That swiftly became my focal point.

The gun had been hanging down at Jason's side, until now. "Bradley." Jason lifted the weapon and tentatively pointed in our direction. "What are you doing here? I don't want to hurt anyone, least of all, either of you. I just need a car. I need help to get out of here," he said frantically. His lip pulsed blood, his face was swelling as we stood there.

"You are the last person I would help, Jason Magnus!" Bradley pushed his chest toward Jason.

"Bradley," I screamed. "Give him the God damn car!" I couldn't bear it if something happened to Bradley. I put my hands up in the air as if to give in. Jason appeared anxious, burdened with something extremely heavy, but he didn't seem to be high. His actions were clear and concise.

"Where have you been for the past ten years?" Bradley ignored my plea and continued yelling at Jason. "How could you just walk out on everything, Jason? How could you leave and never look back? You are a fool, Jason Magnus." Bradley took in a deep breath and raised his voice another octave. He was short and snappy with his words. Fear didn't seem to play a part in his actions. "I don't understand how you could have left another man to raise your child. You had to know Amber was pregnant. How could you have stayed away?" Bradley's veins were bulging from his neck. I never heard this sound come from him.

I stood unmoving, shocked by what I was hearing. I tried to connect the dots, but figuring out their past wasn't my priority. I slowly lowered my hand and searched for my cell phone.

"Why didn't anyone tell me I had a kid?" Jason was taken aback. "I would have come home. I would have never left Amber alone to cope with all that. I thought I was doing everyone a favor by leaving. I thought everyone wanted me to stay away." Both surprise and disappointment tugged on Jason's face.

His features were harder than I remembered. And even though he aimed a gun in my direction, I could still see a gentle soul, a soft man underneath this new exterior. My phone remained in my pocket. I could tell by the way his knees buckled with shock he was remorseful for his past deeds.

"I would have been there for Amber had I known." He started to repeat himself. "All I have ever fucking wanted was the life you took from me, Bradley. You were the one who told me to leave her alone. You said it would be best for me to give her space." He began to weep. "You were supposed to be one of my best friends. You and me and Amber—the Three Musketeers, remember?

"I didn't mean forever, Jason. I meant give her time. All we ever wanted was for you to get it together. All any of us ever prayed for was your sobriety. We all loved you, Jason. She loved you. Amber has always loved you. Have you ever just once in your pathetic life just thought to call?"

"Every single day of my pathetic life I thought to call." He dropped his arms down to his side. The gun now pointed into the ground. He appeared as though he were ready to give up, on everything.

Bradley looked like he was going to slap Jason in the face. He didn't. Instead he continued to badger him with words. "I can see that never happened. You are still a narcissistic ass. Don't you get it? I only married Amber to protect her. I did it to protect you. She never wanted her parents or anyone else to know what you did to her that night. I gave up a life with Ethan to cover your ass, to be a father to your child, and I continued to be a best friend to the woman who has loved you since childhood." Bradley grabbed Jason's collar and began to shake him. The car door was between them as they struggled.

"Stop!" I screamed at the top of my lungs. "Please, Jason—Bradley, stop this! Someone is going to get hurt." I was scared. I stood frozen in the passenger doorway on the other side of the car, one foot on the curb, the other in the street.

Jason jerked out of Bradley's grip. "It is more likely you did it for yourself, Bradley. Admit it." Jason screamed in his face, showering him with years of shame. "You never had the courage to live your own life so you easily stepped right into mine. That is why you told me to leave. That was the only reason you came to visit me in the hospital that day. That was probably just another Bradley manipulation. I just made it too easy, that's all." He pushed hard against the car door, slamming Bradley's chest with the metal frame.

I instantly looked down to dial 911 into my cell phone that was when I heard the shot ring out. The pain, it wasn't instant, I didn't actually feel any pain until the blood appeared. And there was lots of that.

"I've been shot!" I screamed. I fell back onto the curb. My hand clutched the side of my head. The warm blood oozed through my fingers. When I looked up, Jason was kneeling over me.

"I didn't mean to do it! The gun just went off." He was stripping off his shirt and wrapping my head when Bradley violently knocked him to the ground. The gun slid from his waistband off the sidewalk. Jason rolled back up to his feet quickly.

"I'm going to get you to the hospital, Ethan." Bradley lifted me from the ground.

"Let me help you!" Jason grabbed an arm and the two of them hauled me into the back and propped me up against the seat. I clung to the shirt that was now a makeshift bandage and I pressed it hard against my head.

"I don't need your help, Jason." Bradley closed the door and ran around the car.

Blood dripped off my hand. I was feeling oozy. I had the sensation of blood sliding down my neck. *My beautiful shirt*, I thought. My sight began to blur as I watched a shirtless Jason lean over in front of the car. He snatched the weapon from the ground before darting across the street and disappearing. I felt the jerking motion of the car pulling away from the curb and into the street.

Bradley talked to me nonstop the whole time, reassuring me I would be okay. He told me how he loved me, and he reminded me of what a great future we would have together. Bradley maneuvered his hand between the seats and found my leg, stoking it lightly, I could hear him whisper, "I love you Ethan. Please be okay."

My eyesight began to narrow. I was dizzy. Here I was bleeding half to death in the backseat of my lover's car, headed for the emergency hospital, and I felt happy. For a brief moment I thought about Samantha's gift in the front seat. I had hoped I didn't get any blood on it. The ribbon was so pretty. I knew she'd like what I pick out for her. Then I thought about her premonition about me and Bradley, a stranger, I guess she was dead on. I was disappointed I wasn't going to be at the birthday party tonight. I was terribly let down everyone wasn't going to meet my date. Even so, I was finally content. My vision went black.

Chapter Forty

Samantha 'Sam' Green

The employee bathroom wasn't my favorite place to get ready for a party, but it would work in a pinch. Earlier in the day, I used the spray bottle I'd kept on the filing cabinet in the corner of my office to water a Boston fern, to spray the wrinkles out of my outfit, before hanging it in the backroom all day to dry. It worked. My clothes looked almost like they'd been ironed. Madison will be proud. I could see the scared look in her eyes this morning when I stuffed my outfit into my bag. But of course, she is the kind of person to iron her underwear. Well, maybe not that bad, but bad enough compared to me.

When I walked out of the ladies room and into the office breakroom, Todd, the security guard, let out a whistle. Tacky as it was, it made me feel pretty. Especially when he told me how nice I looked. He was headed home and wanted to make sure I knew his replacement wouldn't be in until 8:00 p.m. I waved him on and continued to fuss with my hair. The hairclip I was using was my mother's, and the clasp was a little tricky. The outfit was one I wore to one of Gram's friend's funeral. I never believed in wearing black to a memorial service. I packed up my belongings, set my things on my desk, and walked through the office toward the backdoor.

It turns out Madison was running a little late tonight as well. I looked at the clock on the wall in the backroom near the door. It read 7:25. I stuck my head out the back door to see if Madison was there yet. She wasn't. Instead, leaning against the wall on the backside of the building, in a splash of light from the parking lot, there was a strange man. He had both hands up to his face and he was loudly crying into them. He was shirtless. It was fairly dark and it was getting chilly.

I leaned out a little further. "Are you okay?" I hollered. I could see I startled him.

"No, I'm not all right," he howled. "I haven't been all right for a long time." He sniffled and wiped his hands on his pants.

"One minute." I held up a finger, then shut the door and swiveled around. Literally a minute later I returned with an extra-large man's long-sleeved, light-blue, dress-shirt. It looked brand new. But really, it probably belonged to a man who had plenty of money and several blue shirts he wore only once, and then passed it on. Last Chance kept a clothing donation box in the front lobby, so it wasn't a stretch to think I could help clothe this distressed man.

I opened the door and leaned out again. "Here you go." I gestured for him to take the item draped over my hand. He didn't seem to want to move toward me. "It's a shirt. I thought you might need it. If you want help, you can come around to the front and ring the buzzer. Someone will see you. We have 24-hour staff." I set the shirt just outside the door and closed it. I leaned back on the inside of the door and wondered what must have happened to him to leave him shirtless, crying, and standing in the dark parking lot of Last Chance.

I walked back to my desk and retrieved the cell phone from my purse. I decided to call Madison and tell her to pick me up by the front door. That entrance was well lit. It would be completely dark by the time she arrived. When I reached her she was just a few minutes from pulling into the parking lot. I grabbed my things and headed for the exit. I slung my bag over my shoulder and bumped the door open with my hip.

The cool night air surrounded me with a new fresh newness. It was nice. Right when the automatic locks on the door snapped, closing me out of the building, I heard his voice. Startled at first, I tensed. My heart went into my throat.

"Thanks." His voice was low, soft, filled with appreciation. "I literally gave someone the shirt off of my back tonight. That was why I was shirtless." He stepped out of the shadows. I was alarmed by his appearance. His face had been beaten. Moist blood gathered on his lip and his nose in a few different places.

"Are you okay?"

"Not really. But I just wanted to thank you for the shirt. Thanks for treating me normal, human."

"It fits you nicely." I felt like an idiot.

I don't know why I said that. I am sure he could care less if he looked good right now. He probably cared more to find a bed and a hot meal, besides medical attention. His nose sat awkwardly crooked on his face. I'm pretty sure it was broken.

"Can I help you with something?" I asked. "Maybe I can call someone for you?" I held my phone in my hand and looked toward the street for my car. I thought Madison would have been here by now.

"What is Last Chance?" he asked. His eyes moved nervously around the empty parking lot.

"We are basically a privately funded placement facility or a crisis center if you will, for the homeless, drug and alcohol addicted, and for abused women and children." I watched him hang his head as I spoke. "We help people get off the streets and into a halfway house that fits their needs, hopefully a place that can help them get a fresh start in life."

"Sounds like another place I've heard of called Miracle House. A place I've been trying to get to almost half my life. I don't even know if it still exists." He squinted into the bright headlights that shined directly in his face.

It was Madison. She was finally pulling into the parking lot. I smiled at him. A part of me wanted to offer him a ride to Miracle House. Except the professional part of me knew that wasn't the proper course of action. That side of me also knew I shouldn't have left the safety of the building tonight until Madison was in the parking lot. I touched his arm. The sensation that shot through my body was unidentifiable.

"Miracle House is a great, long-term facility. And yes, it does still exist. I highly recommend it. Good luck." I slung my bag up over my head and across my shoulder.

He touched my arm. "Thanks."

I flung my arm out. "This is my ride."

Madison jerked the vehicle into a parking spot closest to us. In that moment, I questioned her driving. "She usually takes public transportation." I smiled. "It's my car, she borrowed it."

Madison jumped out of the car and started swearing at the stranger. "Stay the fuck away from her."

"Madison!" I yelled. I was embarrassed by her behavior. Suddenly she was standing between him and me.

He held his hands up in the air, as if he were being arrested. "I'm not doing anything wrong. We were just talking." He stood extremely still.

"You can't fool me." Madison wouldn't let up. "I remember you from my courtroom. And I can tell by looking into your eyes you remember me." She stepped up closer to him. Her face was right up next to his. I could see the energy sparking between them. "I read your file, man. It's Jason, right? Jason, how many days have you been out of jail before you went and found trouble? I can tell by looking at you it wasn't long." She held her arms out wide, as if to shield me from him, to protect me from attack, even though he was unmoving and non-threatening. "Get in the car, Samantha!" She pointed to the passenger side.

"Madison, you have it all wrong," I told her. I placed my hand on her arm and lowered it. Then I gently pushed her to take a few steps back to give him some space. I wanted the eyes of the stranger to find my peaceful stare.

He stepped up to Madison. "Like I said, we were just talking. You know, like people do when they exchange useful information." His voice got louder. He was no longer soft spoken or calm. He stepped back and swung in a circle, his hands gripped his head. "Christ!" He screamed, then he looked up into the dark sky. He appeared to actually be calling on God. "I need a fucking break, man. Please! I can't ever do anything right." He began to sob, again. Then he lifted the tail of his shirt and revealed a gun that had been tucked into the waist of his pants. It was promptly in his grip.

"I fucking knew it!" Madison yelled, and she slid her body in front of mine.

I watched him swing the gun upward, toward his heart, a movement I was all too familiar with. I pushed past Madison and lunged at him, pulling his arm back just as the gun discharged. The blast was loud. But the high-pitched piercing shriek that came from Madison was louder.

"I've been hit!" Madison cried, and she gripped the right side of her abdomen. She held her hand up and displayed the blood that was dripping from the wound. Her eyes suddenly lacked luster. Her stare was blank.

"This can't be possible!" He screeched louder than any human could. He dropped the gun to the ground and ran passed me.

I scooped the weapon into my bag and I went to Madison. "We need to call 911!" I grabbed Madison around the waist and held her.

"There is no time for that." He was there beside us, scooping Madison up in his arms. He quickly headed toward my car. "Open the door! Hurry!" he yelled.

I was in shock. I felt as though an ice-pick stabbed at my throat, rendering me speechless. I did as he commanded.

I could hear him mumbling to himself. "Why? It was supposed to be me!" He whimpered as he gently placed Madison in the backseat of the car. "Everyone would be better off if I were dead." He lightly pushed me into the backseat. Go on, get in there with her. Comfort her. I'll drive."

He shut the door then ran around and jumped behind the wheel. The keys were still in the ignition. "Do you have something to stuff in the wound?" He seemed fairly calm for someone who had just appeared to lose his mind.

The bulge I was awkwardly leaning on was my bag that I had draped over my body. "I have something!" I shouted. "Just drive." I had my voice back. "Fast!" I screamed, and repositioned myself. I nervously pulled the gun of my bag and tossed it to the floor on the backseat. The blouse I had on earlier in the day was wadded up inside. I snatched it out and pressed it against Madison's side. She cried in pain.

"I'm sorry," he said. "I never intended for this."

"I know," I told him. There was a spirit around him—a mother figure. She thanked me for saving him, for giving him another chance. "Your mother loves you, Jason. Bertie is here with us right now." I knew it was shocking for most people when spirit would give me their name. This particular spirit made certain I knew not just his name, but hers, too.

"Quit fucking with me." He turned his gaze on me. A look of disbelief was plastered across his face.

"Just drive!" Madison surprised us both. I thought she was out of it. "If she says your mother is here with us you should fucking believe her." She closed her eyes and pressed her head into the backseat of the car and gripped her gunshot wound. "Your party…" Madison said in a faint, whiny tone, "I'm sorry you're missing it. It was going to be awesome." She opened her eyes. There's your present." She gestured to the blouse covering the window opposite of me. A colorful ribbon decorated the hanger.

"It's beautiful. But, Madison, you should rest, just rest," I whispered and then cracked the window to give Madison some air.

We sped through the street toward the hospital, passing the Laundromat, the pawn shop, and one of my favorite Mexican food places. Traffic was heavy but opening up perfectly for us to easily surge by. We were not too far from McDowell and 12th Street. Good Samaritan Hospital.

"Sam. I wanted you to know, I forgive him. I forgive that bastard for killing Lisa. I'm not going to let him hold resentment over me any longer." She leaned her head into my shoulder and gripped her side.

"That is good, but Madison, now isn't the time to worry about this." I could smell the clean scent of her hair. It had the aroma of fresh apples. I ran my fingers through her short hair and along her forehead, and then I pressed the back of my hand to her cheek. She was sweaty, yet her skin was cool. I hugged Madison close. "You'll be all right. I promise. You have to be. I'm gonna need help spending that trust fund of mine. We can move into a nice house and find a much better neighborhood." I said that, only because it was something Madison had said, all the time.

'When I'm an attorney I am moving uptown—no more downtown for me.' She'd say. As we blazed through the streets, flashes of light revealed Madison's pasty color and her sunken eyes. Even though I believed she would be okay, I still felt sick with worry. Doubt had taken ahold of my mind. My throat tightened and I was having trouble breathing. I needed to call Gram. She was going to be disappointed. Yet tapping at my senses, another very strong presence suddenly wanted to be heard.

"Someone wants me to thank you for getting her necklace back." I leaned forward and touched Jason's shoulder. We were just about to turn into the brightly lit emergency room entrance. "I hope this makes sense to you." I saw his eyes in the rearview, they were mystified, yet I could see it registered.

Once the car was stopped, he immediately jumped out and ran through the large double doors. He returned to the car with a group of people in scrubs pushing a gurney. I slid out of the backseat, and then stood and waited as they hauled Madison from the car and rushed into the emergency room. I saw Jason anxiously step back away from the action. I leaned back into the car and grabbed my purse. I glanced at the gun on the backseat floor, thought about putting it in my purse, but instead, I left it right where it lay.

Once I had collected my belongings, I glimpsed down at my birthday, slash, funeral outfit, in order to straighten myself, when I realized I wouldn't be wearing that outfit ever again. I took a minute to make a phone call, and like every other traumatic time in my life, I dialed Gram's house. I leaned over the car door and tried to fill Gram in on as little as possible, while convincing her to get Madison's parents to the hospital. Then I took off after the gurney carrying Madison. Jason stood just outside the entrance, his head in his hands. He was visibly shaken. He had some strong women around him, in spirit. It was too bad he didn't know the strength he could gather from that.

"Your mother wants me to make sure you know, to tell the truth. Tell them everything, she says. 'Honesty,' that seems to be the word she wants me to convey. I hope you understand what she is trying to tell you." I leaned into him, trying to find his eyes. I felt like there was so much more to his story than I knew, but this person who I was certain was his mother, she knew the story.

"Trust her." I glared at him, hoping to get my point across. Well, actually, her point. "By the way, you might want to have someone take a look at this." I pointed to my face, referring to his, as if I had to show him where his pain was coming from. His face oozed blood, and his nose hurt just looking at it.

"Can I borrow...?" He was cut short by my intrusion.

"Here." I handed him my cell phone. I already knew he would be asking for it. His mother was convinced he would do the right thing.

"Thanks." His voice was grave. I knew it couldn't be easy turning yourself into the police.

"Don't worry," I touched his arm and gave it a light squeeze. "I'll tell the cops what really happened. I know you never intended to shoot Madison. That is just the kind of thing that happens when energies collide—bad energy. If it was anyone's fault, it was mine. I was the one to pull your hand away from your heart."

I couldn't help but think of Gram's friend, Evelyn. She said fate could be changed with the right amount of effort. And an enormous attempt was made here tonight to change fate.

"Thank you." He looked through tears of gratitude.

I left him at the doorway and sprinted over to the intake counter of the emergency room. If Madison had not flown out of my car to confront Jason, I would have jumped in the front seat and headed for the party, my party. But instead, Spirit had another thing in mind. I was certain there were no accidents. And this was another reminder there were no coincidences.

Crossroads

Chapter Forty-One

Jason Magnus

My ears pulsed and my palms dripped water. I stood at the entrance of the hospital, staggered and temporarily speechless with bewilderment. I watched as the crew of healthcare workers snatched my victim from the backseat of the car. I could hardly believe my fuck-ups. The poor people who had come into my path.

I rubbed the back of my neck, it throbbed, and so did my face. The past 48 hours had been too much to bear. I never realized the shadow of death trailed so closely. I never would have thought I was the kind of person to want to kill myself, but my stress had led me to a breaking point.

Without awareness, I had just snapped. I wanted to die. I never knew I had the courage to do something so final. Getting off drugs, that was final. Not allowing alcohol to rule my world—that would be final. Not wallowing in self pity, now that would be life-changing. I could now see this self-indulgent belief that my life had been harder and sadder than everyone else's. Life had become a self-fulfilling prophecy. A stabbing pain shot through my belly.

I leaned against the wall, watching the commotion as they strapped Madison to the gurney. I wanted to—I needed to change the vision I had for myself. The misery I had caused so many people, the pain, and the disappointment. The destruction I had left all along my pathway over the years had finally caught up to me. I looked over at the vehicle. When I saw her standing there, I half expected to see wings, a floating halo, maybe even a fucking white gown.

Samantha's hair was twisted up on her head, except for the wild loose strands that trailed along her face. She was gathering her things. I watched as she surveyed her clothing, and I noticed she was not easily sickened. Blood covered the entire front of her blouse and slacks.

The ER team rolled past me, no one cared that I was the shooter, the one who pulled the trigger. After saying the words gunshot victim, they just went into action. I guess save the patients first, ask questions later, was their motto.

To my own amazement, in one frantic moment, I had been ready to check out of this life, finger on the trigger, seconds away from seeing my mother. I was prepared to leave this world, and do absolutely nothing to repair the damage I had done to so many different people. But luckily for me, someone stopped me, from once again being the most selfish individual, and leaving everyone else to pick up the pieces of my fuck-ups. I watched that someone gather herself and begin to head my way. I wiped the tears from my swollen eyes. I couldn't look at Samantha. She was so nice, even after I had caused her such difficulty. And it was even her birthday.

I borrowed her phone. She nicely handed it over with a glitter of concern in her eyes. How could she have known I was going to turn myself into the police? Why was she so nice to me? Could she really be psychic? *She had to be*. I was shocked she wasn't blaming me for what happened. Everyone else would blame me—but not her. When I turned my body to watch Samantha head into the hospital, I could see my reflection in the large sliding glass doors. Even I would have been afraid, yet she wasn't. No one had ever put that kind of trust in me before, no one but my mother and Amber.

I clenched her cell phone in my hand and then I bent over and put my clenched hands on my knees. I began to sob, again. I couldn't get a grip on my emotions. I felt I had lost all control. It brought me right back to my mother's bed, to that very day in the hospital, the day she died. That was the last time I felt this helpless and vulnerable. I thought it might be possible that this could somehow be the higher power I had been promised could take control of my life. Because right now, it seemed I had no other choice—this time, I was ready to *let go, and let God*.

That young woman, Samantha, she seemed to be a very old soul, a powerful person. Her touch still radiated through my body, and so did her soft voice, telling me to have someone look at my injuries. She was right. I probably should get help. But the pounding in my head seemed like perfect punishment for the pain I had caused, not to mention the chunks of blood that kept sliding down the back of my throat.

An ambulance pulled into the drive and unloaded a patient, and then the paramedics ran through the automatic doors, pushing the stretcher on wheels as they went. I glanced over to where I had parked the car and noticed there was a homeless man circling it. He was looking in the windows and then looking around the area. It all seemed rather suspicious to me so I hollered at him to get away.

He yelled out, it sound like he said "Samantha?" He seemed rather crazy. I thought it a coincidence. He turned and walked off, over behind the large pillar near the ambulance entrance. I forgot about him as I collected myself.

I leaned back into the wall and thought about Ethan and I prayed. Then I thought about Madison, the screaming and the blood, all the blood. I prayed some more, begging God not to let anything else bad happen to anyone. "Please, God, help them, please." I whispered aloud. I squeezed my eyes shut and begged my mother to stay with me. It was comforting to know she was there. I fiddled with the cross in my pocket. Then I thought of Raven, I could feel the chain of her pendent wrap the cross in my pocket. I silently apologized to her again. I could almost feel her telling me thanks—thanks for killing Mr. Faranghi, even though it was not my intention. Really, I felt like he killed himself. He was the one left holding the gun when his body stopped moving. It was his finger on the trigger.

My life had been a nightmare and it was time to wake up. My legs wobbled of hunger, of weakness and exhaustion. As I leaned into the wall, smokers came and went lingering at the entrance of the ER. The smell of cigarette smoke filled my nostrils. I found myself taking in a deep inhale, a soothing breath. I was vaguely aware of the searing pain in my face. Again I realized how friends could be found when you least expected it. I had no idea who this woman was that just came into my life. In a non-descript parking lot. Out of sheer desperation, I had looked up to God and prayed harder than ever before, and he listened. He sent me an angel. I looked down at the cell phone in my grip and dialed 911, spent several minutes telling the operator my story, told her where I would be, and I assured her I'd be here waiting.

I hauled myself into the waiting room of the hospital and walked over to the counter, hoping to find someone who could *help*. I returned the phone to Samantha, just as she was disappearing behind a large set of doors labeled: *Restricted Area*. I was immediately taken to a small cubicle around the backside of the admission counter. The nurse called it a triage room. I sat in the chair and she began with taking my blood pressure, my temperature, and then she gathered basic information. She then cleaned the blood from my face and was able to get a much better look at the injuries.

According to her, even though the cut over my eye would require a few stitches, my nose was the worst part of my injury. My lip would heal on its own, and there was little that could be done for the rib pain I was feeling, and as far as the rest of my issues, well, I just kept those to myself. She threw a few adhesive strips on the largest gash, "for now," she said. I suppose because my injuries weren't considered life threatening, I was then shuffled into a small room off to the side of the emergency waiting room. Because I had neglected to tell the nurse I had threatened my own life, the psychiatric wing was never a consideration.

The pine smells in the hospital made me sick—pine over alcohol, pine over throw-up, pine over shit, all odors that evoked memories of my mother's death—a loss, which for me, had finally come full circle. I knew I could no longer degrade the memory of my mother. I had disgraced her for far too long. It was time I made up for that. I could hear the sounds of machines beeping in the background. Faint conversations wafted through the walls. I heard someone being consoled in the room adjacent to mine. Through the wall behind me I could hear someone else being discharged. And in the room right next to me, I could hear the soft voice of a mother. She was explaining to her child how the sling would make his arm "all better."

My heart was suddenly beating in the back of my throat. I recognized that voice. I jumped to my feet and hurried over to the wall and put my ear against it. I heard Bradley's voice. In a sympathetic tone, Bradley was reassuring the child his arm would be as good as new. Then he apologized for not being with him earlier, said he had a friend who needed him. Then I heard Amber. She spoke to the doctor, or nurse, or whatever, they were going over care instructions. My legs began to shake, but I kept my ear nailed to the wall until hearing silence. This could really be *my* son. I wanted to bolt into the room and beg Amber to forgive me. I wanted to claim my son, my past, and my all of mistakes. Instead, I turned and walked over to the door and peered through the window that looked out over the ER waiting room.

That was when I saw them. Ethan, his head was wrapped up like the Grand Ayatollah. He was flamboyantly waving his arms, talking to a man, obviously a plain-clothes cop, sandwiched between two men in uniform. There were other cops over at the counter asking questions. All at once, I felt nauseous from dread and relief. I was happy to see Ethan waving his arms in the air. I was thrilled to see him talking and walking. A ton of bricks just fell from my back. But all the cops standing in the ER reminded me I still had so much more to worry about. I needed to figure out how to get rid of the other ten tons of bricks that remained.

Then I saw her. My knees buckled. I collapsed against the door, my face smashed into the glass as I stared at Amber. All these years without talking, and there she was. Just seeing her up close like that felt like the brokenness inside of me began to heal. I had so much to say, so many regrets to apologize for. I looked like hell, my face, my pants, my shirt, everything was messed up. My life was upside down. I had nothing to offer—nothing to give but my word, which had never been dependable and carried absolutely no value. After ten years, this was never how I dreamed of reuniting. This wasn't the way I wanted it, but this was the way it was.

I remembered the words my mother had written on a note to me, and packed in with a ham sandwich. The simple note read, "You will always have a chance—and there is always a choice." I decided I was going to make the right choice for a change. I was ready to take a chance. I wanted a real life. I wanted to live. Really live. I fixed the collar of my newly acquired shirt, tucked in the bloodiest part, and then pulled my trousers down to my hips, hoping to cover my ankles. Blue was always Amber's favorite color on me. She said it made my eyes look like the ocean. I ran my hand through my hair, took in a deep breath, putting one foot in front of the other and, I stepped into my future. I knew all I could do was take it one day at a time.

Chapter Forty-Two

Ethan Price

Fainting at the sight of blood was such a distinct phenomenon, an occurrence I never thought I'd have to experience. Who knew I would faint at the sight of my own blood? Other people's blood never really bothered me. And whenever I had lost this much blood I had already been knocked out and beaten to a pulp, so it wasn't really like I fainted. But seeing my blood, in quantities large enough to fill a wine glass, made me woozy. And the unsteady feeling didn't pass, not until my earlobe was stitched back together and my head was completely wrapped. Bradley was with me the entire time. Right up until the minute he saw Amber and Jacob in the hallway. I was almost finished, just basically had to sign my discharge papers. I told Bradley to go, be with them, I'd meet him in the lobby.

When I finally looked at my phone and saw it was only 8:30, I was totally surprised so much had happened in such little time. I was also surprised Samantha hadn't tried hunting me down. No missed calls, no messages, no texts. She must have noticed I hadn't shown up for her party. As I looked down at my phone I was reminded the nurse gave me a hospital smock in place of my bloody shirt, which was now stuffed into the plastic bag I was carrying. I had also been given a shot of Demerol for my pain. I looked into the bag, my heart dropped. I loved that shirt. I was totally hot in that shirt. I would most definitely get the blood out of that shirt. When I lifted my gaze there was a familiar face in the lobby. He was flanked by two other police officers, and I saw two others at the admittance desk.

I wrapped it up and sauntered over. "Detective, we need to stop meeting like this. Do you handle every single case in town? You know, you didn't need to bring the calvary with you on this one." I was sure Bradley must have called the police. I looked around at all the uniforms in the lobby. I put my hand out to greet him.

He reached for my hand. "Hello, Mr. Price."

"Did you come to personally tell me that you captured the murderer in my complex?" I didn't correct him on the Mr. Price thing. Right now, Mr. Price sounded pretty good.

"Someone else already beat us to it, Mr. Price."

Then, what he said finally registered with me. "Do tell, Detective?"

"I am glad to see you are doing okay." He smiled and peeled out his notepad and pen. "The caller said you were hit in the head. I wasn't expecting to see you walk out to greet me."

"When he called, Bradley didn't know the seriousness until we were seen by the docs. He was shaken. No head wound." I smiled. "But, the bullet did take out a path along my cheek before ripping through my earlobe." It sounded so dramatic, which was the point.

"The 911 caller didn't say he brought you in. He said Bradley did. Where are the two women?"

"What two women?"

"The shooter said he came in with two women. One of them is another gunshot victim." He was puzzled, staring down at his notes.

"What?" I threw my arms up. "How could he? My shooting was an accident. Please don't tell me someone else got shot." I remembered seeing Jason swoop up the gun as he ran off. It must have been before I fainted. "Wait a minute—you said someone beat you to it. Beat you to what? Did you find Nasreen's murderer?"

"No," he said. "Apparently the guy who shot off your earring had just killed your landlord."

"Get out!" I screamed. "Jason killed Mr. Faranghi?" For a moment I forgot my pain. "No shit..." I was stunned.

"Our team was battling it out with a judge, trying to get the search warrant signed to arrest Mr. Omid Faranghi, just as it appears the 911 caller was allegedly having his altercation with the deceased." He clicked his pen. "You know Jason?" His eyebrow went up.

"We were school friends. Well, really, we weren't even that."

"So you knew he lived in the complex—one building over from yours?" He was writing on his pad.

"No."

"The caller said your boyfriend was there. Is that Bradley?" The detective looked directly in my face. "I'd like to get a statement from both of you."

I looked down the corridor. Bradley was still with his family. I was finally catching on, *the caller* was Jason.

"Here comes Bradley's wife."

The other officers backed away and went and held up a wall by the entrance. The detective didn't blink, nor did he say anything. Amber walked into the center of the lobby where we were standing. Bradley remained in the hall. It appeared he was waiting on something. Jacob was in his arms, resting on his left hip, the little guy's arm was bandaged. *Kind of a big kid to be holding in your arms,* I thought. Bradley swayed his body and continued talking with the intern standing in the room's doorway. I had seen Amber before, but we hadn't ever really met. As she walked toward me a smile of kindness crossed her face. She seemed to know exactly who I was.

She reached out for me. "Ethan, are you all right? Should you be standing?" One of her hands met mine, her other hand found my shoulder. "Bradley was so worried. I am so sorry about what has happened to you." She stepped back and looked at the detective, reached out and introduced herself, only as Amber. I felt like I was in the twilight zone.

"I know Jason. Rather, I knew Jason," she corrected herself. "I am sure he never meant to hurt anyone." She turned back toward me. "I am sorry you ended up in the middle of a quarrel that was not your doing." She tilted her head.

"I knew Jason, too, back in high school." I noticed the detective was scribbling on his pad as we spoke. "He really helped me when I needed it, back then. The kind of help you don't forget." I reached for her shoulder, and slightly turned my back on the detective. "But that was a long time ago." I swiveled back around. "In fact, tonight, Jason gave me the shirt off his back." I watched the detective write that down. I hardly knew Jason, yet I wanted to help him.

"Bradley told me what happened. He said it was an accident." Amber's tone took on a desperate quality. "I am so glad you are going to be okay." Her skin was perfect, her teeth nice and white. But the expression on her face was clear about how she wanted me to report the crime. The car-jacking had become nothing more than a resentful argument. I guess I could leave it to Jason to explain the weapon.

When Bradley revealed to me that Amber carried a torch for someone else, I didn't realize the flame burned so brightly. In fact I thought it was all bullshit. Boy—was I wrong. I was knocked over by her kindness, she was pretty. And I was blown away by the devotion she showed to a man she couldn't possibly think she still knew. I especially liked her spunk. Bradley had always said she wasn't ordinary. And in this short time, I now knew what he meant.

"Amber!" Jason's screech startled us. He appeared from a room off the lobby. Last time I saw him he was shirtless. I rarely forgot a half-naked man. *Maybe that was why I fainted.* Even though the blood had been cleaned, Jason's face looked worse than when I saw him last, more swollen. He was wearing what looked to be a brand new shirt, aged only by the blood smears on the starched blue. I now recognized the high-water pants. *He was the man yelling at the landlord's door.*

"Jason?" Amber's voice exhibited doubt, but her eyes, shocked as they were, slowly revealed recognition.

The detective and I stood silent, in the center of the emergency room, and watched them come together under the bright florescent. Jason was much taller than Amber, his short pants revealed his dirty tennis shoes. Amber was wearing a very casual, purple and yellow dress, three-quarter sleeves, a scoop-neck; her dress lay just above her knees, no nylons, and she had slip-on flats on her feet. The two officers who had followed the detective in were now standing at the exit, one on each side of the door.

"Amber..." Jason reached for her. She opened her arms. "I can't believe I am seeing you right now!"

They embraced. The waiting room full of people seemed to silence.

"Nothing is making sense for me." Jason leaned away from her and stared in her face. "But one thing I am very clear on, Amber—I want to make it up to you. All of it." He gripped her shoulders.

"It has been years, Jason." Amber's voice was soft.

"Everything I ever did to hurt you has haunted me for years," his words were obviously painful. "I am sorry. I wish I could take it back. But, Amber, I am sorry, more remorseful than I would ever be able to put into words. When my mother died, I let that become an excuse to stop living, too. All I ever wanted was a family. I don't know why I chose the path I did, but I am back on track, starting now. I want to move on, Amber. I want a family. I want you in my life again. Whatever role you will allow me—I want to be a part of your life, Amber." Jason never took his stare off her weeping eyes.

I was beginning to feel voyeuristic while staring at their private moment.

Jason continued. "I took the coward's way out—addiction," he admitted. "But I'm ready, now, Amber. I am done. I can tell you I will never, ever do drugs again. Never!" His face was red, it looked painful, dried blood clung to the rim of his nostrils.

Amber didn't say anything. Tears rolled down her cheeks. She lightly brushed his face with the back of her hand. I spied Bradley out of the corner of my eye entering the ER lobby from the intersecting hallway. He paused. Jacob was still riding his hip. He kept his distance, yet had to be close enough to feel the energy of these two people, close enough to hear what Jason had to say. I turned my back on them and looked at the detective. For some reason I wanted to give them privacy, even as they stood in the center of the room, in a busy, public hospital emergency room. At the same time I wanted to hear what they said. My eyes darted around the lobby for some empty chairs. There weren't any, so I stood my piece of ground, eyeing Bradley as he leaned into the wall on the other side of the room.

"I did you a favor when I left. I wasn't ready to be a man."

"You didn't do me any favors, Jason." Suddenly Amber had a voice.

Jason began to cry, causing me to turn back and stare. A huge lump was now in my throat. "I've never so much as kept a car for longer than a year without selling it for drugs. I have lived in so many places I can't count, evicted twice, and I have never once had my security deposit refunded. I've never had a checking account or a valid credit card, I have never had medical insurance, and I don't currently have a job. But I am ready to change. I am more ready to be a man than I have ever been before." He wiped his tears on his sleeve. "I want to be completely honest about everything, Amber. Please," his tone was deep, "let me settle my mess. Let me work through all of this that I have gotten myself into," he waved his long arms out wide, as if to grab ahold of all of his problems, "and let me show you that I have changed. Please, Amber," I was waiting for him to fall to his knees, but he didn't. "Let me be a part of your life, friends, again. I will give you a reason to forget about all the wrong I have done." He looked into her face. "Let me get to know my son?" He looked over at Bradley and Jacob.

Amber never took her gaze off of Jason's. "I'd like that," she said, in the softest tone. Her shoulders shook with sorrow, or happiness, I wasn't really sure. "I'd like to see you get your life together, Jason. I hope you do." She seemed to say yes, without saying yes. "I make no promises."

I glanced over at Bradley. For the first time, I looked—I really looked into Bradley eyes and I saw something I hadn't seen before—he needs me. I don't know why I saw that now, but his need was clear, almost tangible. He set his son on the floor, fixed the arm sling around Jacob's collar, and allowed him to trot over to his mother. She swept him up to her an held him affectionately.

"Jason Magnus?" The detective stepped forward.

"Yes." Jason put his hands out, as if he knew the handcuffs were coming. I watched him stare at the little boy, and Jacob stared back at him, neither of them said anything. Amber's eyes followed Jason's movements.

The detective eyed the other officers who cuffed him. "I would like you to come with us. We have a lot to talk about. You have the right..."

"That's okay. You don't need to go there. Lead the way." Jason fell in behind one of the officers. The other policeman gripped his arms and walked him off.

The detective handed me his card, again. "Please call me in the morning and I can get your statement then." He turned and followed the others through the sliding doors of the hospital entrance.

Jason looked back over his shoulder the entire time. Amber held her son close, and held the stare of Jason, until he disappeared from sight. Before I was able to catch my breath the doors slid back open, and Samantha's grandmother, along with Madison's mother and father came into view. I had rarely even seen Madison's parents over the years, yet I knew exactly who they were. I was shocked they had all come here for me. I looked past them, waiting to see Samantha. She didn't appear. They walked right by me, like I wasn't even there, and approached the admittance counter. I had to admit, the turban was off-putting.

"You-hoo," I waved my arms. "I'm over here."

Samantha's Gram turned back. "Ethan? Is that you? My God, what happened to you?"

"I was shot. How did you know I was here?"

"We didn't." Madison's father stepped forward. He had little concern for me. "Where is Madison?"

"Madison?" I questioned.

"Yes! Madison. My daughter has been shot, too. They brought her in here about a half hour ago." His eyes darted from one area to another. Madison's mother was nervously wringing the handle of her purse.

"Where is Samantha? She said she'd be in the lobby." Samantha's Gram tugged on my arm. "Where are they?"

I was immediately knocked over by a wave of nausea. I couldn't believe Madison had been shot. Bradley was by my side to catch me as I swayed. Then I spotted Samantha pushing through the doors marked, *RESTRICTED*.

Chapter Forty-Three

Samantha 'Sam' Green

So far my birthday had been full of surprises, surprises that had rendered me speechless and shocked, scared and astonished. And not one of them had been wrapped in a box with a pretty pink bow. I met Madison's parents in the ER, then led them halfway through the maze of hallways before learning the guy in the head bandage standing next to Gram was Ethan. I knew Madison's mother and father wanted to see their daughter, so I took a second to kiss my grandmother, before quickly spinning back to Madison's parents. I never really even looked around for any other faces. Madison's parents told me little of what happened to Ethan, other than he was shot. *My vision!* I thought.

We came upon Madison's room. It wasn't really a room per se. It was more like a bed behind a curtain. No chairs for visitors. They had just rolled Madison back into the space, after returning from x-ray. The drugs they gave her for pain made her sleep. So first sight, she was pale, her mouth slightly lay open, and her breathing was loud. The drugs were strong. Her mother leaned over her, while whispering something in Spanish she stroked Madison's face. It sounded like prayers. Her father stood at the foot of the bed and caressed Madison's foot through the bed sheet. His eyes misted when I told them everything, in detail, from the time I met Jason, to our arrival in the emergency room. I heard her father huff when I told them Madison jumped from the car and threaten Jason, for no reason. No reason I knew of. I never liked the boxer, Madison. It was that persona I've tried convincing her came out of fear and resentment. A façade her father encouraged her to keep. A posturing I often warned her would lead to trouble. *I was right.* I kept that to myself.

The curtains around the cubicle rippled from the blowing air. Low voices could be heard, along with the clinking sound of curtains opening and closing. And grief, the sound of grief filtered in from the adjacent room. The doctor had said the amount of blood Madison had lost was significant. Not enough for a transfusion, but enough to make her look seriously ill, which she wasn't. In fact, her prognosis was excellent. The x-ray was a precautionary measure, looking for any bullet fragments that might have remained in her body. But the x-rays had proved the doctors correct.

They said because of the high speed and relatively close range of the shot, and the fact that the bullet found a clear path, it went through and through, hitting her on the front of her right side, and exiting out the back. The entrance and exit sites were to stay left open, packed with damp dressings until they healed. If the bullet had not gone straight through there could be any amount of organ injury. That was when Madison's mom began to sob. Again she began praying in Spanish. We were all staring at Madison's chest rise and fall with her breath. She was snoring, sleeping well, comatose, on morphine. I decided this would be a good time to leave them alone with their daughter.

I returned to the endless maze of crowded hallways in the hospital. The antiseptic smells were overpowering. I stepped around a young man pushing an older woman in a wheelchair, and then scooted passed someone else shuffling along with an IV bag in tow. The lights where bright, casting an odd glow, causing the skin on my arms to appear blotchy red. As I strolled through the corridor, I readjusted the clip in my hair and smoothed all the out-of-control wispies around my face. When I pushed through the doors, I promptly found Gram sitting with Ethan across the waiting room. Gram hurried over, greeting me with one of her hugs that seemed to say so many things. In this case, she was telling me she was sorry for not trusting my visions, pleased I wasn't shot, heartbroken for Madison, and bewildered by Ethan, Bradley, his wife, and their child. We went back over to sit down.

"Ethan! I can't believe I didn't see you earlier. My God, what happened to you?" I reached for him as he stood to hug me.

We clung to each other for a moment. Then I felt Ethan softly push back on me, still holding me, he turned to the man next to him, dressed in a pair of navy blue slacks, a bloodstained, violet, dress shirt, and a black tie that was slightly loosened around his neck.

"Samantha, this is Bradley." Ethan was smiling as if he was announcing an engagement. I found it unusual to see Ethan's shirt was a baggy, doctor's scrub top. I was so used to seeing his physique tightly covered. Together with the head garb, this completely changed his appearance.

My hugs lingered, and so did Ethan's. What had happened tonight made me realize just how lucky we all were. I recognized Bradley the minute I saw him, although he looked better now than I remembered—manlier, filled out, more mature. Under the circumstances, I was impressed with how attentive he seemed to be with Ethan.

By the time I had made it back out to the waiting room, Ethan had introduced Gram to the whole family. I filled them in on Madison's condition. I had learned I just missed the chance to meet Amber and Jacob. Ethan and Bradley told us how Jason was someone they had all known. Ethan brought up the visions I had, telling Gram and Bradley how accurate I had been, in a braggadocio kind of way.

I thought back to Gram's friend in the backyard, Evelyn, telling me that "as we moved through life, the force of fate creates events that we only appreciate when we reflect on our existence," she said. "We are not prisoners of fate, but only prisoners of our own minds." She was right. Today proved to me that everything happens for a reason, including the actions or inactions we take in life. There are no accidents, nothing is a coincidence. I also learned there is a certain order to the events in our lives.

I squeezed in and sat next to my grandmother. Gram went on about how great the party was, before she left, that is. "Everyone who was invited had shown up, plus some that weren't invited came as well." Gram had a crooked smile. "The block was lined with cars," she said. "I left Ms. Beth in charge of things when we all ran out. The fellow she brought with her was grilling the burgers and dogs."

"Guy! What guy?" Together we yelled out at the same time. Ethan and I were both shocked.

Ethan looked at his watch. "It isn't too late to celebrate." He looked at Bradley, then over at me. "Okay, so we would have to change clothes first. We wouldn't want to turn your twenty-fifth into a *Friday the 13th* theme party."

"Ethan!" Bradley elbowed him before I could say a word.

Gram went on to tell us how nice the party was, the balloons and tiki torches, all the delicious food, the music, the laughs, the wine, all the beautifully wrapped gifts. That was when Bradley stood and left for a few minutes, returning with a box, perfectly wrapped, with a ribbon bow. I could tell a gay guy did it, specifically, Ethan. He had a knack for gift-wrapping.

Bradley sat back beside him. I loved my crystal. So did my grandmother. Ethan helped me with my new necklace. It fit perfectly. I put my arm around Gram and we waited—we waited for Madison to wake.

Chapter Forty-Four

Madison Morgan

When I opened my eyes my gut was on fire and my body hurt. My mother and father were staring intently at me. They seemed startled I had opened my eyes, like that was something they hadn't expected. All the pain, all the trouble, the blood, the bandages, and all I basically had was a flesh wound. My father began to sob, something I hadn't seen since Lisa's tragic death. I was still woozy from the pain shots. My mother stroked my head, fed me ice chips, straightened my bedding, and told me I would be fine.

I felt the tightness of the bandages around my midsection. My mouth was like cotton. Mom spoke to my father in Spanish, which he hated, mostly because he rarely understood what she was saying. I knew what she said. She told him to stop crying and to find some strength for his daughter. She didn't realize how touched I was by his tears. Then she turned her attention back to me. Once we found out I would be okay, my mom wanted to get me out of the hospital. She said she wanted to take me home, to her house, so she could feed me, comfort me, nurse me, and love me. She drew the sheets up to my neck and then folded them back. My father was still crying. She turned back and shushed him, told him to leave the room if he couldn't stop. He said he was going to get me a change of clothes so they could get me out of here. Then he stepped through the curtain.

Once he left, my mom pressed one of my hands between the two of hers and brought it to her lips. She kissed my hand, then my arm. Tears finally found their way to her eyes. I had scared her. When it came to her kids she did anything she could to protect us. Mom and I talked. We agreed this brought on bad feelings for all of us. For the first time, my mother admitted to being upset my father wouldn't let her come to New Mexico to be with me when Lisa turned up missing. Instead, she stayed home with my brothers, wishing the entire time she had gone.

"Your Uncle Joe needed his brother," she said. "But my daughter, my only daughter, she needed her mother." Mom drew some tissue from her purse and wiped her eyes. She told me it killed her to now see me on national TV. Back then I was walking around the scene with a bunch of strangers, Lisa's cat in my arms. She mentioned how upset she still was that my father insisted on teaching me hand-to-hand combat, and trying to turn me into a boy. She told me how she fought for me to remain innocent, unmarked by the evil that had touched my life.

My mother lost that battle. Instead, my past had become a part of me, all of it—the whole experience, like the birthmark on my right knee, or the smallpox scar on my upper left arm, and even the fact that I had one green eye and one brown one: it was who I was. Unfortunately I had let what happened to me as a child identify me in the worst way. I don't like that I believed most people were out to get me, or that I assumed *once a loser—always a loser.* I was one of those people who thought most people's motives were ill-intended, which I was sure if you asked Sam, she would tell you it was what caused me to do stupid things, like jump from a car and threaten a stranger.

My father always taught me to think on my feet—"Predicting the bad outcome will help you stay on top," he would say. Hell, that was a mainstay for a good boxer: defense. Sam's argument against that always went back to a person's energy. "If you expect to find the bad in people, you surely will," she said, often. "You get what you give in life, Madison. You give a smile, guess what? You get a smile."

I closed my eyes and gripped my mother's hand. I twisted her wedding ring while trying to gather my thoughts. I believed I had finally come to terms with the anger and the fear that had blazed my trail. But what I really wanted was to begin to expect the best and see the good in people. I knew my father meant well. All he ever wanted was to protect me. But it was time for me to blaze another trail. I wanted to begin to expect good things to happen.

"It's going to be okay, Mom," I said in Spanish. "Things will be better, I promise." She thought I was speaking of my bullet wound. She had no idea I wanted to change the person I had become.

I remembered back to when it happened. Back to the day my life changed course. I was being consoled by strangers, while I sat on the front patio and watched in amazement as Lisa's homicide scene unfolded. Everyone who had put their hearts into the search stood around, gasping for air, trying to come to terms with what that man did to my cousin. Their faces, every one of the expressions worn by each person were still seared into my mind, the disturbing shock, their eyes, their gaping mouths, all of it, as if it were yesterday.

There was something back then that I had promised myself I would never forget from that nightmare. And I had forgotten it for years. In front of my uncle's house, the day Lisa's body was found, one of the reporters stood on the street and he talked into a microphone. In my mind over the years, probably a million times since that life changing day, I had seen him say the words. Except that, I never really listened again, until now. I lay in the hospital bed, my mother stroking my head, and while tears pressed through my eyelids, that reporter's words once again began to flood through my mind. He spoke of Courage saying, *"We, as a society, should have the courage not to turn our backs on each other and so easily cast aside the troubled."* But what seemed to resonate with me was when he said, *"Courage doesn't always roar. Sometimes courage is the little voice at the end of the day that says I'll try again tomorrow."*

I feel as though I am at a crossroads between the past, my present, and my future. I will never forget his face, nor will I ever again forget his words. I had come to the realization that my tomorrow was today, an no matter what, my yesterday will always be a part of my tomorrows.

When I was a child, I wanted to grow up and have a profound impact on society, but what I had realized was that society had had a profound impact on me. I now needed to be the change I wanted to see. Learn to expect the best, plan for the worst, and prepare to be surprised. That is what I wanted for my tomorrows.

The Death Penalty

The United States is the only country in the Western industrialized world that still uses the death penalty. Since 1990, - 30 countries have abolished the death penalty. Among the 74 countries who continue to execute, China, Iran, Vietnam, and the United States account for the vast majority of the world's executions each year. More than three-quarters of killings in the U.S. take place in southern states—and over 35 percent in Texas alone.

The New Mexico Death Penalty

New Mexico Governor Bill Richardson signed the bill abolishing the death penalty in New Mexico on March 18, 2009. New Mexico became the 15th state to abandon capital punishment.

Child Molestation & Sexual Abuse Statistics

Roughly 33% of girls and 14% of boys are molested before the age of 18, according to the U.S. Justice Department. Nearly 2/3 of all sexual assaults reported involved minors and roughly 1/3 involved children under the age of 12. In most cases, however, child molestation goes unreported. Estimates are that only 35% of sexual abuse is reported.

Gay Youth Homelessness

Between 20 and 40 percent of homeless youth in the US identify as lesbian, gay, bisexual or transgender. 26% of gay youth are forced to leave home because of conflicts with their families over their sexual identities.

Crystal Meth addiction

Crystal Meth addiction is a wide spread problem that is sweeping across the United States. Death by overdose from Crystal Meth has been reported as three times higher than overdose from use of cocaine. Crystal Meth addicts never start with the idea that addiction will eventually destroy them and anything around them. Crystal Meth in itself is an addictive substance that tears down its user and surroundings piece by piece. Addiction and continual use are fueled by the avoidance and unwillingness to deal with emotional and personal problems within the user's life.

The Author

Lori Hicks is a freelance writer, magazine columnist, and an award-winning author. She has a knack for writing compelling stories and building characters we can identify with. Lori is an activist for human rights, fair treatment, and equality for all.

Her goal is to help bring to life her characters' experiences and allow her readers to walk in someone else's shoes. Two-time Pushcart nominee for her short stories, Lori has also written and published several personal essays and opinion pieces in a regularly published magazine column.

Undaunted by any subject, as a social advocate Lori has a sense of social responsibility and devotion to community that is expressed in her writing.

Visit Lori's website at: LoriHicks.com
Follow CrossRoads on facebook
http://www.facebook.com/pages/CrossRoads-The-Book-by-Lori-Hicks